THE ARRANGEMENT

By Mary Balogh

The Survivors' Club Series
The Proposal   *The Arrangement*

The Mistress Series
More than a Mistress   *No Man's Mistress*
The Secret Mistress

The Huxtable Series
First Comes Marriage   *At Last Comes Love*
Then Comes Seduction   *Seducing an Angel*
A Secret Affair

The Simply Quartet
Simply Unforgettable   *Simply Magic*
Simply Love   *Simply Perfect*

The Slightly Series
Slightly Married   *Slightly Tempted*
Slightly Wicked   *Slightly Sinful*
Slightly Scandalous   *Slightly Dangerous*

Beloved Classic Novels
A Summer to Remember   *A Precious Jewel*
One Night for Love   *The Gilded Web*
The Ideal Wife   *Web of Love*
The Secret Pearl   *The Devil's Web*
A Christmas Promise
Dark Angel/Lord Carew's Bride
The Famous Heroine/The Plumed Bonnet
The Temporary Wife/A Promise of Spring
A Christmas Bride/Christmas Beau
A Counterfeit Betrothal/The Notorious Rake

THE ARRANGEMENT

Mary Balogh

DELL • NEW YORK

The Arrangement is a work of fiction. Names, characters, places, and incidents are the products of the author's imagination or are used fictitiously. Any resemblance to actual events, locales, or persons, living or dead, is entirely coincidental.

A Dell Mass Market Original

Copyright © 2013 by Mary Balogh

Published in the United States by Dell, an imprint of The Random House Publishing Group, a division of Random House, Inc., New York.

DELL and the HOUSE colophon are registered trademarks of Random House, Inc.

ISBN 978-1-62490-797-5

Cover design: Lynn Andreozzi
Cover and stepback illustrations: Alan Ayers
Printed in the United States of America

THE ARRANGEMENT

When it became clear to Vincent Hunt, Viscount Darleigh, that if he stayed at home for the remainder of the spring he would without any doubt at all be betrothed, even married, before summer had properly settled in, he fled. He ran away from home, which was a ridiculous, somewhat lowering way of putting it when he owned the house and was almost twenty-four years old. But the simple fact was that he bolted.

He took with him his valet, Martin Fisk; his traveling carriage and horses; and enough clothes and other necessary belongings to last him a month or two—or six. He really did not know how long he would stay away. He took his violin too after a moment's hesitation. His friends liked to tease him about it and affect horror every time he tucked it beneath his chin, but he thought he played it tolerably well. More important, he liked playing it. It soothed his soul, though he never confided *that* thought to his friends. Flavian would no doubt make a comment along the lines of its scratching the boot soles of everyone else who happened to be within earshot.

The main trouble with home was that he was afflicted with too many female relatives and not enough male ones—and *no* assertive males. His grandmother and his mother lived with him, and his three sisters, though married with homes and families of their own, came to stay all too frequently, and often for lengthy spells.

Hardly a month went by without at least one of them being in residence for a few days or a week or more. His brothers-in-law, when they came with their wives—which was not every time—tactfully held themselves aloof from Vincent's affairs and allowed their women-folk to rule his life, even though it was worthy of note that none of them allowed their wives to rule *theirs*.

It all would have been understandable, even under ordinary circumstances, Vincent supposed grudgingly. He was, after all, everyone's only grandson or only son or only brother—and *younger* brother at that—and as such was fair game to be protected and cosseted and worried over and planned for. He had inherited his title and fortune just four years ago, at the age of nineteen, from an uncle who had been robust and only forty-six years old when he died and who had had a son as sturdy and fit as he. They had both died violently. Life was a fragile business and so was the inheritance, Vincent's female relatives were fond of observing. It behooved him, therefore, to fill his nursery with an heir and a number of spares as soon as was humanly possible. It was irrelevant that he was still very young and would not even have begun to think of matrimony yet, left to himself. His family knew all they cared to know about living in genteel poverty.

His were not ordinary circumstances, however, and as a result, his relatives clucked about him like a flock of mother hens all intent upon nurturing the same frail chick while somehow avoiding smothering it. His mother had moved to Middlebury Park in Gloucester-shire even before he did. She had got it ready for him. His maternal grandmother had let the lease expire on her house in Bath and joined his mother there. And after he moved in, three years ago, his sisters began to find Middlebury the most fascinating place on earth to be. And Vincent need not worry about their husbands feeling neglected, they had collectively assured him. Their husbands *understood*. The word was always spoken with something like hushed reverence.

In fact, most of what they all said to him was spoken in much the same manner, as though he were some sort of precious but mentally deficient child.

This year they had begun to talk pointedly about marriage. *His* marriage, that was. Even apart from the succession issue, marriage would bring him comfort and companionship, they had decided, and all kinds of other assorted benefits. Marriage would enable them to relax and worry less about him. It would enable his grandmother to return to Bath, which she was missing. And it would not be at all difficult to find a lady willing and even eager to marry him. He must not imagine it would be. He was titled and wealthy, after all. And he had youth and looks and charm. There were hordes of ladies out there who would *understand* and actually be quite happy to marry him. They would quickly learn to love him for himself. At least, *one* would, the one he would choose. And they, his female relatives, would help him make that choice, of course. That went without saying, though they said it anyway.

The campaign had started over Easter, when the whole family was at Middlebury, his sisters' husbands and their children included. Vincent himself had just returned from Penderris Hall in Cornwall, country seat of the Duke of Stanbrook, where he spent a few weeks of each year with his fellow members of the self-styled Survivors' Club, a group of survivors of the Napoleonic Wars, and he had been feeling a little bereft, as he always did for a while after parting from those dearest friends in the world. He had let the women talk without paying a great deal of attention or even thinking of perhaps putting his foot down.

It had proved to be a mistake.

Only a month after Easter his sisters and brothers-in-law and nieces and nephews had returned en masse, to be followed a day or so later by houseguests. It was still only spring and an odd time of year for a house party, when the social Season in London would be just getting into full swing. But this was not really a party, Vincent had soon discovered, for the only guests who were not also family were Mr. Geoffrey Dean, son of Grandmama's dearest friend in Bath, his wife, and their three daughters. Their two sons were away at school. Two of the daughters were still in the schoolroom—their governess had been brought with them. But the eldest, Miss Philippa Dean, was almost nineteen and had made her curtsy to the queen just a couple of weeks before and secured partners for every set at her come-out ball. She had made a very satisfactory debut indeed into polite society.

But, Mrs. Dean was hasty to add while describing her daughter's triumph over tea soon after their arrival at Middlebury Park, how could they possibly have resisted the prospect of spending a quiet couple of weeks in the country with old friends?

Old friends?

The situation had soon become painfully clear to Vincent, though no one bothered to explain. Miss Philippa Dean was on the marriage mart to the highest bidder. She had younger sisters growing up behind her and two brothers at school who might conceivably wish to continue their studies at university. It seemed unlikely that the Deans were vastly wealthy. They had come, then, on the clear understanding that there was a husband to be had for the girl at Middlebury and that she would return to London with all the distinction of being betrothed within a month of her come-out. It would be a singular triumph, especially as she would be securing a husband who was both wealthy and titled.

And who also happened to be blind.

Miss Dean was exquisitely lovely, his mother reported, with blond hair and green eyes and a trim figure. Not that her looks mattered to him. She sounded like a sweet and amiable girl.

She also sounded quite sensible when in conversation with everyone except Vincent himself. She often *was* in conversation with him during the following few days, however. Every other female in the house, with the possible exception of Vincent's three young nieces, did everything in her power to throw the two of them together and to leave them together. Even a blind man could see that.

She conversed with him upon trivialities in a gentle, somewhat breathless voice, as though she were in a sickroom and the patient hung precariously between death and life. Whenever Vincent tried to steer the conversation to some meaningful topic in order to discover something of her interests and opinions and the quality of her mind, she invariably agreed wholeheartedly with everything he said, even to the point of absurdity.

"I am firmly of the opinion," he said to her one afternoon when they were sitting together in the formal parterre gardens before the house despite a rather strong breeze, "that the scientific world has been in a wicked conspiracy against the masses for the past number of centuries, Miss Dean, in order to convince us that the earth is round. It is, of course, quite undeniably flat. Even a fool could see that. If one were to walk to the edge of it, one would fall off and never be heard of again. What is *your* opinion?"

It was unkind. It was a bit mean.

She was silent for several moments, while he willed her to contradict him. Or laugh at him. Or call him an idiot. Her voice was gentler than ever when she spoke.

"I am quite sure you have the right of it, my lord," she said.

He almost said "Balderdash!" but did not. He would not add cruelty to unkindness. He merely smiled and felt ashamed of himself and talked about the blustery wind.

And then he felt the fingers of one of her hands on his sleeve, and he could smell her light floral perfume more clearly, an indication that she had leaned closer, and she spoke again—in a sweet, hurried, breathless voice.

"I did not at all mind coming here, you know, Lord Darleigh," she said, "even though I have been looking forward forever to my first Season in London and do not remember ever being happier than I was on the night of my come-out ball. But I know enough about life to understand that I was taken there not *just* for enjoyment. Mama and Papa have explained what a wonderful opportunity this invitation is for me, as well as for my sisters and brothers. I did not mind coming, truly. Indeed, I came willingly. I *understand,* you see, and I *will not mind* one little bit."

Her fingers squeezed his arm before letting it go.

"You will think I am forward," she added, "though I am not usually so outspoken. I just thought you needed to know that I do not mind. For perhaps you fear I do."

It was one of the most excruciatingly embarrassing moments of Vincent's life, as well as being almost insufferably infuriating. Not that she infuriated him, poor girl. But her parents did, and his mother and grandmother and sisters did. It was quite obvious to him that Miss Dean had been brought here not just as an eligible young lady whom he might get to know with the possibility on both their parts of deepening their acquaintance in the future if they liked each other. No, she had been brought here fully expecting that he would make her an offer before she left. Pressure would have been brought to bear by her parents, but she was a dutiful daughter, it seemed, and accepted her responsibility as the eldest. She would marry him even though he was blind.

She very obviously *did* mind.

He was angry with his mother and sisters for assuming that mental deficiency was one effect of blindness. He had known they wished him to marry soon. He had known that they would proceed to matchmake for him. What he had *not* known was that they would choose his bride without a word to him and then practically force him into accepting their choice—and in his own home, moreover.

His house, in fact, was not his own home—that realization came like an epiphany. It never had been. Whose fault that was must be examined at some future date. It was tempting to blame his relatives, but . . . Well, he would have to think the whole matter over.

He had a niggling suspicion, though, that if he was not master here, the fault lay with him.

But for now he was in an impossible situation. He felt no spark of attraction toward Miss Dean, even though he believed he would very probably like her under different circumstances. It was clear she felt nothing for him but the obligation to marry him. He could not, though, allow both of them to be coerced into doing what neither of them wanted to do.

As soon as they had returned indoors—Miss Dean took his offered arm and then proceeded to steer him along with gentle but firm intent even though he had his cane with him and knew the way perfectly well without any assistance at all—Vincent went to his private sitting room—the only place in the house where he could be assured of being alone and of being himself—and summoned Martin Fisk.

"We are going," he said abruptly when his valet arrived.

"Are we, sir?" Martin asked cheerfully. "And what clothes will you be needing for the occasion?"

"I will need everything that will fit into the trunk I always take to Penderris," Vincent said. "You will doubtless decide for yourself what *you* need."

A low grunt was followed by silence.

"I am feeling especially stupid today," Martin said. "You had better explain."

"We are going," Vincent said. "Leaving. Putting as much distance between us and Middlebury as we possibly can in order to evade pursuit. Slinking off. Running away. Taking the coward's way out."

"The lady does not suit, does she?" Martin asked.

Ha! Even Martin knew why the girl had been brought here.

"Not as a wife," Vincent told him. "Not as *my* wife, anyway. Good Lord, Martin, I do not even *want* to marry. Not yet. And if and when I *do* want it, I shall choose the lady myself. Very carefully. And I shall make sure that if she says yes, it is not simply because she *understands* and *will not mind*."

"Hmm," Martin said. "That is what this one said, is it?"

"With the softest, gentlest sweetness," Vincent said. "She *is* sweet and gentle, actually. She is prepared to make a martyr of herself for the sake of her family."

"And we are running away *where*?" Martin asked.

"Anywhere on earth but here," Vincent said. "Can we leave tonight? Without anyone's knowing?"

"I grew up at a smithy," Martin reminded him. "I think I could manage to attach the horses to the carriage without getting the lines hopelessly tangled up. But presumably I won't have to risk it. I suppose you will want Handry to drive us? I'll have a word with him. He knows how to keep his lips sealed. Two o'clock in the morning, shall we say? I'll come and carry your trunk out and then come back to dress you. We should be well on our way by three."

"Perfect," Vincent said.

They were about one mile on their way when Martin, occupying the seat opposite Vincent's in the carriage, his back to the horses, reported that it was three o'clock.

Vincent refused to feel guilty—and of course was consumed by nothing but guilt. And by the conviction that he was the world's worst cad and coward, not to mention worst son and brother and grandson. And *gentleman*. But really, what else could he have done, short of marrying Miss Philippa Dean or publicly humiliating her?

But would she not be equally humiliated to learn that he had fled?

Arrghh!

He chose to believe that behind any momentary humiliation she might feel would be an enormous relief. He was *sure* she would be relieved, poor girl.

They went to the Lake District and spent three blissful weeks there. It was reputed to be one of the loveliest parts of England, though much of its beauty was lost on a blind man, of course. Not all of it, however. There were country lanes to stroll along, many of them parallel to the banks of Lake Windermere or some other, lesser lakes. There were hills to climb, some of them requiring strenuous effort—and stronger winds and more rarefied air as a reward when they climbed high. There was rain and sunshine and chill and warmth, all the wonderful variety of English weather and countryside. There was a boat ride, on which he could pull the oars himself, and horse rides—with Martin at his side but never touching him. There was even one glorious gallop across flat land, which, in Martin's careful estimation, did not hide any unexpected dips or potholes. There was birdsong and insect croaks and the bleating of sheep and the lowing of cattle to listen to. There were all the myriad smells of the countryside, most notably heather, to many of which he had been oblivious in the days when he could see. There was sitting to meditate or merely to stretch the four senses that remained to him. There were his usual strengthening, body-building exercises to be performed daily, many of them outdoors.

There was peace.

And ultimately there was restlessness.

He had written two letters home—or, rather, Martin had done it for him—the first two days after he left, to explain that he needed some time alone and that he was perfectly safe in his valet's capable hands. He had not explained either where he was at the time or where he was going. He advised his mother not to expect him home for a month or so. He confirmed everything in the second letter and assured her that he was safe and happy and in good health.

Miss Dean and her mama and papa and sisters would presumably have returned to London in time to secure her some other eligible husband before the Season was out. Vincent hoped she would find someone to fulfill the dual demands of duty and personal inclination. He sincerely hoped so, both for her sake and for the sake of his conscience.

He could go home, he decided at last. The Deans would be long gone. So, probably, would all three of his sisters. He would be able to have a frank talk with his mother and grandmother. It was high time. He would assure them that he was more than happy to have them live at Middlebury, where he could know that they were both comfortable and secure. Or he would be equally happy if they wished to move to Bath. The choice must be theirs, but they must not feel compelled to stay for his sake. He did not *need* them, he would explain as tactfully as he could. He did not need their assistance in his day-to-day living. Martin and the rest of his well-staffed household were perfectly capable of catering to all his needs. Neither did he need their assistance in finding him a bride to make his life more comfortable. He would find a wife for himself when he judged the time to be right.

It would not be easy to get his mother to accept the truth of what he would say. She had dedicated herself to learning to be mistress of a large home and estate, and she had done superlatively well. Too well, actually. By the time he had arrived at Middlebury, one year after her, he had felt like a little boy returning from school to the care of his mama. And because it had soothed her to see herself in that role, and because his new home and his new life had bewildered him, even overwhelmed him, he had not made a strong enough effort from the start to assert himself as the man of the house.

He had been only twenty years old, after all.

He did consider going back to Cornwall for a while to stay with George Crabbe, Duke of Stanbrook, as he had done for a few weeks in March—and for a few years following his return home from the Peninsula after losing his sight in battle. George was his very dearest friend. But, though he did not doubt the duke would welcome him and allow him to stay as long as he wished, Vincent would not use him as an emotional crutch. Not any longer. Those days, and those needs, were long past.

His years of dependency were past. It was time to grow up and take charge. It was not going to be easy. But he had long ago realized that he must treat his blindness as a challenge rather than as a handicap if he wished to enjoy anything like a happy, fulfilled life.

Sooner or later, then, he must return to Middlebury

Park and begin the life he intended to live. He did not feel quite ready yet, however. He had done much thinking in the Lake District, and he needed to do more so that he would not return and simply fall back into the old routine, from which he would never be able to extricate himself.

He was done with the Lake District, though. He was restless.

Where else would he go but home?

The answer came to him with surprising ease.

Of course. He would go . . . *home.*

For Middlebury Park was only where he had lived for the past three years, the stately home he had inherited with his title and not set foot inside until three years ago. It was very grand, and he liked it well enough. He was determined to settle there and make it his own. It was not yet really *home,* however. Home was Covington House, where he had grown up, an altogether more modest dwelling, not much larger than a cottage actually, on the edge of the village of Barton Coombs in Somerset.

He had not been there in almost six years. Not since he left for the Peninsula, in fact. Now he had a sudden hankering to go back again, even though he would not be able to see it. It had happy associations. His childhood and boyhood years had been good ones despite the near poverty in which they had lived even before the death of his father when he was fifteen.

"We are going home," he announced to Martin one morning after breakfast. He could hear rain pelting against the windows of the small cottage on Windermere he had rented for a month. "Not to Middlebury, though. To Barton Coombs."

"Mhmm," Martin said noncommittally as he gathered up the dishes from the table.

"You will be glad?" Vincent asked.

Martin too was from Barton Coombs. His father was the village blacksmith there. The two boys had gone to the village school together, for there had been no money for private education for Vincent despite the fact that socially he was a gentleman. The blacksmith fancied having a son who could read and write. Vincent had learned his lessons, as had his sisters, from his own father, who had been the schoolmaster. Often he and Martin had played together. Most of the neighborhood children had, in fact, regardless of social rank or financial status or gender or age. It had all been rather idyllic.

Vincent's well-to-do maternal uncle had returned from a long residence in the Far East when Vincent was seventeen and had purchased a commission for his nephew. Martin, upon hearing the news, had come to Covington House, hat clutched in hand, to ask if he could go too as Vincent's batman. That position had not lasted long, as it turned out. Vincent had lost his sight during his very first battle. But Martin had remained with him as his valet, even during those early years when Vincent had not been able to pay him. He had stubbornly refused to be turned off.

"My mam will be glad to see me," Martin said now. "So will my dad, though no doubt he will make the usual grumbling quips to his anvil about his one and only son choosing to be a gentleman's val*ett*."

And so they went.

They traveled all through the last night of the journey, weary as they were, and arrived at Covington House at first light—or so Martin informed him. Vincent would have known it himself, though, as soon as the carriage stopped moving and the door was opened. He could hear a few birds singing with that almost echoing clarity that was peculiar to the predawn period. And the air had a freshening feel to it that suggested an end to night but not quite a start to day.

There was no real need for secrecy except that Vincent would rather no one know he was at Covington House, at least for a while. He did not want to be a curiosity to old friends and neighbors. He did not want them trekking to his door to pay their respects and to satisfy their curiosity about what a blind man looked like. And he did not want anyone writing to his mother and bringing her hurrying here to look after him. He probably would not stay long anyway. He just needed enough time to get his thoughts in order.

A house key had always been kept above the lintel on the inside of the potting shed behind the house. Vincent sent Handry to see if it was still there. If it was not, then Martin was going to have to climb through the window into the wine cellar. It was very doubtful anyone had thought of mending the catch on it in the last six years, since it had never been mended throughout Vincent's boyhood. It had been a regular middle-of-the-night escape and reentry route, in fact.

Handry came back with the key. It was looking slightly rusty, he reported, but it fit in the lock of the front door and turned with a grinding sound and a little persuasion. The door opened.

The house smelled neither musty nor stale from being shut up, Vincent discovered. The cleaners he paid to come in once a fortnight must be doing a conscientious job. There *was* a smell, though, an indefinable something that brought back memories of boyhood days and of his mother and his sisters as they had been when they all lived here. Even faint memories of his father. It was strange that he had never noticed the smell while he lived here—perhaps because he had not needed to notice smells in those days.

He felt about the hall with the aid of his cane. The old oak table was still where it had always been, opposite the door, the umbrella stand beside it. Both were draped with holland covers.

"I know this house like the back of my hand," he told Martin, pulling the cover off the stand and placing his cane in it. "I am going to explore it on my own. And then I am going to lie down in my room for an hour or two. A carriage is not designed for sleeping in, is it?"

"Not when it has to travel over English roads," Martin agreed, "and there isn't any alternative that I have discovered. I'll go and help Handry with the horses. And then I'll bring your bags inside."

One thing Vincent particularly liked about Martin Fisk was that he cared for all his needs without fuss and bluster. Best of all was the fact that he did not *hover*. If Vincent walked into the occasional wall or door or tripped over the occasional object lying in his path or even once in a while tumbled down a flight of steps or— on one memorable occasion—head first into a lily pond, then Martin would be there to deal with any cuts and scratches and other assorted consequences and to make appropriate or inappropriate comments without any sentiment creeping into his voice.

He even occasionally informed his master that he was a clumsy clod.

It was better—ah, infinitely better—than the solicitous care with which almost everyone else of his acquaintance smothered him.

He was an ungrateful wretch, he knew.

Actually, his fellow members of the Survivors' Club treated him much as Martin did. It was one reason why he loved his annual stay at Penderris Hall so much, he supposed. But then all seven of them had been badly wounded in the wars and still bore the scars inside or out or both. They understood the frustrations of too much sympathetic care.

When he was alone in the house, he made his way to

the sitting room on his left, the room in which all the daytime living had been done. Everything was as he remembered it and *where* he remembered it, except for the fact that all the furniture was covered. He moved through to the drawing room, larger and less used than the other room. Sometimes there had been dancing in the drawing room. Eight couples had been able to form for a country set with some comfort, ten with a little less comfort, twelve at a squeeze.

There was a pianoforte in this room. Vincent found his way to it. Like everything else, it was hidden beneath a cover. He was tempted to pull it off, to lift the lid over the keyboard and play. But the instrument must be horribly out of tune.

It was strange that he had never learned to play it when he was a lad. No one had even thought of suggesting that he might. The pianoforte was for the girls, an instrument of torture peculiarly their own—or so Amy, his eldest sister, had always claimed.

Strangely, now that he was here, he missed all three of them. And his mother. Even his father, who had been gone for eight years now. He missed those carefree days of his childhood and youth. And they were not even so very long ago. He was only twenty-three now.

Twenty-three going on fifty.

Or seventy.

He sighed and decided to leave the cover where it was. But standing there at the pianoforte, his hands resting on the top of it, his head bowed, he was suddenly smitten by a familiar tidal wave of panic.

He felt the blood drain from his head, leaving it cold and clammy. He felt the breath cold in his nostrils and so thin that there seemed not enough of it to inhale. He felt all the terror of the unending darkness, of the sure knowledge that if he closed his eyes, as he did now, and opened them again, as he did *not,* he would still be blind.

Always and forever.

With no reprieve.

No light.

Not ever.

He fought to control his breathing, knowing from long experience of such episodes that if he lost control of it, he would soon be gasping for air and even losing consciousness until he came out of his swoon, perhaps alone, perhaps—much worse—with someone hovering over him. But still sightless.

He kept his eyes shut. He counted his breaths again, trying to concentrate upon them to the exclusion of all the thoughts that teemed and tumbled through his mind.

In. Out.

After a while he opened his eyes again and loosened his grip on the top of the pianoforte. He lifted his head. He would be damned, he thought, before he would allow the darkness to encroach upon his inner being. It was enough that it was there outside himself for all time. His own stupidity in battle had caused the outer darkness. He would not compound that youthful folly by allowing the light that was within him to be doused.

He *would* live his life. He would live it to the full. He would make something of it and of himself. He would not give in to either depression or hopelessness.

He would *not,* by God.

He was desperately tired. That was the problem, he supposed, and it was easily solved. He would feel better after a bit of a sleep. He would continue his exploration of the house after that.

He found the staircase with no trouble at all. And he found his way up it without mishap. He found his room without having to feel his way along the wall. He had done it in darkness on numerous occasions when he had sneaked out of the house and in again before daylight.

He turned the knob on his door and stepped inside the room. He hoped there were at least blankets on the bed. He was too tired to worry about sheets. But when he found the bed, he discovered that it was made up as if he had been expected—and he remembered his mother saying that she had left instructions with the biweekly cleaners that the house always be kept ready for the unexpected arrival of a family member.

He removed his coat and boots and cravat and lay down gratefully between the sheets. He felt as if he could sleep for a week.

Perhaps he would spend a week here, alone and quiet in these achingly familiar surroundings, unencumbered by any company other than Martin's. That should be enough time to get his head firmly on his shoulders so that he could go back to Middlebury Park to *live* and not merely to drift onward.

He had given instructions that the carriage be hidden from sight without delay. He had told Martin to inform anyone who asked that he had come alone to visit his parents at the smithy and that his master had granted him permission to stay at Covington House. Martin would have to tell only one person and within an hour everyone would know.

No one would know *he* was here too.

It all sounded like bliss.

He fell asleep before he could fully enjoy the feeling.

2

❧

$\mathcal{V}$incent's arrival had not gone unobserved.

Covington House was the last building at one end of the main street through the village. To the far side of it was a low hill covered with trees. There was a young woman on that hill and among those trees. She wandered at all times of day about the countryside surrounding Barton Hall, where she lived with her aunt and uncle, Sir Clarence and Lady March, though she was not often out quite this early. But this morning she had woken when it was still dark and had been unable to get back to sleep. Her window was open, and a bird with a particularly strident call had obviously not noticed that dawn had not yet arrived. So, rather than shut her window and climb back into bed, she had dressed and come outside, chilly as the early morning air was, because there was something rare and lovely about watching the darkness lift away from another dawning day. And she had come here in particular because the trees housed dozens, perhaps hundreds, of birds, many of them with sweeter voices than the one that had awoken her, and they always sang most earnestly when they were heralding a new day.

She stood very still so as not to disturb them, her back against the sturdy trunk of a beech tree, her arms stretched out about it behind her to enjoy its rough texture through her thin gloves—so thin, in fact, that the left thumb and right forefinger had already worn through. She drank in the beauty and peace of her surroundings and ignored the cold, which penetrated her almost threadbare cloak as if it were not even there, and set her fingers to tingling.

She looked down upon Covington House, her favorite building in Barton Coombs. It was neither a mansion nor a cottage. It was not even a manor. But it was large and square and solid. It was also deserted and had been since before she came here to live two years ago. It was still owned by the Hunt family, about whom she had heard many stories, perhaps because Vincent Hunt, the only son, had unexpectedly inherited a title and fortune a few years ago. It was the stuff of fairy tales, except that it had a sad component too, as many fairy tales did.

She liked to look at the house and imagine it as it might have been when the Hunts lived there—the absentminded but much-loved schoolmaster, his busy wife and three pretty daughters, and his exuberant, athletic, mischievous son, who was always the best at whatever sport was being played and always at the forefront of any waggery that was brewing and always adored by old and young alike—except by the Marches, against whom his pranks were most often directed. She liked to think that if she had lived here then, she would have been friends with the girls and perhaps even with their brother, although they were all older than she. She liked to picture herself running in and out of Covington House without even knocking at the door, almost as if she belonged there. She liked to imagine that she would have attended the village school with all the other children, except Henrietta March, her cousin, who had been educated at home by a French governess.

She was Sophia Fry, though her name was rarely used. She was known by her relatives, when she was known as anything at all, and perhaps by their servants too, as the mouse. She lived at Barton Hall on sufferance because there was nowhere else for her to go. Her father was dead; her mother had left them long ago and since died; her uncle, Sir Terrence Fry, had never had anything to do with either her father or her; and the elder of her paternal aunts, to whom she had been sent first after her father's passing, had died two years ago.

She felt sometimes that she inhabited a no-man's-land between the family at Barton Hall and the servants, that she belonged with neither group and was noticed and cared about by neither. She consoled herself with the fact that her invisibility gave her some freedom at least. Henrietta was always hedged about with maids and chaperons and a vigilant mother and father, whose sole ambition for her was that she marry a titled gentleman, preferably a wealthy one, though that was not an essential qualification, as Sir Clarence was himself a rich man. Henrietta shared her parents' ambitions, with one notable exception.

Sophia's thoughts were interrupted by the sound of horses approaching from beyond the village, and it was soon obvious that they were drawing some sort of carriage. It was very early in the day for travel. It was a stagecoach, perhaps? She stepped around the trunk of the tree and half hid behind it, though it was unlikely she would be seen from below. Her cloak was gray, her cotton bonnet nondescript in both style and color, and it was still not full daylight.

She saw it was a private carriage—a very smart one. But before she could weave some story about it as it passed along the village street and out of sight, it slowed and turned onto the short driveway to Covington House. It stopped before the front doors.

Her eyes widened. Could it be . . . ?

The coachman jumped down from his perch and opened the carriage door and set down the steps. A man descended almost immediately, a young man, tall and rather burly. He looked around and said something to the coachman—Sophia could hear the rumble of his voice but not what he said. And then they both turned to watch another man.

He descended without assistance. He moved sure-footed and without hesitation. But it was instantly obvious to Sophia that his cane was not a mere fashion accessory but something he used to help him find his way.

She sucked in a breath and hoped, foolishly, that it was inaudible to the three men standing some distance below her. He had come, then, as everyone had said he would.

The blind Viscount Darleigh, once Vincent Hunt, had come home.

Her aunt and uncle would be over the moon with gratification. For they had made up their minds that if and when he came, Henrietta would marry him.

Henrietta, on the other hand, would *not* be gratified. For once in her life she was opposed to her parents' dearest wish. She had declared more than once in Sophia's hearing that she would rather die a spinster at the age of eighty than marry a blind man with a ruined face even if he *was* a viscount and even if he *was* far more wealthy than her papa.

Viscount Darleigh—Sophia was convinced that the new arrival must be he—was clearly a young man. He was not particularly tall and he had a slight, graceful build. He carried himself well. He did not hunch over his cane or paw the air with his free hand. He was neatly, elegantly clad. Her lips parted as she gazed down at him. She wondered how much of the old Vincent Hunt was still present in the blind Viscount Darleigh. He had descended from his carriage without assistance. That fact pleased her.

She could not see his face; his tall hat hid it from her

view. Poor gentleman. She wondered just how disfigured it was.

He and the burly man stood on the driveway for a few minutes while the coachman went striding off to the back of the house and returned with what must be the key, for he bent to the lock of the front door, and within moments it swung open. Viscount Darleigh ascended the steps before the door, again unassisted, and disappeared inside with the larger man behind him.

Sophia stood watching for another few minutes, but there was nothing more to see except the coachman taking the horse and carriage to the stables and coach house. She turned away and made her way back in the direction of Barton Hall. Standing still had thoroughly chilled her.

She would not tell anyone he had arrived, she decided. No one ever spoke to her anyway or expected her to volunteer any information or opinion. Doubtless everyone would know soon enough.

*U*nfortunately for Vincent and his hope for a quiet stay at Covington House, Sophia Fry was not the only person who observed his arrival.

A farm laborer, on his way to milk cows, had the distinct good fortune—of which he boasted to his colleagues for days to come—of witnessing the arrival of Viscount Darleigh's carriage at Covington House. He had stayed, at the expense of the waiting cows, to watch Vincent-Hunt-that-was descend after Martin Fisk, the blacksmith's son. By seven o'clock in the morning he had told his wife, having dashed back home for that sole purpose; his baby son, who was profoundly uninterested in the momentous news; his fellow laborers; the blacksmith and the blacksmith's wife; and Mr. Kerry, who had come in early to the smithy because one of his horses had cast a shoe late the evening before.

By eight o'clock, the farm laborers—and the original farm laborer's wife—had told everyone they knew, or at least those of that category who came within hailing distance. Mr. Kerry had told the butcher and the vicar and his aged mother. The blacksmith's wife, ecstatic that her son was back home in the capacity of valet to Viscount Darleigh, Vincent-Hunt-that-was, had dashed off to the baker's to replenish her supply of flour and had told the baker and his two assistants and three other early customers. And the blacksmith, also bursting with pride even though he spoke with head-shaking disparagement of his son, the *valett,* told his apprentice when that lad arrived late for work and for once did not have to recite a litany of excuses, and Sir Clarence March's groom, and the vicar, who heard the news for the second time in a quarter of an hour but appeared equally ecstatic both times.

By nine o'clock it would have been difficult to discover a single person within Barton Coombs, or a three-mile radius surrounding it, who did *not* know that Viscount Darleigh, Vincent-Hunt-that-was, had arrived at Covington House when dawn had barely cracked its knuckles, and had not left it since.

Though if he had arrived *that* early, Miss Waddell observed to Mrs. Parsons, wife of the aptly named vicar, when the two ladies encountered each other across the hedge separating their back gardens, he must have been traveling all night and was enjoying a well-deserved rest, poor gentleman. It would not be kind to call upon him *too* early. She would inform the reception committee. Poor dear gentleman.

The vicar rehearsed his speech of welcome and wondered if it was too formal. For, after all, Viscount Darleigh had once been just the sunny-natured, mischievous son of the village schoolmaster. He was, in addition to everything else, though, a war hero. And he did now have that very impressive title. Better to err on the side of formality, he decided, than risk appearing over-familiar.

Mrs. Fisk baked the bread rolls and cakes she had been planning in her head for weeks. *Her son,* her beloved only child, was back home, not to mention Viscount Darleigh, that bright and happy boy who had used to run wild with Martin and drag him into all sorts of scrapes—not that Martin had taken much dragging. Poor boy. Poor gentleman. She sniffed and wiped away a tear with the back of her floury hand.

At ten o'clock the young Misses Granger called upon the equally young Miss Hamilton to discover what she planned to wear to the assembly, which would surely happen now that Lord Darleigh had come. The three of them proceeded to reminisce about Vincent-Hunt-that-was winning all the races at the annual village fete by a mile and bowling out every cricketer on the opposing team who had the courage and audacity to come up to bat against him and looking so very handsome with his always overlong fair curls and his blue, blue eyes and his lithe physique. And always smiling his lovely smile, even at *them,* though they had been just little girls at the time. He had always smiled at *everyone.*

That last memory drew tears from all of them, for now Viscount Darleigh would never win any race or bowl at any cricket game or look handsome—or perhaps even smile at anyone. He would not even be able to dance at the assembly. They could conceive of no worse fate than that.

Vincent would have been horrified to know that, in fact, his arrival in Barton Coombs had been expected. Or, if that was too strong a word, then at least it had been looked for with eager hope and cautious anticipation.

For Vincent had forgotten two overwhelmingly significant facts about his mother and his sisters. One was that they were all inveterate letter writers. The other was that they had all had numerous friends at Barton Coombs and had not simply relinquished those friends when they moved away. They might not be able to visit them daily, as they had been used to do, but they could and did write to them.

His mother had not been reassured by the two notes that had arrived, scrawled in the inelegant hand of Martin Fisk. She had not sat back and waited for her son to come home. Rather she had done all in her power to discover where he was. Most of her guesses were quite wide of the mark. But one was that Vincent might return to Barton Coombs, where he had spent his boyhood and been happy, where he had so many friends and so many friendly acquaintances, where he would be comfortable and would be made much of. Indeed, the more she thought of it, the more convinced she became that if he was not already there, he would end up there sooner or later.

She wrote letters. She always wrote letters anyway. It came naturally to her.

And Amy, Ellen, and Ursula wrote letters too, though they were not as convinced as their mother that Vincent would go to Barton Coombs. It was more likely that he had gone back to Cornwall, where he always seemed to be so happy. Or perhaps to Scotland or the Lake District, where he could escape their matchmaking clutches. All three of Vincent's sisters rather regretted the aggressive manner in which they had pressed Miss Dean upon him. She obviously was not for him—or he for her. It had not escaped their notice that rather than looking mortified when it was discovered that he was gone, she had been hard pressed not to look openly relieved.

However it was, long before Vincent actually did arrive in Barton Coombs, there was scarcely a person there who did not know for a near certainty that he would come. The only question that had caused any real anxiety was *when*.

Everyone, almost without exception, was enraptured as the news spread through the village and beyond that the wait was at an end. He was here.

*T*he most notable exception to the general mood of rapture was Henrietta March. She was horror-struck.

"*Vincent Hunt?*" she cried.

"Viscount Darleigh, my love," her mother reminded her.

"Of Middlebury Park in Gloucestershire," her father added. "With an income of twenty thousand a year, at a conservative estimate."

"And two blind eyes and a deformed face," Henrietta retorted. "Yeeuw!"

"You would not have to look at him," her father told her. "Middlebury Park is big enough, or so I have heard. Far larger than this. And you would need to spend time in London as a fashionable viscountess. It would be expected of you. He would hardly go with you, would he? And you would want to visit here. He will not want to come too often to be subjected to that Waddell woman each time, not to mention the vicar and all the other sycophants who live in the neighborhood."

The mouse, who sat in her corner of the March drawing room darning pillowcases, looked sharply and incautiously across the room at him. Sycophants? *Other* people? Had her uncle not looked in a glass lately? But she lowered her head quickly before he noticed her. She certainly did not want to be caught staring, especially staring incredulously. Besides, she needed her eyes for her darning.

She did not particularly mind being the mouse in the corner. She had, in fact, cultivated invisibility for most of her life. While her mother had still lived with her and her father, a time she remembered only dimly, there had been almost daily and nightly arguments and even fights, from which she had withdrawn into the dimmest corner of whatever rooms they had happened to be occupying at the time. And after her mother left, never to return, when she was five, she had kept well clear of her father when he came home in his cups, though he had never been a violent man and it had not happened with any great frequency. More often, it was his boisterous friends from whom she had hidden when they had come home with her father to carouse and play their card games instead of going elsewhere. They had had a tendency to chuck her under the chin and bounce her on their knees when she was young—and she had always looked younger than her years. And then there had been landlords to hide from when they were slipping away from yet another set of rooms for which they were in arrears on the rent, and merchants and bailiffs who came looking for payment of various debts. She had spent most of her childhood, in fact, trying to be invisible and silent so that no one would notice her.

Her father, the younger son of a baronet, had been one of those gentlemen who had looks and charm and even intelligence to spare—he had taught his daughter to read and write and figure—but who lacked any ability to cope with life. His dreams had always been as big and wide as the ocean, but dreams were not reality. They did not put a permanent roof over their heads or a regular supply of food in their stomachs.

Sophia had adored him, occasional drunken sprees and all.

She had been content to be invisible to Aunt Mary, her father's elder sister, to whom she had been sent after his death, even though she was fifteen at the time. For Aunt Mary had raked her from head to toe with one contemptuous look upon her arrival and pronounced her impossible. She had proceeded to treat her accordingly—she had virtually ignored her, in other words. But at least she had allowed her to stay, and she had provided her with the basic necessities of life.

And being ignored was actually better than being noticed, experience had taught her during those years with Aunt Mary. For the only friendship she had ever enjoyed, the only romance that had ever stirred her heart, had been brief and intense and ultimately soul-shattering.

And then Aunt Mary had died suddenly after Sophia had lived with her for three years, and Sophia had been taken in by Aunt Martha, who had never pretended to look upon her as anything more than a glorified maid who must nevertheless be suffered to dine and sit with the family when they were at home. Only very occasionally did Aunt Martha call her by name. Sir Clarence did not call her anything except, sometimes, the mouse. Henrietta seemed unaware of her very existence. But she did not want to be visible to any of them. She did not like them, even though she was grateful to them for giving her a home.

Sophia sighed, careful to make no sound. Sometimes she might almost have forgotten her own name if it were not for the fact that she was the mouse only to the depth of her skin—not even so deep, actually. Inside, she was not a mouse at all. But no one knew that except her. It was a secret she rather enjoyed hugging to herself. Except that she worried sometimes about the future, which stretched long and bleak ahead of her with no prospect of change—the lot of poor female relatives everywhere. Sometimes she wished she had not been born a lady and could have sought employment on the death of her father. But it was not considered genteel for ladies to work, not while they had relatives to take them in, anyway.

"Viscount Darleigh will no doubt be more than happy to marry you, Henrietta," Sir Clarence March said. "He is not quite a marquess, heir to a dukedom, as Wrayburn was, it is true, but he *is* a viscount."

"Papa," Henrietta wailed, "it would be intolerable. Even apart from his wrecked face and his blind eyes, the very thought of which make me feel bilious and vaporish, he is *Vincent Hunt*. I could not so demean myself."

"He *was* Vincent Hunt," her mother reminded her. "He is now Viscount Darleigh, my love. There is a world of difference. It still amazes me that his father lived here all those years as the village schoolmaster, the not very well-to-do schoolmaster, I might add, and we never suspected that he was the younger brother of a viscount. We might never have known it if the viscount and his son had not been obliging enough to die and leave Vincent Hunt the title. Why they stood up to a gang of highwaymen instead of simply relinquishing their valuables, I will never understand. But it is your good fortune that they did and were shot. This is a perfect opportunity for you, my love, and will enable you to hold your head high in society again."

"Again? She never had to hang her head," Sir Clarence said sharply, frowning at his wife. "That dashed Wrayburn! He thought to cut our Henrietta in the middle of a crowded ballroom. Well, she showed him!"

Sophia had not been present at that particular ball. She had never been present at *any* ball for that matter. But she had been in London, and she had pieced together what she believed to be the real story about Henrietta and the Marquess of Wrayburn. When Henrietta and her mama had approached him at the Stiles ball, he had turned his back and pretended not to see them coming, making a loud remark to his group to the effect that it was sometimes near impossible to avoid determined mamas and their pathetic daughters.

After Henrietta had spent half an hour in the ladies' withdrawing room with her mama, where the latter had had to be plied with smelling salts and brandy, she had emerged in order to slink off home—several people had heard that remark, and doubtless by then *everyone* knew of it—and had the misfortune to come face to face with the marquess himself. To her credit, she had stuck her nose in the air and asked her mother if she knew the source of that nasty odor. Unfortunately for her, because it might well have been a splendid set-down, the marquess and his cronies had seen fit to find her remark uproariously funny, and doubtless the whole ballroom found it hilarious within a quarter of an hour.

Sophia had felt *almost* sorry for her cousin that night. Indeed, if Henrietta had told the full truth of the incident—which Sophia learned from listening to the servants—she might have felt all the way sorry for her, at least for a while.

"I shall call at Covington House without further delay," Sir Clarence said, getting to his feet after consulting his pocket watch, "before anyone else gets there first. I daresay that bore of a vicar will be there before luncheon with one of his speeches and that fool of a Waddell woman will be there with her welcoming committee."

And you will be there, the mouse commented silently, *to offer your daughter in marriage.*

"I shall invite him for dinner," Sir Clarence announced. "Have a talk with the cook, Martha. Make sure she puts on something special this evening."

"But what does one serve a *blind* man?" his wife asked, looking dismayed.

"Papa." Henrietta's voice was trembling. "You cannot expect me to marry a blind man with no face. You cannot expect me to marry *Vincent Hunt*. Not after the way he always played the most atrocious tricks on you."

"Boyish high spirits," her father said with a dismissive wave of his hand. "Listen to me, Henrietta. You have just been presented with this wonderful opportunity as if on a platter. It is as if we were brought home early from London for just this purpose. We will have him here this evening, and we will look him over. He won't be able to see us doing it, after all, will he?"

He looked pleased with his little joke, though he did not laugh. Sir Clarence March rarely did. He was too puffed up with his own consequence, Sophia thought with unrepentant malice.

"If he passes muster," Sir Clarence continued, "then you will have him, Henrietta. This year was your third Season in London, my girl. Your *third*. And somehow, though not through any fault of your own, it is true, you lost your chance for a baron the first year, an earl the second, and a marquess this year. A Season does not come cheap. And you do not grow younger. And pretty soon, if it has not happened already, you are going to be known as the young lady who cannot keep a suitor when she has one. Well, my girl, we will show them."

He beamed at his wife and daughter—and ignored the mouse—and seemed totally oblivious to the devastated look on Henrietta's face and the mortified one on his wife's.

And off he went to net a viscount for Henrietta.

Sophia felt sorry for Viscount Darleigh, though perhaps, she conceded, he did not deserve her pity. She did not know anything about him, after all, except what she had learned about his alter ego, Vincent Hunt, when he had been just a boy. Though she *did* know that he was neat and elegant, and independent enough not to have to be led everywhere by his servants.

At least this evening promised to be a little less tedious than life usually was. She would have a viscount to gaze upon, even if seeing his face should make her want to vomit or faint, like Henrietta. And she would be able to observe the early progress of a courtship. It should be mildly entertaining.

She slipped away after Sir Clarence had left and ran upstairs for her sketch pad and charcoal—prized possessions since she was not granted any regular pin money. She had taken them from Henrietta's long-abandoned schoolroom. She would go out to the woods behind the house, where she could be out of sight, and sketch a large, blustering man with huge chest and biceps and puny head and spindly legs towering over a cowering little man with bandaged eyes and holding a wedding ring aloft in a pudgy hand, while two women, one large and middle-aged, the other young and willowy, stood off to one side, the plump one looking triumphant, the young one looking tragic. As always, she would place a grinning little mouse in the bottom right-hand corner.

3

❧

"*I was* firm," Vincent protested, his chin raised as Martin tied his neckcloth in a manner suitable for evening wear. "I refused to go there for dinner. I don't suppose anyone quite understands how tricky it is chasing food about on one's plate without knowing quite what food it is one chases while holding a polite conversation at the same time—*and* wondering if one has dribbled gravy down one's chin or onto one's cravat."

Martin was not to be deterred.

"If you had been firm," he said, "you would not have gone at all. Old *March,* for the love of God! And *Lady* March! And *Miss Henrietta* March! Need I say more?"

"If you do," Vincent said, "you may well run out of italics and exclamation points, Martin. Yes, they were a haughty trio and treated the rest of us lowly mortals as if we were worms beneath their feet. But we had a great deal of sport out of them and must not complain."

"Do you remember the time his nibs set up that stone bust of supposedly ancient Roman origin on a pedestal in his courtyard," Martin asked, "and invited all the neighborhood to gather around at a respectful distance while it was unveiled with great pomp and ceremony? And then, when old March pulled off the cover with a grand flourish, everyone except the Marches themselves collapsed in a heap of mirth? I'll never forget that bright blue, winking eyelid with long black eyelashes, or the scarlet up-curling lips. You excelled yourself with that one."

They snickered and then outright guffawed for a while at the memory of that winking, leering monstrosity of stone.

"Yes, well," Vincent said, "I almost got caught that time, you know, when I was getting back into the house through the cellar window. The keg beneath it wobbled and would have fallen with a crash if I had not hurled myself beneath it and deadened the sound. I nursed a good few bruised ribs for the following week or so. But the suffering was worth it."

"Ah, those were the days," Martin said fondly, indicating with a tap on Vincent's shoulder that he was ready to go. "And now you are going to pay them an evening call. You are capitulating to the enemy."

"I was taken aback when March knocked on the door," Vincent said, "and was not thinking straight. I was still half asleep."

"You must have been," Martin said. "There I was at the door, explaining to his nibs that he was mistaken, that I had come alone to Barton Coombs to visit my mam and dad and was staying here with your permission, and there you were walking down the stairs behind me as bold as brass, in full view from the door, to make a liar out of me."

"It is the mark of a good butler," Vincent said, "that he can lie with a straight face and perfect conviction."

"I am not your butler," Martin reminded him. "And what would you have been even if I were? An optical illusion? You had better come down to the kitchen and have some of the rabbit stew I made and some of Mam's fresh bread before you go. She loaded me down with enough to feed the five thousand."

Vincent got to his feet and sighed—and then laughed again. This morning had been like a well-rehearsed farce and had left him wondering if the village was ringed about twenty-four hours a day with lookouts whose sole task was to give instant notice of the approach of any and all comers. Sir Clarence March had come soon after eleven, all puffed up with his own importance and magnanimity—nothing had changed there in six years. He had left, in some haste, only when a seeming army of ladies had arrived to welcome Vincent home. Miss Waddell had been the spokesperson, but she had named each of the other ladies in a slow, distinct voice and repeated the list after he had invited them all to be seated—just before he remembered the holland covers. But they had been removed, he discovered when he sat down himself. Then, before the ladies could settle into any flow of conversation, the vicar had arrived, though his wife, who was a member of Miss Waddell's committee, had scolded him before everyone with the reminder that he had *known* the ladies were coming at a quarter past eleven and ought to have waited until at least a quarter to twelve before coming himself.

"Poor, dear Lord Darleigh will be feeling quite overwhelmed, Joseph," she had told him.

"Not at all," Vincent had assured them, smelling coffee and hearing the rattle of china as Martin carried in a tray. "How delightful it is to receive such a warm welcome."

He had been rather glad he had not been able to see the expression on Martin's face.

Several minutes later, just as the Reverend Parsons was setting the finishing touches to his windy welcome speech, Mr. Kerry had arrived with elderly Mrs. Kerry, his mother, and the volume of conversation had increased considerably, for she was deaf.

At the first slight lull in the chatter, perhaps twenty minutes after that, Miss Waddell had delivered her pièce de résistance. There was to be an assembly tomorrow evening, she had announced, in the assembly rooms above the Foaming Tankard Inn, and dear Viscount Darleigh was to be the guest of honor.

And at last light had dawned in Vincent's brain. His mother! And his sisters! They had guessed he might come here, and they had probably used a pot of ink apiece writing letters to everyone they knew in Barton Coombs and within a few miles of its outer bounds.

So much for his few days of quiet relaxation.

With a smile on his face and thanks on his lips, he had suffered ladies dashing at him from all directions—to pour his coffee, to position his napkin on his lap, to lift his cup and saucer from the tray and set them on the table beside him where he could easily reach them, to set them in his hand a moment later lest he have difficulty finding them on the side table, to choose the best cake from the plate of Mrs. Fisk's offerings and set it on *his* plate, to set his plate in his other hand, to set his cup and saucer back down on the table so that he would have one hand free to eat his cake—there were some amused titterings over that—to . . . Well, they would have eaten and drunk for him if they could.

He had forced himself to remember that their ministrations were kindly meant.

But *an assembly*?

A dance?

And right now, this evening, a private evening visit to the Marches at Barton Hall.

Perhaps, he thought in one moment of weakness, he ought to have married Miss Dean a month or so ago and put himself out of his misery.

 ℒady March had been relieved to learn that Viscount Darleigh was not coming to dinner. Henrietta was disappointed that he was coming at all. But neither lady had been able to get any further information from Sir Clarence when they had asked about his lordship's appearance and demeanor. He had merely smirked and looked self-important and told them that they would *see*.

"Which is more than Darleigh is able to do," he had added, his smirk widening and deepening, making him look like the cartoon Sophia had drawn of him the evening Henrietta had first danced with the Marquess of Wrayburn.

Henrietta picked at her food during dinner. She was dressed for the evening in her silver shot-silk ball gown, an extravagance for an evening in the country, perhaps, but suited to the grandness of the occasion, her mama assured her. For tonight a viscount was coming to call, and such an opportunity might not come again.

Aunt Martha was looking rather formidable in purple satin with matching turban and tall, nodding plumes. Sir Clarence could not turn his head more than an inch in either direction. If he did, he would be in dire danger of piercing an eyeball with a starched shirt point.

How silly they all looked, especially when their expected guest was a blind man.

Oh, how Sophia's fingers itched for her charcoal.

She herself was wearing one of Henrietta's cast-off day dresses, which she had cut down to size. In the process, of course, she had completely destroyed any style and flow the dress had once had, for she was very much smaller than Henrietta in every imaginable way. Sophia did not go so far as to tell herself that it was a good thing Lord Darleigh was blind. That would be cruel. And it would presuppose the ludicrous notion that he might notice her if he could see. But truly she looked like someone's abandoned scarecrow.

At the precise moment the guest was expected, there were the sounds of carriage wheels and horses' hooves and creaking, jingling harness from the courtyard below the drawing room, and everyone except Sophia leapt to their feet and smoothed out skirts and checked that plumes had not wilted and straightened a cravat and cleared throats and looked nervous and then . . . smiled with gracious ease as they turned in a body toward the opening door.

"Lord Darleigh," the butler announced in tones a majordomo in Carlton House might envy.

And in stepped two men, the one with an arm drawn through the other's before he slid it free and the other took a step back, then disappeared behind the closing door with the butler.

The other man was the burly one who had stepped first out of the carriage this morning.

Sir Clarence and Aunt Martha made a rush for the remaining gentleman and made a great to-do about helping him to a chair and seating him on it. Sir Clarence boomed pompously and Aunt Martha spoke in the sort of voice she might have used to an ailing infant or a harmless imbecile.

Sophia did not notice what Henrietta did in the meanwhile. She herself was too caught up in a personal moment of surprise, and, quite frankly, she stared. It was a good thing he was blind and would not notice.

For Viscount Darleigh was everything she had observed this morning and more. He was not particularly tall, and he was graceful and elegant. He also looked well shaped and well muscled in all the right places, as though he lived a vigorous life and was fit, even athletic. He was dressed for evening with perfect good taste and no ostentation. He was, in fact, really quite gorgeous, and Sophia felt foolishly smitten. And that was just her reaction to what she saw below his neck.

It was what she saw above his neck that caused her to stare in such surprise, though. He had fair hair, a little long for fashion, perhaps, but perfectly suited to him. For it waved softly and was a little disordered—attractively disordered. It looked shiny and healthy. And his face . . .

Well, it was not ruined after all. There was not even the merest scar to mar its beauty. And it *was* beautiful. She did not really consider individual features, but the whole was wonderfully pleasing, for it looked like a good-humored face that smiled often, though he surely could not be feeling very happy at the moment about being so fussed. Surely, once he had been shown to a chair, he could have bent his knees and lowered himself safely to the seat without having to be hauled and maneuvered there.

Oh, but there was one feature of his flawless face upon which Sophia's eyes focused, one feature that raised it above the ranks of the merely good-humored and good-looking and accounted for his almost breathtaking beauty. His *eyes*. They were large and wide and very blue, and they were fringed with eyelashes any girl might envy, though there was nothing even remotely effeminate about them. Or about him.

He was every inch a man, a thought that caught her by surprise and suspended her breath for a moment, for she did not have any idea what the thought meant.

She gazed at him in wonder and awe and retreated a little farther into her corner, if that was possible. She found him utterly, totally intimidating, as though he were a creature who inhabited another world from her own. She had depicted him in her cartoon earlier as a small man with a bandaged face. She would never do that again. Cartoons were for people over whom she wished to indulge a private and not always kindly laugh.

He looked up at his hosts with those blue, blue eyes.

And he looked at Henrietta when Sir Clarence drew her forward to introduce her—or rather *re*-introduce her.

"You remember our dear Henrietta, Darleigh," he said with bluff heartiness. "She is all grown up, leading her mother a merry dance and being a naughty puss for her father. She has been taken to town for the past three Seasons and might have married dukes and marquesses and earls by the dozen—enough of them have sighed over her and paid court to her, I would have you know. But nothing will do but she must hold herself aloof for that special gentleman who will come along to sweep her off her feet. *And you know, Papa,* she says, *I am as likely to find him at our own home in the country as I am in the ballrooms of the* ton *in London.* Can you imagine that, Darleigh? Where is she likely to discover her special gentleman in Barton Coombs? Eh?"

He did not often laugh, Sophia reflected, but when he did, everyone else cringed. Aunt Martha cringed and smiled graciously. Henrietta cringed and blushed—and gazed in raptures at the unmarked face of the man she had declared she would never marry if he was the last man on earth.

He really *was* blind, Sophia decided from her quiet corner of the room. She had doubted it for a moment. It had seemed impossible. But he had got to his feet again in order to bow to Henrietta, and although he appeared to be looking directly at her, in reality he was gazing just above the level of her right shoulder.

"If Miss March is as beautiful as she was six years ago," he said, "and I daresay she is *more* beautiful as she was just a girl then, I am not surprised that she has been so besieged by admirers in London."

He was oily, Sophia thought, frowning in disappointment. Or perhaps he was just being polite.

Everyone sat down and launched into stilted, overhearty conversation—at least, the three Marches did. Lord Darleigh merely made the appropriate responses and smiled.

He was being polite, Sophia decided after a few minutes. He was not oily at all. He was behaving like a gentleman. She was relieved. She felt predisposed to like him.

He had been an officer in an artillery regiment during the Peninsular Wars, she had learned. A very young officer. He had been blinded in battle. It was only later that he had inherited his title and fortune from an uncle. It was a good thing too, for there had been very little money in the family. Recently he had left his home in Gloucestershire after his mother and sisters had tried to force a bride upon him. They had all been agreed that it would be best for him, for any number of reasons, if he had a wife to care for him. Clearly he had disagreed, either with the general principle or with their specific choice. He had stayed away for some time, and no one had known where he was until he had arrived at Covington House this morning, as Mrs. Hunt had predicted he would in letters she had written to various ladies in the village.

He had once been plain Vincent Hunt, and Sophia had weaved stories about him. He had been a leader among the youth of the village, good at all sports and the ringleader of all mischief. One night, for example, after Sir Clarence had boasted of a red carpet he had walked across to enter some grand house in London, he had painted the steps outside the front doors of Barton Hall a scarlet red.

Now he was a very grand gentleman with a different, imposing name. And he was a very well-mannered gentleman too. He scarcely stopped smiling and making polite, noncommittal replies to all the pomposity that was being said to him despite the fact that Aunt Martha and Sir Clarence were almost openly and really quite embarrassingly courting him, and Henrietta was simpering. It was actually rather hard to simper effectively before a blind man, but she was doing quite well at it.

When the conversation finally threatened to flag, Henrietta was sent to the pianoforte to dazzle the viscount with her talent on the keyboard. And then she was directed to sing as she played and went through a repertoire of five songs before remembering that the music for the sixth, her particular favorite, was in her mother's private sitting room, where she had been practicing earlier in the day.

"Go up and fetch it," her mother said, turning her head in Sophia's direction.

"Yes, aunt," Sophia murmured as she got to her feet.

And she was aware of Viscount Darleigh, a look of slight surprise on his face as he raised his eyebrows and turned his eyes her way. She would have sworn he was looking directly at her, though she knew it could not be so. But for that moment, before she left the room, she felt a little less anonymous than usual. And she found, before she reached the staircase, that she was scurrying rather than walking like a dignified lady.

They had not, of course, been introduced.

"When you stepped into the drawing room with me," Vincent asked as the carriage swayed its way over the short distance between Barton Hall and Covington House, "was there someone else there in addition to Sir Clarence and Lady March and Miss March?"

"Hmm." There was a pause, during which Martin was presumably thinking. "Apart from the butler, you mean?"

"A woman," Vincent said.

"I can't say I noticed," Martin told him.

"Someone was sent for more music," Vincent said, "and she said *yes, aunt* before going. It was the first and last I heard of her all evening. She must walk very softly, for I did not hear her return, though the music certainly arrived. She was obviously not a servant. She called Lady March *aunt*. But we were not introduced. Is that not strange?"

"A poor relation?" Martin suggested.

"I daresay," Vincent agreed. "But it would have been good manners to introduce her to a guest anyway, would it not?"

"Not necessarily if you were a March," Martin said.

"*Go up and fetch it,* her aunt told her when Miss March wanted the music," Vincent said. "There was no *please*. And, worse, there was no name."

"Hmm," Martin said. "You are not betrothed yet by any chance, are you?"

"Eh?"

"They have serious designs on you," Martin told him. "Be warned. The servants are not very close-lipped in that house, a sure sign the Marches don't inspire a great deal of loyalty."

"Serious designs," Vincent said. "Yes, I believe the servants may be right about that. I shall tread with great care during the coming days. In particular, if I should happen to hear the fateful words *I understand* and *I do not mind* come from Miss March's lips, I shall flee to the tip of Land's End."

"You had better have a boat with you," Martin said. "That might not be far enough."

They were home already. What a very strange day it had been. He had arrived here before dawn with the happy idea of relaxing quietly for a few days and doing some serious thinking before going back home to Middlebury Park to take command of the rest of his life. And then—

He laughed as Handry set down the steps of the carriage and he climbed down outside his front door without assistance.

"Miss Waddell and her welcoming committees," he said.

"I was upset you did not invite me to come and listen to the vicar's welcome," Martin said.

They both snorted with laughter.

"Actually, you know," Vincent said as he made his way up the steps to the front door, "it was touching. They were all so much a part of the fabric of our childhood, Martin. And kindlier, more well-meaning people one could not hope to encounter. It is unkind of us to laugh at them, except that our laughter is well meant too. We were fortunate to grow up here."

"That we were," Martin agreed cheerfully. "There are some of Mam's cakes left, sir. Would you like one or two with a drink?"

"Hot milk, if there is some, please, Martin," Vincent said, making his way to the sitting room. "And one cake, please. Your mother has certainly not lost her touch, has she? One of her cakes is worth four of anyone else's."

Goodness, he must be feeling nostalgic. What had he just asked for? *Hot milk?*

He was actually glad he had been discovered here. He had been a bit ashamed or embarrassed or . . . or *something* to be seen blind like this when these people had known him as he used to be. But that had been foolish of him. His morning visitors had been kind and, solicitous though they had been over his blindness, they had still treated him as a thinking, functioning adult. They had been happy to reminisce about the past, when his father was schoolmaster here and his mother was active in the church and the community and Vincent and his sisters had been growing up with all the other village children and getting into all sorts of mischief with them. Vincent too had been happy to remember and had joined in the conversation with some enthusiasm.

He sighed as he sat back in his chair by the fireplace. Dash it, but he was tired. Tired without having even exercised today. That, no doubt, was part of the problem.

And tomorrow evening there was to be an assembly at the Foaming Tankard. Vincent grinned as he remembered the petition Miss Waddell had coaxed eleven people to sign protesting the name of the inn when it changed hands—Vincent must have been about six at the time. The inn had once been the respectably named Rose and Crown.

An assembly.

In his honor.

He tipped back his head and laughed aloud. Who but the citizens of Barton Coombs would put on a dance for a blind man?

He must not relax too much into this unexpectedly pleasant interlude, though, he thought as Martin brought in his milk and cake. For Sir Clarence March had made it perfectly clear that his daughter would welcome a marriage proposal from him, and Lady March had extolled her daughter's virtues and accomplishments. Miss March herself had simpered. They all meant to have him, and what the Marches wanted, they often got, though they had obviously failed miserably with a few dozen dukes and marquesses and earls—were there that many in existence, even if one included the married ones?

He was going to have to watch himself.

Henrietta March had been exquisitely pretty as a girl and had shown promise of extraordinary beauty when Vincent last saw her. She must have been about fifteen at the time. She was dark-haired, dark-eyed, and shapely, and she had always been fashionably, expensively clad in clothes made by a dressmaker—or modiste in Sir Clarence's vocabulary—who came down from London twice a year. Miss March had always had a French nurse and a French governess, and had never mingled with the children of the village. The closest she had ever come to conversing with them was at her birthday parties, when she stood in a receiving line with her mama and papa and nodded and murmured graciously in acknowledgment of the birthday greetings of all those who filed respectfully by.

Vincent might have felt sorry for her if she had not embraced haughtiness and an air of superiority quite independently of her parents. And his guess was that she had not changed. Certainly she had shown no sign of it this evening. That music her mother had sent for had arrived, but she had not uttered a word of thanks to the mystery woman who had brought it. Her cousin?

Who was she? She had not even been introduced to him or been included in any of the conversation. Her only spoken words all evening had been *yes, aunt*. But she must have been there all the time.

He felt rather indignant on her behalf, whoever she was. She was apparently a member of the family, yet she had been ignored except when there was an errand to be run. She had sat all evening as quiet as a mouse.

It ought not to bother him.

He reached for his glass of milk, having finished the cake, and drained it.

Good Lord, it had been a ghastly evening. The conversation had been pompous and insipid, the music less than distinguished. While he might happily have endured both if the Marches had been amiable people whom he had once liked, he felt no guilt about looking back on the evening with a shudder of distaste. If he had returned to the village today as plain Vincent Hunt, they would not have deigned to recognize his existence. Did a title make all the difference?

It was a rhetorical question.

It was time for bed.

He wondered how long it would be before his mother was informed of his whereabouts. He would wager that at least a dozen letters had been written and sent on their way today. Everyone would want the distinction of being the first to tell her.

4

There had been several assemblies since Sophia came to Barton Hall to live, but her uncle and aunt and cousin had not attended any of them. It would have been far beneath their dignity to make an appearance and to dance at the Foaming Tankard Inn even if attendance had been reserved to those with some claim to gentility. But village assemblies would not have been worth holding if they had not been open to anyone who cared to go. The thought of rubbing shoulders with a farm laborer or the butcher or the blacksmith was enough to give Aunt Martha the vapors, she had once declared.

Hence Sophia had never attended any of the assemblies either.

All that was about to change, though. For tonight's assembly was in honor of Viscount Darleigh, and Sir Clarence and Aunt Martha had decided that somehow, by fair means or foul, Henrietta was going to become Viscountess Darleigh of Middlebury Park in Gloucestershire with twenty thousand pounds or so a year at her disposal. Since last evening Henrietta herself had done a complete about-face and now declared that the viscount was by far the most handsome, most genteel, most charming, most everything else that was wonderful of all the gentlemen she had ever met. He had certainly changed since the days when he had been "that horrid Vincent Hunt."

"Tonight you must seize your chance in both hands, my love," Aunt Martha said, "for we do not know how long Viscount Darleigh plans to stay at Covington House. He will not dance, of course. You must refuse to dance too, for of course there will be no one else there worth dancing with, and you must spend the time talking with him. If the weather holds—and it looks as if it is going to be a beautiful day—you must suggest a stroll in the outdoors. The assembly rooms are certain to be stuffy. And you must be sure to keep him outside long enough that people will remark upon it. And remark upon it they will, for as the guest of honor he will have everyone's attention focused upon him. He will feel obliged to do the decent thing, you may be sure, and call upon Papa tomorrow morning, for everyone will expect it of him, and he surely values the good opinion of his former neighbors."

"Your mother will plan a summer wedding," Sir Clarence added, clasping the lapels of his coat with both hands and looking pleased with the world. "Perhaps in London with half the *ton* in attendance. Though almost everyone leaves town in the summer, I am sure they would return for such an illustrious event."

Sophia was going to the assembly too. She had not been told she might go, and she had not asked. But the village assemblies were for everyone. No invitations were sent out. She was going to go even if she had to walk to the inn. In fact, that was what she would do anyway, for if Aunt Martha knew she intended to go, she might try to stop her. They could not stop her from going if she was already there, could they? And how could they even express annoyance afterward when everyone else would be there too? And it was not as if she was going to create a scene. She would be going strictly as an observer. She would find an obscure corner and fade into it. She was an expert at that.

She was going to go. Her heart thudded in her chest as soon as the decision had been made while she was sitting at the breakfast table, for she never went anywhere. Not to any social event, anyway. She had gone to London for the last two Seasons, for the simple reason that she could not very well have been left alone at Barton Hall. But she had not attended any of the parties or concerts or balls her aunt and Henrietta had gone to every day. How could she? Aunt Martha had said on the only occasion she had alluded to the fact. It was hard enough being the sister and niece of a gentleman who had been killed in a duel for cuckolding an earl, a shocking and humiliating event that had only been the final chapter in a less than illustrious career. They would *never* be able to hold up their heads if they were seen to be harboring his daughter, especially when she looked as she did.

Sophia had one dress that was marginally suitable for evening wear. It had been made for Henrietta when she was fourteen or fifteen and had been worn once, to her birthday party that year. It had not needed to be altered quite as much as the other hand-me-downs that had come Sophia's way. It was a pink-and-cream striped muslin and still had some shape even after Sophia had shortened it and taken it in at the seams. It was not ravishingly pretty, and its design was no doubt woefully out of date, but this was no grand London ball that she was going to attend. It was a village assembly. There would surely be other women more plainly dressed than she, or at least *as* plainly.

She walked to the Foaming Tankard after the other three had left in the carriage, thankful that it was neither a cold nor a wet night. Nor windy. She felt rather excited.

She did not expect to dance, of course. Or to converse. Nobody knew her in Barton Coombs even after two years. She had never been introduced to anyone and had only ever received some genial nods after church on Sundays. But all she really wanted to do anyway was watch people interacting and having fun.

Oh, and—*admit it, Sophia!*—to see the beautiful Viscount Darleigh again. To worship from afar.

And to make sure, if she possibly could, that Henrietta, aided and abetted by her mama and papa, did not trap him into any compromising situation that would compel him as an honorable man into marrying her. She had never cared about the other gentlemen they had tried to ensnare in London. They had been perfectly capable of looking after themselves, she had always thought, and events had always proved her correct. But was Lord Darleigh as capable? If he was lured outside the inn, would he know if he was led away out of sight of other guests? And would he know that Sir Clarence and Lady March would make good and sure that everyone else noticed the length and impropriety of his absence with their daughter?

It took considerable courage to step inside the inn when she got there and ascend the stairs to the assembly rooms, from which a great deal of noise was spilling down to the ground floor and out onto the street. It sounded as if a merry jig was in progress and as if every inhabitant of the village and its neighborhood was trying to talk to every other inhabitant in a voice loud enough to be heard. And it sounded as if every listener—if there was anyone left to listen—was finding the conversation brilliantly funny and was showing appreciation by laughing uproariously.

Sophia almost turned about and scurried home.

But she reminded herself that she was not *really* a mouse. And that she was, in fact, a lady, and socially at least on a level with more than half the people here. She was not even sure she was naturally shy. She had never had the chance to find out.

She went on up.

She was confronted by the vicar almost as soon as she passed through the doorway. He beamed at her and extended his right hand.

"I do not have the pleasure of your acquaintance, ma'am," he bellowed above the music and the conversation and the laughter. "But may I presume upon the fact that you have sat in a pew in my church every Sunday for a couple of years or so and listened most attentively to my sermons, which put all too many of my parishioners to sleep, alas? I am Parsons, as you must know. And you are—?"

Sophia set her hand within his. "Sophia Fry, sir."

"Miss Fry." He patted the back of her hand with his free one. "Let me have Mrs. Parsons pour you a glass of lemonade."

And he led her past crowds of revelers to a table laden with food and drink. He introduced her to his wife, who nodded genially, tried to say something, and shrugged and widened her eyes and laughed when it became obvious that it was impossible to make herself heard.

Sophia took her glass and went to find a corner of the room to sit in. Well, that had been easier than expected, she thought, sinking gratefully onto a vacant chair. Her aunt was some distance away—there was no mistaking her nodding royal blue plumes—and was gazing at her in some astonishment. Sophia pretended not to notice her. Aunt Martha could not really send her home, could she? And she would be quite happy to be a mouse for the rest of the evening. Well, almost happy. Sometimes her capacity for self-deception disturbed her.

One couple pranced down between the lines, while the dancers who formed those lines clapped vigorously in time to the music. It all looked very jolly. Sophia found that one of her feet was tapping out the rhythm.

It was not easy to see Viscount Darleigh, but it was very obvious that he had arrived. There was a particularly dense crowd of people just to the left of the door, mostly ladies, all focused happily upon someone who was lost in their midst. Sir Clarence was one of the few gentlemen there, and both Aunt Martha and Henrietta were doing their share of fawning. Who else would they be fawning over than the viscount? And she was quite right. After Sophia had been watching for several minutes, the set of country dances came to an end, the dancers drifted off the floor, the dense cluster by the door opened as if it were yet another door, and Henrietta emerged triumphant, on the arm of Viscount Darleigh, whom she proceeded to maneuver in a promenade about the perimeter of the assembly room.

Henrietta was looking resplendent in another of her London ball gowns.

The dancing resumed, a set of more stately dances this time, and Henrietta and the viscount promenaded until their steps brought them to the door and they disappeared through it. Since everyone, with the possible exception of the dancers, had had their eyes riveted upon Viscount Darleigh since his arrival, and no one could fail to follow the progress of Henrietta's shimmering ball gown, their exit was hardly discreet.

Sophia lifted one hand to her mouth and bit the knuckle of her forefinger. There must be a number of other people outside the inn. There had been when she arrived, and people had been coming and going ever since. As Aunt Martha had predicted, the assembly rooms were stuffy. There was nothing improper about their being out there. But between them, Aunt Martha and Sir Clarence on the inside and Henrietta on the outside would find a way of making it seem improper. There could be little doubt about that.

Sophia sat where she was and gnawed on her knuckle for ten minutes before doing anything. It was still not too, too long for a couple to be absent from the room. Except that everyone was almost openly watching for their reappearance, and Sir Clarence and Aunt Martha were talking to people they must have deigned worthy of their notice, and all turned to watch the doorway. They were undoubtedly fanning the flames of speculation.

Sophia got to her feet and slipped outside. As she went, she picked up a woolen shawl from the back of a chair. She had no idea whose it was and hoped the owner would not dash after her yelling *stop, thief,* or something equally alarming. It was unlikely, though. It was unlikely anyone had noticed her leave the room—or even noticed her *in* the room, for that matter.

There was no sign of Henrietta and Lord Darleigh among the small clusters of people standing outside. A few couples were strolling farther along the street, where they were in full view from the inn, but the two people she was looking for were not among them. Where would Henrietta have taken him to be more private, and therefore more indiscreet?

Fortunately, Sophia's first guess was the right one. They were strolling along the back alley behind the buildings on the main street, walking on the grassy verge to avoid the deep ruts made by carts along the middle. She could hear Henrietta's trilling laugh as she hurried up behind them, and the low voice of the viscount.

"Oh, Henrietta," Sophia called as she drew close, "you forgot your shawl."

The two of them turned, and even in the faint light of the moon and stars Sophia could see that Henrietta's eyes were wide with shock and . . . fury. Viscount Darleigh's eyebrows were raised.

"I forgot no such thing," Henrietta said as Sophia held the shawl aloft and waved it in one hand. "And that is not even mine. Take it back to the inn immediately before its owner misses it."

The viscount had cocked his head to one side.

"You are the lady from last evening," he said. "The one who fetched Miss March's music from upstairs. I am sorry—I do not know your name."

"Sophia Fry," she said.

"Miss Fry." He smiled—and, oh, in the near darkness she would swear he was gazing right back into her eyes. "I am pleased to make your acquaintance. How kind of you to bring Miss March's shawl, even if it has turned out to be the wrong one. I have been concerned that she might be chilly. She has denied it, but I do believe she is merely being polite, since I agreed that a breath of fresh air would be very welcome. I must return her—and you—to the assembly rooms without further delay."

And he held out his other arm for Sophia to take.

She gazed at it in wonder and astonishment. And she looked at Henrietta, whose eyes were positively burning with fury and hate.

"I would far prefer to remain out here where it is cool and peaceful," Henrietta said, her voice sweet and quite at variance with her facial expression. "Do let us continue, my lord."

"By all means, if it is your wish," he said. "Miss Fry, will you walk with us?"

He was still offering his arm.

It was the last thing Sophia wanted to do. Henrietta would slay her. More important, Sophia found him beautiful to behold from afar but almost impossibly intimidating from close to. But she had come outside to prevent the jaws of the trap from snapping shut.

She took a few steps toward him and slid her hand through his arm. And—oh, goodness—he was all warmth and solidity, and he smelled of some lovely musky and very male cologne. Sophia had never been more uncomfortable in her whole life. It felt as if the very air had been sucked out of the alley.

"We cannot walk three abreast on this lane," Henrietta said no more than half a minute later, and her voice was betraying her this time. She sounded distinctly petulant. "I am afraid we must go back after all, my lord. Mama and Papa will be anxious at my absence. I did not realize how far you had brought me from the inn. Do let us return."

"They will see that I am with you and be consoled, Henrietta," Sophia said. "They will see, as will everyone else, that the proprieties have been observed."

She could not remember another occasion when she had addressed a whole sentence to Henrietta.

Viscount Darleigh turned his head to smile at her. She was almost sure that she could read relief in his face.

Poor gentleman. Everyone was trying to marry him or arrange for him to marry someone else. During the half hour she had sat alone in the assembly room she had listened to the conversation around her, almost all of which was about Viscount Darleigh. She had already heard again that his mother and his sisters were urging him to marry and were actively matchmaking for him. People here were speculating about who in the neighborhood might suit him, since he had been plain Vincent Hunt until recently and did not appear to be at all high in the instep and might prefer someone who was familiar to him. The names of Miss Hamilton and Miss Granger had loomed large in the speculations. And, of course, the Marches were trying to net him by any means within their power.

Everyone noticed their return to the assembly rooms—

and that was scarcely an exaggeration, if it was an exaggeration at all, for there was no set currently in progress to distract even those who would have been dancing. Everyone turned from their conversations to look from Viscount Darleigh to Henrietta to . . . her, Sophia Fry. Her aunt's and uncle's faces were a sight to behold. They looked first identically relieved and joyful as they beheld their daughter returned after so long in the company of Viscount Darleigh, her arm still drawn through his, and then they looked . . . astonished and chagrined and a number of other things they had not expected to look. For there, her arm drawn through the viscount's other arm, was . . . their mouse.

And this time she was invisible to no one. She felt a curious mix of extreme discomfort and triumph.

The orchestra played a decisive chord as a signal to the dancers that a new set was about to begin, and the moment passed. All was well, depending upon one's perspective, of course. There had been no impropriety after all, for there had been two ladies with the gentleman and so their walking outside, even along a quiet alley, had been quite above reproach.

A fast and furious dance began.

Henrietta hurried toward her mother.

Viscount Darleigh pressed Sophia's hand to his side when she would have slipped it free.

"Miss Fry," he said, "thank you for your concern for Miss March's reputation. It was careless of me to walk so long and so far with her, but she did not wish to return, you see. I ought to have insisted, of course. May I escort you to the refreshment table? I believe I can even remember the way."

He smiled. And she knew, despite his gallant words, that he was thanking her for rescuing him. He must have understood, almost too late, the danger in which Henrietta had placed him.

"Thank you, my lord."

She was about to add a *but* and make some excuse before scurrying away. But she paused to consider. She could walk to the refreshment table with him, perhaps even stand there with him for a few minutes conversing while they ate or drank. She might, for a fleeting moment out of her life, be like any normal woman. No, not a *normal* woman. She might be like a privileged young lady who had attracted the attention of a viscount and a beautiful man, even if only for a few minutes, to be forgotten an hour later.

And then, not having spoken up immediately, it was too late to make excuses. They were on their way across the room together.

Sophia set the shawl over the back of an empty chair as she passed and avoided looking at her aunt and uncle, who were, of course, looking at *her,* as was almost everyone else.

It was a dizzying, alarming, exhilarating experience— to mention but a few of the emotions she could identify.

He was an utter idiot. Why did he forever allow the women in his life to manipulate him and rule him? Sometimes it was benevolent, or at least intended to be. Other times it was distinctly malevolent. Yet the only time in recent memory he had stood up against it, he had done so by *running away*. This time, though he might have stopped when he and Miss March were outside the inn, with the firm and truthful explanation that he would not compromise her by taking her any farther into the darkness, he had allowed her to lead him back to what he remembered as a very dark, deserted alley behind the main street of the village.

Was he never to be a functioning adult, able to think and act for himself, free of the influence of any woman?

He had not always been like this, surely? He had been a distinctly independent boy. He had allowed himself to grow into a weakling—or at least he was in danger of doing so.

He was more grateful than he could say to Miss Fry, who, he suspected, had come very deliberately to his rescue, though he was not sure why. She was Miss March's cousin, was she not? Or was it Miss March she had been rescuing? Either way he was grateful—and intrigued. He had been able to hear her quite clearly just now, he realized, when she had said *thank you, my lord,* though she had spoken in the same low voice she had used to her aunt last evening. She must know the secret of making oneself heard above a din by pitching the level of one's voice below it rather than trying to shout above it, as most people did.

"Here we are," she said just as softly.

"Would you care for a drink?" he asked her. "Or something to eat?"

"No, thank you," she said. "I had some lemonade earlier."

"I am not hungry or thirsty either," he said with a smile. He had no wish to attempt either eating or drinking in such a public setting. He had no doubt there were plenty of eyes fixed upon his every move. "Are there any empty chairs nearby? Shall we sit for a few minutes?"

"A new set has just begun," she said. "There are empty chairs."

And soon they were seated side by side and he half turned his chair so that he would be close enough to hear her and to make himself heard—and, he hoped, to discourage interruption for a short while. He was finding all the attention both touching and wearying.

"You are Miss March's cousin?" he asked.

"Yes," she told him. "Lady March is my father's sister."

"Your father is deceased? And your mother?"

"Yes, both," she said.

"I am sorry."

"Thank you."

"I was sorry," he said, "that we were not introduced last evening."

"Oh," she said, "I am not of any importance."

The music was loud and cheerful, and he could hear the sound of feet pounding rhythmically on the floor. The level of conversation rose above both sounds.

But he had not misheard her. He did not know quite how to reply.

"Perhaps not to your aunt and uncle and cousin," he said. "But in the nature of things? And to yourself? I am sure you must be."

He waited for her answer and leaned slightly closer to her. He could smell soap. It was a more pleasant, more wholesome smell than the harsh perfumes he had been smelling all evening.

She said nothing.

"I daresay," he said, "you are trapped in a life not entirely to your liking by the fact of your parents' death, just as I am trapped in a life that is not always entirely to *my* liking by the fact that I lost my sight six years ago. How long have you been orphaned?"

"Five years," she told him. "My father died when I was fifteen."

She was twenty, then.

"I was seventeen," he said.

"So very young."

"It is hard, is it not," he said, "to have one's life develop quite differently from what one expected and to feel not fully in command of it?"

It was strange. He never spoke like this to anyone, least of all to a stranger, and a female stranger at that. But perhaps that made it easier. Tomorrow they would still be strangers. What they said tonight would be forgotten.

"Yes," she said after a rather lengthy pause.

"What would you do," he asked her, "if you could reshape your life to be exactly as you would wish it to be? If you had the means and the opportunity to do whatever you wished? What do you dream of being and doing? I suppose you do have dreams. We all do. What is yours?"

She was either not going to answer him at all or she was giving the matter some thought. He suspected that Miss Sophia Fry was not someone who chattered aimlessly about nothing. But then, she probably did not have much opportunity to do that. He did not envy her living as a poor relation with the Marches. He liked the idea that she was thoughtful.

Perhaps she considered his questions idiotic—and perhaps they were. They were the sorts of questions an eager boy asked of a girl. A man and a woman were expected to be anchored in reality.

"I would live alone," she said. "In the country. In a little cottage with a garden full of flowers that I could tend. With a vegetable patch at the back and maybe a few chickens. With some friendly neighbors and a cat and maybe a dog. And books. And an endless supply of sketching paper and charcoal. And a sufficient income to supply my needs, which would not be extravagant. Perhaps the chance to learn new things."

He had given her the chance to wish for riches and jewels and furs and mansions and foreign travel and the Lord knew what else. He was touched by the modesty of her dream.

"And a husband and children?" he asked.

Again he felt her hesitation.

"No," she said. "I believe I would be happier alone."

He almost asked her why. But he reminded himself

that she was a stranger and that the question would be an almost intimate one. He must not be too intrusive.

He wondered fleetingly what would have happened if he had asked Miss Dean about her dreams. Would she have answered candidly? He ought to have given her the chance, perhaps. He still felt badly about her.

"It is your turn," she said in a voice so low that he had to lean closer yet. He could sense her body warmth. He withdrew a couple of inches. He would not embarrass her or give the villagers any cause for gossip. "What are your most secret dreams?"

"It seems ungrateful to have any when one seemingly has everything," he said. "I have a title and fortune, a spacious home and a vast park surrounding it. I have a mother and grandmother, sisters, brothers-in-law, nieces and nephews, all of whom love me."

"And a dream," she said when he stopped talking.

"And a dream," he admitted. "A dream, like yours, of being on my own, independent and able to manage my own life, even with all its myriad responsibilities. Of being able to send all my female relatives back to the homes they either neglect far too often now or have actually abandoned for my sake. Of not having to have them running my life for me any longer. Of being fully grown up, I suppose I mean, which I would surely have been long ago if I had retained my sight. I cannot regain my sight, and even dreams have to take *some* reality into consideration. I would live as independently as a blind man can, able to find my way about alone, able to oversee the running of my estate and farms, able to consort with some ease with my neighbors. I dream of a richly lived, independent life. *My* life and no one else's. But perhaps it is not a dream I talk of, Miss Fry, is it, but a goal. Dreams are wishes that will in all probability never come true. I could make my dreams come true. Indeed, I mean to."

He stopped talking, astonished at all that had come pouring out of his mouth. He was probably going to be horribly embarrassed when he woke up tomorrow morning and remembered this conversation—or this particular monologue, anyway.

"And marriage and children?" she asked him.

He sighed. That was a thorny question. Marriage was something that might appeal to him in the future. But not yet. He was not ready. He had nothing of any value to offer—beyond the obvious. He would always have only blindness to offer a potential wife, of course, but he did not want to impose afflictedness as well upon any woman. It would be unfair to her, and he might come to resent her if he must lean upon her—literally as well as in numerous other ways. At present he was still afflicted. He needed to overcome that.

And children? One of his duties was to beget an heir, and he was determined to do his duty. But not yet. There was no urgency, surely. He was only twenty-three. And he would never be able to play cricket with his son . . .

Self-pity was something he had taken ruthlessly in hand a number of years ago, but occasionally it could still seep through his defenses.

"I am sorry," Miss Fry said. "It was an impertinent question."

"Even though I asked it of you?" he said. "I was thinking, considering my answer. We are speaking of dreams, not reality. We are speaking of what we would like our lives to be if we had the freedom to live them as we chose. No, then. No wife. No women at all. Not that I despise your sex, Miss Fry. Quite the contrary. But women are tenderhearted—at least, almost all the women in my life are. They feel sorry for me. They want to help me. They want to smother me. No, in my dream I am free and on my own—apart, I suppose, from an army of servants. In my dream, I have proved to myself and the world that I can do this living business on my own, that I neither need nor permit any pity."

"Particularly from women," she said.

"Particularly from women." He grinned at her and moved back a little farther. "You will think me an ungrateful wretch, Miss Fry. I *do* love my mother and my grandmother and my sisters. Very dearly."

"We are talking of dreams," she said. "We may be as ungrateful as we wish in our dreams."

He laughed softly and then felt a hand on his shoulder.

"You must be hungry, my lord," the hearty voice of the vicar said.

He was about to deny it. But he had taken enough of Miss Fry's time. Already she had missed dancing this set and probably the one before it when she came to rescue him—or her cousin. Besides, he did not wish to cause her any embarrassment by monopolizing too much of her time. He did not doubt there was not a person in the assembly room who was unaware of the two of them sitting here tête-à-tête.

"Yes, indeed." He got to his feet, smiling. "Good night, Miss Fry. It has been a pleasure talking with you."

"Good night, my lord."

And he was borne away to the refreshment table.

$\mathcal{V}$incent started his morning with an hour of vigorous exercise in the drawing room. He was feeling the enervating effects of a few days of merely sitting or standing—and eating far too much of Mrs. Fisk's fine baking.

After breakfast he went outside into the back garden, using only his cane for guidance. He knew the garden and was unlikely either to get lost or to come to great grief. He smelled the absence of the vegetable garden immediately. Not that he had been very aware of the smells when he was a boy, but he noticed them now when they were not there, especially the mint and sage and other herbs.

There were no flowers either. At Middlebury he had been trying to differentiate among the smells of different flowers and the texture and shape of their petals and leaves and stems.

The garden had not been completely neglected, though. The gardeners he paid to come in twice a month had swept the path that ran between the former flower beds. The stone bench that encircled the copper urn in which his mother had used to set a great pot of flowers each year was free of rubble. Martin had told him that the grass on the lawns had been scythed short and the hedges had been trimmed.

Vincent sat down on the bench and propped his cane beside him. He lifted his face to the sky. It must be cloudy, though there was no dampness in the air. And it was not a cold day.

If he decided to remain here for another day—and he was not at all sure he would—he would get Martin to come for a long walk in the country with him this afternoon. No matter how strenuously he exercised various muscles in the house, he always craved fresh air and the feeling of his legs moving under him, preferably in a lengthy stride. Ah, how he would love to run!

He wanted to stay a little longer. The last two days had been surprisingly enjoyable. In all the upheavals of the past six years, he had forgotten how very fond he was of the people of Barton Coombs. He had forgotten how many friends he had here, or he had assumed that for various reasons they could be his friends no longer. Several of them had promised last night at the assembly that they would call upon him here.

Yet a part of him wanted to leave without further ado. For his blindness was more apparent to him here than it was elsewhere. This was a place and these were people he had known with his eyes. Penderris Hall and his more recent friends of the Survivors' Club, as well as Middlebury Park and his neighbors there, were places and people he had come to know only through his other senses. They were in some ways easier to deal with, easier emotionally, anyway.

Here he found himself repeatedly fighting panic. He had thought those days were past or at least receding.

And he was not sure if his desire to stay here was a genuine need to reconnect with old friends and old haunts while he made definite plans for the future or just procrastination, the knowledge that when he went home to Middlebury he must not fall into the old pattern of passive dependence. He had asserted himself in some ways—his music, his physical exercises, his ability to find his way about familiar places with just a cane or sometimes without even that. But they were just a drop in the ocean to what his life ought to be like and could be.

He sometimes wished he did not love his mother so much. She had been hurt enough as it was. He desperately did not want to hurt her more. Perhaps the answer *was* a wife, perish the thought, but one of his own careful choosing. Very careful.

The clouds must not be in a solid mass, after all. A ray of sunshine had just found him. He could feel its warmth and tipped his face to it, closing his eyes as he did so. He did not want to damage them with direct light from the sun, after all, did he? He smiled at the absurd thought and even chuckled to himself. That was what Flavian had said to him once at Penderris on a particularly sunny day—Flavian Arnott, Viscount Ponsonby, one of the members of the Survivors' Club.

He missed them with a sudden ache of longing for them all to be back, safely cocooned, in Cornwall, himself included. He wondered if Hugo had gone in pursuit of Lady Muir, who had spent a week at Penderris earlier this spring after spraining her ankle down on the beach. Hugo Emes, Lord Trentham, was the one who had found her and carried her up to the house. He had then proceeded to fall head over ears in love with her—*that* had been obvious even to a blind man—and then, in typical Hugo fashion, he had convinced himself that the social gulf that separated them was far too wide to be breached. Hugo was a military hero and as rich as Croesus, but because he was of middle-class origin and proud of it, he was one of the most insecure men Vincent had ever known.

He would be willing to wager Lady Muir had fallen for Hugo too.

Had Hugo gone after her?

The ray of sun had already been swallowed up by

cloud again. There was a coolness against his face where there had been warmth. Well, it had felt good while it lasted.

And the thought of a wife, a carefully chosen wife, reminded him of another reason why he really needed to get away. He had almost fallen into a neat trap last evening. It had been foolish and naïve of him, especially as he had known the Marches were out to net him. And even if he had not known it himself, Martin had warned him. When he had stepped out of the inn with Miss March because she complained of the stuffy heat of the assembly room, he had reacted as she must have known he would, like a puppet on a string. He had been desperately thankful for the arrival of Miss Fry in that deserted alley.

Miss Fry. Sophia Fry. A small lady with a light touch. And a soft, slightly husky voice. And a strangely appealing conversation that had replayed itself in his mind when he lay down after returning home. An exchange of dreams, which in many ways were not dissimilar, though their circumstances were as different as they could be. According to Martin, who had danced all night, she had not danced at all and had disappeared early, soon after talking with him.

Without her intervention, he might be in danger today of finding himself a betrothed man. Betrothed to Henrietta March, of all people. He had not liked her as a girl. He did not like her now. She had spoken last evening of nothing but her well-born friends and her beaux and her connections with the highest echelon of the *ton,* and she was the star of every anecdote and had had the last, witty word in every remembered altercation. Sir Clarence March he abhorred as much as he ever had. Lady March was enough to raise the short hairs along the back of his neck.

He had had a narrow escape. Was he now safe? Now

that he was fully on his guard? But he had been on his guard before.

He could hear footsteps approaching along the path from the house—the firm tread of Martin's boots, and someone else's. Male, almost definitely. Ah, and a third tread, lighter, more feminine.

"Here are Sam and Edna Hamilton to see you, sir," Martin said.

"Sam!" Vincent got to his feet, a smile on his face, his right hand outstretched. "And Edna. How good of you to come. Do sit down. But is it warm enough out here for you? Should we go into the parlor instead?"

"Vince!" His old friend and partner in crime gripped his hand and pumped it up and down. "We hardly had a chance for a word last evening. You were swaddled about by Miss Waddell's ladies."

"Vincent," Edna Hamilton, the former Edna Biggs, said, and she stepped forward to hug him and set her cheek against his for a moment. "I might have waited for you if I had known just how handsome a man you were going to grow into."

"Hey, hey," Sam protested as Vincent laughed. "None of that. I am not so bad looking myself."

"Do let us sit out here," Edna said. "The clouds are about to move off entirely, and it is beautifully warm in the sunshine. My feet are sore from last evening. I very nearly danced them off the ends of my legs."

"Vince will think you very ungenteel, Ed," her husband commented. "Ladies are not supposed to admit that they even *have* legs."

They talked of the assembly as they settled on the bench, and they reminisced about the childhood they had all shared. They laughed a great deal. And then Edna changed the subject.

"Oh, Vince," she said, "have you heard what has happened to that little mouse of a woman who lives with the Marches?"

"Miss Fry?" Vincent said, frowning.

"Is that her name?" she asked. "You took pity on her last evening and spoke with her for a few minutes, did you not? No one even knew for a long time whether she was a servant at Barton Hall or a poor relation, but the servants disowned her when asked. We should have known, of course, for she is always far more poorly dressed than any of them. Anyway, she has been turned out. The Reverend Parsons found her in the church this morning, sitting pale and silent in one of the pews, a pathetically small bag beside her. He took her into the vicarage, and Mrs. Parsons gave her breakfast and a room to lie down in—she was turned out last night, apparently, and spent what was left of it in the church pew. But no one knows what will become of her, poor thing. No other servants are needed at the vicarage—and she is not a servant anyway. I suppose *someone* will help her somehow."

"She is better off away from the Marches, if you were to ask me," Samuel said. "Anyone would be. We came to invite you to our house this evening, Vince. We will try to gather more of the old crowd there too and have a rollicking good time. We will even get Martin to come, if we may. What do you say?"

It took Vincent a few moments to comprehend what had just been said to him.

"What?" he said. "Oh, yes. Certainly. My thanks to both of you. That would be splendid. What time?"

They went on their way a short while later, and Vincent sat where he was a few minutes longer before going in search of Martin. He found him in the kitchen. He was about to warm up the remains of yesterday's stew and butter some bread. Luncheon would be ready in a quarter of an hour or so, Martin told him.

Vincent had no appetite.

"I need to go to the vicarage," he said. "The sooner, the better. Will the food spoil?"

"I haven't actually started getting it yet," Martin said. "I did not know how long you would be. Sam was always a talker. So was Edna."

"I need to go now," Vincent said. "Lend me your arm, Martin. It will be faster than tapping my way along the street with my cane."

"Confessing your sins will not wait, will it?" Martin asked him.

Surprisingly, Sophia had slept, though she had no idea for how long. She sat on the edge of the bed after waking, not knowing what else to do. Mrs. Parsons found her there and took her down to the parlor, where they sat drinking coffee and eating freshly baked biscuits until the vicar came in from his study, beaming and rubbing his hands together and looking awkward.

She would take the stagecoach to London, Sophia assured them when they asked if she had any plans. Sir Clarence March had given her money to get there. And yes, she would be fine, and yes, she knew people there. They would help her find employment. They must not worry about her. They had been very kind.

Her mind had been numb all night as she sat in the church. Now it was a great tumble and jumble of thoughts and anxieties and blank terror, all of which she must hide from these kindly people. She had no intention of becoming a burden to them.

She was accustomed to hiding from people, even when she was in their plain sight.

She knew no one in London, no one she would care to seek out, anyway. She did not know how to go about finding employment, though perhaps she ought to have found out as soon as her father died. She had been fifteen, after all. But she had gone to Aunt Mary instead, as any gently born lady would, and had been trapped in dependency ever since. There were employment agencies. She would have to find one and hope that her family background and lack of experience and total absence of recommendations would not make it impossible for her to find something. Anything. But what would she do while she searched? Where would she go? Sir Clarence knew the cost of a stagecoach ticket to London, and he had given her that exact amount with nothing extra, even for light refreshments on the journey.

She tried to picture herself getting down from the stagecoach in London, her journey at an end, and succeeded all too well.

She wondered if anyone in Barton Coombs needed help. The landlord at the Foaming Tankard, perhaps. Would he give her employment, even if her only payment was a broom cupboard to sleep in and one meal each day?

It was as if the vicar had heard her thoughts.

"I have made inquiries, Miss Fry," he said, his kindly face full of concern, "but there seems to be no employment to be had anywhere here in Barton Coombs for a young lady. Or for any sort of female for that matter. My dear wife and I would be happy to have you stay with us for a day or two, but . . ."

His voice trailed away, and he turned his head to look helplessly at Mrs. Parsons.

"Oh, but I would not dream of imposing upon your hospitality any longer than necessary," Sophia said. "I shall go on tomorrow's stagecoach if I can discover what time it leaves."

"I will pack a bag of food for you to take with you," Mrs. Parsons said. "Though there is no big hurry. You may stay for a night or two if you wish."

"Thank you. That is—"

Sophia did not complete the sentence, for there was a knock on the outer door, and both the Reverend and Mrs. Parsons turned their attention all too eagerly to the door of the parlor, as though they believed the knock had been upon it. And then indeed there was a tap on the door and the housekeeper opened it from the other side.

"It is Viscount Darleigh, ma'am," she said, addressing Mrs. Parsons.

"Ah." The vicar rubbed his hands again and looked pleased. "Show him in, then, show him in. What an honor and a pleasant surprise, I must say. I am delighted that I am home."

"Indeed," his wife agreed, smiling warmly as she got to her feet.

Sophia cringed back in her chair. It was too late to flee the room, though where she would flee to if she could, she did not know. At least he would not be able to see her.

His man brought him to the door and then left. The vicar hurried across the room and took his arm.

"Viscount Darleigh," he said, "this is an unexpected pleasure. I trust you enjoyed last evening's little festivities? It is always good to celebrate occasions like homecomings with one's friends and neighbors, is it not? Come and have a seat, and my good wife will go and make sure the kettle has been put on to boil."

"You are kind," Viscount Darleigh said. "I realize how ill-mannered it is of me to come without warning when you must be about to sit down for luncheon, but I particularly wished to talk with Miss Fry. May I? Is she still here at the vicarage?"

Oh, Sophia thought, mortified, as she clutched her hands very tightly in her lap, he had *heard*. He must have come to apologize—not that anything was his fault. She hoped he would not offer to go and intercede with Sir Clarence on her behalf. It would be useless. Besides, she would not go back there now even if she could. She had been an abject nobody for too long. Destitution was better than that—a rash and foolish thought, when nothing could possibly be worse than destitution. Her stomach somersaulted within her, or felt as if it did.

Being a poor relative was about the worst thing in the world to be, she had sometimes thought. But there was worse.

"Miss Fry is here now in this very room, my lord," the vicar said, indicating her with an arm the viscount could not see.

"Ah," Lord Darleigh said. "And you are here too, are you, Mrs. Parsons? My manners have certainly gone begging. Good day to you, ma'am. May I beg the favor of a private word with Miss Fry? If she is willing to grant it to me, that is."

Sophia bit her lip.

"You have heard what happened, have you, my lord?" Mrs. Parsons asked. "I do not care what Miss Fry did to cause Sir Clarence and Lady March to turn her out at gone midnight last night—she will not say and we have not pressed her on the matter. But it is a disgrace that they did it, and Miss Waddell is getting up a committee of ladies to go and tell them so. We do not usually interfere—"

"My dear," the vicar said, interrupting her.

"We will leave you to have a private word with Miss Fry," Mrs. Parsons said, nodding and smiling encouragingly in Sophia's direction.

And she and the vicar left the room after the latter had led Viscount Darleigh to a chair.

He did not sit down on it.

Sophia gazed up at him in some dismay. He was the

very last person on earth she wanted to see today. Not that she blamed him for what had happened. She most certainly did *not*. But she did not need his sympathy or his offer to intercede with Sir Clarence on her behalf or . . .

Why *had* he come?

She found his presence, especially his *standing* presence, horribly intimidating. She could hardly believe she had actually talked with him last evening, told him her most secret dreams, listened to his, just as if they had been equals. In a sense they *were* equals. She sometimes forgot she was a lady born.

"Miss Fry," he said, "this is all my fault."

"No."

His eyes turned unerringly her way. "You were turned out because you foiled a plan involving me last evening. I ought to have been able to foil it myself and am ashamed that it fell to you to rescue me, a perfect stranger. I am deeply in your debt."

"No," she said again.

He wore a form-fitting coat of green superfine, buff-colored pantaloons, and shiny Hessian boots, with white linen and a simply tied cravat. As usual, there was nothing ostentatious about his appearance, only perfect correctness. Yet somehow he looked so suffocatingly masculine and powerful that Sophia found herself trying to press back farther into her chair.

"Can you tell me," he asked her, "that that is *not* the reason you were turned out? *And*, I suppose, the fact that I lingered at your side after we returned to the assembly room."

She opened her mouth to speak, thought of lying, thought of telling the truth. . . .

"No, you cannot." He answered his own question. "And what are your plans now? Do you have other relatives to go to?"

"I shall go to London," she told him, "and seek employment."

"Do you know someone who will take you in and help you in the search?" he asked.

"Oh, yes," she assured him brightly.

He stood there, frowning down at her, his steady blue gaze only slightly to one side of her face. The silence stretched a little too long.

"You have nowhere to go, do you?" he said. It was not really a question. "And no one to help you."

"Yes," she insisted, "I do."

Again the silence.

He clasped his hands behind his back and bent slightly at the waist.

"Miss Fry," he said, "you must allow *me* to help you."

"How?" she asked. And then, more hastily, "But it is quite unnecessary. I am not your responsibility."

"I beg to disagree," he told her. "You need employment if you have no other relatives to take you in. Genteel employment—you are a lady. I could ask my sisters—but it would take too long. I have a friend in London. At least, it was his plan to go there this spring. He has vast and prosperous business interests there and will surely have something suitable to offer you or be able to find you something elsewhere if I provide you with a letter of recommendation."

"You would do that for me?" She swallowed. "Would he listen to you?"

"We are very close friends." He frowned. "If only I could be perfectly sure he was there. The Duke of Stanbrook also talked of spending part of the Season in London. Perhaps he will be there even if Hugo is not. But where would you stay while you wait to be settled into employment?"

"I—" But he had not believed in her mythical friends.

"Hugo would perhaps take you in for a short while," he said. "If he is there."

"Oh, no."

"His stepmother and his half sister live with him in his London home," he explained. "They would surely not mind—"

"No," she said, feeling quite distressed. It was one thing to knock upon someone's door with a letter of recommendation and a plea for employment. It was quite another to beg to be given lodgings in a stranger's house. "Oh, no, my lord. It is impossible. You and I are strangers. You do not know me well enough to vouch for me to that extent, even to your closest friend. It would be rash of you, it would be an imposition upon him and his mother and sister, and it is something I could not possibly bring myself to do."

He still frowned down at her.

"I am not your responsibility," she said again. But her stomach was feeling decidedly queasy. What *was* she going to do?

The silence stretched between them. Should she say something to dismiss him? But perversely she did not want him to go, she realized suddenly. There was a terrifying emptiness yawning ahead, and she was not sure she wanted to be alone to gaze into the abyss. She gripped the arms of her chair more tightly.

"I think you must marry me," he said abruptly.

She gaped inelegantly, and it was surprising she did not push herself right out through the back of her chair.

"Oh, no."

"I hope," he said, "that is an exclamation of surprise rather than an out-and-out rejection."

And suddenly, surprisingly, she was angry.

"It was not my intention," she said, her voice breathless. "It was *never* my intention, Lord Darleigh, to be in a sort of competition with Henrietta to see who could trap you first and most effectively. That was *never* my plan."

"I know." He was still frowning. "Pray do not distress yourself. I am well aware that you have set out no lures for me, that what you did last evening was done out of the goodness of your heart."

How could he possibly know that?

"And you think you must show your gratitude by *marrying* me?" she asked him.

He stared silently for a few moments.

"The thing is," he said, "that I *am* grateful and that I *do* feel responsible. If I had used my head, I would have refused to budge from just outside the door of the inn with Miss March and you would not have had to come to the rescue and thereby incur the wrath of your aunt and uncle. I *am* responsible for you. And I like you, even though that liking is based purely upon the strength of what you did and our short conversation afterward. I like your voice. That sounds ridiculously lame, I know. But when you cannot see, Miss Fry, sound and the other senses become far more acute. Normally one likes the look of someone to whom one feels attracted. I like the sound of your voice."

He was offering her marriage because of her *voice*?

And was he saying he found her *attractive*?

"It is a good thing," she said, "that you cannot see me."

He stared again.

"You look like a gargoyle, then, do you?" he asked.

And then he did something that had Sophia gripping the arms of her chair even more tightly. He smiled slowly, and then the smile developed into something else. A mischievous grin.

Oh, all those stories about his boyhood must be true. But he looked suddenly human, a real person shut up inside all the pomp and trappings of a viscount. And a handsome, elegant viscount at that.

And he had dreams.

"If I did," she said, "people would notice me. Nobody ever notices me, my lord. I am a mouse. It is what my father used to call me—Mouse. Never Sophia. And for the last five years there has always been a *the* placed before the word so that it has no longer been even a name but a simple label. I am not a gargoyle, but a mouse."

His grin had faded, though the smile remained. His head had tipped slightly to one side.

"I have been told," he said, "that the best and most famous actors are invisible people—or mice, perhaps. They can project the character they play on stage to perfection, but in their own right they can be quite un-remarkable and can escape detection even from admir-ers who are looking for them. And yet all the richness of their talent is contained within themselves."

"Oh," she said, somewhat startled. "Are you saying that I am not *really* a mouse? I know that. But . . ."

"Describe yourself to me, Miss Fry."

She rubbed her hands along the arms of her chair.

"I am small," she said. "Five foot nothing. Well, five foot two. I am small in every way. I have the figure of a boy. I have a nose my father used to describe as a button and a mouth that is too wide for my face. I cut my hair very short because . . . well, because it curls too much and is impossible to control."

"The color of your hair?" he asked.

"Auburn," she said. "Nothing as decisive as blond or raven. Merely auburn."

She hated talking about her hair. It was her hair that had led to the destroying of her soul—though that was a ridiculously theatrical way by which to describe a lit-tle heartbreak.

"And your eyes?"

"Brown," she said. "Or hazel. Sometimes one, sometimes the other."

"Definitely not a gargoyle, then," he said.

"But not a beauty either," she assured him. "Not even
nearly a beauty. Sometimes when my father was alive, I
dressed as a boy. It was easier when . . . Well, never
mind. No one ever accused me of being an impostor."

"Has no one ever told you that you are pretty?" he
asked.

"I would only have to look in the nearest glass," she
said, "to know that they lied."

He did one of those silent stares again.

"Take a blind man's word for it," he told her, "that
you have a pretty voice."

She laughed. She felt absurdly, pathetically pleased.

"*Will* you marry me?" he asked.

Suddenly she was engulfed in a tidal wave of temptation. She gripped harder. She would be leaving permanent indentations in the arms of the vicarage chair if she
was not careful.

"I cannot do that," she said.

"Why not?"

Only for a thousand reasons. At least.

"You must know," she said, "that the whole village is
buzzing with talk about you. I have not heard much of
it, but I have heard enough. It is said that you left home
a while ago because your relatives were trying to make
you marry a young lady you did not really *wish* to
marry. It is said that they have set their minds upon
finding you a wife. Everyone here has been speculating
about who, if anyone, will suit you among the young
ladies with whom you are familiar. And, of course, my
uncle and aunt made a determined effort last evening to
catch you for Henrietta. You are set about by people
who are scheming to get you married, though their mo-

tives differ widely. I will not add to that crowd, Lord Darleigh, by marrying you just because you are kind enough to feel responsible for me. You are *not* responsible. Besides, you told me yourself last night that your dream does not include a wife."

"Do you have any active aversion to marrying me?" he asked her. "My blindness, for example?"

"No," she said. "The fact that you cannot see *is* a handicap, but you do not seem to treat it as one."

She did not know him. But he really did look fit and well muscled. She knew he had been blind for several years. If he had sat in a chair or lain on a bed most of that time, he would not look as he looked now. His face was weather-bronzed too.

"Nothing else?" he asked. "My looks? My voice? My . . . Anything?"

"N-no," she said.

Except that he was a titled, wealthy, privileged gentleman despite the blindness, and lived in a mansion far larger than Barton Hall. And that he had a doting mother and sisters. And twenty thousand pounds a year. And that he was handsome and elegant and made her want to cower in a corner, worshiping from afar— even from within her mouse hole. Actually, that would make a splendid cartoon, except that she would have to capture his splendor without satire and she was not sure she could do that. Her charcoal almost always viewed the world through a satirical eye.

"Then I beg leave to press my suit," he said. "Miss Fry, please marry me. Oh, very well. We are both young. We both admitted last night that we dream of independence and of being alone to enjoy it, unencumbered by spouse or children. But we also recognized that dreams are not always reality. This is reality. You have a frightening problem; I feel responsible for helping solve it, and I have the means of solving it. But our dreams need not completely die if we marry. Quite the contrary. Let us come to some sort of *arrangement* that will benefit us both in the immediate future and offer us both hope for the longer term future."

She stared back at him. Temptation gnawed at her. But she did not understand quite what he offered.

"In what way," she asked him, "would marriage to me benefit *you*, Lord Darleigh, either in the shorter term or the longer? Apart from soothing your conscience, that is. It is perfectly obvious how it would benefit me. There is not even any point in making a list. But what would such an arrangement, as you call it, offer you? And what do you mean by that word—*arrangement*? How does it differ from just plain marriage?"

Marriage to her would offer him absolutely nothing whatsoever. That was what. Again, there was no point at all in making a list—there would be nothing to put on it. It would be a blank page with a wistful little mouse gazing up at the emptiness from a bottom corner.

He felt behind him for the arms of the chair to which the Reverend Parsons had led him and sat down at last. He looked a little less intimidating. Or perhaps not. For now there was an illusion, as there had been last evening, that they were just two friendly equals having a cozy chat. Yet . . . Well, there was nothing equal about them except a basic gentility of birth.

"If one considers the facts purely from a practical and material perspective," he said, "ours would be an unequal match. You have nothing and no one and nowhere to go and no money. I have property and fortune and more loving relatives than I know what to do with."

And that was that. There was really no more to be said.

She stared into the abyss and felt as though her stomach had already descended into it.

"There is no other perspective," she said.

"Yes, there is." He was silent again for a few moments. "I ran from home six weeks or so ago, as you have heard. I have not made a good start on my life as Viscount Darleigh of Middlebury Park. I have allowed myself to be ruled by all the well-meaning people surrounding me there. And now they have decided it is time I married, and they will not be satisfied until the deed is accomplished. I want to change things, Miss Fry. How much easier it would have been if I had asserted myself three years ago. But I did not, and there is no going back. So where do I start now? Perhaps in taking a wife home with me. Perhaps I will have the courage to start again and start differently if I have someone at my side who is undeniably mistress of Middlebury. Perhaps it is the very thing I need. Perhaps you will be doing me as great a favor as I will be doing you. If I can persuade you to agree, that is."

"But to choose a stranger," she said.

"It is precisely what my relatives wished me to do six weeks ago," he said. "She had been brought to Middlebury by parents who needed to marry her well. She had no personal wish to be there. We had no previous acquaintance. She was a sacrificial lamb. She told me she *understood* and she *did not mind*."

"Ah," she said. "But clearly she did?"

"Would *you* mind?" he asked her.

"Marrying a blind man? No," she said. But what was she saying? She was not agreeing to marry him. "But I would mind forcing you into something you do not want to do, with someone you do not know and someone who could bring nothing into the marriage except, perhaps, that she really *would* not mind."

He ran the fingers of one hand through his hair and looked as though he was searching for words.

"Was this the *arrangement* you spoke of?" she asked.

"That you offer me material comfort and I offer you the courage to become the master of your own domain?"

He exhaled audibly.

"No," he said. "Remember our dreams."

"Our impossible dreams?" She attempted a laugh and then wished she had not when she heard the pathetic sound she made.

"Perhaps not so impossible." He sat forward suddenly, and his face looked earnest and eager and boyish. "Perhaps we can have both them *and* marriage."

"How?" They seemed mutually exclusive concepts to her.

"Marriages," he said, "perfectly decent ones, are undertaken for all sorts of reasons. Especially marriages of the upper classes. Often they are alliances more than love matches. And there is nothing wrong with an alliance. Often there is a great deal of respect, even affection, between the partners. And often they live lives that are quite independent of each other even while the marriage survives. They see each other from time to time and are perfectly amicable with each other. But they are free to live their own lives. Perhaps we could agree to such a marriage."

The very idea chilled her.

He was still looking eager.

"You could eventually have your cottage in the country," he said, "with your flowers and your chickens and cats. I could eventually prove to myself that I can be master of Middlebury and of my life alone. We could have a marriage now, when we both need it, and freedom and independence and a dream come true in the future. We are both young. We have plenty of life ahead of us—or we can hope for plenty."

"When?" She still felt chilled—and tempted. "When could we move from the one phase of our marriage to the other?"

He stared past her shoulder.

"One year?" he said. "Unless there is a child. It is a real marriage I propose, Miss Fry. And the begetting of an heir is a duty I must look to sometime. If there is a child, our dream will have to be postponed, at least for a while. But a year if there is no child. Unless you would rather make it longer. Or less. But I think we would need a year to establish ourselves as Viscount and Viscountess Darleigh of Middlebury Park. And we ought to do that. Would you agree to a year?"

She had not agreed to anything. She felt a little as though she were about to faint. She could be married *and* have her life of quiet contentment? Could the two coexist? She needed time to think, and lots of it. But there *was* no time. She lowered her chin to her chest and closed her eyes.

"It would be madness," was all she could think to say.

"Why?" He sounded anxious. Anxious that she would say no? Or that she would say yes?

She could not *think*. But one thought popped free.

"What if there was a child," she asked, "and it was a girl?"

He thought about it and then . . . smiled.

"I think I would rather like to have a daughter," he said, and then he laughed. "Another female to rule my life."

"But what if?" she persisted. "What if you were still without an heir?"

"Then . . . Hmm." He thought again. "If we became friends during our year together, and I see no reason why we should not, then we would not have to be strangers for the rest of our lives, would we? We would not be *separating,* only living apart because it suited us to do so. Perhaps we would both be quite happy to come together again from time to time."

For enough time to have a child? Or *another* child?

She still felt light-headed. She tried to think ratio-
nally.

"What if the time should come, Lord Darleigh," she
asked, "when you wished to marry someone with whom
you had fallen in love?"

"I am unlikely to meet any such person at Middlebury," he said. "I hope to become less reclusive than I
have been for the past three years—indeed I am determined to be—but it is a quiet village. Besides, it is a risk
run by everyone who marries, is it not? The danger that
one will meet someone one wants more? When one
does marry, however, one pledges one's loyalty to the
person one marries and that is that."

There had to be a hole in that argument large enough
to drive a stagecoach and four through. And she thought
of one. Men had *needs,* did they not? She had learned
that during the years she had lived with her father and
his friends. What about Lord Darleigh's needs? According to the arrangement he suggested, she would be
leaving him when he was twenty-four unless she was
increasing.

How would he satisfy his needs after that? Mistresses?

She opened her mouth and drew breath, but she could
not bring herself to make the point.

He made it for her.

"We could get together occasionally anyway," he
said. "We need not be strangers. Provided it was by mu-
tual consent, of course."

There was another of those short silences.

"What if *you* should meet someone and fall in love?"
he asked her.

"I would turn away from it," she told him. "I would
be loyal to my marriage."

And by her answer had she crossed the line into seriously considering his proposal?

Oh, she *must* not take it seriously.

But what was the alternative?

She hugged her hands about her arms, as though she were cold.

"You do not even know me," she said, realizing too late that she did not need to make that point if she was *not* considering saying yes. "I do not know you."

He did not immediately reply.

"What happened to you?" she asked.

"To my sight, you mean?" he said. "My mother's brother came home from long years in the Far East. He is a merchant and a businessman, very prosperous. My father was not very long deceased at the time and my mother was struggling harder than ever to make ends meet. My uncle wanted to take my sisters to London to find them eligible husbands, which he actually did with great success, and he wanted to take me into the business. But the thought of sitting behind a desk all day, even if only for a few years until I had earned promotions, depressed me. I begged him to purchase a commission for me instead, and I went off to war with an artillery regiment at the age of seventeen. I was bursting with pride and eagerness to prove myself, to show that I was as brave, as resourceful, as steadfast as the most seasoned of veterans. In the first hour of my first battle in the Peninsula, I was standing beside one of the great guns when it was fired. Nothing happened, and I stepped slightly forward, as though I thought to see the problem and set it right and win the whole war then and there for the allies. The gun fired, and the last thing I saw was a bright flash. I really ought to have been blown to glory. There ought to have been so many pieces of me raining down upon Spain and Portugal that no one would have found and identified a single one of them. But, when I was carried off to a field hospital, I was perfectly intact except for the fact that when I recovered consciousness I could neither see nor hear."

Sophia gasped in horror.

"Hearing returned after I had been back in England awhile," he said. "Sight never did, and never will."

"Oh," she said. "What was it like—"

But he had held up a staying hand, and the other, she noticed, had curled tightly about the arm of his chair, just as her hands had about the arms of hers a few minutes ago. His knuckles were white.

"I am sorry," he said, and his voice sounded unaccountably breathless. "I cannot talk about that, Miss Fry."

"Forgive me," she said.

"And what ought I to know about you?" he asked her. "What can you tell me that will have me dashing for the door and freedom?"

"I am not respectable," she said. "My grandfather was a baronet and my uncle, his elder son, now has the title. But both of them disowned my father long before I was born. He was the black sheep of the family. He was an adventurer and a gambler and a—a rake. Sometimes he won a fortune and we lived in sudden luxury. But it never lasted longer than a few days or weeks at most. He lost more money than he ever possessed, and we often spent weary weeks and months fleeing from bailiffs and other men to whom he owed large debts. He was handsome and charming and . . . and he drove my mother away, I suppose, with his philandering, though when she left, when I was five, she went with a lover and without me. It was a great scandal. She died in childbirth three years later. My father was killed in a duel five years ago. He was shot by an enraged husband. It was not even his first duel. He was notorious in so many ways. It would not be good for you to be associated with me."

She bit her lip and closed her eyes again.

She heard him sigh.

"Miss Fry," he said, "you are neither your father nor your mother."

He got to his feet and took a few tentative steps in her direction, afraid perhaps that there was some obstacle between his chair and hers.

"Miss Fry." He reached out his right hand. "Will you set your hand in mine?"

She got reluctantly to her feet, closed most of the distance between them, and set her hand in his. When he raised his other hand, she set her right one in it, and his fingers closed, warm and strong, about both.

And he went down on one knee before her.

Oh!

He bowed his head over her hands.

"Miss Fry," he said, "will you do me the great honor of marrying me? Will you give us both a chance to realize our dreams?"

How could she think straight when she was looking down on the soft, shining waves of his hair bowed over her hands and when she felt his warm, strong clasp?

He was an impulsive man, she suspected. He would live to regret it if she said yes. Especially if—when?—he found himself all alone in one year's time with no prospect of marrying anyone else unless she died before him. His dream was all very well for a year or two. But forever? She guessed that he was the sort of man who would eventually want a warm, loving family about him.

And what about her? But she had no choices. Or at least, she did. She could choose between two alternatives—the imperfect marriage arrangement he had suggested and destitution. That was really no choice at all.

God help her, there was really no choice.

"I will," she whispered.

He lifted his head. And, his eyes right on hers, he smiled.

It was an intensely sweet smile.

6

❦

*M*artin was not talking to him, if one discounted the fact that he was *yes, my lord*ing or *no, my lord*ing Vincent's every question or remark, his voice almost vibrating with stiff formality. He was sulking after the quarrel they had had on the way home from the vicarage.

"You are *what*?" he had bellowed when Vincent told him he was betrothed to Miss Fry. "What the blinking devil? Are you out of your bleeding *mind*? She looks like a boy, and I am not even sure that is being kind to boys."

"Don't make me hit you, Martin," Vincent had said.

Martin had sneered—audibly.

"You know I can," Vincent had reminded him. "Remember the split lip and bloody nose you got when you doubted me before?"

"Sheer luck," Martin had said. "And you did not play fair."

"Fair is exactly what I did play," Vincent had told him. "Don't make me prove that it was not sheer luck. The lady is my betrothed, and I will defend her against any insult."

Martin had sneered a little more quietly and retreated into an injured silence.

The Reverend and Mrs. Parsons had not been quite so frank in their reactions. But there had been amazement, even stunned incomprehension, in their voices when

Vincent had summoned them back into the parlor and made his announcement. Their congratulations had been hesitant, as if they had not been sure it was not all a joke, and then had sounded overhearty when they were sure he was serious. But they had agreed to allow Miss Fry to remain at the vicarage for another night or two until he had made other arrangements for her.

The trouble was, he did not know quite what arrangements to make. He had hoped, as he hurried toward the vicarage on Martin's arm earlier, that he would discover that Miss Fry had plans, that she would have somewhere to go, some other relatives who would welcome her or at least some friends. Then all that would have been called for was a heartfelt apology for the trouble he had caused her and perhaps an offer of his carriage with Handry to take her where she chose to go. In the meanwhile, he would stay at Covington House and enjoy visiting his friends for a few more days while he awaited the return of his carriage, and prepare himself for returning to Middlebury Park.

Somewhere way back in his mind he had thought he might have to offer her marriage if there was no alternative, but he had not really expected it would come to that.

But it had.

The trouble was, he had not thought further than the proposal.

No, the trouble was, he had not even thought *as far* as the proposal!

Martin was right. He *was* out of his bleeding mind.

Should he now take her home to Middlebury with him? And marry her there? He imagined the consternation into which he would throw his mother. And soon his sisters would be swooping down upon him, and his life and his wedding would not be his own. His wedding was always going to be like that, of course, whomever he married. But with almost any other bride, there would be her family swooping from the other side as a sort of balance to his own. There would be no one to speak for Miss Fry or to fuss over her and make sure that the wedding was about her as much as it was about him, or even more so, because she was the bride and he the mere bridegroom.

It would not be fair to take her straight home with him.

And he kept remembering Edna Hamilton saying that Miss Fry had been found in the church this morning with a pathetically small bag on the pew beside her. Had she left the bulk of her belongings at Barton Hall simply because she could not carry more than one bag with her? Or did the bag, in fact, comprise all her belongings?

He wished he knew how she had been dressed—at Barton Hall when he visited there, at the assembly last night, at the vicarage this morning. He would be willing to wager, though, that she needed clothes and lots of them. And then he remembered Edna's saying that she could not be mistaken for a servant at Barton Hall because she was not as well dressed as they.

Perhaps he should have the banns called here and marry her at Barton Coombs. But that would mean a whole month of kicking his heels here, and he would have to beg the vicar and his wife to extend their hospitality to Miss Fry that long. His mother and his sisters would have time to descend upon him here, and the wedding would be no different than if he took his bride to Middlebury Park. And the Marches might cut up nasty and cause trouble. He would not put it past them to make public the less-than-savory past of Miss Fry's mother and father. And she would need clothes even here. Any bride ought to be married in a pretty dress. Where would she find one here?

If he was not going to return to Middlebury Park, then, and was not going to remain here, where would he go to marry?

There really was only one alternative.

London.

She could shop for a bridal outfit and bride clothes there. They could marry quickly and quietly, by special license. It really would be the best plan.

It gave him a bit of a pang to think of marrying without even informing his mother and his sisters, but on the whole it seemed best for Miss Fry herself. It would put them on a more equal footing.

It would be altogether better, anyway, to present his family with a fait accompli, he decided, remembering uneasily how Martin and the vicar and his wife had reacted to his choice of bride. His mother and sisters did, after all, want to see him married. They would surely be overjoyed for him once they had recovered from the first shock of finding that he had gone out on his own and chosen a bride and married her. And if they were not, well, then, he and they would have something of a quarrel on their hands.

Good Lord, he never quarreled with his family.

How would Miss Fry shop for clothes in London with no one to guide her? Would she know where to go? How would he acquire a special license? One had to go to Doctors' Commons, did one not? Well, even without eyes, he would find his way there. He had servants, after all, and he had a tongue in his head. How did one then arrange a wedding, though? *He would find out.* Where would they stay for the day or two or three while all this was being arranged? A hotel? A single man and a single lady?

The questions and their less-than-satisfactory answers swirled around in his head as he ate some of the rabbit stew Martin had warmed and a piece of the buttered bread. There was no point in asking Martin's opinion. He was ignoring anything that could not be answered with a simple affirmative or negative.

At least thinking about the practical problems that needed to be solved kept his mind off the larger issue. He had offered her—he had *promised* her—both marriage and freedom. He had offered her the sort of marriage he had always deplored.

And then he thought of something that brought his mind back to practicalities. Actually he had thought of it when he was with her, though in a different context. The Survivors. Hugo—Hugo Emes, Lord Trentham, that was—had been planning to spend at least a part of the spring in London. And even if he was not there, his stepmother and half sister almost certainly would be. Miss Fry would not stay with them as a mere supplicant for employment, but she surely could have no objection to doing so as his betrothed. And perhaps Mrs. or Miss Emes would be willing to accompany her when she went shopping.

Vincent half smiled to himself. Most problems had a solution if one was determined to find it. And he *was* determined. It was infinitely more difficult to live independently and to assert oneself when one had lost one's sight, of course, but it was by no means impossible. He suddenly felt quite eager to go home and start tackling the bigger challenges of his life.

"I do believe the stew tasted better today than it did yesterday, Martin," he said. "And the bread could not be fresher if it tried."

Actually he had scarcely tasted either.

"Thank you, my lord."

Ah, a variation on a theme. He was usually *sir*.

"I will need my hat and my cane, please, Martin," he said, getting up from the table. "I promised Miss Fry that I would take her for a walk this afternoon. It is not going to rain, is it?"

A pause, presumably while Martin looked out through the window.

"No, my lord."

"I will not need you to accompany me to the vicarage," Vincent told him. "I have the way memorized."

"Yes, my lord."

"Martin," he said ten minutes later as he went out through the front door and located the steps with his cane, "I will be married to Miss Fry within the week, I expect. All the sulks in the world will not change that. Perhaps at some time in the next five years or so you will find it in yourself to forgive me."

"Yes, my lord."

Well, it was better than *no, my lord*.

Vincent found his way safely down the steps and a short way along the driveway. But then he stopped at the sound of a carriage approaching along the village street, drawn, if he was not mistaken, by four horses. There was far too much noise and clatter and clopping for two. Unless it was a stagecoach or something else passing through, there was only one person in Barton Coombs to whom it could belong.

It slowed and turned in toward Covington House. Vincent stood where he was and hoped that if he was in the middle of the drive the horses would not run him down before he was seen.

He need not have worried.

"Ah, Darleigh," the jovial voice of Sir Clarence March called. He must have lowered one of the windows on the carriage. "Taking a stroll up the driveway and back, are you? Do be careful."

Vincent inclined his head without replying, and he listened as a thud of boots announced the descent of the coachman and then a carriage door opened and steps were let down. He heard a great commotion of descent and understood that Sir Clarence was not alone.

This was an afternoon call—in a traveling carriage and four?

"My dear wife and daughter wished to take a drive out in the country on such a lovely afternoon," Sir Clarence said, "and how could I not indulge them, Darleigh? When you have a wife and daughters of your own, though it is to be hoped you will have sons too, you will understand what it is like to be a husband and father trying to put his foot down and live his own life. It cannot be done. One's very happiness depends upon indulging one's womenfolk. My womenfolk thought you would enjoy a drive in the country with us and perhaps even a stop somewhere for a little walk. My legs are not all they used to be, and Lady March is unable to walk far without becoming breathless, but young people are made of sterner stuff. Henrietta will be happy to walk with you if you should wish to take the air later in the afternoon. You must come back with us for dinner afterward. Just a simple, informal repast between friends."

Ah. He was going to enjoy this, Vincent thought.

"I thank you for your kind invitation," he said. "Unfortunately, I must decline it. Samuel and Edna Hamilton have invited me to spend the evening with them and a few of our other childhood friends. And this afternoon I have arranged to take my betrothed walking."

There was a brief, almost loud silence, apart from some jingling of harness and snorting of horses and pawing of gravel.

"Your betrothed?" Lady March said.

"Yes." Vincent smiled. "Had you not heard? I would have thought everyone in Barton Coombs knew by now. An hour or two ago Miss Fry accepted my hand in marriage. I trust you will wish me happy."

"Miss—*the mouse?*" Sir Clarence's voice was almost a roar.

"*Sophia?*" Lady March said almost simultaneously.

"What?" Miss March said, sounding bewildered. "*Mama?*"

"We will be marrying in London as soon as I can make the arrangements," Vincent told them, "and then I will be taking my new viscountess home to Middlebury Park. You must not worry about your niece, Lady March. She will be quite safe in my keeping. And cherished. Ah, I have just remembered something. *Martin?*"

He hoped the door behind him was still open. But he guessed that Martin had been keeping an eye on him while he was still in sight, to make sure he did not trip over any stone larger than a pebble or collide with a gatepost.

"Yes, my lord?"

"Martin," Vincent instructed him, "fetch my purse, if you would be so good, and count out the cost of a stagecoach ticket. Sir Clarence will tell you the exact amount. You were kind enough to give your wife's niece the fare when she left Barton Hall last night, sir, but it is not needed after all, and it is my pleasure to return it to you with my thanks."

He continued to make his way along the driveway, hoping he was not going to mar his grand exit by tangling himself up with horses or slapping into an open carriage door.

"Mama?" Miss March said again from behind him, her voice tremulous.

"Oh, do be quiet, Henrietta," her fond mama said crossly. "That hussy. After all I have done for her."

Vincent felt the gatepost with his cane and passed safely through onto the street. He could remember games like this—one child with bandaged eyes being led a merry dance by another child and having to guess at the end of it all where he was. Vincent had always cheated, of course, as he supposed all the other children had done, by peeping below the blindfold. He wished he could do the same now. But the vicarage was not far away. He would find it.

He would always find his way, he thought, despite a dull feeling in his stomach that he had acted with haste on his first visit here today and would have to live with the consequences for the rest of his life.

Just before he reached the vicarage, he heard the carriage and four returning along the street in the direction of Barton Hall. It would seem that the afternoon drive and walk had been abandoned.

And so he had played one more prank upon Sir Clarence March, he thought. The last and by far the most satisfying.

And he had done *something* to avenge his lady.

"Do you go walking often? Do you have a favorite place to go?" Vincent asked Miss Fry as they left the vicarage a short while later. "I used to enjoy turning along the narrow lane beyond the smithy and then climbing over the stile and crossing the meadow to the bank of the river. As boys, we all used to fish and swim there. Usually swimming was forbidden, but we did it anyway, even at night."

"I do walk," she said. "Sometimes I go just into the woods in the park at Barton Hall, where I can be alone, and sometimes I go farther afield, wherever my footsteps lead me. I know the place you speak of."

She had taken his offered arm, but she must have realized, as she did last night, that he could not lead her anywhere with any confidence. It was more likely to be the other way around despite the fact that he had his cane in his free hand.

He turned them in the direction they would need to take, and almost immediately they were hailed by Miss Waddell, who lived next to the vicarage. And she just happened to be in her front garden, she explained, trimming the dead heads off some of her flowers.

She must have seen him arrive, Vincent thought, for the second time today. And, like everyone else, she would know about the vicar's finding Miss Fry in the church this morning and taking her to the vicarage. She would know too that Miss Fry had been tossed out of Barton Hall in the middle of last night. Had Mrs. Parsons not mentioned that she was planning to lead a delegation of protest to Barton Hall?

"It is a fine afternoon, Lord Darleigh," she continued. "And Miss . . . Fry, is it not? You are Lady March's relative, I believe, but are staying at the vicarage."

Her voice bristled with curiosity, and Vincent realized in some surprise that the vicar's wife had done as he asked and not told anyone of the engagement.

"You must hear the happy news from my own lips, then, Miss Waddell," he said. "Miss Fry has made me a happy man today. We are betrothed."

"Oh, my." For a moment she seemed lost for words. "Then congratulations are in order. Well, bless my soul, this is unexpected news. Only this morning the vicar was asking everywhere about the possibility of genteel employment for . . . Well. Oh, my. Well, how delightful, I must say."

It was not as difficult to get away from her as it had sometimes used to be. Vincent guessed that she was itching to spread the word before anyone else could.

"I do apologize," he said when he was alone with Miss Fry again. "I made the announcement without first consulting you. I hope you did not mind?"

"No, my lord," she said.

"I told Sir Clarence and Lady March and Miss March

too, as I was leaving home a short while ago," he said. "They had come to invite me to take a drive in the country with them and perhaps take a walk with Miss March somewhere along the way. It gave me enormous satisfaction to explain to them that I would be walking with my betrothed instead. I wish you could have been there to see their faces when I informed them just who that was. I am sure they must have been a sight to behold. Oh, and I had Martin Fisk, my valet, return the stagecoach fare to Sir Clarence."

"Oh," she said.

"We used to play merciless pranks on him when I was a boy," he told her. "I say *we,* though almost invariably I was both the mastermind and the ringleader. Once we climbed onto the roof of Barton Hall the night before Sir Clarence was expecting a visit from a titled naval admiral and his wife—he had boasted of it for days beforehand. We flew a large sheet, painted with skull and crossbones, from the tallest chimney and hoped no one would notice it before the admiral's arrival. No one did, and as good fortune would have it, there was a brisk breeze blowing that morning. If servants are to be believed, and they usually are, the first thing the admiral did after stepping down from his carriage was draw in a deep breath of fresh air and look up to where the sheet was flapping merrily in the wind."

She laughed, a light, happy sound that delighted him.

"Were you ever caught?" she asked.

"Never," he said. "Though there were a few close calls. Sir Clarence always knew who the culprits were, of course, but he could never prove his suspicions, and though some of us had stern parents, I have the feeling they investigated all complaints from the Hall less than vigorously."

She laughed again.

"You had a happy childhood, then, my lord?" she asked.

"I did."

He turned his head toward her and almost asked about her own childhood. But he knew it had been a difficult one and perhaps—no, probably—a very unhappy one, and he was trying to set her at her ease.

He guessed that they must be drawing close to the smithy, and, sure enough, he heard Mr. Fisk hailing him, and then he heard the approach of heavy footsteps before his right hand was caught up, cane and all, in a great big ham of a hand and pumped up and down.

"Vincent Hunt," the blacksmith cried in his great booming voice. "I could not get near you last evening with my good wife. You are looking quite the grand gentleman. But still a rogue at heart, I have no doubt. Hello, missy. Don't you live at Barton Hall? No, wait a minute. You are the one the vicar was asking about this morning. Wanted to know if my missus needed a helper in the house. Staying at the vicarage, are you? Well, I daresay you are better off there than where you were. I would not recommend the Hall to my worst enemy."

"Miss Fry and I are newly betrothed," Vincent told him.

Mr. Fisk pumped his hand even more heartily.

"Ho," he cried, "you work a fast courtship, lad. But you never were a laggard, were you? I could tell you a thing or two about this rascal, missy, that would make your hair stand on end. But he was always a good lad despite it all, and he will make you a good husband, I do not doubt. I am glad you chose a little country lass, Vincent—or *my lord,* I suppose I ought to call you now—and not one of them fashion dolls that the nobs usually marry. I wish you both happy. The missus would wish you happy too, but she is busy baking more bread and cakes for our Martin and is not looking out through the window. She thinks he needs fattening up like his dad."

"I hope she understands, Mr. Fisk," Vincent said, "that she has been fattening me up too. Her bread is the best I have tasted, and her cakes spell death to any good intentions of eating sparingly."

He moved on with Miss Fry, and they turned almost immediately onto the quiet lane that ran parallel to the river but some distance from it.

"A little country lass," he said. "Is that what you are? Were you offended?"

He knew her so little. Again he had that hollow feeling in his stomach of having done something impulsive and rash but irretrievable.

"Not when the alternative was to be 'one of them fashion dolls the nobs marry,'" she said. "It sounds like a very undesirable thing to be if one wants to win the approval of blacksmiths, does it not?"

He laughed. Her answer surprised and delighted him. It showed both spirit and humor.

"Mr. Fisk is my valet's father," he explained to her. "Martin and I grew up together. When I was going away to war, he asked if he could come as my batman. After I was wounded, he insisted upon staying on as my valet, and I have not been able to get rid of him since. I have tried, especially in the early years, when I could not afford to pay him and all he got was room and board at the home in Cornwall where I convalesced. He flatly refused to go."

"He must love you," she said.

"I suppose he does," he agreed. He had never thought of it that way before. He doubted Martin had either. "The stile must be quite close."

"About twenty more steps," she said.

He had not given much thought to how he would get over it. He had done much more rugged walking than this in the Lake District, of course, but there he had had Martin with him. Not that Martin ever hauled him bodily about, but they were accustomed to each other and comfortable together. Martin knew just what instructions and warnings to give and when to give them.

He could remember this stile. He had climbed over it a thousand times.

"I'll go first," he said when they came to it. "Then I can at least make some pretense of helping you over."

He hooked his cane over the top bar. He was glad she did not try to take it from him or insist upon going ahead of him so that *she* could help *him*. A man must retain some dignity.

He felt self-conscious and actually rather terrified that he was about to make an idiot of himself. There were two wooden bars, one about three feet from the ground, the other about two feet above that—the one over which he had just hooked his cane. Beneath the lower bar there was a third, flatter one, passing underneath it but not at a ninety-degree angle. There was grassy verge this side. The other side was lower, more worn, and it had a dip in the center where thousands of feet had landed when descending from the stile. It was always full of mud—a boy's paradise—after a rain. Fortunately, there had been no rain in the past few days. On either side of the stile there were high hawthorn hedges. Beyond was a grassy meadow, usually liberally dotted with daisies and buttercups and clover. And beyond that, at some distance, was the river.

He wondered if children still came here. He could not hear any now. But perhaps they were at school, that bane of the existence of boisterous youth.

He need not have worried. He got over the stile without incident, though he was glad he had remembered the dip on the far side so when he jumped down he did not go plunging farther than he expected. He turned back to the stile, found the post of the lowest board with the inside of his boot, and reached up a hand.

"Madam," he said, "allow me to assist you. Do not be afraid."

She laughed again, a pretty, trilling sound that seemed lighthearted, as if she was enjoying herself. And then he felt her small hand in his, and she jumped down beside him.

"Do we have the meadow all to ourselves?" he asked, though he was almost sure they did.

"We do," she said, withdrawing her hand. "Oh, this is a beautiful time of year. The very best, with spring just turning to summer. The meadow is like a colored carpet underfoot. Would you like me to describe it to you?"

"In a little while," he said. "Though you need not always feel obliged to do that. I am learning to experience the world through the other senses rather than straining always to imagine what I cannot physically see. When you describe a scene to me, I shall describe it right back to you, but my scene will be filled with sound and smell and sometimes touch. Even taste. Does that make sense to you?"

"Yes," she said. "Oh, yes, it does. And it explains why you are not a victim."

He raised his eyebrows.

"Why you do not *act* like a victim," she explained. "I admire that."

He tipped his head to one side.

"Have you felt like a victim sometimes?" he asked her. "We all do, you know. At least, I assume most of us do at some time or other in our lives. There is no shame in that, for sometimes we *are* victims. Sometimes, though, if we are fortunate or diligent, we can rise above self-pity. It has been made easier for me than it might otherwise have been, of course, for I inherited a fortune two years after I was blinded. That has given me a freedom for which I will always be grateful."

"And I am marrying *you*," she said breathlessly.

So that it would be easier to set herself free of being one of life's victims? Though there was always more than good fortune involved in the shedding of self-pity. Sometimes, self-pity was so ingrained in people that nothing could persuade them to take joy out of living. *Was* Miss Fry self-pitying? He did not know her well enough to answer his own question.

"I cannot see you," he said. "I have only heard you— and touched your hand and felt it within my arm. I have smelled the faint fragrance of your soap. I would know you a little better, Miss Fry."

He could hear her draw a breath through her mouth.

"You want to . . . touch me?" she asked him.

"Yes."

Not with any lascivious intent. He hoped she would understand that. He could not bring himself to say it aloud.

She was close to him, though she did not immediately touch him, and he did not reach for her. He could hear the rustle of fabric and guessed that she was removing her bonnet and perhaps her cloak too. He heard the slight scrape of his cane against the bars of the stile. She must have hung her garments beside it.

They were standing to one side of the stile. He hoped they were far enough over that they were in the shelter of the hawthorn hedge and invisible to anyone passing along the lane. Not that it was ever a well-used lane.

She had moved to stand in front of him. He could sense her there. And then he felt her fingertips feather-light against his chest. He raised his hands and found her shoulders. They were small and thin and yet sturdy. He slid his hands in until he felt the warm, smooth flesh of her throat. He could feel her pulse beating steadily beneath his left thumb. His hands moved up the sides of a slender neck, over small ears, and into her hair—thick and soft and curly and really very short, as she had said it was.

She looks like a boy. . . .

He bent his own head closer. The soap fragrance he had noticed last evening was coming most noticeably from her hair. She must have washed it recently. He could feel the warmth of her breath against his jaw.

He explored her face with his fingertips. A smooth, rather broad forehead. Arched eyebrows. Eyes that were closed—sometimes brown, sometimes hazel, she had said. With auburn hair. But he was no longer interested in color.

She had long eyelashes. A short, straight nose—but he could feel no resemblance to a button. Warm cheeks as smooth as rose petals, with well-defined cheekbones. A firm jaw, tapering to what felt like a pointy little chin.

"Heart-shaped," he murmured.

With his hands cupping the underside of her jaw, he found her mouth with his thumbs. Wide. With soft, generous lips. He ran his thumbs lightly along them and kept them resting against the outer corners.

She had not moved or uttered a sound. Her facial muscles were relaxed. He hoped that the rest of her was too. He did not want to embarrass or frighten her. But his fingertips were his eyes.

He moved his head forward again until he felt her warmth and her breath against his face. She neither drew back nor voiced a protest. He touched his lips to hers.

It was not really a kiss. Merely a resting there. A feeling. A tasting. A recognition that they had agreed to a betrothal just a short while ago.

Her lips trembled against his for a moment and then relaxed again. She did not really kiss him either. But she rested against him. Accepted, perhaps, that they would belong together.

He drew back a little, raised his hands to her hair again, ran his fingers through it, and took a half step forward to draw her face against his cravat. He slid one hand down along her spine to draw her against him.

Small. Thin, or at least very slim. No really discernible curves, though he did not—would not—explore her body more intimately with his hands. He did not have the right. Not yet.

She yielded to his touch without pressing against him. Her hands held his coat on either side of his waist.

And they stood there like that, for how long he did not know.

She had described herself accurately. She was not voluptuously shaped. She might even, as Martin had said, look like a boy. She was surely not beautiful or even pretty. She almost certainly did not have the sort of figure that would draw male eyes. But, feeling her warmth and the softly yielding pressure of her body against his, and breathing in the soap scent of her, he did not care a single damn what she looked like.

She was to be his, and though he knew his mind would run the gamut of misgivings when he was alone again later, he felt curiously . . . moved by her.

"Miss Fry," he said against the top of her head—but that sounded all wrong when he was holding her, getting to know her in a manner more intimate than with a mere passing acquaintance. "Or may I call you Sophia?"

Her voice when she answered was muffled against the folds of his neckcloth. "Will you call me Sophie?" she asked. "Please? No one ever has."

He frowned slightly. There had been some pain in that plea. No, perhaps not *pain* exactly. But some yearning, surely.

"You will always be Sophie to me, then," he said. "Sophie, I believe you are pretty. And before you protest that it is not so, that your glass tells a different story, that I would say no such thing if I could *see* you, let me add that a pearl probably does not look so very remarkable either while it is still hidden inside its shell."

He heard a soft gurgle of laughter against his chest, and then she drew free. A moment later he felt his cane against the back of his right hand and took it from her.

Had he said the wrong thing?

"We should walk down by the river," she said, "and perhaps sit on the bank. I shall make a daisy chain, and you can insist that the daisies are as lovely as the most costly of rosebuds. What shall I call you, my lord?"

"Vincent," he said as she busied herself, presumably with putting her cloak and bonnet back on.

He smiled. Perhaps what he was doing was not so very rash after all. He had the distinct feeling that he might grow to like her—not just because he was determined to do so, but because . . .

Well, because she was likable.

Or seemed to be.

It was too soon to know for certain. Would she grow to like him? Was he likable? *He* thought he was.

It was too soon to know if she agreed with him.

And it was too soon to think about the long-term future he had so rashly offered. It always was. The future had a habit of being nothing like what one expected or planned for.

The future would take care of itself.

❧

7

"*W*ill you come to Covington House for tea before I return you to the vicarage?" Lord Darleigh asked when they were making their way homeward later. "We need to make some plans."

We.

Nothing on the subject of their future had been broached during their walk along the river bank or while they sat there. He had talked about Barton Coombs and his boyhood here, and she had made a daisy chain, which he had touched and explored when she announced she was finished. Then he had taken it from her hands and looped it rather awkwardly over her head and about her neck after it had stuck on the brim of her bonnet.

They had both laughed.

That was what she had found so incredible—that they had laughed together more than once. Oh, and there were other things too, even more incredible. He had *touched* her. She knew he had done it only because he could not see her, but he had touched her nevertheless, with fingers that had been warm and gentle and respectful. And with his lips . . .

And he had held her. That had been most incredible of all. He had held the whole length of her body against his. And while there had been the shock of his hard-muscled maleness, there had also been the wonder—ah, the sheer *wonder*—of just being held. As if he cared. As if somehow she was precious to him. As if somehow she had an identity for him.

This had been an incredibly strange day. How could a day that had begun so disastrously—it had started just after midnight, when Sir Clarence and Aunt Martha and Henrietta had returned from the assembly some-time after her and had all come into her bedchamber without knocking, even though she was already in bed with the candle extinguished. How could a day that had begun that way end this way? And it was not even over yet. He wished to discuss their plans for the future over tea at Covington House.

Without a chaperon. She did not suppose that mat-tered, though. They were betrothed, and it was full day-light. They had not been chaperoned during their walk. Indeed, she had never thought of chaperons in connec-tion with herself.

"Thank you," she said.

She rather believed she was going to like him, and the thought brought tears welling into her eyes and a sore-ness to her throat. There had been so few people to like in the past five years and precious few even before that. Oh, and what sort of self-pitying thought was that! She had learned long ago that self-pity was also self-defeating. She had turned it to satire and had found an outlet through her sketches. There was nothing satirical about Viscount Darleigh, nothing to laugh at—not even the fumbling way he had draped the daisy chain about her neck.

She wondered if *she* was likable. She had never asked herself the question before.

When they arrived at Covington House, Mr. Fisk, Lord Darleigh's valet, opened the door to them. His eyes held Sophia's while the viscount asked him to bring them tea to the drawing room. His face was expression-less, as the faces of servants usually were. But Sophia read accusation, even dislike, in his eyes. She would have been intimidated by him even without that. He was taller and broader than his master and looked more like a blacksmith than a valet.

Sophia did not smile at him. One did not smile at servants. They would despise one. She had discovered that when she went to live with Aunt Mary.

The house, about which she had woven fantasies of family and friendship for the past two years, was more imposing on the inside than she had expected. The drawing room was large and square with some comfortable-looking old furniture, a big fireplace, and French windows opening out onto what must once have been a flower garden and was still neatly kept. There was a pianoforte at one end of the room and a violin case on top of it.

"Do have a seat," Lord Darleigh said, gesturing in the direction of the fireplace, and Sophia made her way to an armchair on one side of it. She already recognized the slight tilt of his head when he was listening intently. He made his way unerringly to the chair on the other side of the fireplace and sat down.

"I believe we ought to go to London to marry, Sophie," he said. "By special license. It can be done within a week, I would think, and then I will take you home to Gloucestershire. Middlebury is a vast, stately mansion. The park is huge and is ringed by farms. It is a busy, prosperous place. It is a daunting prospect for you, I know. But—"

He stopped as Mr. Fisk came in with the tea tray. He set it down on a small table close to Sophia, looked directly into her eyes, his own still expressionless, and withdrew.

"Thank you, Martin," the viscount said.

"Sir."

Sophia poured the tea and set a cup and saucer down

beside Viscount Darleigh. She set a small currant cake on a plate and put it in his hand.

"Thank you, Sophie," he said. "I am sorry. I did say *we* needed to make plans, did I not? And then I told you what they were."

"Within a week?" she said.

Reality was threatening to smite her. She was going to leave here with Viscount Darleigh. They were going to go to London and get married there. Within a week. She was going to be a married lady—Lady Darleigh. With a home of her own. And a husband.

"It would be the best plan, I believe," he said. "I have a close and loving family, Sophie. They are especially loving and protective of me because I am the only male and I am the youngest. And to top it off, I am blind. They would suffocate me if they were allowed to arrange our wedding. You have no family of your own to balance their enthusiasm, to fuss over and suffocate you. It would be unfair to take you directly to Middlebury."

She had two aunts, two uncles, and two cousins, if one counted Sebastian, who was Uncle Terrence's stepson. But he was right. She had nobody who would be interested in coming to her wedding, let alone helping to plan it.

"Sophie," he said, "that bag you had with you in the church this morning. I was told it was not large. Did you leave most of your clothes and belongings at Barton Hall? Do I need to send Martin over there to fetch your things? Or did you bring everything?"

"I left behind a few clothes," she said.

"Do you want them?"

She hesitated. She had almost nothing without them, but they were all hand-me-downs from Henrietta, and they were all ill-fitting. Some of them were shabby. She had her sketch pad and charcoal in her bag and a change of clothes.

"No."

"Good," he said. "Then you will have everything new. London is the place to buy whatever you will need."

"I have no money," she said, frowning. Her cup clattered back onto her saucer. "And I cannot ask you—"

"You did not," he said. "But you are to be my wife, Sophie. I will care for all your needs. I will certainly clothe you in a manner befitting your station."

She set her cup and saucer back on the tray and sat back in her chair. She bit down on one side of her forefinger.

"I would love to be able to whisk you off to London, send you shopping while I acquire a special license, and marry you all within one day," he said. "But it will not be possible to do things quite so quickly. I am confident, though, that you will be welcomed in the home of my friend Hugo, Lord Trentham. I mentioned him earlier."

The very thought of it all terrified her—and filled her with such excitement that she felt almost bilious and was glad she had not eaten a cake.

"Sophie?" he said. "I am dictating to you, after all, am I not? But I cannot think of any alternatives. Can you?"

Only getting on the stagecoach tomorrow and riding off alone into the unknown. But she knew she would not do that. Not now that she had an alternative that was all too tempting.

"No," she said. "But are you sure—"

"Oh," he said, "I am quite, quite sure. We will make this work. We will. Tell me you believe me."

She closed her eyes. She wanted this marriage so very badly. She wanted *him* very badly—his sweetness, his sense of honor, his dreams and enthusiasms, even his vulnerability. She wanted someone of her own. Someone who called her by name and held her for comfort and laughed with her. Someone beautiful and achingly attractive.

Someone to give her back her shattered image of herself.

And someone who—

"You intend to support me even after I have left you?" she said.

"Even after you have—" He stared in her direction. "You will always be my wife and therefore my responsibility, Sophie. And I shall, of course, make adequate provision for you in my will. But—must we think of the distant future already? I would prefer to think of the immediate future. We are about to wed. Let us think about *marrying* and going home, and leave the rest to take care of itself. Shall we?"

He looked eager and anxious again.

And she was anxious too—not that her dream might not come true, but that it might.

"Yes," she said, and he smiled.

"We will leave in the morning, then," he said. "Will that suit you?"

So soon?

"Yes, my lord."

He tipped his head to one side.

"Yes, Vincent."

"Shall I play my violin for you?" he asked. "Which is another way of announcing that I will play it for you, for I am sure you are far too polite to voice a protest."

"That is your violin?" she asked. "I would like it of all things if you will play for me."

He laughed as he got to his feet and made his way across the room to the pianoforte, feeling his way there but not by any means groping.

He opened the violin case and removed the instrument. He positioned it beneath his chin, took the bow in his hand and tightened it, adjusted the tuning, and then played, half turned toward her. She thought it might be Mozart, but she was not sure. She had not encountered much music. It did not matter. She clasped her hands, held them to her mouth, and thought she had never heard anything even half as lovely in her life. His body moved slightly to the music, as though he was completely engrossed in it.

"They say at Penderris Hall," he said when he had finished his piece and was putting the violin back into its case, "that when I play, I set all the household and neighborhood cats to howling. They must be wrong, do you not think? I do not hear a single cat howl here."

He had told her during their walk about Penderris Hall in Cornwall, home of the Duke of Stanbrook. He had spent several years there after his return from the Peninsula, learning to cope with his blindness. And a group of seven—six men and one woman, including the duke—had formed a close friendship and called themselves the Survivors' Club. They spent a few weeks of each year together at Penderris.

How very cruel of those friends, Sophia thought, to mock his playing. But he was smiling as if the memory of the insult was a fond one. They would have been joking, of course. They were his *friends*. He had told her how they all encouraged and teased one another out of the doldrums if any of them sank into a depression.

How lovely it must be to have friends. Friends who would even take the liberty of teasing.

"Perhaps," she said, "that is because there *are* no cats here."

Her heartbeat quickened.

"Ouch!" He winced theatrically and then laughed.

"You are as bad as they are, Sophie. I am unappreciated, as all geniuses are, alas. I daresay the pianoforte is dreadfully out of tune. It cannot have been played for a number of years."

She felt absurdly pleased. She had made a joke and he had laughed and accused her of being *as bad as his friends*.

"You play the pianoforte too?" she asked.

"I have taken lessons for both instruments in the last three years," he said. "I am proficient at neither, alas, but I am improving. The harp is another matter. There are just too many strings, and I have been sorely tempted on more than one occasion to hurl the thing through the nearest window. But since the fault is mine, not the harp's, and I would not particularly enjoy being hurled through a window myself, I usually conquer the urge. And I am determined that I *will* master the harp."

"You did not learn to play the pianoforte as a boy?" she asked.

"No one ever thought of it," he said, "including me. It was for the girls. On the whole, I am glad I did not learn then. I would have hated it."

He sat down on the long pianoforte bench and raised the lid. Sophia watched as his fingers felt along the black keys until he found the middle white note with his right thumb.

He played something she had heard Henrietta play—a Bach fugue. He played it more slowly, more ploddingly than Henrietta, but with perfect accuracy. The instrument *was* out of tune, but only to a degree that made the melody sound rather melancholy.

"You may hold your thunderous applause until the recital is at an end," he said when he lifted his hands.

She clapped her hands and smiled.

"Is that a hint that the recital is already ended?" he asked her.

"Not at all," she said. "Applause usually calls for an encore."

"And *polite* applause usually signals the end of a recital," he said. "That applause was decidedly polite. Besides, I am about at the end of my repertoire. Do *you* want to try to coax music out of this sad instrument? Do you play?"

"I never learned," she said.

"Ah." He looked her way. "Was that a wistful note I heard in your voice? Soon, Sophie, you may do anything you please. Within reason."

She closed her eyes briefly. It was too vast a notion to comprehend. She had always wanted to . . . oh, simply to *learn*.

"Do you sing?" he asked. "Do you know any folk songs? More specifically, do you know 'Early One Morning'? It is the only song I can play with any degree of competency."

He played the first few bars.

"I do know it," she said, crossing the room toward him. "I can hold a tune, but I doubt I will ever be invited to sing at any of the world's great opera houses."

"But how devoid of music our lives would be," he said, "if we allowed the making of it only to those of outstanding talent. Sing while I play."

His hands—those hands that had touched her face—were slender and well-shaped with short, neatly manicured nails.

He replayed the opening bars, and she sang.

"Early one morning, just as the sun was rising, I heard a maiden sing, in the valley below."

His head was bowed over the keys, his eyelids lowered over his eyes.

Why were almost all folk songs sad? Was it because sadness tugged far more strongly upon the heartstrings than happiness did?

"Oh, don't deceive me, oh, never leave me. How could you use a poor maiden so?"

She sang the song from beginning to end, and when she was finished, his hands rested on the keys and his head remained bowed.

There was a soreness in her throat again. Life was so often a sad business, full of deceptions and departures.

And then he played again, a different tune, more haltingly, missing several of the notes. And he sang.

"On Richmond Hill there lives a lass, more bright than May-day morn . . ."

He had a light, pleasant tenor voice, though he would surely never sing on the stage of any opera house either. She smiled at the thought.

". . . I'd crowns resign to call thee mine, sweet lass of Richmond Hill."

He was smiling when he finished.

"The language of love can be marvelously extravagant, can it not?" he said. "And yet it can smite one here." He patted his abdomen with the outside of a lightly closed fist. "Would you believe a man who told you he would resign crowns for your sake, Sophie?"

"I doubt any man would," she said. "He would have to be a king, would he not, and they tend to be in short supply. But I might believe the sentiment if I were sure he loved me above all else. And if I loved him with an everlasting kind of love in return. Do you believe in that kind of love, my lord?"

She could have bitten out her tongue when it was too late to recall the words.

"I do," he said, playing a scale softly with his right hand. "It does not happen to everyone, or even perhaps to most, but it does happen. And it must be wonderful when it does. Most people settle for comfort instead. And there is nothing wrong with comfort."

She was feeling decidedly *un*comfortable.

He looked up at her then and smiled.

"I had better return you to the vicarage," he said. "I suppose it was not quite proper to bring you here, was it? But we are betrothed and will be married very soon."

"You do not need to walk back with me," she said.

"Ah, but I do," he told her, getting to his feet. "When my lady needs to go somewhere beyond my home or hers, I will escort her whenever I am able."

It sounded a little excessively possessive, but she understood his need not to be handicapped by his disability.

My lady.

Was that what she was now—his *lady*?

Most people settle for comfort instead, she remembered as they left the house together. *And there is nothing wrong with comfort.*

Oh, there was not.

But . . . comfort instead of the everlasting kind of romantic love about which he had sung?

And even the comfort might not last.

*T*hey were on their way to London, in the middle of the second day of their journey. It had been tedious, as all journeys were. They had scarcely talked.

Vincent tried not to regret everything he had done in the past few days, starting with his acceptance of Sir Clarence March's invitation to spend an evening at Barton Hall. Or perhaps starting with his decision to go to Barton Coombs instead of returning home.

He had offered marriage to a stranger—and not even a normal marriage. It was that last part that weighed most heavily upon him. He was going to have the doom of a possible separation hanging over his head from the first moment. Impulsive behavior had always been his besetting sin. And he had often lived to regret it. He had once impulsively stepped forward to see why a large cannon had not fired.

He had, though, felt a desperate need to persuade Sophia Fry to marry him, and there had seemed no other way to get her to say yes. She had *needed* to say yes.

The near silence in which they had traveled for a day and a half was as much his fault as hers. More so. He believed she was a little intimidated by him and his grand carriage and the grandeur of the life she was facing. And by the fact that she was stepping into the unknown.

Last night could have done nothing to help her relax. They had stopped at one of the more obscure posting inns, chosen by Martin and Handry between them, and had taken two rooms, one for Martin and one for Mr. and Mrs. Hunt. He had slept in Martin's room, but all night he had worried about the impropriety and possible danger of Sophia's having to huddle all alone in her room, without even a maid to lend her countenance.

He tried to think of something to say, some conversational opener that would elicit a response, perhaps even a laugh. She had a pretty laugh, though he had been given the distinct impression the day before yesterday that laughing was something she rarely did. She had led a brutally lonely life, judging by the little she had told him of it.

Before he could speak, she did.

"Just look at that church spire," she said, her voice bright and eager. "I have noticed it before, and it always amazes me that something so very tall and slender can remain standing in a strong wind."

He waited for realization to hit her, as it did very quickly. He heard her draw a sharp inward breath.

"I am so sorry," she said, her voice far more subdued.

"Tell me about it," he said.

"It belongs to a church in the little village we are approaching," she told him. "It is a remarkably pretty village. But that tells you absolutely nothing of any significance, does it? Let me see. There are some old whitewashed, thatched cottages along the sides of the road here. Oh, one of them is bright pink. How cheerful it looks. I wonder who lives in it. The church is farther in. There, now I can see the whole of it. It is on one side of the village green and is really quite unremarkable except for the spire. I daresay the villagers were so dissatisfied with the church and so ashamed in the company of people from other, more fortunate villages that they decided to build the spire to restore their pride. There are some children playing cricket on the green. You used to play cricket. I have heard people talk about it."

He listened with interest. She had a sharp eye and the imagination with which to embellish details in an amusing way. And there was warmth and animation in her voice.

"I cannot tell you the name of the village," she continued. "There is nothing to say. Perhaps it does not matter. We do not have to give a name to everything that is pretty, do we? Do you realize that a rose does not call itself a rose? Nor do any of the flowers and trees surrounding it."

He found himself grinning in her direction.

"How do you know?" he asked her. "Do you speak rose or flower language?"

She laughed, the light, pretty sound he remembered from two days ago.

He hesitated, and then decided to trust what he was beginning to suspect about her.

"I believe it was one of those boys on the village green," he said, "or actually it was probably his father, or even his grandfather, who once hit the ball in such a high arc that it landed on the church roof. That was before the spire was built, of course."

"But you do not even know what village that was," she protested, sounding a little bewildered.

Ah. Perhaps he was wrong.

"The parishioners," he continued, "were so annoyed with the boys for climbing up the ivy on the church walls to retrieve the ball, and leaving it patchy-looking and not at all picturesque—the ivy, that is—that they decided to build the spire and prevent any repetition of the sacrilege."

There was a short silence.

"And they built it extra high," Sophia said, "to discourage Bertha from climbing it."

Bertha? He grinned.

"Bertha was the girl, was she," he asked, "who climbed everything in sight even before she could walk? No one could stop her?"

"The very one," she said. "She was a severe trial to her parents, who were forever rescuing her from trees and chimney tops and were terrified that one day she would fall and break her head."

"Not to mention her neck," he said. "And of course it did not help that she could climb *up* but never *down*. Indeed, she could not even bear to *look* down."

"And then came the fateful day," she said, "when the very same cricketer, who was brilliant at hitting the ball as high as he could without ever realizing that it was distance, not height, that really counted, impaled it on the very tip of the church spire."

"And as fate would have it," he said, "Bertha, who was supposed to be visiting her maternal grandparents twenty miles away on that day, had *not* gone after all because the grandfather had a chill and the incompetent physician who examined him pronounced his ailment to be typhoid and put the whole village into quarantine."

"And so Bertha climbed the spire," Sophia said, "and tossed the ball down while all the children cheered wildly and all the adults held their hands over their eyes and held their breath at the same time, and the vicar and the whole church choir went down on their knees to pray. Those members of the choir, that was, who were not cheering."

"And then," Vincent said. "And *then*. Blind-as-a-bat Dan, who had been looked upon as the village idiot all his seventeen years because he could not see even . . . well, a bat, to coin a pun, finally came into his own and was forever after the great hero of village myth. There is even a statue of him somewhere, though not on the village green at the special request of several generations of cricketers. He climbed onto the roof and shinned up the spire and brought Bertha down because he, of course, did not fear heights, as everyone else did, for the simple reason that he could not see them. She might still be up there if Dan had not climbed to her rescue."

"By that time," she said, "Bertha was sixteen, going on seventeen. And of course she fell in love with Dan, upon whom she had never really looked fully before. She discovered that he was wondrously strong and handsome and that he was not, of course, an idiot at all, only as blind as a bat. And he confessed that he had adored her in secret all his life because she had a voice like an angel. They married in the church with the great spire and lived happily ever after."

"And she never climbed upon anything higher than a chair ever again," Vincent said, "and even then it had to be a sturdy chair and only if a mouse ran underfoot. For she knew that Dan would always come to her rescue, and she feared that he might fall and kill himself and she would lose the love of her life. Their children were all cheerfully earthbound and never showed any inclination to climb even out of their cradles."

"The end." Sophia sighed.

"Amen," Vincent said solemnly.

They both collapsed into laughter and snorts and giggles, until something—astonishment, perhaps, or embarrassment—hushed them.

"Have you always told stories?" he asked her after a short silence.

"I *see* stories," she said. "Well, not real stories, with a beginning and middle and end. But moments in time. Foolish ones. I sketch them. Caricatures."

"Do you?" He turned his head in her direction. "Of people you know?"

"Always," she said, "though I believe I may try sketching a series of pictures of Bertha and Dan and the church spire. It would be an amusing new challenge."

He smiled at her.

"And maybe I shall write the story to go with the pictures," she said. "You must help with your parts of it. You have a way with words. Do *you* tell stories? Other than this one, I mean?"

"I used to invent fantastic stories to put Ursula, my youngest sister, to sleep when she was frightened by the dark or ghosts or thunder—there was always something," he said. "Though she was older than me. And I can still invent bedtime stories for children. At Easter time, when all my family was at Middlebury Park, one of my nieces asked me to read them all a bedtime story. I could hear Amy, my oldest sister, shushing her, and I could imagine that she was also flapping her hands and making faces and otherwise trying to remind her daughter that *Uncle Vincent is blind*. I told the children about a dragon who freed a field mouse from a trap by breathing fire on the cords that held it imprisoned. Every evening after that I had to invent another adventure for the dragon and the mouse."

"Oh," she said, "I wonder if I could draw a dragon. I have a mouse in almost all my sketches—a little one in the corner."

"Your signature?" he asked her. "Have you always been the little mouse observing the absurdities of life around you, Sophie?"

"The mouse in my sketches may be small," she said, "but it does not always look meek and docile. Sometimes it has a wickedly gleeful smirk on its face."

"I am glad," he said.

They fell silent again, but for only a short while. The carriage swayed suddenly into a sharp turn, and Vincent, grasping the strap beside the door so that he would not bump against his companion, could hear the horses' hooves clopping over cobblestones, presumably in the yard of a posting inn.

"It is a bit sooner than need be for a change of horses," Martin said as he opened the carriage door and set down the steps. "But there is going to be a deluge any minute now, and it was in my own interest to persuade Handry to stop early since I have been forced to ride up alongside him on the box. Shall I bespeak a private parlor for you and Miss Fry, sir? And order luncheon?"

At least Martin was talking again, even if only with a clipped formality.

"Yes, please, Martin," Vincent said, and he took his cane from the seat opposite, descended the steps without assistance—both servants knew not to offer any—and turned to hand Sophia down.

If only he could *see* her, he thought. And her sketches—her caricatures.

If only he could *see*. Just for one minute. He would not be greedy. Just one minute.

He concentrated upon his breathing. In. Out. In. Out.

He was something of an expert now at warding off these sudden, quite unpredictable bouts of panic. Not a total expert, though, he thought ruefully. Once his breath was under control, he had to fight the quite igno-minious urge to shed tears, even to weep noisily with frustration and self-pity.

He smiled and offered his arm.

8

❦

$\mathcal{T}$he carriage had entered London, where Sophia had spent most of her life before two years ago. And she had spent last spring here and part of this one, while her aunt and uncle took Henrietta on a round of social events in pursuit of a noble husband and Sophia remained in their rented lodgings and walked in the various parks.

This time she was coming here to be married.

It was a dizzying thought. She was not sure that even yet she comprehended the full reality of it.

They were on their way to the London home of Lord Trentham, Lord Darleigh's friend, to ask if she might stay there until her wedding. Sophia dreaded the moment of their arrival. What would Lord Trentham and his relatives think of her? And of this situation? Would Lord Trentham look at her as Mr. Fisk did? Would he think that she was a fortune hunter taking advantage of a blind man?

But how could he *not* think that?

She felt helpless and a little sick.

The carriage rocked to a stop outside a solidly respectable-looking house on a long street. Sophia looked out to see Mr. Fisk jump down from the box and run up the steps to bang the knocker against the door panel. It opened after a few moments and he spoke to the man who stood in the doorway—a servant, obviously. He peered out at the carriage and then disappeared from view, leaving the door ajar.

"I believe a servant has gone to see if someone is at home," she said. "Oh, they will think this is very presumptuous of me."

His hand reached across the seat and covered the back of hers.

"Hugo is one of my dearest friends in the world," he said.

That, she thought, *might be part of the trouble.*

It was not the servant who appeared next in the doorway, filling it. But the man who stood there, looking at Mr. Fisk and then at the carriage, and then came bounding down the steps and across the pavement, surely could not be Lord Trentham. He was a great giant of a man with a fierce, frowning face and unfashionably close-cropped hair.

Whoever he was, he was going to tell them all about their presumption, and he was not going to mince words in the telling. She could see that in his eyes.

He tore open the carriage door and leaned inside.

"Vince, you damned rogue," he bellowed while Sophia cowered in her corner, glad she was not sitting on his side of the carriage, "what is the meaning of this? Eh? You are two days late. You might as well turn around and go back wherever the devil you came from for all the good you are to me now."

Lord Darleigh's face lit up with smiles.

"I am delighted to see you too, Hugo," he said. "Or at least, I would be if I was able."

The fierce giant *was* Lord Trentham.

"Get out of there," he bellowed, stooping briefly to set down the steps while the coachman hovered helplessly in the background. "If you are not going to drive away again, as any decent man would who was two days late, get out here so that I can go up one side of you and down the other. Why the devil did you not get here in time?"

And he half dragged, half helped Lord Darleigh down onto the pavement, where he proceeded to draw him into a bear hug that looked as if it would surely crush every bone in his body. But Lord Darleigh, rather than being alarmed, was laughing and hugging the giant back.

"In time for what?" he asked. "Two days late for what?"

"My *wedding*," Lord Trentham roared. "You missed my wedding and ruined my day. Ruined my *life*, in fact. George came, and Imogen and Flavian and Ralph. Ben is staying with his sister in the north of England and so had a half-decent excuse for neglecting me, especially when he does not have the legs with which to dash back here. But you had disappeared off the face of the earth without any thought to the wedding invitations you might miss. No one at Middlebury Park knew where you were. Not even your mother."

"Your wedding?" Lord Darleigh said. "You are *married*, Hugo? To . . . Lady Muir?"

"None other," Lord Trentham said. "Lady Trentham now. I had the devil's own job persuading her, but how could she resist me forever? No woman in her right mind could. Come inside and see her, Vince. Or *not* see her, to be more accurate. She can add her reproaches to mine. You have blighted both our lives."

It was at that moment that he glanced up at the carriage and his eyes met Sophia's.

"I have brought someone with me," Lord Darleigh said at the same moment.

"As I can see." Lord Trentham's eyes remained upon Sophia. "I beg your pardon, ma'am. I did not see you sitting there. Have I used any language I ought not to have used in a lady's hearing? Doubtless I have. Do forgive me."

Lord Darleigh turned toward the carriage, and Sophia could see how he located the step with the inside of his boot, moved his foot along to the edge of the step, and then held out a hand to help her alight—just as he had done at the stile a few days ago.

Lord Trentham appeared even larger when she was standing on the pavement looking up at him. And he was frowning and looking strangely embarrassed.

"This is Hugo Emes, Lord Trentham, Sophie," Vincent said. "Hugo, I would like you to meet Miss Sophia Fry, my affianced bride."

Sophia half curtsied.

"Affianced bride," Lord Trentham said, his eyebrows almost meeting over the bridge of his nose. "Is this sudden, lad, or were you being very secretive at Penderris a few months ago?"

"No, you might call it a whirlwind affair," Lord Darleigh said. "We are going to be wed, probably the day after tomorrow. It is why we are in London. I have to purchase a special license first. I was hoping your stepmother would be willing to allow her to stay here for the next two nights. Now that permission will have to be asked of Lady Muir—Lady Trentham."

"Havey-cavey stuff, is it, then?" Lord Trentham asked, looking doubtfully at Sophia. "You had better come inside, the two of you. Four paces forward, Vince, and five steps up to the front door. Where is your cane? Ah, here comes Fisk. He will see to you. Miss Fry?"

He was offering her his arm and favored her with a steady stare, which she found more than a little frightening. But of course, most of Lord Darleigh's friends of the Survivors' Club had been military officers in the late wars. They must all be formidable gentlemen.

A lady was hurrying into the hall by the time they got

inside, limping rather heavily as she came. She was small and slender with blond curls and an exquisitely lovely face. She was smiling warmly.

"Lord Darleigh!" she exclaimed. "I looked out through the sitting room window to see who the visitor was, and I could see it was you. How delightful, even if you did miss our wedding. Hugo was disappointed about that, but now he will be happy again."

She was approaching Lord Darleigh as she spoke, and somehow he seemed to know that both her hands were outstretched toward him. He raised his own and they squeezed each other's hands. He was smiling directly at her.

"I feared Hugo might be too much of a slowtop to go after you when he left Penderris," he said. "I am glad I misjudged him. I thought you perfect for him from the moment I met you. And what could be more romantic than his finding you wounded down on the beach and carrying you all the way up to the house? I wish you happy, Lady Trentham. May I kiss the bride, Hugo, even though I am two days late?"

He drew her closer without waiting for permission and kissed her, half on one cheek, half on her nose.

They both laughed.

"Thank you," she said, and turned to look with polite inquiry at Sophia. "And your friend, Lord Darleigh?"

"Miss Sophia Fry," he said. "I have brought her here in the hope that she may stay for a couple of nights until we can marry by special license the day after tomorrow."

Lady Trentham raised her eyebrows and looked fully at Sophia, who wished she could be anywhere else on earth but where she was. Even her dark corner of the drawing room at Barton Hall suddenly seemed infinitely desirable. The smile in the lady's eyes had died. She spoke politely, however.

"You look exhausted and apprehensive and even downright frightened, Miss Fry," she said. "I do not doubt there is an interesting story behind this unexpected announcement and plea for shelter, but we will not demand to know it at this very moment, will we, Hugo?"

And she came closer and linked an arm through Sophia's. She was not a tall lady, but even so she was half a head taller than Sophia.

"Of course you may stay here," she said. "If you are a friend and even a betrothed of Lord Darleigh's, that is a good enough recommendation. Let me take you up to a guest room and get you settled. Hugo, your stepmama will not mind my taking charge?"

"You are the lady of the house now, Gwendoline," he said, "and you know she loves you. I'll take Vincent up to the drawing room to meet her and Constance—and my uncle. They will be charmed. Everyone loves Vincent. He does not frown and frighten little children the way I do."

"Oh, Hugo," she said, laughing, "you do *not*. Children take one look at you and know you are just a cuddly bear."

He pulled a face, and she drew Sophia away in the direction of the staircase.

"You look on the verge of collapse," she said quietly as they began to climb. "Let us get you settled, and I will leave you alone to rest if you wish, or we will sit down if you would prefer and you may tell me everything, or as much as you wish to divulge. You are quite welcome here. You may relax and rest. Have you traveled far?"

That slack, almost hostile look with which she had first favored Sophia when she learned of her relationship to Lord Darleigh had been dropped and replaced with perfect good manners.

And she *was* exhausted and on the verge of collapse, Sophia realized.

"From Barton Coombs in Somerset," she said. "And I know what you are thinking. I know that I am plain and unattractive and dressed like a fright. Yet here I am about to marry a wealthy viscount who is charming and kind and beautiful—and conveniently *blind*. I know that you must despise me as the very worst kind of adventurer."

And she did something that she never, ever did. She burst into tears.

It was a pretty room to which Lady Trentham had brought her. The bedcover and the curtains were made of the same floral print on an ivory background. It was a cheerful room.

And here she was, standing in the middle of it, as out of place as a scarecrow in a *ton* ballroom.

"Come and sit on the bed," Lady Trentham said as Sophia blew her nose into her handkerchief, "or lie down on it. Do you wish me to go away for a while? There are two hours before dinner. Or do you want to tell me how it came about that Lord Darleigh offered you marriage and brought you here to marry you by special license? And please forgive me for the shock I must have shown when I was first told downstairs that you were Lord Darleigh's betrothed. I know better than to make instant judgments based upon appearance alone. Give me a chance to make up for my rudeness, even if I can do it at present only by leaving you alone to rest."

Sophia sat on the edge of the bed. Her feet dangled a few inches above the floor.

"He persuaded me," she said, "that there were as many advantages to him in our proposed marriage as there were for me. That is absurd, of course, for I would be alone and destitute without him, and that fact weighed heavily in my decision, though I did try to fight my baser nature. I said no more than once, and meant it each time. Though I suppose I could not have done so, could I, or I would not have ended up saying yes."

She swiped at her wet cheeks and spread her hands over her face.

"I am sorry," she said. "I am so sorry. How you must hate me. You and Lord Trentham are his friends."

Lady Trentham, who had sat down beside her, patted her knee and got to her feet again to pull on the bell rope beside the bed. She stood there in silence until a light tap on the door preceded the appearance of a maid.

"Bring tea and some cakes, please, Mavis," she said, and the maid disappeared again.

Sophia dried her cheeks with her damp handkerchief and put it away.

"I never cry," she said. "Well, almost never."

"I think you have probably earned a good weep," Lady Trentham said. "There are two chairs over by the window. Shall we sit there and have some tea? Tell me how this all came about, if you will. I do not hate you. My husband and your future husband are close friends. You and I are likely to meet many times in the future. I would far prefer to like you, even to be fond of you. And I would hope you will like me and be fond of me. Who are you, Miss Fry?"

"My uncle is Sir Terrence Fry," Sophia explained as she seated herself on one of the chairs. "Though he has never had anything to do with me. He is a diplomat and is gone from the country more than he is here. My father was killed in a duel by an outraged husband five years ago, and I have lived with two different aunts since then. I am a lady by birth, but we did not live a respectable life, my father and I, after my mother left when I was five—or even before she left. My father was a rake and a gambler. He was forever in debt. We were always moving and hiding, hiding and moving. I never had a governess or went to school, though I did learn to read and write and figure—my father insisted upon that. I never had a maid. I am not . . . worthy of Lord Darleigh."

"Did your aunts cherish you during the past five years?" Lady Trentham asked.

"Aunt Mary ignored me for three years until she died," Sophia said. "She took one look at me and pronounced me hopeless. Aunt Martha, Lady March of Barton Hall, gave me a home after her sister died, but she has a daughter of her own to bring out and marry. And Henrietta is beautiful."

The maid returned with a tray, which she set down on a small round table close to Lady Trentham before withdrawing quietly and closing the door behind her. Lady Trentham poured a cup of tea for Sophia and set two little pastries on a plate, which she handed to her.

"It was there, at Barton Hall, was it," she asked, "that Lord Darleigh met you?"

"In a way," Sophia said, and she proceeded to give Lady Trentham an account of everything that had happened in the last week. Not even quite a week, in fact. How amazing that was. That first sight she had had of him arriving at Covington House seemed as if it must have happened months ago.

"So perhaps you can understand," she said in conclusion, "how tempting the offer was for me, especially when he repeated it after I had said no. I ought to have held firm. I know I ought."

She had almost finished drinking her tea. Her plate, she noticed in some surprise, was empty apart from a few crumbs.

"I can understand," Lady Trentham said. "I believe I can also begin to understand why Lord Darleigh persisted after you had said no. I can see that he saw something in you that he liked."

"He said he liked my voice," Sophia told her.

"There are voices that are lovely for various reasons or annoying for other reasons, are there not?" Lady Trentham said. "But when we can see, a voice is often of secondary importance. How very important it must be to someone who is blind. Permanent blindness is very hard to imagine. It is easy to understand, though, that your voice is of greater significance to your betrothed than your looks."

"But I have no figure," Sophia said. "I look like a boy."

Lady Trentham smiled and returned her empty cup and saucer to the tray.

"Is that why you wear your hair so short?" she asked. "Do you cut it yourself?"

"Yes," Sophia said.

"An expert hairdresser could make it look prettier," Lady Trentham told her. "And the right clothes with the addition of stays can make even the most slender of figures appealing. Do you have better fitting dresses than the one you are wearing?"

"No," Sophia said.

"I wonder," Lady Trentham said, "if Lord Darleigh has thought of your need for bride clothes?"

"He has," Sophia assured her. "He hoped that perhaps Mrs. Emes or Miss Emes would go shopping with me tomorrow."

"I imagine either or both of them would be delighted," Lady Trentham said. "But may I come instead?"

"I cannot so impose upon your time," Sophia said.

"Oh." Lady Trentham's smile deepened. "Ladies love to shop, Miss Fry. Often we shop when there is really no need to, and end up buying bonnets and fripperies for the sake of buying. It will be a wonderful treat to shop with someone who needs simply everything. Lord Darleigh is willing to foot the bill?"

"He says so." Sophia flushed. "It does not seem right, though."

"It would be worse," Lady Trentham told her, "if he were to take his bride home to meet his family dressed in clothes even servants would reject—forgive me. You owe it to him to dress well, Miss Fry, and to allow him to pay the bills. I believe he is a wealthy enough man not to suffer from the expense."

Sophia sighed. "You are being very kind," she said. "I am so . . ."

"Weary?" Lady Trentham suggested, getting to her feet. "I would advise you to lie down and rest for an hour. I will send my maid to you when it is close to dinnertime. May I please lend you a dress to wear this evening? You are smaller than I am, but not hopelessly so. My maid is very skilled at making hasty and temporary adjustments. Will you be offended?"

"No," Sophia said, not knowing quite how she felt. She was actually feeling numb and more tired than she had ever felt in her life. "Thank you."

And then she was alone in the pretty guest room. She kicked off her shoes and stretched out on top of the bed to think. But fortunately, given the confused state of her mind, she had no chance to do so. She fell instantly and deeply asleep.

Hugo took Vincent to the sitting room and introduced him to Mrs. Emes, his stepmother; Miss Emes, her daughter and Hugo's half sister; and Mr. Philip Germane, his uncle. Hugo explained to them that Vincent's newly betrothed was upstairs with his wife, too tired to be sociable for a while. She was to stay with them for a few days.

"We have come here to be married," Vincent explained as Hugo led him to a chair. "Sophia has no family and I do. It seems to me that it is fairer to her that we marry quietly in London by special license and then go home. But I do beg your pardon for the intrusion."

"You are one of Hugo's friends from Cornwall, Lord Darleigh," Mrs. Emes said. "You are always welcome here."

"Hugo was disappointed that you were not here for his wedding," Miss Emes said. "He is beaming with pleasure that you have come now."

"I am sorry to have missed it," Vincent said. "Do tell me all about it."

Miss Emes needed no further encouragement.

"Oh," she said, "it was at St. George's on Hanover Square, and I am quite sure *everyone* was there, even though Hugo insists that only family and close friends were invited. Gwen was wearing pink, a gorgeous shade of deep rose, and . . ."

Vincent smiled and listened with half his attention. With the other half he wondered and worried about Sophia. She had been looking exhausted and apprehensive and frightened, Lady Trentham had said. This must all be quite overwhelming for her. But better, surely, than the alternative. She had been fully intending to take the stagecoach to London with no plan for where she would go or what she would do when she got here. The very thought was enough to make him break out in a cold sweat.

Germane took his leave after a while, and Hugo suggested that Vincent accompany him to his study.

"It's a grand notion, is it not?" he said, clapping a hand on Vincent's shoulder as they walked. "Me with a study. But I owe it to my father to show an interest in all the businesses, Vince, and actually I *am* interested. More than that, I am getting involved. And my father was quite right about the man he left in charge of everything. He is an intelligent, earnest, conscientious soul who manages the businesses with meticulous care—except that he has not one grain of imagination. Nothing will ever change with him in charge, and everything in life must change or stagnate and wither away, as we all very well know. Sit here and I will sit behind this large oak desk of mine. It is a pity you cannot see. I now look quite important and imposing, and you look like a lowly supplicant."

"You are going to settle here in London as a businessman, then, are you, Hugo?" Vincent asked. "How does Lady Trentham feel about that?"

He heard Hugo sigh.

"She loves me, Vince," he said. "*Me*. Just as I am, without any conditions attached. It's the grandest feeling in the world. She would accept it even if I *did* want to stay here all my life. I don't, though. I want to spend most of my time in Hampshire, at Crosslands, and Gwendoline has all sorts of ideas on how to transform the house into a home and the large garden into a park. I have turned into that most embarrassing of all creatures, you know—a happily married man. Easy to say, I suppose, when I have been married for all of two days. But I am confident it will last. You may call me naïve for believing so, but I *know*. And Gwendoline knows the same thing. And that brings us to you."

"I ran away from home," Vincent told him. "That is why no one knew where I was when you sent your invitation. I ran because my mother and sisters had decided that I will be far more comfortable if I am married. They began the campaign in earnest after Easter by inviting a young lady and her family to Middlebury, and it soon became obvious that she had come, not to be courted, but to accept my addresses. She even told me that she *understood* and that she *did not mind*."

Hugo chuckled, and Vincent too smiled. Had he expected words of sympathy?

"So I ran," Vincent said. "Martin and I went to the Lake District for a few weeks of sheer bliss, and then I went, on impulse, to the old house in Somerset. My intention was to relax there in quiet solitude, not to let anyone know I was home. I was quickly disabused of that notion."

He proceeded to give Hugo a brief account of everything that had happened after his arrival.

"And so here I am," he concluded. "Here *we* are."

"And you could think of no alternative to marrying her," Hugo said.

"None that was satisfactory," Vincent told him.

"And so Lord Darleigh rode blindly to the rescue," Hugo said.

"I need a wife, Hugo," Vincent explained. "I will have no peace from my family until I wed. Sophia needs a home and someone to care for her. No one ever has really cared, you know. It will work. I will make it work. *We* will."

Even if that meant giving each other the freedom eventually to live alone—stupidest of stupid ideas.

"You will." Hugo sighed. "I have every confidence in you, Vince."

The library door opened at that moment.

"Am I interrupting anything?" Lady Trentham asked.

Vincent turned his head. "Is Sophia with you?"

"She is lying down," Lady Trentham told him. "I suspect she is already asleep. She will come down for dinner. While you are busy tomorrow making arrangements for your wedding, Lord Darleigh, I shall take Miss Fry shopping for bride clothes if I may. She needs a great deal, as well as a good haircut. May I assume that we have carte blanche to spend whatever needs to be spent?"

"Of course," Vincent said. "And please do not allow her to persuade you that she needs only the very barest of necessities and the plainest and least expensive of everything. I am sure she will try."

"You may depend upon me," Lady Trentham said. "She will look presentable when I am finished with her."

"She tells me she is not ugly enough to turn heads," Vincent said. "But she believes she is hopelessly unattractive."

"She is not ugly enough to turn heads, lad," Hugo assured him. "I did not even notice her in the carriage when you first arrived."

"Not many women are astonishingly pretty," Lady Trentham said. "Even fewer are ravishingly beautiful. But we women are experts at making the most of what we have. I will do my best tomorrow to show Miss Fry how to make the most of her assets. Her hair is a lovely color, and she has the eyes to go with it. She has a wide mouth and a lovely smile, though I have seen it only once. And she has a slight figure that will look light and dainty when she is wearing the right clothes. But I understand, Lord Darleigh, that you have already discovered one of her finest assets. She does indeed have a pretty voice, low and a little husky. I may not have noticed if she had not mentioned that you had told her so. We sighted people are often neglectful of the power of sound."

Vincent smiled at her.

"If you are trying to reassure me, ma'am," he said, "I thank you. But there is no need. I do not care what Sophia looks like. I like her."

"It is she who needs the reassurance," she told him. "And you should care what she looks like, Lord Darleigh. Every member of your family and all your friends will see her and respond to her appearance. And she will respond to what she sees in her glass and in the eyes of those who behold her. You need to care. But of course, you are already doing so, for you have brought her here to shop. She looks like the veriest waif, you know. Her aunt should be thoroughly ashamed of herself for passing on clothes even her servants would scorn to wear. And she cuts her own hair and has made a horrid mess of it. And she looks somewhat undernourished. Her eyes are too large for her face. You need to care how she looks."

Vincent frowned. She was right, he decided. It was all very well for him to assure Sophia that he did not care. But *she* probably did.

"Will you stay here tonight?" Hugo asked. "You will be very welcome."

"I'll take a room at a hotel if you can recommend one," Vincent said.

"We will go over to George's after dinner," Hugo suggested. "He is in town for a week or two. And Imogen is staying with him. She came for the wedding, to my eternal surprise and gratification. Flavian is here somewhere too—he was my best man, in fact. And Ralph is in town. George will no doubt persuade you to stay with him. You were always his special pet."

When Vincent had first arrived at Penderris Hall, deaf as well as blind, it was George Crabbe, the Duke of Stanbrook himself, who had spent almost every minute of every hour of every day in his room with him, stroking his hand and his head, often cradling him in his arms for hours on end so that he would know the only human contact he could experience—touch. He had fought those cradling arms like a madman on more than one occasion, lashing out with all the strength of his terror, but the arms had never fought back or tensed or tried to imprison him. They had never abandoned him.

Vincent doubted he would have survived without George. Or if he had, he would have been a raving lunatic long before his hearing returned.

"It will be good to see him again so soon. And Imogen," he said. Imogen Hayes, Lady Barclay, was the only woman member of the Survivors' Club, having lost her husband to torture in the Peninsula, a torture she had witnessed. "And you too, Hugo. I have wondered if you went after Lady Muir when you left Penderris. I am so glad you did."

"Well, I am too, lad," Hugo said, "though she did not make it easy for me."

"If you had heard his first proposal to me, Lord Darleigh," Lady Trentham said, "you would not wonder at it."

Vincent grinned. They sounded very pleased with themselves, the two of them. He could hear the smile in both their voices.

9

⚜

Sophia was having her hair cut, an absurdity, she had thought when Lady Trentham first suggested it to her, for her hair was very short already. But here she was, at the mercy of Mr. Welland and his scissors and his flying fingers.

"He cuts my hair when I am in town," Lady Trentham had explained. "I chose him, as I chose my dressmaker, because he does not speak with a French accent. I have no objection whatsoever to a French accent on the lips of a Frenchman or -woman, but you would not believe, Miss Fry, how many Englishmen and -women affect one in the belief that it will suggest superior skill and draw superior customers."

Like Sir Clarence and Lady March, Sophia had thought.

Mr. Welland had clucked over Sophia's hair and declared in a distinctly cockney accent that her last stylist ought to be flogged to within an inch of his life at the very least.

"The last stylist was me," Sophia had confessed rather sheepishly.

He had clucked once more and gone to work.

They were not alone in his workroom. Lady Trentham sat facing them and watching with apparent interest. So did the Countess of Kilbourne, her sister-in-law, who had sent a note last evening to ask if Lady Tren-

tham would be at home for a call this morning and who
had been invited to join the shopping trip instead.

"You must not be overawed by her title," Lady Trentham had assured Sophia. "There is no one less high in
the instep than Lily. She grew up in the tail of an army
as a sergeant's daughter and married my brother when
her father died. A long, long saga followed that event,
but I will not trouble you with the full story now. May
I invite her to accompany us?"

"Yes, of course," Sophia had said, awed anyway.

And this morning after she had arrived at Lord Trentham's house and greeted her sister-in-law with a hug
and bidden Mrs. and Miss Emes a good morning with a
beaming smile, the countess had been introduced to Sophia and had looked her over frankly from head to toe.
Sophia was wearing one of her own dresses, having declined Lady Trentham's offer of one of hers.

"You are to be Viscount Darleigh's bride?" she had
asked. "Oh, my dear, we are going to have such *fun* this
morning. Are we not, Gwen?"

And she had startled Sophia by darting forward and
hugging her. She was herself exquisitely lovely, with a
face that looked as if it always smiled.

Finally Mr. Welland seemed to be finished. Sophia
was alarmed at the amount of hair that had fallen to the
floor about her feet. Was there any left on her head? He
had not placed her before a mirror, as she had expected.

"I have shaped your hair and thinned out the bulk,
you will understand," he told her now, handing her a
glass and inviting her to hold it up before her face.
"That does not mean I *wished* to cut your hair shorter.
It ought to be longer."

Sophia gazed at her image in some astonishment. Her
hair hugged her head in soft curls and framed her face
with wispy waves. It looked neat and tame and not at
all its usual wild bush.

"It is very chic," Lady Kilbourne said. "It shows up your heart-shaped face. And the color is adorable."

Lord Darleigh had explored her face with his hands when they were on their way to the river and had said, when he came to her chin, that her face was heart-shaped. Sophia had always thought it was round.

"If the lady wishes to look like a cherub, she will keep her hair this way," Mr. Welland said. "But she will not show off the best feature of her face if she does. I will show you what I mean."

And as Sophia watched in the glass, he pressed his fingers through her hair at the sides and held it back from her face so that it looked smooth over her temples and ears.

"See the classic lines of the cheekbones?" he said. "If the lady wears her hair back like this and piled on top, these cheekbones will be cast into prominence and her neck will look more elegant and her eyes will be more alluring. So will her mouth."

Sophia stared at herself in the glass and saw someone who looked, by some illusion, if not actually pretty, at least womanly.

"Oh, goodness, you are quite right, Mr. Welland," Lady Trentham said. "But it is for Miss Fry to decide if she will grow her hair. Even if she does not, there is a great deal to be said for cherubs."

"Especially well-dressed cherubs," Lady Kilbourne added, getting to her feet, "which is what Miss Fry will be by the time the three of us have finished with her today. Shall we move on?"

The bill was to be sent to Lord Darleigh, Sophia knew. She had no idea how large that bill would be, but if Mr. Welland had a titled lady for a client, it probably would not be insignificant. She felt uncomfortable about it, but what choice did she have? Being wealthy was something she would have to grow accustomed to. Perhaps it would be easier after she was married.

There followed hours of shopping for everything under the sun, or so it seemed to Sophia. There were stays and other undergarments and nightgowns and stockings and shoes and bonnets and gloves and garters and parasols and reticules and fans and cloaks and spencers, among other things. And, of course, there were the dresses, which fell into two categories, those that were ready-made and needed only minor alterations, all of which must be done today or tomorrow at the latest, and those that were to be made from patterns and sent on to Middlebury Park at a later date.

"I cannot possibly need so many," she protested when Lady Trentham listed all she would need *to start with*.

"But they are not just for your personal comfort and pleasure," Lady Kilbourne reminded her gently, a hand on her arm as they sat in the carriage, moving from one shop to the next. "They are for your husband's pride and pleasure too. Oh, I know he is blind and will not see any of your dresses and other finery. But he has hands and will feel them."

Sophia felt herself blushing.

"And other people will see you," the countess added. "You are going to be Lady Darleigh, you must remember. Your appearance will reflect upon your husband."

"They will think I married him for his title and money," Sophia protested. "They will think I trapped him because he is blind."

Lady Trentham looked assessingly at her.

"But of course they will," she surprised Sophia by saying. "I must confess that for the merest moment yesterday, I thought it too. And what are you going to do about it, Miss Fry?"

Sophia stared at her wide-eyed, waiting for the answer to be provided for her. Had Lady Kilbourne thought it too? Did she still? Did Lady Trentham still have doubts about her? Unconsciously she lifted her chin.

The countess exchanged a glance with her sister-in-law, and her eyes danced with merriment.

"Precisely," she said. "That is *exactly* what you must do."

"I *like* him," Sophia said fiercely. "And I am enormously grateful to him. I am going to make his life so comfortable that he will not even *miss* his sight. I am going to—Oh, people may say what they wish. I will not care. And *he* will not care. He will be too busy enjoying the comfortable life I will provide for him."

For one year.

And he did not *want* yet another woman fussing over him.

"Oh, bravo," Lady Trentham said, laughing. "Lily, we must stop provoking the poor lady."

"But we got the answer we expected," Lady Kilbourne said, laughing too. "Little people are often more fierce than their larger counterparts, and you are very little, Miss Fry. Even smaller than Gwen and me. We should perhaps form a league of little people. We would terrify the world. And then rule it."

And, surprisingly, Sophia laughed too. Oh, how *good* it felt to share laughter and absurdities with other people.

"I shall sketch a picture," she said, "and we will use it as a banner when we march upon . . . What shall we march upon?"

"White's Club," Lady Kilbourne said without hesitation. "That bastion of male pride and supposed male superiority that no respectable woman dares walk near. The Little League will march on it and demand equal rights."

They all enjoyed a gleeful laugh.

Sophia endured being measured and poked for what seemed like hours, and she looked through pattern books until all the designs began to look alike. She selected fabrics and colors and trims until she felt she could do it no more. And all the time she listened to the advice and opinions of her companions, though they were never domineering and always deferred to her final judgment. They did quite firmly steer her away from vivid colors, however, which she was inclined to choose at first since it seemed to her that every garment she had owned in the last five years was faded and near colorless. But bright colors, Lady Trentham explained, would swallow her up and make her invisible within them.

"And I believe," she said, "you have been invisible long enough, Miss Fry."

And they steered her away from heavy fabrics, like brocades and some velvets, which she would have chosen for several garments, for it seemed to her that she had been cold most of her life. But heavy fabrics would drag her down, Lady Kilbourne told her, and her smallness and daintiness were assets she ought to emphasize. She discovered that fine wool, thin of texture and light of weight, was just as warm as some of the heavier fabrics. And shawls and stoles—ah, there were so many pretty ones, she discovered—were marvelous for warmth and could look attractive and dress up an otherwise plain gown.

She bought ready-made day dresses and one evening gown and a walking dress and a traveling outfit. All had to be shortened and taken in at the waist and bosom. And she ordered so many different dresses to be made to suit so many different types of occasions that she simply lost count and relied upon the judgment of her two companions, whom she trusted, little as she knew them. Afterward, she did remember one outfit more than any other simply because it had made the dressmaker raise her eyebrows almost to her hairline and had had Lady Kilbourne smiling in such a way that it would be more accurate to say she grinned. Sophia ordered a riding outfit that included breeches as well as a skirt.

"You ride?" Lady Trentham asked her. "Astride?"

"Neither," Sophia admitted. "But Lord Darleigh has told me I may do whatever I wish to do when we are married, and I have always wanted to ride. He must have horses in his stables."

"I think he must," Lady Trentham agreed.

And then there was the one outfit that was bought ready-made and had to be altered before anything else so that it could be delivered to Lord Trentham's house before evening today.

Her wedding outfit.

"But it is to be just Lord Darleigh and me and the clergyman," she had protested at first. "By special license."

"It is to be your wedding day nonetheless," Lady Trentham said. "It is the day you will remember most vividly for the rest of your life, Miss Fry. And you will always remember what you wore. You are to be a *bride*."

Sophia blinked back the tears that had sprung to her eyes and protested no more.

"Lord Darleigh stayed at the home of the Duke of Stanbrook last night," Lady Trentham said. "Lady Barclay is staying there too. She came to London for our wedding. I would not be at all surprised if after Lord Darleigh has obtained the special license today he will find a few other members of the Survivors' Club at the duke's house too waiting to greet him. Hugo has gone there. You know about the Survivors, I suppose?"

Sophia nodded.

"I am sure they will all want to attend Lord Darleigh's

wedding," Lady Trentham said. "They all adore him, you know. He is the youngest among them, and the sweetest. And I know Hugo's stepmother and half sister would love to attend. So would I. And from the way Lily is looking at me, I would guess that she would like to be there too with my brother. I would like to put on a wedding breakfast for you after the ceremony. Will you allow it, Miss Fry? I do not wish to bully you into anything you do not want. You must say if you would prefer to have a completely private wedding. And of course, Lord Darleigh's wishes must be consulted too. But . . . will *you* allow it?"

"Please?" Lady Kilbourne added. "It is *ages* since I was last at a wedding. It is three days since Gwen's."

Sophia sat in the carriage staring from one to the other of them. She was the mouse. No one ever saw her or spoke to her. She had never had friends—well, almost never. No one had ever loved her, except her father in his own careless way, though he had never been more demonstrative about it than to ruffle her hair occasionally as he told her that they would have to tighten their belts again for a while as he had just had a run of bad luck at the tables or the race track.

Yet now about ten people wished to attend her wedding? One of them wanted to put on a wedding breakfast for her? It was all for Lord Darleigh's sake, of course. She understood that. But Lady Kilbourne, as far as Sophia knew, had never even met him. Mrs. Emes and her daughter had met him only briefly yesterday while they had spent all evening with her and part of this morning too.

Lord Darleigh had sacrificed a wedding with his family about him for her sake, she knew. Now he had a chance to have a few of his very closest friends with him for the occasion. And she had a chance to have with her at her wedding some ladies who appeared to like her. It seemed incredible. Did her new hairstyle have something to do with it? But Mrs. Emes and Constance Emes had not seen it yet, and they had been kind and amiable both last evening and at breakfast this morning.

Was it possible to have friends at last? She bit her lower lip.

"Oh, yes," she said, "if it is what Lord Darleigh wishes."

The two ladies exchanged identically satisfied smiles.

The shopping expedition was over at last and they returned home. She would need to get busy, Lady Trentham declared. She had a wedding breakfast to organize. Though she must write a note to Lord Darleigh first to send over to Stanbrook House.

The Survivors' Club had only ever met as a body at Penderris Hall in Cornwall during the spring. It seemed strange and wonderful to be together here in London, which was such an unknown to Vincent. Only Ben—Sir Benedict Harper—was absent. He was in the north of England, staying with his sister.

Vincent had spent the evening at Stanbrook House on Grosvenor Square with the Duke of Stanbrook and Imogen, Lady Barclay, his distant cousin, and they had sat up late talking before going to bed. And today, after spending the morning procuring a special license from Doctors' Commons in company with George, and then making arrangements for the nuptials to be solemnized the next morning at St. George's on Hanover Square, they had returned to Stanbrook House to find Hugo and Ralph—Ralph Stockwood, Earl of Berwick—there too as well as Flavian Arnott, Viscount Ponsonby.

Miss Fry had been borne off, as planned, Hugo reported, to be outfitted from head to toe for her wedding and her new life. His wife had gone with her, and so had the Countess of Kilbourne, her sister-in-law.

Vincent hoped Sophia would not feel overwhelmed.

"They will look after her, lad," Hugo assured him as though he had read Vincent's thoughts. "Woman power or something hideous like that. It is better to stay far away from it and let them do what they must do."

"Goodness me," Flavian murmured on a sigh. "Is this you, Hugo? The hero of Badajoz? The ferociously scowling giant? Is this what three days of marriage have done to you? One can only shudder at the p-prospect of what one week will do."

"It is called the acquiring of wisdom, Flave," Hugo said.

"Heaven defend me," Flavian said faintly.

"You would deny women all power, Flavian?" Imogen asked sweetly.

"Oh, not you, Imogen," he said hastily. "No, no, not you. I have no wish to be fixed with your steely look every time I glance at you. Your steely look is nasty and is inclined to interfere with my digestion. Let us change the subject. Tell us about your b-bride, Vince, my boy. And tell us why you are marrying in such indecent haste. Imogen has refused to divulge a single detail. It is not her story to tell, she assured us before you came back with George. A hopeless gossip *she* makes."

Vincent told them everything, with the omission of the maddest of the details, of course. By the time he had finished, he was surprised to find that one of his hands was in both of Imogen's. She was not normally the demonstrative sort.

"Marrying Miss Fry is what I want to do," he said as if there had been a chorus of protests from his friends. "It may sound as if I was coerced into offering for her, and I admit that if circumstances had not been what they were, I would not be doing what I am about to do.

But I am not sorry it has happened. And I want to make it perfectly clear—to *all* of you." He moved his head about the room as though he could see them all. "I want to make it clear that she did not *in any way whatsoever* maneuver matters so that I would be obliged to marry her. She is utterly blameless. I had the devil's own job getting her to accept my offer even though she faced a bleak future if she said no."

"You look, Vince," Ralph said, "as if you are about to challenge us collectively to pistols at dawn."

Vincent relaxed a bit and laughed.

"Is she a b-beauty?" Flavian asked. "Or have you *heard* she is? Hugo? You have seen her."

Significantly, Hugo said nothing.

"It may surprise you to know, Flave," Vincent said, "that I do not care the snap of two fingers what she looks like except how her looks may affect her happiness. She describes herself self-deprecatingly. She is small and slender. That I do know. She has short curly hair, which is auburn, and eyes she cannot identify as definitely either brown or hazel but a bit of both. She has smooth-skinned cheeks and a wide mouth. She has an attractive voice. I like it and I like her. Hugo, anything to add?"

"Not when you ask me in that tone, lad," Hugo said hastily. "Gwen and Lily will see to her, you may depend upon it. I believe a hairdresser was first on the agenda this morning. And then lots of dressmakers. The aunt with whom she has been living deserves to be horse-whipped. Her dresses look like half-threadbare sacks and she looks as if she has not been eating all that she could. But those things can be put right."

"Yes," Vincent said. "Can and will."

Imogen was patting the back of his hand.

"Vince," Ralph said, "you are too good for the rest of

us. You are too good for this world. Were you this bad when your eyes worked?"

"I intend to be happy, you know," Vincent told him, grinning. "Marriage does sometimes bring happiness, it seems. Look at Hugo. I can't do that literally, of course, but I can *hear* him."

"Nauseating, is it not?" Ralph said.

Vincent continued to grin. "And soon there will be two of us. The Survivors' Club may not survive the shock."

"We survived the wars," George said. "I daresay we will survive a couple of decent marriages too. Since your family will not be in attendance at your wedding tomorrow, Vincent, and Miss Fry has none worth speaking of, may we all come? Or would you rather we did not?"

A wedding with no guests seemed like a bleak thing— though a necessary one, he had thought when he planned it.

"I would indeed like you all to be there," he said. "But I will have to ask Sophia if she minds. The whole point of coming here rather than returning to Middlebury Park for our wedding was that the balance of guests would not be all on my side."

There was a tap on the drawing room door at that very moment and George's butler murmured to him that a letter had just been delivered by private messenger—for Viscount Darleigh.

"My wife's handwriting," Hugo said.

Vincent got abruptly to his feet. Had something happened to Sophia?

"Will someone read it to me?" he asked. "George?"

He heard the rustle of paper. There was a brief pause, presumably while George scanned the contents.

"Ah," he said. "Lady Trentham asks, Vincent, if you have any great objection to her organizing a wedding breakfast for thirteen persons at her home and Hugo's tomorrow. Thirteen? Goodness me. Ah, she has listed names here, and we are all included. So are Mrs. and Miss Emes, Mr. Philip Germane—your uncle, I believe, Hugo—and the Earl and Countess of Kilbourne. Apparently Miss Fry has already approved both the breakfast and the guest list."

Vincent smiled and sat down again.

"Then it seems you are all invited to a wedding tomorrow," he said. "St. George's at eleven o'clock. I could not get here in time for your wedding, Hugo, so I shall compensate by having one of my own."

"The devil," Flavian said. "*Another* wedding? I may not survive the ordeal. But for you, Vince, I shall take the risk. I will be there."

"*You* complain, Flavian," the duke said. "There is yet another wedding in a little less than one month's time, and I will of necessity have to remain in town for it. So will Imogen, since it concerns family. My nephew."

"The heir, George?" Ralph asked.

"None other," the duke said. "Julian was a bit of a scamp as a boy, but he has found someone of whom he seems genuinely fond. He brought her here the day before yesterday for my inspection, I suppose. Not for my approval, I am happy to say. He did not ask. The poor girl was clearly awed."

"Of course she was," Imogen said. "You always tend to poker up on such occasions, George, and you are formidable enough even when you are *not* pokered up. Poor Miss Dean. I felt for her."

"Miss Dean?" Vincent asked, arrested.

"Miss Philippa Dean, yes," George said. "You do not know her, do you, Vincent?"

"Ah, I believe her family is from Bath," Vincent said. "My grandmother lived there for years before moving to Middlebury Park to keep my mother company. The Deans were her close friends."

"Shall I write to Lady Trentham for you, Vincent?" Imogen asked. "I daresay she would like a quick answer to her question. A wedding breakfast to organize in less than twenty-four hours is not an easy thing."

. . . someone of whom he seems genuinely fond.

Oh, Vincent hoped so and that the fondness worked in both directions. Guilt concerning Miss Dean had been niggling at him ever since he fled from home. And she was marrying a duke's heir? Her family would be pleased.

"No need, Imogen," Hugo said. "I'll go home and tell Gwendoline myself. I have the feeling I have married a woman who will take this sort of thing in her stride."

"If your chest was puffed out any farther, Hugo," Flavian said, "you might discover you cannot see your feet. I'll be on my way too, George. All this talk of matrimony has given me a c-craving for space and fresh air."

"I'll come with you if I may, Hugo," Vincent said. "I want to hear from Sophia's own lips that all this is not overwhelming her."

"I promise not to poker up tomorrow when I meet her at your wedding, Vincent," George said. "Apparently I look formidable enough anyway."

"You are not going to let me forget that, are you?" Imogen commented.

Good Lord, Vincent thought as Hugo took his arm, tomorrow was his wedding day.

Tomorrow!

10

Three of Sophia's dresses had been delivered early in the evening, her wedding dress among them.

She was wearing it now, the following morning, and she was peering timidly into the full-length mirror that had been squeezed into her dressing room, where Lady Trentham's maid had just finished with her. She looked— different. She did not look like a boy. Or a waif. Or a scarecrow.

The dress was a pale sage green, almost silver. It was a shade that brought out the red in her hair. It was simply styled, its high waist caught beneath her bosom with a matching sash, the skirt falling in soft folds almost to her ankles, where it ended in two small flounces. The neckline was low but modestly so, the puffed sleeves trimmed with miniature versions of the hemline flounces. She wore dull gold slippers and gloves. A small-brimmed straw bonnet trimmed with tiny white rosebuds lay on the dressing table, ready to don.

Perhaps the most remarkable item of her wedding outfit was something that could not be seen—her stays. She had never worn them before. They were not uncomfortable, as she had expected they would be. Not yet, anyway. Lady Trentham and Lady Kilbourne had together persuaded her into trying them, and when she had them laced beneath the dress and the dressmaker had pinned it to fit her, she had known why they had done so. She knew it now. Somehow, despite her basic shapelessness and despite the straight lines of the skirt, the stays gave her a waist and hips. Most of all, though, they gave her something of a bosom, pushing her breasts upward as they did. It was not a very impressive bosom. But at least it *was* a bosom, and for once in her life she thought she looked like a woman.

These stays might, of course, prove to be uncomfortably warm. It was going to be a hot day, Lord Trentham had reported at breakfast, frowning fiercely at Sophia and then surprising her with a grin.

"It is a good thing you never thought of earning your living as a hairdresser, lass," he had said. "Your hair looked like an uncultivated bush that had passed through a hurricane this time yesterday."

"Oh, my dear Hugo!"

"Hu-go!"

Mrs. and Miss Emes had spoken simultaneously.

"Which is merely Hugo's way of saying, Miss Fry," Lady Trentham had said, "that your hair looks very fetching today."

"That is exactly what I said," he had agreed, beaming down at his wife.

She would do, Sophia decided now, gazing wistfully at her image. Indeed, if she abandoned all modesty for a moment in the privacy of her own mind, she thought she would do very nicely indeed. She smiled.

And reality swept over her. This was her wedding day. To Viscount Darleigh. Vincent. She had seen him briefly at dinner the evening before last, before Lord Trentham took him to Stanbrook House. And she had seen him briefly for tea yesterday afternoon. Neither time had she been alone with him. Neither time had they had any sort of private conversation with each other. It felt a long time since they had talked.

He felt like a stranger.

He *was* a stranger.

For a moment panic threatened. She should never have agreed to this. Just think of his friends—Lord and Lady Trentham, the Duke of Stanbrook, Lady Barclay, Viscount Ponsonby, the Earl of Somewhere she could not remember. All of them titled and from a world far different from her own. Later today she would be expected to meet them. She had agreed to a wedding breakfast here.

She ought not to do it. It was not fair to him.

But he had once been just Vincent Hunt, she reminded herself, who had been educated at a village school by his father, the schoolmaster, and whose playmates had been the other children of the village. She was the granddaughter and the niece of a baronet. She was a lady.

And then she wished she had not thought of who she was. She had family. There was Sir Terrence Fry, whom she had never met, and there were Aunt Martha and Sir Clarence and Henrietta. None of whom were here for her—just as none of Lord Darleigh's family were here. But in their case it was simply because they did not know about the wedding. But her uncle did not know either. If he did know, would he come? He was probably not even in England.

She gave her head a shake. Almost at the same moment, she was distracted by a knock on the door. It opened to reveal Lady Trentham, Miss Emes behind her, peering over her shoulder.

"Oh, Miss Fry," the latter cried, "how pretty you look. Do turn and let us see you properly."

Sophia turned obediently and looked anxiously at them.

"Will I do?" she asked.

Lady Trentham smiled slowly.

"I keep remembering Mr. Welland's saying that if you keep your hair short you will look like a cherub," she said. "He was right. You look like a small, dainty fairy creature, Miss Fry. You will do very well indeed."

"Shall I assist you with your bonnet?" Miss Emes asked, coming inside the dressing room. "You do not want to squash your curls entirely, do you? Oh, how pretty and dainty it is. There. It suits you perfectly. Have I tied the bow at the right angle, Gwen?"

"Poor Hugo will be wearing a path in the tiles of the hallway if we do not go down soon," Lady Trentham said. "Apparently he was very nervous on our wedding day just four days ago, and now he is nervous all over again because he has the responsibility of giving you over into the care of that rogue and rascal Lord Darleigh—his words, not mine. And spoken purely in fun, of course. But he does feel his responsibility since you have no family to stand with you. Shall we go down?"

Her words, unconsciously spoken, brought back that pang of loneliness and abandonment again. But it was easy enough to brush off. Sophia had not expected a normal wedding—not that she knew a great deal about normal weddings. She had expected a brief ceremony with only her and Viscount Darleigh and the clergyman present. Oh, and one or two witnesses, perhaps Mr. Fisk and Mr. Handry. But suddenly it was to be a real wedding after all. There were to be guests and a best man—the Duke of Stanbrook—and someone to give her away. Lord Trentham had offered last evening and she had accepted. He terrified her—and did not. She had not quite figured him out yet. He looked like a fierce, dour warrior, yet he could catch Lord Darleigh up in a bear hug and gaze at his new wife sometimes as though the sun rose and set upon her. She suspected he was a man who felt most comfortable hidden behind the mask of fierceness so that his tender side would not be on public display and open to ridicule or hurt.

She might have sketched a caricature of him if she had disliked him. But she did not. She was only a little afraid of him.

He was indeed pacing the hall at the bottom of the staircase. He came to a halt when he saw them descending, his booted feet slightly apart, his hands clasped at his back, his posture ramrod straight, like a soldier on parade, not quite at ease. His eyes passed over his wife and his sister with obvious approval and then came to rest upon her.

"Well, lass," he said, "you are looking very fetching indeed. It is a pity Vince will not be able to see you."

She paused two steps from the bottom. The other two ladies were down already. Lord Trentham took two strides toward her, and his eyes were only just above the level of hers as he gazed into them with a look that surely must once have had his soldiers quaking with terror.

"He is very precious to me," he said softly.

He continued to look at her, and she almost retreated to the third stair. But she held her ground and lifted her chin.

"He is going to be even more precious to me," she said. "He is going to be my husband."

There was a beat more of eye-searching on his part, and then he smiled and really looked quite unexpectedly handsome.

"Yes, he is," he said. "And again I say it is a pity he can't see you this morning. You look like a little elf."

At least she did not look like a mouse on her wedding day.

"The carriage is outside waiting, Hugo," Lady Trentham said.

She and Miss Emes were to accompany them to the church. Mrs. Emes had left earlier with Mr. Philip Germane, Lord Trentham's uncle, who, Sophia suspected, was courting Mrs. Emes.

Lord Trentham handed Sophia into the carriage and insisted that she take the seat facing the horses beside his wife.

This was it, she thought. Her wedding day. A hot summer day. The sky was deep blue with not a cloud visible. No bride could ask for anything better.

Sophia turned her head to the side as the carriage rocked on its springs and moved forward. She did not want to engage in conversation. She wanted to . . . to feel like a bride, to put aside all her misgivings, to be excited and only a little anxious, but in a good way.

Lady Trentham had come to her last evening and explained about tonight. Humiliatingly, considering the fact that she was twenty, Sophia had had little idea. Lady Trentham had assured her that it sounded a great deal worse—more embarrassing, more painful, more utterly terrifying—than it was.

"Indeed," she had said, her cheeks a rosy red, "I will be going to Hugo for the fourth night of our marriage when I leave you, Miss Fry, and really I can hardly wait. It must be . . . No, it *is*, beyond any doubt at all, the most glorious thing in the whole wide world. You will see. You will soon come to welcome it."

Sophia thought she might be right. For her very deepest, most secret dream . . . Well, she had not shared *that* at the Barton Coombs assembly. How could she? She had been talking to a man.

The man she was about to marry.

Lady Trentham took her hand and squeezed it.

They were turning into Hanover Square.

* * *

$\mathcal{V}$incent was having all kinds of second thoughts, which meant, he supposed, that by the time he had finished with them they would be thirty-sixth or fifty-eighth thoughts.

He really ought not to be thinking at all.

Except that trying not to think was no more effective than trying to hold back the tide would be.

It had turned into a proper wedding with guests at the most fashionable church in London, yet his mother and grandmother and sisters did not know about it. They did not even know his bride. He did not really know her either, though, did he? They were virtually strangers.

He did not even want to be married.

Except that if he must marry—and he would have no peace from his relatives until he did—he would just as soon it be Sophia. He actually did like her—or thought he did.

He did not *know* her.

Or she him.

Yet today was their wedding day.

And in some perverse way—thank God!—the thought excited him. His life was about to change, and perhaps he would change with it—for the better.

"Do you have the ring?" he asked George, who was seated beside him in the front pew of the church.

"I do," George said. "Just as I did when you asked three minutes ago."

"Did I?"

"You did. And I still have it."

His wedding day. His best man was beside him. His friends were behind them. Although they were not talking loudly, some of them were whispering, and he could hear the rustle of their movements and the occasional cough. He could smell candles and traces of incense and that cold stone and prayer book smell peculiar to churches. He knew the great organ was going to play.

There was to be a wedding breakfast afterward at Hugo's, a mildly terrifying thought even though he would be eating with friends. He did not like taking his meals in public.

And there was to be a wedding night at Stanbrook House. It had all been arranged without any consultation with him. Imogen was going to stay at Hugo's after the breakfast, and George was going to spend the night at Flavian's lodgings. Vincent and Sophia were to have Stanbrook House to themselves for the night, apart from servants, of course.

That at least he could look forward to.

"Do you have the ring?" he asked. "No, forget it. I have asked you before, have I not? Is she late, George? Will she come?"

"She is two minutes from being late," George assured him. "Indeed, I do believe she is two minutes early. Here come Lady Trentham and Miss Emes."

But Vincent had heard the slight commotion at the back of the church for himself. And he heard the clergyman clear his throat. He rose to his feet.

The great organ began to play, and it was too late for seventy-second thoughts. He was about to get married.

She and Hugo would be making their way along the nave toward him. His bride. He could hear the slow, steady click of Hugo's boot heels on stone. He wished he could see her. Ah, he *wished* he could. She would be wearing new clothes. Pretty clothes. Would they make her feel better about herself?

He smiled though he could not see her. She must see that he was welcoming his bride. How many second thoughts had plagued her this morning?

And then he smelled her, that faint soap scent he had begun to associate with her. And he felt the slight warmth of a human presence on his left side.

The anthem faded away.

"Dearly beloved," the clergyman said.

Ah, let him be adequate. Let him be a worthy husband for this damaged little waif he was marrying. Let him be a good companion and friend. Let him be a decent lover. Let him protect her from harm all the days of their lives. She was blameless. She had come to his rescue that night of the assembly and would have suffered her punishment for the rest of her days if he had not persuaded her to marry him. Let her never regret marrying him. Let him cherish her. Let him put aside second and ninety-second thoughts from this moment on. He was in the process of getting married. Let him *be* married, then, and glad of it. Let him never, even for a single moment, allow himself to feel regret, whatever the future held. Let him cherish her.

He had spoken his vows, he realized, without remembering a word. She had spoken hers without him hearing a word. He had taken the ring and slid it over her finger without fumbling or dropping it. And the clergyman was telling them that they were man and wife.

And it was done.

There was a murmuring from the pews.

There was still the register to sign. All would not be legal and official until that was done. Sophia slid an arm through his and guided him to the vestry without hauling him. He had noticed that during their walk together in Barton Coombs. Very few people of his experience could trust him to follow slight cues.

The clergyman did not expect him to be able to sign his name, but of course he could. He sat before the register, and George handed him the quill pen and guided his hand to the beginning of the line where he would write. He scrawled his name and stood.

Sophia signed her name followed by the witnesses—George and Hugo. And then she slipped an arm through his again and led him back into the church. The organ began a joyful anthem and they proceeded the short distance across the front of the church and then along the nave. Vincent could sense his friends there. He smiled from left to right.

"Lady Darleigh," he said softly.

"Yes." Her voice was a little higher pitched than usual.

"My wife."

"Yes."

"Happy?" he asked. It was probably the wrong question.

"I don't know," she said after a short pause.

Ah, honesty.

They walked on in silence, and then he felt a different quality to the air, and she drew him to a halt as they stepped out through the church doors into the fresh air outside, and the sound of the organ receded somewhat.

"There are steps," she said.

Yes, he remembered that from when he came in.

"Oh, and there are people."

He could hear them, talking, laughing, whistling, even cheering. There were always people gathered outside St. George's, he had been told, to watch society weddings.

"They have come to see the bride," he said, smiling and lifting his free hand in acknowledgment of the greetings. "And today that is you."

"Oh, and there are two men," she said.

"Two men?"

"They are grinning," she said, "and they are both holding handfuls of . . . oh!"

And Vincent felt at least two light, fragrant missiles flutter past his nose. Rose petals?

"No point in c-cowering there, Vince," Flavian called.

"Come and bring your bride to your carriage. If you dare," Ralph added.

"An open barouche," Sophia said. "Oh, it is all decorated with flowers and ribbons and bows."

Vincent could feel the heat of the sun.

"Shall we go down?" he suggested. "Those are two of my friends. Are they armed with rose petals?"

"Yes," she said and laughed—that light, pretty sound he had heard a few times before. "Oh, dear, we are going to be covered."

She told him where the steps were and then clung to his arm as they hurried the short distance to the barouche, making it seem that he was leading her rather than the other way around.

"We are there," she said as rose petals rained about them and upon them and Vincent could hear that their other guests had emerged from the church.

But instead of scrambling inside the barouche without further ado, she waited while he located the lowest step and offered his hand. She set her own in it and climbed inside. He followed her in and made sure he sat beside her, not on her.

The church bells were ringing.

"Well, Lady Darleigh." He felt for her hand and squeezed it tightly in his own. She was wearing soft gloves. "Does it look as much like a wedding as it feels?"

"Yes."

He heard the door of the barouche close and felt the dip of the springs as the coachman climbed back to his perch.

"Are you overwhelmed?"

"Yes."

"Sophie," he said, "don't be. You are a bride. All eyes are upon you today."

"That is precisely the trouble," she said, laughing breathlessly.

"Describe what you are wearing," he told her.

She told him, starting with her straw bonnet. Before she got to her feet, the barouche rocked into motion and moved away from the church—with an unholy din.

"Oh!" she cried.

He grimaced and then grinned. An old trick, one in which he had participated more than once as a boy. "I believe we have all the utensils from someone's old, derelict kitchen trailing behind us. Now you are *really* on view."

She did not reply.

"You sound charmingly clad, Sophie," he said, having to raise his voice above the din. "Is everyone watching back there?"

He felt her turn to look.

"Yes."

"May I kiss you?" he asked her. "It is what they are all hoping for."

"Oh," she said again.

He took the single word as assent. He knew she really was overwhelmed, and the realization made him feel tenderly toward her.

He reached across himself with his free hand and found her face beneath the stiff little brim of the straw bonnet she had described. He cupped her soft cheek with his hand, found the edge of her mouth with the pad of his thumb, lowered his head, and kissed her.

It was more of a real kiss this time, though he made no attempt to deepen it. His lips were slightly parted. Hers were full and soft and warm and moist—she must have just licked them.

He felt a stirring in the groin and a pleasant anticipation of bed tonight.

Even over the hideous din of several kettles and pans or whatever the devil was being dragged along the road behind them, he could hear a rousing cheer.

"Sophie." He lifted his head but did not remove his hand from her cheek. "If you cannot tell me you are happy, can you at least assure me that you are not *unhappy*?"

"Oh, no," she said. "I am not unhappy."

"Or sorry? You are not sorry?"

"No," she said. "I do not have the courage to be sorry."

He frowned.

"I am only sorry that *you* may be sorry," she told him.

He had expected that any woman he married would be the one who might regret doing it, for he was blind and could not live a fully normal life or see and appreciate her. But this bride, he realized, was almost totally lacking in self-esteem, even now when she had been clothed well and expensively and when her hair had been properly styled and she was Viscountess Darleigh.

He had *known* she was damaged. Perhaps he had not realized how deeply. Was she *too* damaged? But he remembered her making a daisy chain and laughing as he tried to loop it over her head. He remembered her joking about cats when he played his violin. He remembered the absurd story of Bertha and Dan they had concocted on the way to London and her admission that she sketched caricatures of people she knew.

"Never," he told her. "I will never be sorry. We will find contentment with each other. I promise."

How could one promise such a thing?

But he could promise to try. He had no choice now anyway. They were married. And he would do all in his power to restore her self-esteem. If he could do that for her, he would be contented.

"I suppose," he said, sitting back in his seat, "we are attracting quite an audience."

"Oh, yes," she said—and laughed.

He squeezed her hand.

11

*T*he Duke of Stanbrook was a tall, elegant, austere-looking gentleman with dark hair just turning to gray at the temples. Viscount Ponsonby was a blond god with a slight stammer and a mocking eyebrow. The Earl of Berwick was a young man, perhaps only a few years older than Lord Darleigh, and would have been entirely good-looking if it were not for the wicked-looking scar that slashed diagonally across one side of his face. Lady Barclay was tall and coldly beautiful with smooth, dark blond hair and high cheekbones in a long oval face. With Lord Darleigh and Lord Trentham and the absent Sir Benedict Harper, they were the Survivors' Club.

Sophia found them terrifying despite the fact that they all bowed courteously to her before the wedding breakfast and kissed the back of her hand—except Lady Barclay, of course, who merely wished her happy.

She thought they had all looked at her and found her wanting. They all thought her an opportunist, a fortune hunter, someone who had taken advantage not only of good nature but also of *blind* good nature. And they were his dearest friends. As close as sister and brothers, he had told her. Perhaps that was the problem. Perhaps they felt protective toward him and therefore suspicious of her. She felt chilled.

The Earl of Kilbourne, Lady Trentham's brother, was also a handsome, formidable-looking gentleman. He also had been a military officer.

Everyone was courteous. Everyone made an effort to keep the conversation moving, to keep it light in tone, to keep it general so that they could all participate. Mrs. Emes was a shopkeeper's daughter and widow of a prosperous businessman. Miss Emes was their daughter. Mr. Germane was also a businessman, a member of the middle class. They were not excluded from the conversation, Sophia noticed. Neither were they made to feel inferior.

But she, who was a gentlewoman by birth, felt suffocated by the grandeur of her wedding guests, her husband's friends.

Her husband!

As yet it was only a word—and a heavy feeling in the pit of her stomach. Strangely, foolishly, it was only while the wedding service was proceeding that she had fully understood that she was getting *married,* that she was consenting to become a man's possession for the rest of her life. She did not want to think of her marriage that way. Lord Darleigh was not *like* that. But church law was. And state law was. She was his possession, to do with as he would, whether he ever exercised that power or not.

She wanted to feel joyful. For a few fleeting moments during the day she had done—when she had walked along the nave of the church this morning while the organ played and she saw Viscount Darleigh waiting for her, a warm smile on his face; when they had stepped out of the church to sunshine and a group of cheering onlookers and a shower of rose petals; when she had first heard the pots and pans clattering and clanging behind the barouche; when Lord Darleigh kissed her; when an elderly gentleman stopped on the pavement to watch the barouche go by and raised his hat to her and winked.

But the wedding breakfast was nothing short of an

ordeal. Try as she would, she could not force herself to participate in the conversation and replied in monosyllables whenever a question was directed specifically at her. She was not giving a good impression, she knew. How could she expect to be liked?

She ate scarcely anything. She tasted nothing.

Lord Trentham rose to propose a toast to the bride, and Sophia forced a smile to her face and forced herself to look about the table and nod her thanks to everyone. Viscount Ponsonby rose and toasted her husband and elicited a great deal of warm laughter. Sophia forced herself to join in. Lord Darleigh rose and thanked everyone for making their day a memorable and happy one, and he reached out a hand for hers and bent over it and kissed it to a few murmurings from the ladies and applause from all.

Sophia relaxed a little more when they all withdrew to the drawing room, for Constance Emes came to sit beside her.

"It *is* awe-inspiring, is it not?" she said, speaking low for their ears only. "All these titles? All this gentility? Hugo has taken me to several *ton* balls and parties this year, at my request. I was frightened out of my wits the first time or two, and then I came to see that they are all just people. And some of them, though not the ones here, are really quite uninteresting because they have nothing to do but be rich and try to amuse themselves for a lifetime. I have a beau, you know—well, a sort of beau. He insists I am too young for a formal courtship, and he thinks I ought to aim higher, but he will come around in time. I love him to distraction, and I know he loves me. He owns the ironmonger's shop next to my grandparents' grocery shop, and I am never so happy as when I am there, in one shop or the other. We have to find what will bring us happiness, do we not? I think Lord Darleigh is one of the sweetest gentlemen I have ever met. And he is gloriously handsome. And he likes you."

"Tell me about your ironmonger," Sophia said, feeling herself relax.

She smiled and then laughed as she listened—and caught the steady, considering gaze of Lady Barclay on her. The lady nodded slightly before turning away to reply to something the Earl of Kilbourne had said to her.

And then, after tea had been served, it was time to leave. The butler had just murmured in Lady Trentham's ear that the barouche was waiting at the door. Sophia's wedding night was to be spent at Stanbrook House, one of the grand mansions on Grosvenor Square. Fortunately, the duke himself was not to be there. Neither was his guest, Lady Barclay. Sophia's new clothes had been packed up by Lady Trentham's maid this morning after they left for the church and sent to Stanbrook House. Directions had been given for the other new clothes still to be delivered today to be sent directly there.

Sophia counted back days in her head. Yesterday was the shopping day. The day before was the second day of the journey, the day before that the first. Then there was the day of the proposal, then the day of the assembly, then the day when she had walked out just before dawn and watched Lord Darleigh's arrival at Covington House.

Six days.

Less than a week.

She had still been the mouse a week ago. Still the scarecrow, with her chopped hair and ill-fitting second-hand clothes.

Less than a week.

Now she was a bride. A wife. Her life had changed,

suddenly and drastically. And she was behaving like a bewildered mouse.

Sometimes one had to make a determined effort if one was not to drift on in life unchanging. Change had come to her life, and she had the chance to change with it—or not.

She got to her feet.

"Lady Trentham, Lord Trentham, Mrs. Emes, Miss Emes," she said, looking from one to the other of them, "I do thank you with all my heart for opening your home to me, for being so kind, for arranging this wonderful wedding breakfast. And Mr. Germane, Lord and Lady Kilbourne, Lady Barclay, Lord Ponsonby, Lord Berwick, Your Grace, thank you for coming to our wedding, for coming here. We expected a quiet wedding day. It has been anything but that, and I will always remember it with pleasure. Your Grace, thank you for letting us use your home until tomorrow."

All conversations had stopped abruptly. Everyone was looking at her—in surprise, she thought, and she wondered if her heart would stop hammering or if it would simply stop. She was even smiling.

Viscount Darleigh was on his feet too.

"You have taken the words out of my mouth, Sophie," he said, "and there is nothing left for me to say."

"You said enough at the breakfast table, Vince," Lord Ponsonby told him. "It is your wife's turn. P-personally, I hope you are the last Survivor to wed for at least a week or two. My v-valet will be running out of dry handkerchiefs to hand me."

"It is my pleasure, Lady Darleigh," the Duke of Stanbrook said, giving her a look that was both penetrating and . . . approving?

And then they were all on their feet, and Sophia found herself being hugged by the ladies—even Lady Barclay—and having her hand kissed again by the gentlemen. Everyone was talking and laughing, and she and Vincent were somehow swept out to the street and into the barouche.

"Are the pots and pans gone?" Lord Darleigh asked.

"Yes," she told him.

"And everything else?" he asked. "There were ribbons and bows, I suppose? And flowers? No, *they* are not gone. I can smell them."

"They all remain," she said.

"You are a bridegroom only once, Vince," Lord Trentham reminded him. "And Lady Darleigh is a bride only once. Enjoy having the whole world know it."

And amid much laughter and cheering and good wishes, they were on their way.

"Thank you," Lord Darleigh said, taking her hand in his. "Thank you for what you said, Sophie. It was lovely. I know you found the whole thing an ordeal."

"I did," she agreed. "But I realized suddenly that I was seeing it all through the eyes of the mouse I have been most of my life. Timidity is not appealing, is it?"

"The mouse is to be banished forever, then?" he asked her.

"To reappear only in the corner of some of my sketches," she said. "But that mouse is usually a saucy little thing, winking or leering or looking frankly nasty or self-satisfied."

He laughed.

"Have you seen anything satirical today?" he asked her.

"Oh, no, my lord," she assured him. "No. There was nothing to ridicule or laugh at today."

There was a short silence.

"There was not," he agreed. "But am I to remain *my lord*, Sophie? You are my wife. We are traveling toward our wedding night."

She felt a strange, sharp stabbing of sensation to the

lower part of her body and found herself clenching inner muscles and fighting breathlessness.

"Vincent."

"You find it difficult to say?" he asked.

"Yes."

"Even though your grandfather was a baronet, your uncle *is* a baronet, and your father was a gentleman?"

"Yes."

She wondered what Sir Terrence Fry would say if he knew she had married Viscount Darleigh today. Would he ever know? A notice had, apparently, been sent to the morning papers. Was he even in the country? And would he care if he saw the notice? Would Sebastian see it? What would *he* think? Would he let his stepfather know?

Vincent lifted her gloved hand and held it against his lips. Passers-by were smiling at the barouche and pointing it out to one another with smiles and even a few waves, she could see.

"Think of me as that naughty boy Vincent Hunt, who used to sneak out of Covington House at night through a cellar window in order to swim naked in the river," he said. "Or, if that is too shocking an image, think of me as that very annoying Vincent Hunt who used to hide in the branches of trees when he was seven years old, stifling giggles and raining twigs and leaves and acorns down upon the unsuspecting heads of villagers as they passed beneath."

She laughed.

"That is better," he said. "Say it again."

"Vincent."

"Thank you." He kissed her hand. "I have no idea what time it is. Is there still daylight? Is it afternoon or evening?"

"Somewhere between the two," she told him. "It is still full daylight."

"It ought not to be," he said. "It ought to be dark. It ought to be time when we arrive at Stanbrook House to take my bride to bed."

She said nothing. What was there to say?

"Does it worry you?" he asked her. "The wedding night?"

She bit her lower lip and felt that unfamiliar raw feeling low down again.

"A little," she admitted.

"You do not want it?"

"I do," she told him. And of course she spoke the truth. "Yes, I do."

"Good," he said. "I look forward to getting to know you better. In all ways, of course, but at the moment I mean specifically in the physical sense. I want to touch you. All over. I want to make love to you."

He would be bitterly disappointed, she could not help thinking.

"Have I shocked you?" he asked her.

"No."

He kissed her hand again and held it on his thigh.

*T*hey had changed their clothes and partaken of a light dinner. They sat together in the drawing room afterward, talking about the day. She described the clothes some of their guests had worn; he described the smells inside the church. She described the way the barouche had been decorated; he described the sounds on the streets—what he had been able to hear of them above the din of the hardware they were dragging behind them, that was—and the smell of the flowers. She told him about Constance Emes's young man and Mrs. Emes's budding romance with Mr. Germane. He told her about Lord Trentham's first meeting with the then

Lady Muir down on the beach at Penderris. They both agreed that it had been a memorable day.

"Is it dark outside yet?" he asked at last.

"No."

It was early summer, of course. It did not get dark until well into the evening.

"What time is it?" he asked.

"Just coming up to eight o'clock."

Only eight o'clock?

She had taken his arm to come into the house and to go in to the dining room and to return to the drawing room afterward. Apart from that, they had not touched each other. Yet it was their wedding day.

"Is there a time," he asked her, "before which one is not allowed to retire to bed?"

"If there is a law," she said, "I have not heard of it."

He was humming with the desire to consummate his marriage, and although she had admitted that she was a little worried, she had also assured him that she wanted it too. The longer they sat here, the more worried and nervous she was likely to become.

Why had he felt obliged to sit out the rest of the day until a decent bedtime? A certain nervousness of his own, perhaps? He had never been with a virgin. And this was not just an experiment that need not be repeated if it was not to his liking—or hers. It was important that he get it just right. Not too much this first time—he did not want to frighten her or disgust her or hurt her. But not too little either. He did not want to disappoint her, or himself.

It was important to get it right.

"Shall we go to bed?" he asked.

"Yes."

She had said in the barouche on the way here that she must cast off the mouse, her alter ego. It was not going to be easy for her, he realized. And he half smiled at the memory of the determined little speech she had delivered just before they left Hugo's. It had been gracious and pretty, and the attentive surprise of his friends and the other guests had been almost tangible.

"Take my arm, then," he said, getting to his feet.

"Yes." She took it.

And then she surprised him again when they had passed out of the drawing room and ascended two of the stairs to the floor above. She stopped and spoke to someone else—presumably a servant.

"Send Mr. Fisk up to Lord Darleigh's dressing room, if you please," she said, "and Ella to mine."

Ella must be the maid George had assigned to her for tonight.

"Yes, my lady," a man's voice murmured respectfully.

"*My lady*," she said softly.

"I still find myself wanting to look over my shoulder when people address me as *my lord*," he told her. "I probably would if I could."

He knew the way to his room, *their* room for tonight. He always memorized directions and distances quickly when he was in unfamiliar surroundings. He did not like the feeling of being lost, of being dependent upon others to take him wherever he needed to go.

He paused when he judged he was outside his dressing room. The door of the bedchamber came next and then her dressing room, which had not been needed until today.

"I can go the rest of the way alone," she told him.

"Let us compromise," he said. "I will stand here until I hear your door open and close. And I will see you in the bedchamber in half an hour's time? Less?"

"Less," she said, slipping her hand from his arm.

He smiled and listened for her door. As he heard it close, he could hear Martin's firm footsteps coming along the corridor behind him. Martin had been stiffly formal this morning—and ever since the announcement of the betrothal.

"Martin," he said as his dressing room door opened and he preceded his valet inside. "Did you come to my wedding as I asked?"

"I did, sir," Martin said.

Vincent waited for more, but all he could hear was Martin setting the water jug down on the washstand and preparing his shaving gear. He sighed. Had he gained a wife and lost a friend? For that was what Martin was, what he had always been.

"She did not look like a boy today," Martin said abruptly as Vincent slipped off his coat and waistcoat and Martin helped him with his neckcloth before hauling his shirt off over his head. "She looked like a little elfin creature."

It was stiffly, grudgingly said. And *little elfin creature* sounded like more of a compliment than an insult.

"Thank you," Vincent said. "She did not do this deliberately, you know, Martin. I, on the other hand, did."

"I know," Martin said. "Idiot that you are. Keep your head still now or I'll be slicing your throat. And you will be wondering if I did it deliberately. If you are still alive to wonder anything at all, that is."

"I trust you." Vincent grinned at him. "With my life."

Martin grunted.

"It's just as well," he said, "since I get to come at you with an open razor at least once a day. Take that grin off your face or you are going to get an uneven cut to take to your lady."

Vincent sat still and expressionless.

Peace, he supposed, had been declared.

A little elfin creature. He remembered holding her against him on the far side of the stile in Barton Coombs. Yes, he believed it. She was just the opposite of voluptuous. He had always favored voluptuous women—as what red-blooded male did not? But he was eager for his bride anyway.

A little elfin creature.

He opened the door into the bedchamber after he had dismissed Martin. He knew the room. He knew where the bed was, the dressing table, the side tables, the fireplace, the window. And he knew as soon as he stepped inside that he was not alone.

"Sophie?"

"Yes, I am here." There was a soft laugh. "Do you know where *here* is?"

"I believe," he said, "you are standing at the window. And it is still not dark, I suppose?"

"The room looks out on the back of the house," she said as he made his way toward her. "Onto the garden. It is very pretty. One could almost forget one was in London."

He reached out and touched the windowsill. He could feel the warmth of her close by.

"Would you like to forget?" he asked her. "Do you not like London?"

"I prefer the country," she said. "I feel less lonely there."

A strange thing to say, perhaps, when one considered the relative number of people in the town and the country.

"I feel less of a lone being," she explained, "and more a part of something vast and complex. I am sorry. That does not make much sense, does it?"

"The emphasis is too much upon humanity alone in town?" he suggested. "And more upon humankind as part of nature and the universe itself in the country?"

"Oh," she said, "yes. You do understand."

He thought of her dream cottage with its pretty garden and a few friendly neighbors. Ah, Sophie.

He reached out and touched her shoulder. His hand

closed about it and his other hand about the other, and he drew her against him. She was wearing a silky night-gown, he could feel. One item of her bride clothes? He hoped so. He hoped she was feeling pretty and desirable. He could feel her draw a slow inward breath.

He was wearing just a light brocaded silk dressing gown. Perhaps he ought to have had Martin dig out a nightshirt for him—if there was one to dig out, that was. It was possible none had been packed when he left home, for he always slept naked.

He moved his hands inward, lifted her chin with his thumbs, and found her mouth with his own—that lovely wide mouth he remembered with its generous lips. He licked his own just before they joined hers, waited for the trembling in hers to cease, and stroked the tip of his tongue across the seam of her lips until they parted. He slid his tongue into her mouth and felt a shiver of desire as she moaned softly deep in her throat.

He moved his hands to thread into her hair. It was soft and silky and not nearly as thick as it had been last time he felt it. It was very short.

"Sophie." He kissed her softly on the lips. "Are we putting on a display for anyone who happens to be strolling in the garden?"

"Probably not," she said. "But I will close the curtains."

He heard them sliding along the rail after she had turned from his arms.

"There," she said. "Now no one will see."

And she moved back against him and slid her arms about his waist. Ah. She was not reluctant, then.

"I am glad you cannot see me either," she said. She drew breath audibly. "Oh, I did not mean to be offensive."

"Because you are not worth looking at?" he asked

her. "Sophie, who destroyed all your sense of self-worth? And don't tell me it was your looking glass. Well, I cannot see you and never will. I can never contradict you—or agree with you. But I *can* touch you."

"That," she said, "is almost as bad."

He laughed softly, and she did too, rather ruefully, he thought.

"You are so beautiful," she said.

He laughed again and slid his hands beneath her nightgown at the shoulders and pushed it off and down her arms. He stood back and straightened her arms with his hands and heard the garment slither all the way to the floor.

She inhaled audibly.

"Do not worry," he said. "I cannot see you."

Her breath shuddered out.

He touched her. He explored her with light hands and sensitive fingertips—thin shoulders and upper arms, small breasts that nevertheless fit softly and warmly into the palms of his hands, a tiny waist, hips that hardly flared below it, a soft, flat belly, a slender bottom with cheeks that fit his hands as her breasts had done, legs that were slender and yet sturdy as far down as he could feel.

Her skin was soft and smooth and warm. She did not have the boniness and angularity of many thin people. She was just small and not particularly shapely. Not at all voluptuous. He could feel himself harden into arousal anyway. She was his bride. She was *his,* and there was a certain exultation in the thought. He had found her himself and married her himself, without any help from anyone. Eyes were not always necessary.

He returned his hands to her face, cupping it and kissing her lips again.

"Have the bedcovers been turned back?" he asked her.

"Yes."

"Lie down, then," he said.

"Yes."

Was she being the mouse again? Her voice was higher pitched than usual.

Or just a virgin bride on her wedding night?

He removed his dressing gown before lying down beside her. It was impossible to know if the sight of him was shocking her. Her breathing had been audible and slightly ragged from the start.

His hands explored her again. He lowered his head to kiss her mouth, one cheek, one ear—he drew the earlobe between his teeth and nipped it. He kissed her throat, her breasts. He suckled one while he rolled the nipple of the other gently between his thumb and forefinger.

She remained passive, though her breathing was more labored and her skin was warmer and her nipples hardened beneath his touch.

He kissed her stomach, found her belly button, and swirled his tongue about it while his hand slid between her warm thighs and moved upward to find the core of her femininity. She was hot and surprisingly moist.

She drew a sharp inward breath and stiffened.

"Sophie." He raised his head above hers, though he did not remove his hand or stop stroking her lightly, parting folds with his fingers, circling the tip of one about her opening. "Are you afraid? Embarrassed?"

"No." Her voice was definitely high pitched now.

He suspected she was both.

And he suspected she considered herself physically undesirable.

He took one of her hands in his and moved it to his erection. He curled her fingers about it and held them there.

"Do you know what this means?" he murmured into

her ear. "It means that I want you, that I find you desirable. My hands, my mouth, my tongue, my body, all have touched you and been well pleased. I want you."

"Oh." Her hand was still about him and then released him.

He was not lying to her either.

"I am going to come inside you," he said. "I am afraid I will hurt you this first time, though I will try not to."

"You will not hurt me," she said. "Even if there is pain, Vincent, you will not *hurt* me. Oh, please. Come."

He smiled his surprise. She wanted him too.

She reached for him as he moved over her and lowered his weight onto her. She parted her legs before he could nudge them apart with his, and when he slid his hands under her, she lifted herself and snuggled her bottom into his hands. And when he positioned himself at her opening, she pressed her legs against his and tilted herself.

His arousal became almost painful. He wished suddenly that he was not so large. She was such a little thing. And when he pressed slowly into her, he met a tightness and a heat that filled him with the warring reactions of elation and terror. Elation because a man could not ask for any sensation more erotic and filled with promise; terror because she was too small for him and he was about to tear her apart and cause her a pain she could not disregard.

She was moaning and pressing toward him.

He felt the barrier. It seemed to him that it was impenetrable. He was going to harm her.

"Come," she was urging him. "Oh, please come."

And he forgot about gentleness. He drove inward with one firm thrust, and he was sheathed in her to the hilt, and she was first gasping and tense and then gradually relaxing about him—before she clenched inner muscles and inhaled slowly.

"Vincent," she whispered.

He found her mouth with his, kissed her open-mouthed, plunging his tongue deep.

"Sophie," he said against her lips. "I am sorry."

"I am not," she said.

And he raised himself on his forearms so as not to crush her while he worked, and he took her with hard, deep strokes, holding back his pleasure because he knew there was more of it to be had and because he knew she wanted the whole of it even though she was going to be very sore afterward.

He could hear the erotic wetness of the consummation.

She was all sweet, hot, wet woman. She smelled of sweat and sex. And she was his.

She was his wife.

A little elfin creature.

And packed full to overflowing, every inch of her, with hot sexuality.

He worked in her for long minutes until he could hold back no longer. He pressed inward, held deep, and let his seed flow until he was drained and utterly relaxed.

His selfishness was the first thing that struck him when he returned to himself a couple of minutes or so later. He had intended being gentle and somewhat re-strained with her this first time. Instead, he had been vigorously engaged in her for far too long. And now his whole weight was on her. She felt deliciously warm and damp. She smelled enticing.

He disengaged from her as gently as possible and moved to her side. He found her hand with his own and curled his fingers about it.

"Sophie?" he said.

"Yes."

"Did I hurt you terribly?"

"No."

He turned onto his side to face her.

"Talk to me."

"About what?" she asked. "I was told it was going to be lovely. Lady Trentham told me. It was lovelier even than that."

Would she never cease to surprise and delight him?

"I did not hurt you?"

"You did," she said. "You hurt me at the beginning and you hurt me toward the end. And I am hurting now. It is the loveliest feeling in the world."

What?

"Lovely?"

"Lovely," she repeated. "Some pain is lovely."

"Are you serious?" He was grinning at her.

"Yes," she said. There was a short pause. "Did I disappoint you?"

Ah, they were back to that, were they?

"Do I look disappointed?" he asked her. "Did I *feel* disappointed?"

"I have no figure," she said. "I am almost as flat as I was when I was a girl. Someone—God?—forgot to let me grow."

It would be comical if it were not also sad.

"Sophie," he told her, "you felt every inch a woman to me. I could not possibly have enjoyed that more than I did."

"How kind you are," she said.

"I am only sorry," he said, "that it cannot be repeated tonight."

"It is not even tonight yet," she said. "It is still only dusk."

What was she saying? Had she really enjoyed it too, pain and all? He was not a very experienced lover—a bit of an understatement—and was doubtless nowhere near the world's best lover. Perhaps that did not really matter, though. They were both lonely people—yes,

sexually speaking he *was* lonely. The comfort and pleasure they could give each other would surely outweigh
experience and expertise.

"Perhaps when tonight has become almost tomorrow,
then," he said, "we will try again, will we? But only if
you feel up to it. Only if you are not too sore."

"I will not be," she said with such conviction that he
laughed and drew her into his arms and against his
chest. And then he stopped laughing and rested his
cheek against the top of her head. Suddenly he felt more
like weeping.

That damned *arrangement*. Would he ever be able to
put it from his mind? Would she? Would they ever be
able to just relax into their marriage?

"Sleep now," he said. "Our wedding day is officially
ended, Sophie. It was a good one after all, was it not?"

"Yes." She snuggled against him, and incredibly was
almost instantly asleep.

And so began the rest of his life—as a married man.

For better or worse.

He tried not to wonder which it would be.

12

❧

*W*hen Sophia awoke, she was warm and cozy and slightly uncomfortable. She tried to ignore the discomfort. His arms were about her, she could hear from the evenness of his breathing that he was asleep, and she was snuggled against him. Against all that masculine, hard-muscled beauty and virile strength.

And he was hers. He was her husband.

She did the counting-back thing again—twice, lest she had forgotten a few days somewhere along the way. But no. It was almost morning—she was aware of the slight graying of dawn beyond the window curtains. Almost exactly one week ago, then, she had been standing among the trees above Covington House, watching the arrival of the carriage everyone had been expecting, and watching first Mr. Fisk and then Viscount Darleigh alight outside the front door.

A stranger, then. Her husband now.

It was *only a week ago.*

Sometimes—most times, in fact—a week could go by and she would look back and not be able to remember a single thing of any significance that had happened. This had not been one of those weeks.

She did not want to move. She wanted to hug the moment to herself lest it somehow steal away and be lost forever. He had touched her all over. He had come inside her and had spent long minutes there. He had not been repelled by her. He had enjoyed her. And he had held her in his arms all night. They were still both naked.

She closed her eyes and willed herself to go back to sleep, or at least to lie in drowsy warmth, enjoying the feeling of being held, of having been enjoyed. But comfort grew more and more elusive, and finally she could ignore her bodily needs no longer.

She slipped out of his arms and out of bed without waking him and picked up her new silk nightgown, which was probably horribly creased after a night of lying on the floor. She let herself into her dressing room and relieved herself. She was a little sore but not in a really painful way. It felt actually rather pleasant when she considered what had caused it. Fortunately, there was some water left in the jug on the washstand, though it was not warm, of course. And there were clean cloths and towels. She washed herself off and patted herself dry. No, there was no sharp pain, only the dull throb of having been a bride the night before.

She pulled her nightgown on over her head and enjoyed the feel of it slithering into place down her body. It was by far the loveliest night garment she had ever possessed.

She hoped she had not disturbed him. She hoped she could crawl back into bed and snuggle against him and warm up and remember. Last night had been their wedding night. The consummation had been the culmination of the ritual of the day. Perhaps it would never be the same again. Perhaps . . .

No, she would not think like that. She would get back into bed and just remember. Remember what he had looked like in his silk dressing gown. How could a man look so suffocatingly male when dressed from neck to feet in a silk *gown*?

She got carefully back into bed and wormed her way across it and against him. His one arm was flung out beneath her pillow. She rested her head on it, and he murmured something incoherent and closed it about her. His hair, she could see in the half-light, was endearingly rumpled. His chest and shoulder and upper arm muscles were well defined, indicating that he found some way to keep himself fit and more than just fit.

She closed her eyes and remembered how she had felt when he removed her nightgown and she was naked before him—even though he could not see her. She remembered the touch of his mouth and his hands. Everywhere. Warm and searching and . . . approving? How had she known that? She had detected no disappointment in him as he kissed her and touched her; she had seen none in his face. And afterward, when she had asked him, he had confirmed it in words.

She remembered what he had looked like when he removed his dressing gown. Magnificent and well proportioned and beautiful. And . . .

Strangely, she had not been frightened even though that part of him had looked huge to her. And though it had been rock-solid to the touch. No, rock was a poor comparison, for it had also been warm and silky beneath her fingers and damp-tipped. And every hard, thick inch of it had stretched and hurt her as it came into her—and thrilled her beyond words to describe.

He had hurt and hurt her during the minutes that followed. It was strange that pain should feel so like pleasure. Intense pain, intense pleasure. She had been terribly sore when it was over and terribly sad too, for she had not wanted it to end and was left with a feeling almost of incompletion.

She was greedy in her needs.

She could never expect such a night again, she supposed. But she did expect her marriage to continue, at least for a while—this part of it as well as the mere fact of it. He needed a wife and companion, and she was both. He needed this. Men did, and she was the woman available to him. He wanted children, specifically an heir. It was on her he would get them or on no one. For no other woman was his wife or would be while she lived.

She was going to do everything in her power to make him happy, or at least contented, while she was with him.

Was it possible?

Everything was possible.

"Is the bed tipping?" a voice asked softly against her ear.

"Hmm?"

"You are clinging tightly," he said. "I thought perhaps the bed was capsizing."

"Oh." She loosened her hold on him. "No. I am sorry."

Now she had woken him and her wedding night was at an end. Foolish her.

"Is it morning?" he asked.

He had asked her a few times last evening if it was dark. Just one of the myriad disturbing aspects of blindness must be the disorientation it would bring regarding time.

"Not quite," she said. "It is just starting to get light. It gets light early at this time of year."

"Mmm." He sighed sleepily. "You are wearing your nightgown again."

"Yes."

"Did you feel naked without it?" He rubbed his nose in her hair.

She laughed.

"It is one of the loveliest things I have ever owned," she said. "I might as well wear it. And you paid for it."

"Did I?" he said. "I must be enamored of my bride."

It was just nonsense talk. It still warmed her to her toes.

"I hope so," she said. "You have spent a fortune on me."

"Have I really?" He settled his cheek against the top of her head. "Do I detect the influence of Lady Trentham? I must remember to thank her."

"I was shocked," she told him. "I would have been happy with two or three new dresses. I would have been over-the-moon happy, in fact. But she reminded me that I would no longer be just Sophia Fry, but Viscountess Darleigh, and that it would reflect badly upon you if I did not dress well. I owe it to you to look my best, she told me. Though even at my best—"

One of his fingers had come to rest firmly across her lips.

"You promised yesterday to obey me," he said.

"Yes." She swallowed awkwardly.

"Here is one command, then," he said. "And I will demand absolute obedience, Sophie. I will be genuinely angry if you disobey. You will stop, as of this moment, belittling yourself. I cannot see you, but I take your word for it that you are not beautiful as feminine beauty is judged. Perhaps you are not even startlingly pretty to the casual observer, though by your own admission you are not ugly either. You are small in stature, and you have the slight figure to go with your height. You have small breasts and slender arms and legs and a small waist, which is nevertheless not much smaller than your hips. You hacked your hair off in order, I suppose, to look more like a boy since you thought you looked like one anyway. I note it has been tamed even though it is even shorter than it was. To my hands and my body, Sophie, you are a woman, with pleasing proportions and warm, smooth skin and a mouth any woman might envy. You smell of woman and soap-cleanliness. And inside you are hot, wet, soft, welcoming womanhood. You are mine, and you are all the beauty I could crave. I will not have you belittle what is mine. I will not have you threaten the well-being and happiness of what is mine. Do you understand?"

She had never heard him speak sternly. She held her eyes tightly closed and pressed her forehead against his chest.

I will not have you threaten the well-being and happiness of what is mine.

She was his.

"Yes." Her voice sounded small and high pitched. She felt so ridiculously happy she could have wept.

"I will not be forever demanding obedience," he said after a minute or two of silence. "It is not how I see marriage. I see it as a partnership, a sharing, a companionship."

Yes, companionship. There were worse outcomes of marriage.

"Lady Trentham's hairdresser thinks I ought to grow my hair," she told him. "He thinks a longer, smoother style will show my cheekbones to greater advantage. He called them classic. And he said that a smooth, swept-up hairstyle would emphasize the length of my neck and the largeness of my eyes. Ought I to grow it, do you think?"

He ran his fingers slowly through her curls.

"It feels lovely like this," he said. "It would feel lovely long too. What do *you* want to do with it?"

"I think I will grow it," she said.

"Good." He kissed the top of her head again. "Has it always been short?"

"No."

"When did you cut it?"

"Four years ago."

She waited for the next question, and wondered how she would answer it. But it did not come.

"I think I will grow it," she said again.

It was still very early. There was a clock on the mantelpiece, she remembered. She turned her head and looked at it, just visible now in the growing daylight. It was a little before six o'clock.

Perhaps when tonight has become almost tomorrow, then, we will try again, will we?

"Tonight is almost tomorrow," she said. "It is almost six o'clock."

She tipped her head back to look into his face. He knew what she was saying, she could see.

"I was rougher than I intended to be last night, Sophie," he said, "and I hurt you."

"It was lovely." She could hardly believe her own boldness.

He smiled. "But it might not be lovely this morning. Perhaps we had better—"

"I think it would," she said before he could finish.

She could feel him stirring to life against her abdomen.

"It feels greedy," he said.

"Yes."

He grinned.

"I am glad you want it too," he said. "I could not bear it if it was merely a duty."

"It is not," she assured him.

His hand came beneath her chin, cupping it between his thumb and forefinger.

"You must stop me if I hurt you," he said. "Promise?"

"I promise."

And he kissed her and she kissed him back in that lovely way men and women kissed, in that way she had not even known about until last night—all open-mouthed and wet and tongue-in-mouth and a hard, deep thrust and withdrawal that had her clenching inner muscles against a sudden ache of anticipation that was almost pain and a rush of wetness between the thighs.

She might have gone all her life without this. She had expected to, though she had had no idea what *this* was. It had always been no more than a vague, unhappy longing.

He turned her onto her back and she opened to him and lifted to him, and when he came into her, she felt both the sharp soreness and the wonder of such intimacy. She clenched her muscles about him.

"Sophie," he said. "Am I hurting you?"

"Yes," she said. "Don't stop. Oh, please don't stop."

It was slower, gentler than last night. And because there was not the shock of something so strange and unfamiliar, she was able to feel him, the hardness and length of him, the firm rhythm of his movements, the ache of longing that built inside her and seemed to spread upward, to her breasts, into her throat, even up behind her nose. And when he was finished and she felt that gush of heat deep inside that she remembered from last night, she held him and let the feelings subside and wondered if they would ever lead anywhere else other than to a slight and vague . . . disappointment.

But how could she be disappointed? She felt— wonderful.

He disengaged from her and moved to her side, taking her with him.

"Comfortable?" he asked.

"Mmm."

"Can I take that as a yes?"

"Mmm."

The next time she knew anything, it was half past eight.

He was stroking the fingers of one hand gently through her hair.

The Duke of Stanbrook arrived home, by pre-arrangement, at ten o'clock, Lady Barclay with him, though she might as easily have come with Lord and Lady Trentham, for they had been invited for breakfast. The Earl of Berwick and Viscount Ponsonby had been invited too.

"Never let it be said," Viscount Ponsonby said when they were all seated at the table, "that any of us were ever allowed to s-slip off with quiet dignity on a journey when there were other Survivors ready at hand to give him a grand send-off. Or her, I will add, Imogen, before you can correct me."

"The grand send-off today will be welcomed, Flave," Vincent told him, "provided it does not come accompanied by old pots and kettles."

"Pots and kettles?" Viscount Ponsonby frowned. "Who would be so dastardly? People would turn their heads as you rattled by. That would be a m-mite embarrassing."

"Has anyone heard anything of Ben?" the Earl of Berwick asked of the table in general. "Apart from the fact that he is in the north of England with his sister, that is?"

No one had.

"I wish he had been here," Vincent said. "He could have danced for my wedding."

There was general laughter.

"Sir Benedict Harper had both his legs crushed under his horse," Lord Trentham explained to Sophia, "and refused to have them amputated on the field, as he was strongly advised to do. He was told he would never walk again, but he does, after a fashion. He swears that one day he will dance, and none of us dares doubt him. A fierce lad is our Ben when he is crossed. Or even sometimes when he is not."

"More important, Lady Darleigh," Lady Barclay said, "is the fact that we really do not doubt what he says. If he says he will dance, then he will. We all believe it."

"We would all b-believe there were fairies at the bottom of your garden too, Imogen," Lord Ponsonby said, "if you told us there were."

"Well, there you are, Flavian," she said. "But I would not say any such thing, would I? Our trust in one another has been earned through honesty."

"Unless you really did see them, Imogen," Vincent said, grinning.

"Granted," she said. "Lady Darleigh, you will think us quite frivolous. Fairies at the bottom of the garden, indeed!"

"I do not," Sophia told her. "I have a lovely mental image of them. I believe I must sketch them and Vincent will make up stories about them for his nieces and nephews. We will make up the stories together, in fact."

She had leaned forward in her place and was looking eagerly from face to face. She met astonishment and amusement. And she heard the words she had spoken and observed the posture of her body and the expression on her face as though she were looking at and listening to a stranger. Oh, they would all think she had taken leave of her senses. She subsided back into her seat.

"Sophie is a caricaturist," Vincent explained. "I have not seen her sketches, of course, but I would be willing to wager they are wickedly satirical. And now she wants to turn her talent to storytelling and illustrating."

Sophia could feel her cheeks flood with hot color. She was being regarded by a duke, an earl, a viscount, a baron and his wife, a nobleman's widow, and her own blind viscount.

Just a week ago . . .

But this was not a week ago.

"It is just foolishness," she murmured against her napkin.

The duke's austere face looked at Vincent with unmistakable affection and then at Sophia with . . . well, surely with some kindness. Everyone else was looking at her in much the same way. No one was frowning or sniggering at her stupidity or gawking as if she had sprouted an extra head—or forgotten her rightful place in the corner.

"Enthusiasm and creativity are never foolish," Lady Barclay said.

"Neither is shared enjoyment," Lady Trentham added, "especially when it is with a loved one."

"And how l-long have you been married, Lady Trentham?" Viscount Ponsonby asked. He waggled his eyebrows at Lord Trentham. "Hugo, you rogue, you."

"Do you really tell stories, Vince?" the Earl of Berwick asked.

Vincent looked sheepish. "Well," he said, "when one's nieces and nephews beg to have a bedtime story read and one's sister shushes them in great embarrassment and no doubt with significant gestures in the direction of my eyes while mouthing *Uncle-Vincent-is-blind* at her offspring, one must, out of sheer self-respect, become inventive."

"Keep him storytelling, Lady Darleigh," Viscount Ponsonby said. "He may forget about his v-violin."

"But I will not let him forget," Sophia assured him.

Breakfast lasted for a mere hour. Sophia had started it feeling horribly self-conscious, especially as she was seated at the foot of the table, opposite the duke at the head. She finished it feeling a little less in awe of the

Survivors and just a little bit proud of herself for not being entirely mute, as she had been during the meal yesterday.

And she felt a little less of a fraud. Perhaps her marriage would not be a temporary thing after all. Vincent had said they must stop thinking that way, and she felt as he did. She ought not to have agreed to such a thing in the first place. Marriage was marriage. It was not right to stretch it and twist it to suit one's own purpose.

Lady Trentham slid an arm through hers a short while later, when Vincent's carriage had drawn up outside the door and footmen, under the direction of Mr. Fisk, were loading it with more baggage than they had arrived with, and they were surrounded with all the bustle of farewells.

"Lady Darleigh," she said, "that new traveling dress is very smart indeed, and I insist upon taking at least a part of the credit for it. I cannot take credit for *you,* however. You must always smile and look happy, my dear, as you do this morning. And *pretty.* Please do be happy. I scarcely know Lord Darleigh, but I have a great fondness for him because he was kind to me at Penderris Hall and because Hugo loves him."

Sophia felt horribly embarrassed. If she was looking different this morning from the way she had looked yesterday, everyone would think . . .

Well, of course they would.

But . . . *pretty?*

"I am going to make him happy," Sophia said impulsively. "I have never before had a chance to make anyone happy."

"But you must be happy too. And as for your husband, remember Lizzie's dog," Lady Trentham said, patting her hand before letting her go to be hugged by Imogen and to have her hand kissed by all the gentlemen until the Duke of Stanbrook drew her into a hug and murmured in her ear.

"I am hopeful," he said. "Indeed I am distinctly hopeful this morning that you are the angel for whom I have been praying for my Vincent, Lady Darleigh."

She had no time to do any more than glance at him, startled. It was time to board the carriage. Vincent was already standing at the open door, waiting to hand her inside.

Lizzie's dog, she thought as she settled into her seat and made room for Vincent beside her. Lady Trentham and Lady Kilbourne between them had told her the day before yesterday about their cousin's blind daughter who dashed about the house and park where she lived with great daring and only the occasional tumble, courtesy of an energetic dog that nevertheless seemed to understand that he had the child's safety at his mercy when he was on his leash. With a little more training and discipline, Lady Kilbourne had explained, Lizzie's dog could free her as no cane or careful memory ever could to live a life that was hardly any more restricted than a sighted person's.

Mr. Handry climbed onto the box, followed by Mr. Fisk, and the carriage rocked into motion. Sophia leaned closer to the window to wave to the duke and his breakfast guests, all of whom were gathered on the steps or pavement to see them on their way. Somehow they looked a little less formidable than they had yesterday. Vincent too smiled and waved.

"Sophie," he said as the carriage turned out of Grosvenor Square. He leaned back in his seat, took her hand in his, and rested it on his thigh. "I brought you to London so that you would not be overwhelmed by my family, at least until after we were married. Instead, I exposed you to all the boisterous energy of my friends. Have you minded terribly?"

"No," she said. "They were kind. And I have been able to practice not being a mouse."

"I have noticed," he said, "and have appreciated your efforts. Has it been hard?"

"Yes," she said. "I expect every time I open my mouth either to be ignored or to be regarded with utter incomprehension or amazement. Or outrage."

"My friends like you," he said.

Her first instinct was to deny it. But she had made a promise last night—a promise to obey the only command he had given her so far in their marriage and perhaps the only one he ever would. Besides, it was true. Or at least, it had the possibility of being true. Lord and Lady Trentham had looked upon her with distinct wariness when she had first appeared in their house. The other Survivors had looked upon her yesterday with considerable reserve and a not-quite-carefully-enough-concealed concern for their friend. This morning they had noticeably warmed toward her. All of them, even the formidable cynic Viscount Ponsonby, and the austere Duke of Stanbrook, who clearly loved Vincent as a son.

Indeed I am distinctly hopeful this morning that you are the angel for whom I have been praying for my Vincent, Lady Darleigh.

My Vincent.

She had felt a little as though the bottom had fallen out of her stomach when he had said that.

"And I like them," she said. "Will Sir Benedict Harper ever dance?"

"He walks with two canes," he told her. "Sometimes he will take a few steps without them. Apparently, it is a painful sight to behold. And inspiring too, for he was told that his legs would be useless appendages for the rest of his life and might even become diseased and threaten his life. He will dance, Sophie. I have no doubt whatsoever that he will."

"And you?" she asked him. "Will you dance?"

He turned his head sharply in her direction and then smiled.

"In the dark?"

"Why not?" she said. "I have never danced myself, though I have watched others dance. I watched at the assembly last week. And I watched Henrietta and her dancing master. He taught her to waltz. I think it must be one of the loveliest feelings in the world to waltz. I would dance it if I had the chance, even in the dark."

"Oh, Sophie," he said, "would you? I have never waltzed either, though I did see it performed at a regimental ball before . . . Well, before my single glorious battle hour. I thought it would be a lovely dance to perform with the right partner."

She gazed wistfully at him.

13

❧

𝒯raveling was a tedious business, especially when one could not watch the passing countryside. It was also uncomfortable, even when one owned a well-sprung carriage with thick, soft cushions. Even so, Vincent was in no hurry for the journey to end.

He was a coward.

Though part of him was excited too at the prospect of being home, of starting an entirely new life. And it would be new, partly because the circumstances of his life had changed, and partly because he was determined not merely to drift onward in the same vein as before.

They rode in silence much of the time. But it was not an awkward silence. They did talk too. She described features of particular interest that they passed, and once she held forth for what must have been close to half an hour on everything that was *not* of interest—a gray, cloudy sky; a whole copse of trees with black trunks and branches and no leaves; a fly-infested dung heap; cows too indolent to stand up in their meadow; a field full of dozens, perhaps even hundreds, of sheep, not a single one of which was black; a stretch of flat land without even a molehill to break the monotony—until he was helpless with laughter.

She had a marvelous eye for the ridiculous. And a gift of humor—quiet, dry, and irresistible. It was the sort of thing he might expect from Flavian—and it amazed him that his wife and that particular friend could have anything whatsoever in common.

"You have convinced me, Sophie," he said. "Sight is not everything."

"Not having it," she assured him, "saves you from having to observe a whole lot of dullness."

She told him more about her father when he asked—handsome, charming, charismatic, ever hopeful of winning his way to untold riches, always with the words, "One day my ship will come in, Mouse," on his lips. And forever having to flee from unpaid landlords, unpaid merchants, and irate husbands. But, after his wife left him, he had fed and clothed and housed his daughter except when he was in particularly dire straits, and he had educated her at least to the degree that she could read and write and figure well enough to work out that their meager, precarious finances would never enable them to settle to a stable existence. And then, one day, he had not fled fast enough from a wronged husband and had had a glove slapped in his face—literally. In the ensuing duel he had been shot right between the eyes before he had even raised his own pistol to the firing position.

"Did you know about the duel beforehand?" Vincent asked her.

"Yes."

There was a long silence, and he felt her bleakness.

"I was waiting," she said. "And praying. And trying to think about other things. And waiting. And praying. Nobody came for a long time. Not until late in the afternoon, though the duel was at dawn. I suppose they forgot about me."

That day must have seemed a month long. The feeling of abandonment and perhaps worthlessness must have seeped permanently into her bones.

"He had written three letters," she said, "and Mr.

Ratchett, his friend and his second at the duel, had been instructed to deliver them should he die. They were to his brother, Sir Terrence Fry, and to his sisters, Aunt Mary and Aunt Martha. Sir Terrence was out of the country, as he almost always is. Aunt Martha did not reply. Neither did Aunt Mary, but she lived in London and Mr. Ratchett took me to her and I stayed."

"She took you in willingly once you were there?" he asked.

"She did not turn me away," she said. "I do not know what I would have done if she had. But I rarely saw her. She told me I was hopeless as soon as she saw me. She bought me clothes when I needed them, and she gave me pin money from time to time, which I used mainly to buy paper and charcoal. She spent most of her time in her own sitting room or away from home with her friends."

"There were no cousins?" he asked. "She had no children?"

There was a short pause.

"No," she said. "She was childless."

He had become sensitive to sound, or, sometimes, the absence of sound. And to atmosphere, to that slight charge of something inexplicable and indefinable that could hang in the silence or even occasionally in the noise.

Why that short pause when the answer was simply no?

He did not ask.

"And then she took a chill," she said, "and died after three weeks. She left her money to charity."

"And Lady March took you in."

"She and Sir Clarence were at the funeral," she said, "and a group of Aunt Mary's friends commended her for coming to take *that mousy girl* home with her. They were influential ladies. All sorts of nasty gossip originated with them almost daily. They could slay a reputation with one word in the right ear."

"And so she was obliged to take you," he said. "Do you have a caricature of the gossips?"

"Oh, yes, indeed," she said. "With long bodies and long necks and waving lorgnettes and quivering noses and Aunt Martha cowering on a level with their knees."

"And the mouse in its corner?" he asked.

"With folded arms and glum expression," she said. "I was eighteen. I ought to have looked for employment. I just—I had no idea how to go about it. I still do not. I ought to have gone to London last week. On the stagecoach, I mean. To look for work."

"You do not like our arrangement, then?" he asked her—and wished immediately he had not used that particular word.

"It is passive at present," she said. "It has been all take and no give. My clothes alone have cost you a fortune."

"You were not altogether passive on our wedding night," he reminded her. "Or last night."

They had made love three separate times in their inn room, and though she had not been a particularly active partner, neither had she been unwilling. She had certainly given every indication of enjoying what they did.

"Oh, that," she said dismissively—and perhaps a little sheepishly.

"Yes, *that*." He frowned. "And do not tell me, Sophie, that you have not liked it. I would be forced to be quite ungentlemanly and call you a liar. And even apart from your own enjoyment or lack thereof, you have given me pleasure."

"But that is not much," she said.

If he had not been concerned about this further evidence of her lack of self-esteem, he might have grinned.

"Not much?" he repeated. "I suggest you know little

about men, Sophie. You do not know how very central sex is to our lives? Pardon me for my blunt use of the word. I am twenty-three years old. Now at last I have a wife. I hope I will never come to think of you only as a convenient supplier of regular sex, but it will never ever be just *oh, that,* or *but that is not much* to me."

He became aware that she was laughing softly, and he joined her.

"This is not the sort of conversation a gentleman imagines having with his bride two days after the wedding," he said. "It is indelicate, to say the least. Forgive me."

Several minutes of silence ensued, but he realized at the end of it that her thoughts had been continuing along the same path.

"What will you do," she asked him, "after the year is over?"

He closed his eyes as though he could shut out thought as well as sight.

"Will you take a mistress?" she asked when he said nothing.

His eyes snapped open and he turned his head her way. "I am married to *you*."

"Yes," she agreed. "But if we are living apart from each other—"

"I am married to *you*," he said again, feeling his temper rise.

But what *would* he do if she left? After one year. After five. After ten. Good Lord, he would be only thirty-four even then.

"Will you take a *lover*?" He had reached the point of fury, he realized.

"No."

"Why not?"

"Because I am married to you," she said, her voice low and flat.

"Would you *want* to?" he asked.

"No. Would you?"

"I do not know," he said brutally. "Perhaps so. Perhaps not."

The ensuing silence bristled with tension.

Perhaps he *would* need to employ mistresses. He was no monk, after all. But the thought only infuriated him more.

A stormy silence ensued.

"Was that our first quarrel?" she asked softly.

"Yes, dash it all, it was," he said.

He felt her hand creep into his, and he laughed ruefully.

"We will be home soon," he said a short while later, "and you will no longer feel that our marriage is all give on my part and all take on yours. I am going to need you. In personal development I have made progress I can be proud of, but I have not done as well in my role as master of Middlebury Park. I have allowed others to look after me and to rule my world for me, and changing that will not be easy, because those others either love me or feel the benevolent wish to make my life easier. But changing the way things are will be done. I am determined on that. I will need your help, though."

"To take over from those others?"

"No," he said. "I do not intend to transfer dependence upon my mother and my steward to dependence upon you. I merely want you to help me reach that point at which I will not need—"

"Even me?" she asked when he stopped abruptly, having realized that those final words would probably sound insulting, though that was not what he had intended.

"I just do not want to be *dependent* upon you, Sophie," he said. "Or upon anyone else."

"And yet," she said, "I am totally dependent upon

you. Without you, I would be starving in the streets of London now."

"It is the nature of marriage, Sophie," he said with a sigh. "A wife is always dependent upon her husband for the material things in life. And he is dependent upon her for other things, some of them tangible, most not. But I hate that word *dependence*. It should be struck from the English language. I prefer to think of marriage as an equality of give and take."

They lapsed into silence again.

Her shoulder touched his after a while and he could hear from her breathing that she was almost asleep. He turned, wrapped one arm about her shoulders, and slid the other beneath her knees. He lifted her across his lap and braced his feet against the seat opposite.

She sighed again and nestled her head on his shoulder, and he dipped his head and kissed her. She kissed him back with warm, languid mouth—mouth, not just lips. And he would refuse to believe, even if someone with perfect vision told him so, that she did not have the loveliest woman's mouth ever created. He was not aroused, nor did he want to be. Not here. But his mouth lingered on hers, and his tongue lazily explored her lips and the smooth flesh behind them. Her free hand was on his shoulder and then behind his neck.

"I have never done anything with my life," she said. "I have merely endured and observed and dreamed—and laughed at the foolishness I see around me. I have always lived on the outer fringes. Now I am to be mistress of Middlebury Park. No, not *to be*. I *am*."

"Frightened?" he asked.

He felt her nodding against his shoulder. It would be strange if she was not.

She yawned and he tucked her head beneath his chin and settled her more comfortably on his lap. He closed his eyes and drifted toward sleep.

It was not even a major rut in the road. They had jarred through far worse in the past day and a half. But it happened just when he was hovering between wakefulness and sleep, and he jolted awake, completely disoriented, and opened his eyes to see what was the matter.

And was assaulted with a massive dose of panic.

He could not see.

He could not breathe.

He *could not see.*

"What is the matter?" a voice was whispering in his ear.

Could she not speak louder? *Louder?* LOUDER!

He thrust her from him and leaned forward until he could paw at the front panel behind the seat. He felt sideways until he found the window and then the leather strap hanging beside him. He grasped it and clung to it and gasped for air. There was not enough air.

There was not enough air.

"Vincent? What is the matter?" She sounded alarmed. Horribly alarmed.

Could she not *speak up*?

She touched his arm, and he flung her hand away. He clawed at the seat opposite, clung to the edge of it, bowed his head over it.

There was no air.

He could not *see.*

"Vincent? Oh, dear God, Vincent? Shall I stop the carriage and call Mr. Fisk?"

Martin would set one arm across his chest and beneath his chin and pat his back firmly with the other hand. And he would tell him bluntly and calmly that he was blind. That was all. He was blind.

There was a certain magic in Martin's treatment. He might even go so far as to tell Vincent that he was being a silly clod. All that was the matter was that he was blind.

But it was humiliating, after all this time, still to have to have Martin to calm him down.

"No," he gasped. "No."

And he found his breath and concentrated his whole attention upon it lest he misplace it again. He could hear the air rasping in through his nose, shuddering out through his mouth.

In. Out.

"I am sorry," he said.

He felt the tentative touch of her hand on his back. When he did not shrug it away, she moved it in light, soothing circles. She did not speak—or make any move to stop the carriage.

In. Out.

There was plenty of air. Of course there was.

The reason he had not heard her voice clearly was that she had spoken softly, even whispered the first time, and the horses and the carriage wheels were making enough racket to drown her out. But *he had heard the racket*. All that was wrong, as Martin would have told him, was that he was blind.

It was a manageable affliction.

Life was still worth living, still rich with meaning and possibility.

He was no longer concentrating upon his breathing, he realized. He was breathing by instinct.

Had he hurt her? Either physically or emotionally? Had he frightened her?

"I am sorry," he said again, still hanging his head over his hands clenched on the edge of the seat opposite. "Did I hurt you, Sophie?"

"No." But her voice sounded a little thin.

He sat back in his seat. He could feel his heart pounding in his chest, but it was slowing.

"I am sorry," he said once more. "For a few months—"
Ah, he never spoke of it. For a moment, his breath
threatened to go again. "For a few months I was deaf as
well as blind. And there never seemed to be enough air.
Ahhh. I am sorry. I cannot—"

She had one of his hands in both of hers and was
holding it against one cheek.

"You do not need to," she told him.

"After an eternity," he said, "there were arms. The
same arms all the time. They held me and fed me and
gave me air."

"Your mother's?"

"George's," he told her. "The Duke of Stanbrook's.
He held me to life and sanity, though that would surely
have gone anyway if my hearing had not returned. But
it did, at first faintly and fuzzily and then fully. I am
blind. That is all. I can live with that. But sometimes—"

"You have attacks of panic," she said. "Do you need
to be held when it happens, Vincent, or left alone?"

She would need to know. She was his wife. It would
surely happen again when he was with her. And he
could never predict exactly when.

"A human touch usually helps me back after the first
few moments," he said. "Beware of getting hurt in those
first moments, though. Oh, Sophie!"

She kissed the back of his hand.

"I am glad I am not the only needy one in our marriage," she said. "I do not mean I am glad you are blind
or glad that you have these attacks. But I am glad you
are not some sort of superhuman pillar of strength. I
would not be able to prevail against it. I am too weak,
too fragile. In each other's weaknesses, perhaps we can
both find strength."

He was feeling too tired to comprehend what she was
saying to him. But he felt soothed, wondrously comforted. At the same time he felt he could weep.

"Come back on my lap," he said. "If you trust me not to fling you off again, that is."

She scrambled across him and snuggled against him, one arm about his neck. He braced his feet against the seat opposite again, twined his fingers in her curls, and felt safe. And somehow cherished.

He slept.

℔ophia was warm and comfortable despite the jolting of the carriage. She was curled up in Vincent's arms, her head nestled in the hollow between his shoulder and neck, her arm about him. She did not sleep even though he did. She pictured him as he had been the first few times she saw him. Not that he had changed in the week since. Only her perception of him had.

Elegant, beautiful, courtly. A *viscount*. Someone to admire from afar. Someone from a different world than her own. Someone quite untouchable. She remembered her consternation when he had offered his arm outside the assembly rooms and she had touched him for the first time.

It had felt like touching a god.

Now she was his wife. She knew him intimately— *very* intimately. And though he was beautiful almost beyond belief, he was just a man. Just a person. Like her, he was vulnerable. Like her, he had been living a life that was in many ways passive. Like her, he felt the need, the intense desire, to *live*. To prevail against life rather than merely to endure. To be free and independent . . .

They were not as unequal as she had thought.

And now they were on their way *home*. She savored the word. She had lived in numerous rooms and houses during her first fifteen years, some of them grand, most of them shabby. And then there had been Aunt Mary's house in London and then Barton Hall. But there had never been rooms or a house that she had called *home*.

Home had always been a place to dream of.

But *would* Middlebury Park be home? Or would it be just another house in which she lived for a while before moving on? But she would not think of that—moving on, that was. He had been right on their wedding day. They were married *now*. Middlebury Park was to be her home *now*. She wished—oh, she *wished* she had not told him her dream at the assembly, for it had been based entirely upon her belief that she would never marry, that no one would even *want* to marry her. And it had always been one of those impossible dreams anyway, apparently harmless for that very reason.

They would be arriving anytime now. She had heard Mr. Handry say the last time they stopped for a change of horses that that would probably be the final time.

She was terrified.

So what was she going to do about that? Hide in a corner somewhere where it was safe?

Or pretend that she was not afraid at all?

She was about to discover who she was, she realized, and what she was made of.

She had a sudden mental image of the next picture in her sketch pad—a huge mouse, almost filling the page, blank terror in its eyes as though a giant cat were bearing down upon it, a silly, sick grin on its face. And a series of straight lines leading from it to converge on the bottom corner, where the exact same mouse, hugely reduced in size, cowered in cowardly safety.

She smiled and felt her body shake against Vincent's as she quelled the bubble of laughter that threatened to erupt in sound.

"Mmm," he said. "Was I snoring?"

"No."

"*Something* was funny."

"Oh," she said. "Not really."

"Did you sleep?" he asked her. "I believe I did."

"I was too busy feeling comfortable," she said. "There is one advantage to being small. I can snuggle up to you on your lap."

This was one thing she had discovered about herself. She could relax with him and talk with him. She was not quite paralyzed in his presence as she had been a week ago.

"You may do so anytime you choose," he said. "Well, within reason, I suppose. My steward might be a trifle disconcerted if you were to snuggle up when I was in consultation with him in his office. But touch is important to me, Sophie, perhaps more important than it is to most men. Never be afraid to touch me."

She had not thought of his need in quite that way. For a moment she thought she might well weep. But she was distracted when she realized the carriage was slowing and then turning.

"Oh." She sat up and her stomach lurched.

"We must be there," he said. "Describe it to me, Sophie."

"Tall stone gateposts," she said, her eyes widening, "with wrought iron gates. They are open so we do not have to stop. A stone wall stretching to either side, though it is half hidden beneath moss and ivy. A shaded driveway with woods on either side. I see oaks and chestnuts and other trees whose names I do not know. I am hopeless on the names of plants."

"Which does not matter," he said, "since plants do not name themselves. Or so you informed me once upon a time."

The grounds must be huge. There was no sign yet of the house or of any cultivated park. They seemed to be in the depths of the countryside.

"I can see water," she said then, clambering off his

lap and sitting beside him, the better to see through both windows. "There must be a lake, is there? Oh, yes, there it is. A big one. There is even an island in the middle of it with a little temple or something on it. How picturesque! And a boathouse. And reeds. And trees."

"I have been out in one of the boats," he told her. "I have to have someone with me, of course, or I am inclined to row into banks and marshes and islands and other assorted obstacles that insist upon getting in my way."

"You need to learn to look where you are going," she said. "Better yet, take me with you and *I* will look where you are going. I shall scream when you are about to collide with something. Oh. Oh, Vincent."

Wonder and terror clutched at her in equal measure.

The house had come into view. House—ha! It was a mansion. It was a *palace*. It was . . . It was Middlebury Park. It was her new home. She was mistress of it.

"Oh, Vincent."

"Struck dumb by my charms, are you?" he asked her. "Or are you seeing something else that has tied your tongue in knots?"

"The latter," she said. "I can see the house. The driveway straightens here on a direct axis with the front doors, and there are lawns on either side with some small topiary trees on either side. And up ahead I can see parterres with more little trees and flowers and statuary. And the house. Oh, *how* can I describe it?"

"It has a high, imposing central block," he said, "with twelve steps leading up to massive double doors. There are long wings to either side and round towers at the four corners. The stable block is off to the left. We will turn to the right very soon and drive between the lawn and the parterres and so approach the house from the east side. Behind the house the park rises into hills, and there are many more trees covering them and descending almost to the kitchen gardens. It is a bit of a wilderness back there. Each side of the park is two miles long—eight miles all told. It would take two and a half hours to walk around the outside of the wall at a fair pace. I have done it in three and a half. The farms are beyond the walls."

"You peeped when no one was looking," she said.

"My secret is out." He took her hand in his. "Are you impressed with your husband's great consequence, Sophie?"

Impressed? That did not nearly describe how she felt, but no other word in her vocabulary did either.

"Oh, Vincent," was all she could say. The carriage had indeed turned right and then left and left again until it drew to a halt at the foot of a flight of marble steps. She would take his word for it that there were twelve.

"Do I take that to be yes?" he asked her.

"I am impressed at *my* consequence," she told him, desperately trying to convert terror to humor. "I am mistress of all this, am I not?"

The great front doors, she could see now that they were close, had opened, and a lady had appeared in the doorway. She moved to the top of the steps as Sophia watched.

Vincent's mother?

Mr. Handry had jumped down from his perch and was opening the carriage door and lowering the steps.

Sophia raised her chin—what else was there to do?

14

❧

𝒱incent stepped down from the carriage and was immediately engulfed in his mother's embrace. She had seen the carriage approaching, then. She must have been watching for it. She had probably had a dozen or more letters from Barton Coombs and had been hovering near a window for days.

He felt a familiar rush of guilt and love.

"Vincent," she cried. "Oh, at last you are safely home. I have worried myself to a shadow." She clung to him wordlessly for a while and then loosened her hold and held him by the shoulders. "But what have you done? Tell me it is not true. Please tell me you did not do anything so foolish. I have been sleepless with worry since I heard. We all have."

"Mama."

He turned slightly and must have given her a view of the carriage behind him. Her hands fell away from his shoulders and she went silent. He raised a hand to help Sophia alight.

"Mama," he said, "may I present Sophia? My wife? My mother, Sophie."

Her hand came to rest on his. She had pulled her gloves on, he could feel.

"Oh, Vincent," his mother said faintly as Sophia came down the steps. "You *have* married her, then."

"Mrs. Hunt." He could feel Sophia dip into a curtsy.

"I would not believe it," his mother was saying, "even

when Elsie Parsons herself wrote to me. I expected that you would come to your senses before it was too late."

"Mama," he said sharply.

"Here come your grandmother and Amy," she said. "Whatever will they think?"

Amy was the first to arrive.

"Vincent," she cried, pulling him into a tight hug. "You wretched boy. Mama has been beside herself ever since you disappeared in the middle of the night like a naughty schoolboy, and she has been beside herself all over again since hearing about your newest escapade. Whatever were you *thinking*?"

Sophia always had been virtually invisible, according to her. The quiet mouse in its quiet corner.

"Vincent. Dearest boy." It was his grandmother's voice, warm with affection, and Amy relinquished her hold on him so that their grandmother could hug him in her turn.

"Grandmama," he said, "and Amy. Allow me to present my wife, Sophia. My grandmother, Mrs. Pearl, Sophie, and my eldest sister, Amy Pendleton."

"Oh, you *have* married, then," Amy cried. "I would not believe it even though Anthony said you would if you had compromised her to the extent of taking her to London without a chaperon."

He might have known that one at least of his sisters would be here, summoned, no doubt, to help deal with this new family crisis involving him. And Amy was the closest geographically. The other two were probably on their way.

The first one to recover her manners was his grandmother.

"Sophia, my dear," she said, "you are looking pale enough to fall over. You are looking as I always feel when I have been compelled to take a long carriage journey. I daresay you need a nice hot cup of tea and something to eat, and we will find both for you up in the drawing room. That is a pretty little bonnet you are wearing. I suppose it is the very height of fashion, since you have been in London."

"Mrs. Pearl," Sophia said, her voice soft and a little trembly. "Yes, we went there to marry, and Vincent insisted that I have new clothes since . . . Well. Yes, a cup of tea would be lovely. Thank you."

"Sophia," Amy said in stiff greeting. "You are a niece of Lady March's, we understand?"

"Yes," Sophia said. "My father was her brother."

"Well, what is done is done," Vincent's mother said briskly, "and we must all make the best of it. Sophia, do go inside with my mother. Amy and I will help Vincent in."

One on each arm, no doubt, walking rather slowly, propelling him along, keeping him safe from any obstacle that might hurl itself into his path. He already felt the old slight irritation. Though that was unfair. They meant so well. They loved him.

"You must not trouble yourself, Mama," he said. "Martin? My cane, if you please. Sophie?" He held out his arm, and he felt her hand slip through it. "I'll take you up to the drawing room while our bags are being carried to our rooms. A cup of tea would indeed be just the thing, Grandmama. It has been a long journey. I am sorry I caused you such anxiety, Mama, though I did have Martin write to you a time or two. We were in the Lake District. I'll tell you about my travels when we are sitting down, and about our wedding, though I daresay Sophia will do a better job of telling you about that. Have you arrived just recently, Amy? Are Anthony and the children with you?"

"They are," she said. "We arrived late yesterday. We came as soon as we heard. Though I was convinced you would not actually get married in such haste. Indeed, I was sure you would not, especially when you ran from the mere prospect of matrimony such a short while ago."

"That was Miss Dean, Amy," he said, "and this is Sophia. Miss Dean was not my choice of bride, while Sophia was. And is."

He was walking as he spoke. When Martin had set his cane in his hand, he had also by a slight touch turned him in the right direction. He felt the rise of the bottom step with his cane and counted as he climbed while talking at the same time.

"I believe the sun must be shining," he said. "Is it?"

"It is," Sophia said.

"I can feel its heat on my back," he said. "I am glad about that. You will be seeing Middlebury Park at its finest, Sophie, though there is far more to see, of course, than just the parterres and the front façade of the house and the woods and the lake."

He stopped when they were inside the hall. He knew it was impressive. The floor was tiled with black and white squares and there was a great deal of white marble with classical busts set in alcoves. The ceiling was painted with scenes from mythology, and the frieze was gilded. There was a large marble fireplace on either side so that when one entered the house on a chilly day, one was met with at least the illusion of warmth and the cozy crackle of logs and the smell of the wood.

"Well?" he said.

"Oh," she said, almost in a whisper. "It is *magnificent*."

Yes. It was also intended to inspire awe in lowly visitors. Not necessarily, though, in its own mistress.

"It is one of the finest halls in England, Sophia, or so I have been told," his mother said.

He moved forward, counting his steps silently again—

through the high arch at the back of the hall and to his right until his cane touched the bottom stair of the marble staircase. Sophia's hand on his arm somehow assured him that she would correct any serious misstep, but it was a subtle, unobtrusive guide.

The drawing room was above the hall, at the front of the house, its three long windows looking out along the straight part of the driveway between the parterres to a small rose garden and trees in the distance. It was a magnificent view in a room that was flooded with light in the daytime.

Or so it had been described to him. He was glad he had once been able to see. At least he could imagine. And who knew? Perhaps the home he pictured in his mind was more magnificent than the reality.

"All the living quarters are here and in the west wing," he explained as they climbed the stairs. "The east wing is seldom used. It houses the state apartments, the gallery, and the grand ballroom. There were once lavish entertainments there, and balls."

A servant must have been waiting outside the drawing room doors. He heard them open and led his wife inside.

"Oh," she said, stopping on the threshold, and he heard her inhale rather sharply.

"Vincent, my lad!" It was the hearty voice of Anthony Pendleton, his brother-in-law. Vincent could hear him striding across the room, and then his right hand was caught up in a firm clasp after his cane had been whisked away. "And what is all this we have been hearing? What mischief have you been up to when there were no mother and sisters to keep you under their wing and under control, eh? You have really done the deed, by the look of it, as I assured Amy you would. Or is this merely your betrothed or a casual acquaintance on your arm?"

"Anthony!" Amy sounded mortified.

"Sophie," Vincent said, "this is Anthony Pendleton, Amy's husband. My wife, Anthony. Yes, the deed is done—*was* done two days ago, in fact, in London, at St. George's on Hanover Square. We are married."

"And proud I am of you," Anthony said, slapping him on the shoulder. "You really are a tiny little thing, aren't you, Sophia, just as all those gossips said you were in their letters." Vincent heard a smacking kiss.

"Mr. Pendleton," Sophia said.

"You must call me Anthony since you are my sister-in-law," he said.

"Anthony," she said.

"St. George's?" Vincent's mother said. "It was not some clandestine affair, then, as we feared? But could you not have waited, Vincent? It is too late now, though." Her voice had turned brisk again. "Sophia, go and sit by the fireplace. The tea tray will be here in a minute. Let me take your gloves and your bonnet. Anthony will set them down somewhere. Oh, goodness me, your hair *is* short. I was told it was. Well, at least it curls quite prettily. Mother, go and sit beside Sophia. Vincent, come and sit in the wing chair by the window, where you can feel the heat of the sun. I know it is your favorite."

She took a firm hold of his arm.

He almost went.

"Thank you, Mama," he said instead, "but I have been sitting forever in the carriage and need to stretch my legs. I am going to stand in front of the fireplace, close to Sophia."

He walked toward it on his own, without his cane. He hoped he was not about to make an idiot of himself and either miss it by a mile or crash into it, though he knew the room well enough. He reached out one hand

when he thought he was close and was relieved to discover the mantelpiece only a little farther ahead of him
than he had expected. He set one hand on it and half
turned to face the chair where his wife sat.

"It is indeed short," his grandmother was saying, presumably referring to Sophia's hair. "But it is a beautiful
color."

"Thank you, ma'am," Sophia said. "Lady Trentham,
who is married to one of Vincent's friends, took me to
her own hairdresser and he tamed it for me. I have always cut it myself, but not very well. He advised me to
grow it."

"Then maybe you ought," his grandmother said,
"and so display its color to greater advantage."

"I really think you ought," Amy said. "I can see why
they thought at Barton Coombs that you look like a
boy."

Anthony cleared his throat.

"Not that you do now," Amy added. "But you look
very . . . young. Have you always kept your hair short?"

"No," Sophia said. "But it was hard to manage."

"A good maid can manage any hair," Vincent's
mother said. "You did not bring a maid?"

"No, ma'am," she said. "I have never had one."

"Well, neither had we," his mother said, "until my
girls married and then I moved here. Except for Mrs.
Plunkett, that is, who was our housekeeper at Covington House and did duty also as cook, nurse, lady's
maid, finder of missing items, hider of guilty culprits
from being caught—yes, Vincent!—and a number of
other things."

"She was always my closest ally," Vincent said. She
had lived with them all the time he could remember.

"I was quite sad that she decided to retire when I
came here, and went to live with her sister," his mother
said. "One of the chambermaids here is my own maid's

sister, Sophia, and apparently it is her greatest ambition
to be a lady's maid too. She did my hair very nicely one
evening when I had sent my own maid to bed with a
cold. Perhaps you would care to give her a try and see if
she suits you."

Vincent looked in her direction with gratitude. She
was recovering herself. She might be upset—undoubtedly
she was—but she would follow her own advice and
make the best of things as they were. His mother had
always been good at that.

"Thank you, ma'am," Sophia said.

"That had better be Mama," his mother said.

"Yes, Mama."

"Ah, here comes the tea tray," Amy said as Vincent
heard the drawing room door open. "Shall I pour,
Mama? No, pardon me. Shall I pour, Sophia?"

"Oh," Sophia said. "Yes, please do, Mrs. Pendleton."

"Amy, if you please," Amy said. "We are sisters-in-
law. Oh, how strange that sounds. I have two brothers-
in-law but no sister-in-law until now. Vincent, you
wretch. I will never forgive you for running off to London to marry and depriving us of all the fuss and an-
guish of organizing a wedding. Ellen and Ursula will
not be happy with you either. Just wait and see."

"While Amy is pouring and Anthony is handing
around the cakes," Vincent's mother said, "I want to
hear about your wedding. Every single detail of it."

"Starting with your wedding outfit, if you please, Sophia," his grandmother said.

Sophia did most of the telling, her voice thin and
breathless at first but settling to a greater steadiness.
She told of her shopping trip with Lady Trentham and
Lady Kilbourne, of her wedding outfit and his, the appearance of the church, the guests, the way he had
signed the register and the astonished look on the cler-

gyman's face as he did so, the tears that had been sparkling in the eyes of Lord Trentham and the Duke of
Stanbrook as they left the church, the small, cheering
crowd outside, the sunshine, the rose petals and the
gentlemen who threw them, the decorations on the barouche and din of the pots and pans, the wedding
breakfast, the toasts. Vincent filled in the gaps, explaining the presence of his friends in town for Hugo's wedding and their request to attend his and to put on a
wedding breakfast for them.

"And I am so *very* sorry that you could not all be
there too," Sophia added, sounding breathless again.
"But Lord Dar— But Vincent was very sensitive to the
fact that I had no family of my own—or no family to
speak of. And he was concerned that I had no decent
clothes and looked like a scarecrow and was in no fit
state to be brought here to be presented to you. And he
did not want the long delay of inviting you all to come
to London, for I had nowhere to stay, though as it
turned out, I believe I could have stayed longer with
Lord and Lady Trentham. They were very kind. But we
did not know that ahead of time. I am *very* sorry."

"I am sorry too, Sophia," his mother said with a sigh.
"And I am sorry the two of you did not take longer to
become acquainted in order to be sure that you will suit
each other for a lifetime. But it is too late to worry over
those things now."

"Sophia and I are not worried, Mama," Vincent said
as someone—Anthony, he believed—took his empty
plate from his hand and replaced it with a cup and saucer. "We did what seemed best to us, and we have not
known a moment's regret since."

He hoped he spoke the truth—for both of them.

"In two days of marriage, Vince?" Anthony chuckled. "That is good to hear."

"I will try to make up for the fact that we did not

come here to marry," Sophia said, her voice noticeably shaking. "I suppose the neighbors would have been invited if we had? I will call on them, if I may. Is that the correct thing to do? And perhaps they will call here. Perhaps at some time in the future, we will invite a number of people here for a sort of reception. Perhaps even a ball, like the ones there used to be."

There was a slight, stunned silence.

"Oh, my dear," his mother said, "I will accompany you if you wish to pay some calls, but we do not encourage anyone to come here. Vincent does not . . . mingle. It is not easy for him. Any sort of lavish entertainment here is out of the question."

He *had* been something of a recluse here at Middlebury. He had made no active move to mingle with local society, and that was entirely his own fault.

"And yet," he said, "it happened at Barton Coombs less than two weeks ago. Half the citizens descended upon me there at home, and Martin served us all coffee and his mother's cakes. There was an assembly at the Foaming Tankard in my honor, and I rather enjoyed it even though I could not dance."

"But that was Barton Coombs," his mother said. "You know everyone there."

"And I ought to know everyone here," he said. "I have lived here for three years, after all. My uncle was, I believe, a sociable man. I must be a disappointment to the people living near."

"Oh, but they will understand, Vincent," Amy said.

"Understand what?" he asked her. "That I am blind and therefore totally incapacitated and mentally feeble as well? I will call on our neighbors with you, Sophie. It is time I made myself known. And this is the perfect opportunity. Middlebury Park has a new viscountess— the first in eighteen years if I have been properly informed. We will even begin to think about the possibility of a reception and ball."

"Good for you, Vince," Anthony said. "I always suspected you had more in you than was apparent. There are all those stories from your boyhood, after all."

"Everyone will be enchanted," Vincent's grandmother said. "Everyone feels the deepest sympathy for you, I know, especially since it was in battle that you were wounded. Nevertheless, I have heard whispers that many people long for the good old days when the viscount was not locked away inside Middlebury Park and everyone else was locked outside."

It was appalling. *He* had been appalling.

"Thank you, Grandmama," he said. "I am going to have to change all that. *We* are. Sophia and I."

He looked down in her direction and smiled. She had started this. Was she up to carrying it through? But she would not have to do it alone.

"Sophia," Amy said, "are you too tired to meet my children? They have probably already heard that Uncle Vincent is home and will be bouncing with excitement, especially if they know he has brought a new aunt with him. William is four and Hazel three, and they are bundles of endless energy except when they are sleeping."

"I am not too tired," Sophia said.

"My love?" Amy said, presumably to Anthony. "Shall we go and fetch them down? Will *you* mind, Vincent?"

She was *asking* him? His female relatives usually told him. Though it had not always been so. He had been very much his own person once upon a time.

"It has always seemed strange to me," he said, "that in great houses children are confined to the nursery most of the time. *We* were not, were we?"

"I might have fewer gray hairs now if you had been, particularly *you*, Vincent," his mother said, and they all laughed.

And it struck Vincent that there had been very little laughter in his home during the past three years. There had used to be, surely, when they all lived at Covington House.

He drank his tea and waited for the onslaught of children.

 Sophia sank down into the comfortable cushions of a sofa in Vincent's private sitting room, now hers too. Their apartments were in the southwest tower, and no one else came here without an invitation, he had told her, except Martin Fisk and now Rosina, her new maid.

The first few hours after her arrival at Middlebury Park had been a dreadful ordeal. The house itself filled her with awe, and she felt uncomfortable with the family, even though they had been polite after the first few minutes and had even gone out of their way to be kind to her. If she had been ignored and allowed to retire into herself, she would have been far more comfortable, but of course that was out of the question—both for them and for her. She was Vincent's wife and they loved him. They could not ignore her. And she was quite determined to do what she must to become mistress of Middlebury Park. She could not tell herself that she would do it tomorrow or next week or next month. If she did not assert herself from the start, she never would.

She was exhausted.

She loved the east tower on sight. It was round and so was the sitting room. The shape gave the illusion of coziness despite the fact that it was not really small. On the floor above there were two bedchambers and two dressing rooms occupying the same amount of space. Long windows in the sitting room looked out on the garden and park in three different directions. Tomorrow she would discover what was to be seen through those windows.

"Tired?" Vincent sat down beside her.

It was not late. After dinner in the large dining room in the west wing, they had gone along to the nursery, as they had promised at teatime, to bid Amy and Anthony's children good night, and had stayed to tell them two stories. Vincent, by request, had told the original one of the dragon and the field mouse, and together they had told the story of Bertha and Dan and the church spire to much interest and a few gasps of anxiety and a million questions. They had drunk tea in the drawing room afterward, and then Vincent had made their excuses. Everyone had seemed agreed that they must be weary after their long journey.

"I am," she said now.

He took her hand.

"This has been a very busy day for you," he said. "A rather lengthy journey and then a new home and a new family."

"Yes."

They loved him, his family, and he them. They had hung on his every word at dinner when he had described his weeks in the Lake District. So had she. He had actually climbed steep hills. And ridden a horse.

"The children are a delight," she said. She had almost no acquaintance with children. She had been surprised by their energy, their affection, their very brief attention span, their very direct questions. "They adored the stories, did they not? I am going to draw illustrations for them and put them into books with the stories. Do you think they will like them? Though I am sure they will always prefer the stories you tell straight from your imagination."

"The stories *we* tell," he said. "I think the Bertha and Dan story was their favorite."

"We are going to have to rethink that one," she said. "We must not be in a hurry to marry them and doom poor Bertha to an earthbound existence for all of the rest of her days, poor thing. It was good that we did not mention their marriage this evening."

"They ought to have more adventures, then?" His head was turned her way, and he was grinning. She liked that expression of his. It made him look boyish—and handsome, of course.

"Like the time the kitten ran up the tree," she said.

"Because it was so adorable that everyone wanted to pet it and it just had to get away somewhere to be alone?"

"Yes, precisely," she said. "And of course, no one could coax it down and it was mewing most pitiably and night was coming on."

"Enter Bertha, stage left?"

"At a trot," she said. "And up she went after the poor kitty. It was not easy. The tree was very tall, but whereas the trunk was sturdy most of the way up, it was thin and not at all sturdy looking at the top."

"But she got there, swaying in the breeze, and tucked the kitten under one arm, and then froze."

"But the kitten did not," she said. "It was still unhappy about being touched, the ungrateful little thing, and it wriggled free and ran down to the ground. Which left Bertha in the same plight as the kitten had just been in. Except that she could not simply run down. Or even look down."

"Dan to the rescue?"

"He had to be *very* brave," she said. "For though he could not see how high they were and how far away the ground was beneath them, he could *feel* the tree swaying. In fact, by the time he got to the top and had an arm firmly about Bertha's waist, the wind was howling about his ears and the tree was bowing from side to side just like a giant rocking horse. In fact—"

"—it rocked so far over," he said, "that it bowed almost to the ground, and all of Bertha's friends were able to pluck her from Dan's arms to instant safety before he shot up to the vertical again."

"And he stayed up this time," she said, "because there was less weight for the trunk to bear and the wind suddenly died. And he climbed down safely and was rewarded with a great round of applause and a great deal of backslapping, and a great big hug from Bertha."

"And a kiss?"

"Definitely a kiss," she said. "Right on the lips. The end."

"Amen."

They chuckled, and their shoulders touched.

"All those people are going to be strangers," she said.

He looked mystified for a moment at the abrupt change of subject and tone.

"Our neighbors?" he said. "They more or less are to me too. But we will remember who we are—Viscount and Viscountess Darleigh of Middlebury Park. We are by far the grandest family for miles around. Under normal conditions they would have expected me to be in the very forefront of social life the day after my arrival here three years ago. I have been a disappointment. That must change. And perhaps I will be forgiven. I was, after all, a single man dealing with a relatively new affliction. Now I have a young viscountess. Everyone will be dying of curiosity and hoping that things will change here."

"Oh, dear," she said. "I am not at all sure—"

He squeezed her hand.

"I have no idea how to be a viscountess and mistress of somewhere so vast and stately," she continued in a rush. "And I have *no idea* how to be gracious and sociable."

"I have every confidence in you," he said.

"It is a good thing one of us does," she said—and laughed.

He laughed with her.

"I realized something this afternoon at tea," he said. "And it would partly explain why I have never been quite . . . happy here at Middlebury Park in three years, despite the fact that I have been surrounded by family, who have lavished their care on me and whom I love dearly. It has been a place without laughter, Sophie. Everyone has been oppressed by my blindness and the necessity of being *cheerful*. I laugh a great deal when I am at Penderris Hall. I have laughed with you, almost from the time we met. And you and I are not the only ones who have laughed here since our arrival."

"Everyone did at tea," she said, "when I was describing standing on a raised dais while the dressmaker and her helpers poked and prodded me with pins. It was not funny."

"But you made it funny," he said, "and we all laughed. It felt good, Sophie. We used to laugh as a family."

"I suppose," she said, "Miss Dean was pretty."

"I was assured that she was beautiful."

"They wanted someone lovely for you," she said. "Because you are beautiful too."

"And instead," he said, smiling, "I found for myself a wife who definitely does not look like a boy, despite what some people from Barton Coombs might have said, but who does look very young. And like a little elfin creature, someone told me on our wedding day."

"Oh, who?"

"Never mind," he said. "It was a compliment."

She sighed and changed the subject again.

"Are there any dogs here?" she asked him. "Or cats?"

"There are probably some mousers in the barns," he said. "Domestic cats, do you mean, though? And house dogs? They were never allowed when we were growing up, though Ursula and I were forever begging our parents to allow them, a cat for her, a dog for me. My mother used to say that there were enough of us to look after without having our pets underfoot too."

"There should be a cat," she said, "to sit on the windowsills in this room, sunning itself. And to sit purring on your lap or mine. And a dog to lead you about so that you need not be dependent upon a human guide or even your cane."

He raised his eyebrows.

"Lady Trentham and the Countess of Kilbourne have a cousin whose daughter has been blind from birth," she told him. "She has a dog who leads her about and stops her from colliding with objects or tumbling down steps or coming to grief in a hundred other ways. She did not really train it and it is sometimes unruly and does not always keep her from harm. Her father is training a larger dog to be less exuberant and more obedient and responsible. Imagine having a dog to be your eyes, Vincent."

Just talking about it made her feel excited.

"And they let her go about on her own?" he asked.

"Not on her own. With her dog. Her father is the Marquess of Attingsborough."

"What sort of dog?" he asked.

"I don't know," she admitted. "Not anything too small and excitable, I suppose. Not a poodle. Perhaps a sheepdog. They herd and guide sheep and have to be intelligent and resourceful as well as obedient."

"There must be sheepdogs around here," he said, half turning in his seat. "There are certainly sheep. And the cat for you? You told me before that you would like one."

"There was an old cat at Aunt Mary's—Tom," she told him. "He was not allowed out of the kitchen area. He was to keep mice away from the pantry. But sometimes I sneaked him upstairs and we would purr together with contentment. But he got to be too old to catch mice. He was of no further use to anyone. He was . . . taken away."

"Poor Sophie," he said. "We will find a kitten, will we?"

"Yes," she said. "Oh, *may* I have one?"

He sat back on the sofa and sighed.

"Sophie," he said, "you may have anything in the world you want. You are not poor any longer."

"A kitten or even an older cat will do," she told him. "For now, anyway."

"And a dog for me." He lifted his free arm and rubbed his brow just above his eyes with the back of his wrist. "Will it work, do you think? Oh, do you think, Sophie?"

She bit her lower lip hard and blinked her eyes. There were such wistfulness and longing in his voice. Oh, she was going to give him back his eyes, or the next best thing, if it took her the rest of her life to do it. He wanted her to help him become independent so that he would no longer need her. Very well. She would do it. She would find a hundred ways or more. He had given her so much already—nothing short of her life, in fact. She would give him his independence in return.

"I do indeed," she said. "And we can but try."

He released her hand, slid his arm about her shoulders, found her mouth with his own, and kissed her.

"I think you are going to be good for me," he said against her lips. "I only hope it can work both ways."

His words filled her with such yearning that her throat ached.

"Is it time for bed?" he asked. "Do not, please, look at a clock and tell me it is too early. Just say yes."

"Yes."

It was twenty-five minutes past nine.

15

❧

*W*hen Sophia half awoke and tried to snuggle back into the warmth that had been next to her all night, she discovered only a cool emptiness. She woke all the way up and opened her eyes.

He was gone. There was daylight, but it had an early look to it. She lifted her head and peered at the clock. A quarter past six. She grimaced and lay back down.

Wherever—?

But she knew the answer. He had gone down to the cellar to exercise. Why it had to be the cellar when there must be any number of unused rooms aboveground she did not know, but he had told her that was where he always went.

She considered closing her eyes and drifting back to sleep. But now that she was awake her stomach churned slightly. Not with hunger. Indeed, she could not even think of breakfast yet. But there was a new life to be lived out there beyond their private apartments, and she had committed herself to living it rather than to creeping into a corner and observing it through a satirical eye.

She pushed back the bedcovers and sat up on the edge of the bed—and shivered in the early morning chill. Sleeping without even a nightgown was fine until there was nothing to cover one at all.

She pulled on her sadly creased nightgown, which had been discarded beside the bed again, and crossed the room to pull back the curtains from the one long window.

It looked southwest. She could see the stable block over to one side and a wide expanse of lawn dotted with ancient trees. It sloped away gradually to the lake. Centered in the view was the little island in the middle and its temple folly. The other side of the lake was dense with trees, lushly green at the moment. They must be a sight to behold in the autumn.

The lake, large though it was, must be man made. It had been very carefully positioned, as had the island and temple, to create just this view from the master bedchamber.

Sophia was smitten with a sudden and unexpected wave of grief for her husband, who would never see it.

On a more practical note, though, how could he ever get to that lake unless someone took him? The lawn undulated in rises and dips that were pleasing to the eye and even to someone strolling over it, she guessed, provided that person could see.

She frowned and considered the problem.

The window in the other bedchamber, nominally hers, must look in the other direction, southeast across the formal part of the park, the parterres and the topiary garden. She would look through it sometime, but right now there was something else she wanted to do. She wanted to go and see Vincent and find out what sort of exercises he did. She had no idea where the cellar was. She had no idea where almost anywhere was, but there was no point in feeling daunted. She would find out. She had a tongue, and it struck her that the servants here would not simply look through her as though she did not even exist. She was Viscountess Darleigh, their mistress.

Somehow it was not a reassuring thought.

She did not summon Rosina to help her dress. The

idea seemed rather absurd when she had been dressing herself all her life. Besides, it was still not quite half past six. She washed her hands and face in last night's cold water, put on one of her new ready-made dresses without stays, and pulled a brush through her hair.

The cellar was beside the butler's pantry in the kitchen area. It was easy to find. She merely walked along to the main hall and startled a footman, who was unbolting the front doors, and he took her himself and showed her the cellar door.

"Shall I call his lordship up, my lady?" he asked her.

"No, thank you," she said. "I do not want to disturb him."

The staircase was very dark, but there was light below. Sophia crept down a few of the stairs until she could see all the way down and then sat on one of them, hugging her knees.

Vincent and Mr. Fisk were down there, in a large, square room. In the light of three lamps she could see that there was an inner room, its walls lined with shelves and stacked with bottles. It was the wine cellar, of course, by the butler's pantry.

The lamps were presumably for Mr. Fisk's use. The horrible thought struck Sophia that a place like this, which must be totally dark without the lamps, would be no different to Vincent than the light-filled drawing room above. For a moment her breathing quickened and she feared she might swoon. It was no wonder he suffered bouts of panic.

He was stripped to the waist and barefoot—they both were, in fact. All he was wearing was a pair of tight, form-fitting breeches. He was lying on his back on a mat on the floor, his feet hooked beneath the bar of a bench, his hands clasped behind his head, and he was sitting up and lying back down in quick succession, the muscles of his chest and abdomen rippling as he exerted himself, and glistening with sweat.

Mr. Fisk was skipping with a rope, increasing and decreasing the speed, crossing the rope in front of him, and never getting tangled up in it.

Sophia counted fifty-six sit-up exercises before Vincent stopped—and he had started before she came down. How could he possibly . . .

"Ho," he said, his voice breathless, "I am out of practice, Martin. I can manage only eighty today."

Mr. Fisk grunted and set aside his rope. "The bar next, is it? Twenty-five repetitions?"

"Slave driver," Vincent said, getting to his feet.

"Weakling."

Sophia raised her eyebrows, but Vincent just laughed.

"Twenty-six," he said. "Just to prove a point."

There was a metal bar suspended horizontally from the ceiling. Mr. Fisk led Vincent to it, and he reached his hands under and over it, gripped it tightly, and hauled himself up until his chin was level with the bar. He lowered himself without touching his feet to the floor and raised himself again—twenty-six times.

It looked like sheer torture.

His ribs and abdomen were like a washboard, Sophia thought. His shoulder and arm muscles bulged. His legs were together, feet pointed.

He was not a large man. He was neither as tall nor as broad as his valet, but he was fit and beautifully proportioned and gloriously masculine.

Sophia lowered her chin to her knees.

"You have made your point," Mr. Fisk was saying. "No weights today, though. I've worn them out myself, anyway. Have you had enough?"

"Bring out the pads," Vincent said. "I'll see if I can hurt you through them today."

Mr. Fisk snorted and said something rude that turned

Sophia's cheeks warm. He picked up two large leather pads, fitted them over his arms, and held them up in front of himself as a sort of shield. Vincent reached out and touched them, felt the tops and the outer edges. Then he curled his hands into fists and took a fighter's stance. He punched one of Mr. Fisk's padded arms with his right hand.

It was almost like watching a dance. Mr. Fisk moved nimbly, ducking and weaving, while Vincent danced on light feet, jabbing with his left hand, occasionally punching hard with his right. Some of his punches missed altogether, but his valet grunted as one jab got past his guard and connected with his shoulder. Then he laughed.

"I got you that time, Martin," Vincent said. "Admit it."

"A chicken punch," Mr. Fisk said, and Vincent pummeled the padded arms, moving in close, using both fists hard.

"Just say when you have had enough," he said, panting. "I would not want to leave you with too many bruises. Or crack a rib or two. I might be accused of abusing my servants."

He laughed and Mr. Fisk laughed too and swore foully—before looking up and seeing her despite the darkness in which she sat.

"We have company," he said, dropping his voice. "My lady?" He lowered his arms and ducked out of sight.

"Sophie?" Vincent turned unerringly to the staircase, his eyebrows raised.

"Oh." She scrambled to her feet, horribly chagrined. "I am so sorry to disturb you. I was curious."

She had intruded upon a purely masculine domain, she realized too late.

He had found his way to the foot of the stairs, one hand reaching out to touch the wall, and looked up.

"I did wake you after all, then, did I?" he asked. "Forgive me. I tried not to. How long have you been there?"

He started up toward her.

"I have been sitting and watching," she said. "I ought not to have been. I ought to have gone away." The words his valet had just spoken—not intended for a lady's ears, of course—were still ringing in hers. She knew they were foul and profane—she had heard them back in her father's day, though never from her father himself.

He stopped a few stairs below her. His hair was plastered to his head and hanging in wet curls along his neck. He was all sweaty. He ought not to have looked appealing but he did. Though truth to tell, she could hardly see him for the dark.

"We have finished for today," he said.

"I am leaving," she said at the same moment. "I am going to step outside and look around."

"I'll go and get bathed and dressed," he said, "and join you there. The family of one of the scullery maids took in a stray cat a week or so ago but does not know what to do with it, since they already have several of their own. He is a tabby, a bit on the thin and scruffy side, a year or two old, probably not a great beauty."

"Oh," she said, "you asked already?"

"And the cook's brother, one of the tenant farmers," he said, "has a litter of collies. Their mother is a good sheepdog, and the father is one too. They are recently weaned, and all but one of them are spoken for. Perhaps that means he is the runt of the litter, but she assured me he has all his limbs in the right places as well as his eyes and ears and bark."

"And now they are *all* spoken for?" she asked him, clasping her hands to her bosom.

"And now they all are."

She beamed at him.

"I do not want to come any closer to you, Sophie," he said. "I reek. I can even smell myself."

"Yes," she agreed, "you do. I am going."

And she turned and left the cellar.

She was going to have a cat. A thin and scrawny tabby, which was not at all beautiful. She loved him already.

And he was going to have a dog. A sheepdog, which would guide him instead of sheep and give him back much of his freedom. She was sure it could be done.

She smiled at the thought, and the footman, the same one, who was back in the hall, smiled a little uncertainly back at her and opened the double doors when it was obvious to him that she wished to go outside. As though she could not have opened one of them for herself! No one had ever opened doors for her either at Aunt Mary's or at Sir Clarence's.

It was a fresh morning, she discovered, and she would probably be more comfortable wearing a cloak, but she did not want to go all the way back to her dressing room to get it. It did not occur to her to send the footman.

She stood at the top of the steps looking around. The park stretched in every direction, as far as her eye could see and beyond. It was designed for visual splendor and for the leisurely exercise and pleasure of those who could see where they were going. It had certainly not been designed for a blind man. More important, in the three years Vincent had been here, it had not been modified for a blind man's use. Could it be?

She looked about with closer attention.

Vincent stood out on the top step, his cane in his right hand, Sophia's cloak in his left. It was only half past seven or so. The rest of his family would not be up for a while yet.

Martin had been surly, a result of acute embarrassment, Vincent had realized.

"I am not wearing any more than you are," he had said after the cellar door closed behind Sophia. "And she heard what I just said."

"We were two men together with no expectation of being either seen or overheard by any woman," Vincent had reminded him. "She will understand that. I will apologize for you."

Martin had grunted as they left the cellar and had handed Vincent his cane before hurrying off ahead of him to make sure the bathwater had been brought to his dressing room.

"I am here." It was Sophia's voice. "In the parterre garden."

Interestingly, she did not come hurrying toward him to help him find his way there too. Dash it, but he liked that.

He counted twelve steps down and then crossed the graveled terrace—ten medium strides or twelve shuffles. He did it in ten and felt the side of the stone urn, which, with its companion on the other side, formed the entrance to the formal flower gardens. There were no steps here. Nothing to fall down or collide with except the urns themselves.

"Oh, you have brought my cloak," she said from close by. She took it from him. "Thank you. The air is a little brisk." She slipped an arm through his when he offered it. "Do you wish to stroll or sit on the seat here?"

"Stroll," he said and turned them to the right, feeling for the edge of the graveled walk with his cane. "The roses are blooming."

"They smell lovely," she said. "And there are so many

colors, all of them beautiful. I cannot decide which is my favorite."

"The yellow ones," he said.

"Do you think?" He could hear the smile in her voice.

"Sunshine," he said. "To match you."

"That is a very kind compliment," she said.

"What?" he said. "No reference to mirrors and what they tell you when you look in them?"

"I am under orders," she reminded him.

"And I was a *very* ferocious military officer," he said. "Men jumped to my command even before I barked it out."

They both laughed. Ah, yes, he liked having her here with him. Life felt—different.

His cane lost the edge of the path suddenly and discovered only loose soil ahead. A corner. He turned it and strolled south. She had not hauled him about the turn. Bless her heart.

"When you come outside on your own," she said, "what are the bounds of the park?"

"The parterres," he said, "and the topiary garden. I can negotiate them without breaking my neck or feeling as though I had wandered off the edge of the universe. I can find my way to the stables and back too, though I sometimes need my nose and the enticing smell of manure to keep me on course. I am not confined to the house."

He sounded a bit defensive, he thought.

"Perhaps the dog will make the park larger for me after I have trained it," he said, "so that I do not have to call upon you or Martin or my mother when I fancy walking farther afield."

"You may call upon me anytime," she told him. "But you should not need to. Has anyone thought of modifying the park?"

"Modifying?" They had reached another corner. He

turned east. There was a bench just here, positioned to face back toward the house. "Shall we sit for a while?"

"Three more steps," she said.

They sat, and he propped his cane beside him.

"If a graveled path or even a paved one was set out between the terrace and the lake," she said, "and if a fence or a rail was constructed along it, you would be able to walk down there whenever you wished. Do you swim? Yes, of course you do. You used to swim in the river at Barton Coombs—at night. Have you swum here?"

"No," he said, "though I have been out in a boat. Twice."

"All your exercising is done in darkness, then," she said.

"Yes. Always in darkness."

"Oh." She sounded mortified. "I am sorry. But I meant underground as opposed to rooms aboveground, where a window can be opened. Or, better yet, out-doors, where there are all the sounds and smells of nature and nothing but fresh air."

"I walked and climbed and rode in the Lake District," he reminded her. "And rowed. It all felt wonderful. Movement—forward movement—is so much more ex-hilarating than static exercises. We even galloped our horses once, Sophie. You cannot imagine how thrilling that felt. And you cannot imagine how I long to stride out and even *run*."

He frowned at the tone of his own voice. He did not usually allow himself to sound wistful. People who pitied themselves were not particularly attractive to others.

"Oh," she said, "how wonderful it must feel just to *ride*! To be on a horse's back, up on top of the world, being borne along by all that power and beauty."

There was wistfulness in her voice too.

"You have never ridden?" he asked her.

"Never," she said. "But I scandalized Lady Trentham's dressmaker by having a riding outfit made with breeches as well as a skirt. I thought perhaps you could teach me."

"To ride? Astride?" He grinned at her. Who but Sophia would believe a blind man could teach her to ride? "Of course I can. And will."

"And the path to the lake?" she said. "It will not spoil the look of the park, I assure you. Indeed, if it bends with the undulations of the lawn, it will look very attractive. And with a wrought iron rail, it will be elegant. Will you have it built?"

How freeing it would be to be able to walk all the way to the lake and back on his own if he wished. Why had no one thought of such a thing before? Why had *he* not thought of it?

"I will," he said. "I will be seeing my steward this morning. I need to have a talk with him. Many talks, in fact. I need to take more of an active hand in the running of my estate even if the bulk of the work will still be his. I'll mention the path and rail and give the order for it to be started."

"I am to spend the morning with your mother," she told him. "We are to meet with the housekeeper and see the whole house and . . ." Her voice trailed away.

He searched for her hand, found it, and held it.

"My mother will come to love you, Sophie," he said. "She will want to do it for my sake, but she will end up doing it for yours. You must not worry. Please do not. I am not sure she has ever truly enjoyed being mistress here. She was happy at Covington House. She talks about it frequently. All her dearest friends are at Barton Coombs. She came here because she thought I needed her. And she was right. I did. But she will be quite relieved to turn over her responsibilities."

"Will she?"

"Feeling overwhelmed?" he asked.

"We are sitting here," she said, "and I can see the house. It is . . . *vast*. And behind us is the village, and all around us are neighbors who must be called upon and conversed with and invited here. And I am looking over at the state apartments and remembering that there used to be grand entertainments and balls there and that we are now master and mistress here. And I am thinking that we really ought to put on some of those entertainments again, and I am—I do not rightly know *what* I am."

"Overwhelmed." He squeezed her hand. "I know the feeling. But everything does not have to be done in a day, you know. Or even a week or a month. Shall we pay our first visit this afternoon? Just one? To the vicarage, perhaps?"

"Yes," she agreed. "Very well. Perhaps the vicar and his wife are as kind as Mr. and Mrs. Parsons."

"I have met them," he told her. "They are amiable."

He squeezed her hand once more and released it.

"Shall we go in for breakfast?" he suggested. "Ah, and I promised to apologize abjectly on Martin's behalf—both for his appearance this morning and for his particular choice of vocabulary in your hearing."

"It looked to me," she said, "as if you were both thoroughly enjoying yourselves."

"Oh, we were," he assured her. "We always do. There are worse parts of one's body to lose, Sophie, than one's eyes."

Perhaps it was even true. He thought of Ben Harper and the rages he had sometimes been unable to control during those years at Penderris Hall because his legs were useless and unwilling to obey his commands.

He stood and picked up his cane and offered his arm.

"You may inform Mr. Fisk that he is forgiven," she

said, "and you will beg his pardon from me, if you will, for I ought not to have been there. I will not go again. I will respect your privacy and his. You may assure him of that."

Trust Sophia to be concerned about the feelings—and privacy—of a servant. For that was what Martin was officially, though in reality he was Vincent's dearest friend. Or coequal with the Survivors, perhaps, though he spent considerably more time with Martin than he did with them.

16

*T*he first month of her new life at Middlebury Park was exhausting, often bewildering, for Sophia. She learned to find her way about the house; she became acquainted with the servants, particularly the cook and the housekeeper, with whom she had dealings almost every day; she studied household inventory and accounts until she understood them and could even talk intelligently about them; she visited her neighbors with Vincent and was visited in return. She got to know her new family. Ellen and her husband and children had arrived three days after them, and Ursula and her family came one week after that.

She had tramped alone about the huge park and viewed every part of it with a critical eye. Construction of a graveled path to the lake was almost complete despite a wetter-than-usual month. There had once been a wilderness walk through the hills behind the house, she had discovered, though by now it was far more wilderness than walk. It could be cleared out again, though, she decided, made safe and level underfoot, and bounded by a wrought iron rail—or perhaps a more rustic wooden one would be better for terrain that was supposed to resemble a wilderness. And there could be fragrant trees and bushes planted there— rhododendron, lavender, and others. She *wished* she knew more about plants. But fragrant plants would be important since picturesque prospects from the hill over the park and surrounding countryside were not going to mean anything to her husband.

Vincent meanwhile was no passive member of the family and household, as he seemed to have been before his marriage. He spent a great deal of his time closeted with his steward and various tenants or traveling about the estate with the former. And he was becoming acquainted with neighbors he had scarcely known before.

They were doing for each other what they had agreed to do. Sophia was well cared for. She was no longer the mouse, though often she longed to be quiet and alone. She was *Sophia* or *Sophie* or *my lady*. And Vincent was no longer cosseted at every turn. Soon he would be able to move about far more freely.

Their marriage could be deemed a success. And there were the times they spent alone together, though they seemed rare enough to Sophia—except for the nights, of course, which had continued lovely. She had even accepted the incredible fact that he found her attractive.

One afternoon Vincent's sisters and their families had taken a picnic tea to a castle a few miles distant, and Vincent and Sophia were in the music room, where he had been giving her a lesson on the pianoforte. It had not been much more successful than the others, though she had learned how to pick out a correct major scale no matter which note she began on. Why there had to be both white and black notes to confuse the issue, she did not know.

Miss Debbins, Vincent's music teacher, was spending some time with her brother in Shropshire, though she was due back soon. Vincent was sure she would be delighted to take on Sophia as a pupil too.

"More than delighted actually," he had said. "You can *see* and she will be able to teach you to read music. She has had to be endlessly patient and inventive with me."

He was playing his violin now while Sophia sketched fairies at the bottom of a garden. She found them more difficult to do than a dragon and a mouse but not as difficult as Bertha and Dan, who never looked on paper quite as she imagined them in her head. But she would persevere. The children loved the stories she and Vincent told them almost every evening, and they screamed with glee over the pictures.

Once in a while she stopped to watch her husband and to stroke a hand over Tab's back. Her scrawny, ugly tabby cat had turned sleek in the weeks he had been here.

Shep was not living with them yet. When the farmer who owned the dog had known what Viscount Darleigh wanted it for, he had insisted that the animal would need some basic training first and that he was the best one to do it, since he had a lifetime of experience. Once that was done, then he would come over daily, with his lordship's permission, and together they would work out the finer points of the training while dog and master familiarized themselves with each other.

He was enthusiastic about the idea and did not see any reason why it would not work though he had never trained a dog for just such a purpose before.

"If a dog can be trained to respond to a whistle or a shout of command and take a whole herd of sheep to a particular spot over a long distance and past all sorts of obstacles and even through narrow gateways," he had said, "then there is no reason he cannot do it for a man holding his leash, is there? I'll stake my reputation on it as the best sheepdog trainer in the county. And no one ever accused me of modesty." He had laughed heartily and pumped Vincent's hand up and down and beamed at Sophia.

"That sounds a good enough guarantee to me, Mr. Croft," Vincent had said. "Thank you."

"Ouch!" Sophia said now as he played a sour note. He was trying to learn something Ellen had played over and over for him on the pianoforte last evening, something by Beethoven.

He lowered his violin.

"Tab is not howling," he said. "My playing cannot be that bad, Sophie."

"I heard one bad note out of how many?" she said. "Five hundred? Of course, one bad note is all it takes to ruin the effect of the whole thing."

"A critical audience is all I need," he grumbled, "when I am trying to learn something new. My repertoire is woefully small."

"Play it again," she told him, "and play that note correctly."

"Yes, ma'am."

She smiled as she sketched an upturned flowerpot with a little door and a round window with checked curtains fluttering out of it—a fairy shelter. A fairy wand propped the door open. She loved teasing him—and being teased. They liked each other. It was a wonderfully warming feeling. It sustained her through days that were frequently not easy for her. His family was kind, even affectionate, and they were careful to defer to her as Vincent's wife. She liked them all, without exception.

But they were not her *own* family.

Only Vincent was her own.

She liked almost all the neighbors they had met. And those people seemed actually glad to know them. They looked with sympathy and some admiration upon Vincent, who was well able to be charming. And they received her with deference, as though she were doing them some honor. How could she *not* like them all?

The viscount before the last—Vincent's grandfather—had opened the park to all comers once a week, they had been told by some of their older neighbors, so that everyone could enjoy strolling on the lawns and having a picnic by the lake and relaxing in the summerhouse and trudging up over the hills. Vincent had suggested that it happen again, and Sophia had agreed with him— and added the suggestion that perhaps next summer they would organize a picnic for everyone, with games and contests and entertainments and prizes. The neighborhood was apparently already abuzz with both items of news. The park was to be open on Saturdays as soon as the lake path had been completed.

It was only afterward that it struck Sophia—she might not be here next summer.

Someone had mentioned too the grand balls that had occasionally been put on in the state apartments, and Sophia herself had promised that they would happen again. Perhaps even this year, Vincent had added. Perhaps after the harvest, when everyone would be in a mood to celebrate if the crops were good, as they showed every promise of being.

As with their storytelling, they seemed to thrive upon building on each other's ideas. But how *on earth* was she to go about planning a harvest ball and a summer picnic—if she was here to plan it, that was? Sometimes she almost lost her courage. But she would not allow herself to do that. She had been given this one chance to . . . to *live* her life, and she would not squander it.

She had had a few riding lessons. She had worn her breeches, to the obvious shock of her mother-in-law and the amusement of Vincent's grandmother. So far she had ridden only a quiet pony and only in the paddock behind the stables. Vincent had taught her how to check the pony over, and he had taught her how to mount and sit correctly. He had adjusted the stirrups so that her feet fit comfortably in them. He had taught her how to hold the reins and what they were for—they were *not* to clutch as though her life depended upon not letting them go. She had felt alarmingly far off the ground—and he had laughed when she had said so and reminded her that she was on the back of a *pony.* He had walked her about the paddock, his free hand trailing along the fence. After a while, he had let her go on her own. But of course, the head groom had kept a very careful eye upon her, as he had from the start. Vincent had taught her how to dismount. By now she was mounting and riding alone, but still only in the paddock and with both the groom and Vincent hovering over her.

She was proud of herself nevertheless and exhilarated by her own courage. But how could anyone be reckless enough to climb onto the back of a real horse and coax it into a *gallop* or even a canter?

All her new clothes had arrived from London, and Rosina had gone into raptures over them as she unpacked them and hung them lovingly in the wardrobe or folded them neatly into drawers.

"Enough for one day," Vincent said now, lowering his violin. "I am going to have to beg Ellen to play that piece again so that I know I am learning it correctly. I would not want to do poor Beethoven a greater disservice than I am doing him anyway by choosing his music. Once I have it properly learned, then I will be able to enjoy it and start to feel it. I will awe you with my talent. Can you swim?"

"No." She was woefully lacking in accomplishments.

"Do you want to learn?"

"Now?"

"It is not raining again, is it?" he asked. "Amy and Ellen were convinced the sun was going to shine all day."

"It is still fine out there," she said. "I think I am a little afraid of water."

"All the more reason to learn to swim," he said. "On the far side of the island the land slopes gradually into the lake, or so Martin told me when we went there once. The water is likely to be shallow enough back there not to terrify you. Of course, we would have to get to the island. Can you row a boat?"

"No." She laughed.

"Then I will have to do it." He grinned at her as he put his violin in its case and snapped it shut. "That should be an adventure."

"I will close my eyes and cover them with my hands," she said, "so that I will not see disaster looming."

"Me too," he said. "Let us go and get some towels."

"What are we going to swim *in*?" she asked him.

"Apart from water?" He raised his eyebrows. "I suppose you can swim in your shift if you are afraid I will see too much should you not wear even that. Leave your stays behind, though."

Tab jumped down from the love seat and accompanied them back to their own apartments, darting ahead and then waiting for them to catch up. He took up residence on the sunniest windowsill in their sitting room while they went upstairs to get ready.

It was indeed a lovely day. A group of gardeners were erecting the wrought iron rail beside the pathway to the lake. Sophia took Vincent's arm and they walked farther out onto the lawn before turning down toward the boathouse.

"Are you feeling more in command of your own estate than you used to be?" she asked.

"I am," he told her. "Oh, I know my people are always going to make sure that I am well protected from everything that poses even the slightest threat to my person, from raging bulls on down to pecking chickens. But I have insisted upon knowing what is going on with my farms, and I have insisted upon being taken about in the gig to see for myself, as it were, and to talk to my people. I still feel very stupid when I ask questions whose answers must seem glaringly obvious to them, but I will keep asking. Only so I can get to the point at which I do not need to ask. I shall grow into a very dull squire, Sophie, who can discuss nothing more interesting with his guests than the price of corn or the newest sheep-shearing methods."

"*Are* there different methods?" she asked.

"I have not the faintest idea."

They both laughed.

"Mrs. Jones has asked me to be honorary president of the women's sewing circle," she said. Mr. Jones was the vicar.

"No!" He stopped walking to look in her direction in mock astonishment. "Is that a huge honor, Sophie?"

"Well, you may make a joke if it," she said, "but I am sure it is just that. Not strictly an honor, perhaps, but a reaching out. So few people have ever reached out to me. I do not quite know what the 'honorary' part means, of course. I shall have to ask. If it merely means that they can throw out my name and title to dazzle women's groups from other villages, then I shall decline. But if they want me to sit in their circle sewing with them, then I shall accept, even though my skill with a needle is nothing to boast of. I have never, *ever* had a woman friend. Not that the women here will want to be my bosom friends, I suppose. They will think, very foolishly, that I am too far above them. But friendly acquaintances, let us say."

She was babbling a bit and they had still not resumed walking. And actually Lady Trentham had written to her several times and was in the way of becoming her friend. But at a distance.

"Oh, Sophie," he said, "I am sorry. I have Martin—and yes, he is a friend and has been since my childhood—

and I have the Survivors, and there are numerous friends at Barton Coombs I have neglected for six years. I had not thought that of course I am not enough for you."

"Oh, that is not—" she began.

"No, I know it is not what you meant," he said. "But I do not think you would be enough for me either, Sophie."

She felt a stabbing of hurt and disappointment. And there it was. The reminder that they would never be all in all to each other, that despite their easy companionship, they would never really be even friends, let alone . . .

"We all need friends or at least friendly acquaintances of our own sex," he said. "There is a different sort of relationship with friends of one's own sex than with someone of the opposite sex, and it is one we all ought to cultivate. What I mean is that I understand and am glad for you, Sophie. I am sure you will enjoy the sewing circle. And the quality of your silence suggests to me that I am digging a deeper hole for myself with every word I speak. I have not hurt you, have I?"

"No, of course not," she said. "I am the one who said I wish to join the sewing circle because I want the companionship of other women."

There was a brief silence, during which neither of them moved.

"I like your companionship too," he said. "We rub along well enough together, do we not?"

He looked a bit anxious.

We rub along well enough . . .

Yes, they did. She smiled a little sadly.

"We do," she said. "Shall we face the terror of the boat ride? Or shall we stand here for the rest of the afternoon?"

"Oh, the boat ride, by all means." He offered his arm

again. "Just be thankful that we do not have a whole ocean to cross."

"We might discover a new continent," she said.

"Atlantis?"

"Or something completely unknown," she said. "But for this afternoon I think I shall be happy just to reach that island safely."

"You have put yourself into capable hands," he told her.

"It is not your hands I am concerned about," she said.

He laughed as they resumed walking.

Sophia felt a bit like crying.

Sophia ought to have been far more worried than she was, considering the fact that she could not swim. But she was too busy giving instructions to feel nervous. He was rowing with great energy and skill, except that he had no sense of direction, of course. At first it did not seem to matter as long as he pulled in the general direction of the island, but she could see after they were out on the water that there was a little jetty for them to pull into. Elsewhere the bank looked rather steep.

With his skill and her guidance they landed safely, and he climbed out and took the rope from her hand and tied it to a stout post.

"Madam?" He bowed and offered his hand, for which she was thankful. The boat had swayed alarmingly when she had tried to climb out unassisted.

"Oh, goodness," she said. "And later we have to row back again."

"We?" He waggled his eyebrows at her and bent to feel around for the towels. "Or you can swim home if you prove to be a more than usually adept pupil."

She took the towels from him and slipped a hand through his arm. He had left his cane in the boathouse.

"I believe the temple was built as a folly purely for picturesque effect when viewed from the house," he told her as they made their way up to it. "However, a former viscountess, or perhaps it was her mother—one of my ancestors, anyway—was a pious soul, or so I have been told, and made it into a little shrine. She was Catholic."

Sure enough, there was a door on the temple and stained glass windows, and inside there was a crucifix on the wall and candles and an old leather-bound prayer book on a table beneath it. There was a chair beside it, a rosary hooked over the back. Nothing else. There was no room for more.

"I wonder if the lady rowed," she said.

"Or swam."

"I daresay," she said, "she had a faithful retainer who brought her across whenever she wished to come. Our ancestors always had faithful retainers, did they not?"

"If they lived in stories they did," he agreed. "I wonder how Martin would like the title of faithful retainer."

Sunlight was beaming through one of the windows and casting multicolored light over everything. The effect was glorious.

"It smells a bit musty in here," he said.

"Yes," she agreed. "Where is this shallow water?"

It was behind the temple, on the far side of the island, where the land sloped more gently into the lake than it did on the near side. Sophia still did not like the look of it.

"Perhaps," she said, "we should just sit and sun ourselves. That rowing looked like strenuous business."

"Was clutching the sides of the boat with whitened knuckles just as strenuous?" he asked her.

"There is *no way*," she retorted, "you could have seen that, even if it were true, which it is not. What are you doing?"

It was a foolish question to ask since there was nothing wrong with her eyesight. He was undressing.

"Have no fear." He looked her way, grinning. "I shall leave on my drawers entirely to save your blushes. And you may leave on your shift lest I peep."

She opened her mouth to argue and shut it again. He was not going to be moved, was he? And if he was going to go in the water, she had to go with him. He could not *see*. Sometimes she almost forgot that.

She undressed down to her shift. Why did being unclothed, and not even fully unclothed, seem far more wicked outdoors than it did in their bedchamber? There was no danger of being watched. There was no vantage point from which they could conveniently be seen even if someone had been looking for them.

Sunlight lit him up like a god—a very fond and foolish thought. But if there was any muscle in his body that was not fully developed and honed through frequent and strenuous exercise, she had certainly not seen it. And yet he was slender and slight of build and not particularly tall. It was a good thing for her that he was not.

He was perfect.

"You are very quiet," he said. "Are you cowering?"

No, just admiring.

She took a few steps toward him and set her hand in his.

She had expected the water to be cold. She had steeled herself against the shock. It was—

"It is *freezing*!"

"It is rather," he agreed. "It feels quite chilly on the ankles. I wonder how it will feel on the knees and the hips."

They soon found out. The land dipped more sharply than had been apparent. It was a thousand times worse.

Sophia gasped and did not know how to expel the breath.

"I think we should go b-b-b-back," she managed to say through chattering teeth.

Without letting go of her hand, he held his nose with his free hand and went straight under until only his hair was wafting on the surface. He came up again and shook his head. Droplets of icy water rained on Sophia's shoulders.

"Ah," he said. "It is better under than out. Or will be."

He went down again and reemerged moments later.

"It is better under," he said. "Trust me. Is that your teeth I hear clacking?"

Hardly. She had them too tightly clamped together.

"Oh, bother," she said and bent her knees and went straight down until she felt the water close above her head.

She came up sputtering.

"Liar!" she cried. "Oh, liar."

He was laughing.

"Under," he said, grasping her other hand. "At least up to your neck. Let your body adjust to the water's temperature. Oh, Sophie, this feels *so* good."

Despite her own discomfort, she looked fully at him. His hair was plastered to his head, water droplets were running down his face, his eyes were wide open, and he looked radiant. Carefree. Her heart melted.

She went under until the water covered her shoulders. Already it felt not quite so cold. Sunlight danced across its surface. How lovely, how freeing it must be to be able to swim.

"Come," he said. "Let us go a little deeper, and I'll teach you to float."

"Oh," she said, "I wish it were possible, but I fear it is not."

But she waded deeper with him just because of that look on his face. He was enjoying this so much.

"Oh, ye of little faith," he said. "Lie on the water. I'll hold you. Like this. No, no need to cling or bring up your knees. That is the surest way to sink like a stone. Stretch along the water. Put your head back. Reach out your arms. Now relax. I won't let you go. Just relax. Imagine you are on the softest, most comfortable of mattresses."

It was incredibly difficult to relax, knowing there was only water beneath her—and his hands. It *did* feel lovely, though. And she trusted those hands and his word that he would not let her go.

She kept her eyes tightly closed.

"You are not fully relaxed," he told her.

Well, there were the muscles that were holding her eyes clenched. And stomach muscles too, she discovered when she mentally checked them.

She opened her eyes and turned her head a fraction. His head was half bent over her. And—

Oh, *God,* she loved him.

She stared up at him, shaken—and yet relaxed.

For of course she loved him. He had rescued her. He had married her. And he was beautiful and sweet and kind. It would be very strange if she did *not* love him. It was not such an earth-shattering revelation.

And it made no difference to anything.

Except to make her heart hurt a little bit more.

"There," he said softly. "Now you have it. Trust yourself. Trust the water."

And she felt his hands slide away from beneath her.

She kept her eyes on his face. She did not sink. And she did not need his hands. She would never allow herself to need them. Or him, except in a purely material way, for she would starve without his support. But not in any other way. She might *want*, but there was a difference between wanting and needing.

She could float alone.

She could live alone.

He floated beside her, his hand occasionally touching hers, and she looked up at the sky. It was a vast, deep blue, with a few puffs of white cloud.

So relaxed. So beautiful. With a dull ache in the throat.

She turned her head to look at him, swallowed a mouthful of water, and scrambled and splashed her way to her feet. The water came to her chin. They must have floated outward. There was a moment of near-panic as she coughed and waded closer to the shore, drawing him by the hand.

"You must have floated on your own for all of five minutes," he said. "Well done. Once you can float, you can learn to swim in a trice."

"Not today, though," she said. "Allow me to bask in the triumph of one mighty achievement at a time."

"I am going to swim," he said, and he turned back into the water and began to swim away into the lake with powerful strokes.

Sophia, standing knee-deep and watching, could almost feel his pleasure.

But how was he going to find his way back, foolish man? He did not have Mr. Fisk beside him today.

She left the water and wrapped a towel about her shoulders. But she did not sit down or take her eyes off him. She shaded them with one hand against the sun.

17

*F*or several minutes Vincent knew what a bird or a wild animal must feel like when it escaped from its cage. He expended all his pent-up energy on the exercise, reveling in his freedom and the power of his own muscles and the cool wonder of the water.

It was a euphoria that did not last, of course. For even though at first even the absence of Martin added to his exuberance, it did not take him long to realize how reckless he had been.

Where was he exactly? How was he to get back to the island? He had no idea how far he had swum or in which direction.

He stopped swimming and trod water. He could not feel the bottom. The temptation was to panic. But panic was not going to do him any good, and this was not like the familiar attacks that assaulted him out of nowhere and for no discernible reason. This was a potential panic based upon reality. It was something under his control.

The comforting thought flashed through his mind that at worst he could swim until he collided with a bank. He would not know where on the bank he was, but he could at least climb out and wait for someone to find him. It was not as though no one knew whereabouts he was.

But poor Sophia would be stranded on the island.

He would feel an idiot—at the very least.

"I am here," Sophia's voice called from what seemed a considerable distance away.

The trouble was that outdoors it was not so easy to know exactly where a voice was coming from, especially when it was some distance away.

"Here," she yelled.

He chose a direction and swam.

"To your left," she called and he adjusted his course.

It took a while. But she guided him in with a voice that gradually diminished from a yell to a volume not far above a speaking voice.

"You ought to be able to touch the bottom now," she said at last. "Wade to your left. I am here."

She did not come to get him. He was thankful for that.

Had he frightened her? He would wager he had.

When his feet were on firm, dry ground, she threw a towel about his shoulders.

"Oh, I do look forward to the day when I can swim even half as well as you," she said. "It must be the loveliest feeling in the world."

And yet there was a slight tremor in her voice.

"Thank you for guiding me in," he said. "Without you, I might have landed on the far bank and wandered off to the most distant corner of the park."

"I did not fancy rowing myself home," she said. "Though it is actually lovely back there, Vincent. I thought there were only trees beyond the lake, but they must have been planted for pictorial effect, so that they would reflect in the water. Beyond them are more lawns and an alley and summerhouse. There is more space than anyone would know what to do with. Though I have an idea."

There was still a tremor in her voice. She knew he had been in potential trouble. And she could neither have come to his rescue nor run for help.

"Oh?" he said as he toweled himself dry. "What?"

"I am not going to tell you," she said. "It is a secret. A surprise. Maybe just foolishness, though I think it can be done."

"I hate surprises when I have to wait to know what they are," he told her.

She laughed. She had sat down on the grass, he realized. He spread his towel and stretched out beside her.

"I am sorry, Sophie," he said after a minute or two.

"Sorry?"

"For causing you anxiety," he said. "For forcing you to keep an eagle eye on me while I was out there frolicking. It was irresponsible of me. It will not happen again."

"Oh, you must not make such promises," she said. "You may feel obliged to keep them. I know just how you felt."

"Do you?" He turned his head her way.

"Some people climb impossible mountains," she said. "Some people go exploring impossible places. And they do it for no better reason than that they simply cannot ignore the challenge of danger or of attempting the seemingly impossible. Sometimes you cannot resist the urge to be free of your sightlessness or at least to push it to its limits."

"Perhaps," he said meekly, "I simply wanted to swim."

"Oh. So much for my fine speech." She laughed.

Martin would not have made excuses for him. He would have called him a string of names, none of them complimentary—and he would have meant every one of them.

He felt good after the exercise, though—a different sort of good from what he always felt after a session in the cellar. And he felt drowsy. He could smell grass and water. Birds were singing at a distance, probably among the trees on the far bank. There were insects chirping and whirring closer at hand. Somewhere a bee droned.

Life at its sweetest.

Fingers, warm and feather light, moved damp hair back from his forehead. He lay very still until they were gone again. She was sitting rather than lying beside him. She must be looking down at him.

Marrying her had been a good move, he realized. He was always able to relax with her. He enjoyed their conversations. He loved her humor. He was comfortable with her. He liked her. He believed she liked him. He enjoyed having sex with her.

How foolish they had been to imagine that dreams conceived when they were both single and none too happy would survive a marriage that was bringing them a great deal of contentment.

He hoped those dreams were well and truly dead and would never be referred to again.

He turned his head her way and reached out a hand. It encountered her bare knees, and he realized that she was kneeling up beside him and looking down at him.

Why?

"Sophie," he said.

She took his hand in both of hers.

Something blocked out the sunshine on his face and she kissed him.

If there was a sweeter mouth to kiss than Sophia's, he could not imagine it. He wound his arms about her, and she collapsed down half over him and spread her hands on his shoulders. They kissed warmly, lazily for a while, their tongues exploring, their teeth gently nipping. Enjoying each other.

"Mm," he said.

"Mm," she agreed.

"I suppose," he said, "every gardener in my employ and a few of the indoor servants for good measure are lined up about the perimeter of the lake enjoying the show?"

"Not a single one," she said. "They would have to hack their way through the jungle across from us and we have the folly behind us."

"We are quite private, then?"

"Yes." Her lips were touching his. "Quite private."

He reached down to remove his drawers, but she was kneeling up beside him again, and her fingers went beneath the band and pulled them downward for him. He lifted his hips, and she slid them all the way off.

When had she grown so bold?

She bent over him and kissed his navel. She moved her lips upward, kissing him as she went until she kissed his lips again.

Mm indeed!

"The ground would not make a soft mattress for your back, Sophie," he said. "Come on top of me."

He was very unadventurous, he realized with a little twinge of shame. Their lovemaking had never seemed routine or monotonous. Every encounter had been different from every other. Yet she had always lain on her back. He had always come on top of her. He would never win any prizes as one of the world's most innovative lovers.

He drew her over him, and she lay on him, small and sweetly warm and smelling of lake water and summer heat. He kissed her again and moved his hands down over her bottom to grasp her upper thighs and spread her legs on either side of his own. Her shift was not a long one. She wore nothing beneath.

She bent her knees and raised herself onto them. She lifted her body too so that she was kneeling astride him.

He felt rather as if someone must have dropped a few more logs onto the sun to make its fire blaze higher. He felt as if he had relinquished some control, and he hardened into further arousal, if that was possible. He bent his own knees and slid his feet up the grass. He set his hands on her hips to position her.

But she was already touching him, the fingers of both hands moving over him so lightly that he thought he might well go mad. He tipped back his chin, pressed his head into the grass, and let her lead the way.

She drew him into position against herself, and she came down onto him in one firm, smooth motion. He almost disgraced himself and came in her without any further ado.

She made a low sound deep in her throat.

She lifted herself off almost to the brink and came down again—and repeated and repeated the motion until she was riding him with firm, sure rhythm. She was working inner muscles into it too, and after a few moments she rotated her hips in time with the ride.

This was *Sophie*?

If he ignored the near pain of being so fully aroused, and he *did* ignore it for a while, the pleasure was exquisite. She was hot and wet and pulsing about him.

He pushed into her descents and withdrew to her ascents and matched her move for move until he felt her break rhythm, felt that she was reaching for something she did not know or understand. He grasped her hips more firmly and drove upward and withdrew and drove and held. She tensed and cried out and came all to pieces about him. And he drove again with reckless energy until he followed her into that glorious state of sexual release.

She was still up on her knees. He moved his hands to her waist and brought her down to lie on top of him. He straightened her legs on either side of his. He threaded his fingers through her hair and held one side of her face against his shoulder.

Good God!

"Happy?" he asked her.

"Mm," she mumbled against his shoulder.

He rather believed they had both dozed off when he woke up to feel less than comfortable.

"Sophie?"

"Mm?"

"We are horribly hot and sweaty, are we not?" he said.

They were quite slick with wetness. Even her shift was clammy.

"Mm."

"Up, then, woman," he said, "and lead me to water."

He splashed her when they were waist deep, and she splashed him back. She had the advantage, of course, because she could see what she was aiming at. On the other hand, he was able to swim beneath the water and clip her behind the knees so that she fell under and came up sputtering.

He slapped her on the back and wrapped an arm about her shoulders.

"Do you plan to survive?" he asked her.

"If I can ever stop coughing," she said, and coughed again. "Did I swallow the whole lake?"

"I can't tell," he said. "I can't see."

"But you can feel." And her left foot got him behind his own knees when he was least expecting it, and he made the personal discovery that she had not, in fact, swallowed the whole of the lake.

She was laughing—really quite gleefully—instead of commiserating when he came up.

*M*iss Debbins was quite a miracle worker. After two music lessons and an hour a day of practice between times, Sophia was able to make sense of the lines and symbols and little notes with their variously feathered tails on a sheet of music. More important, she was able to reproduce the sounds of those notes on the keyboard of the pianoforte and even play with two hands. That seemed impossible to her at first, when each hand was expected to play something different, but it *was* possible even though she was playing but the simplest of exercises.

Moreover, Miss Debbins had the patience to help Vincent improve on the harp to the point at which he could play some simple melodies without making a single mistake.

The playing of music would never be her first love, though, Sophia soon realized. She persevered because she could and because she was so lacking in the accomplishments expected of any lady. And because a musical instrument created sound, lovely, harmonious sound if it was played properly, and sound was of such importance to her husband.

Her first love could never bring him joy, except that he *did* enjoy her talking about it. Her first love would always be sketching. Miss Debbins had brought back with her from her brother's house a younger widowed sister, who was intending to live permanently with her. And Agnes Keeping was a painter. She worked primarily with watercolors, and her favored subject matter was wildflowers. Sophia found her work quite exquisite, and Agnes marveled over Sophia's caricatures and laughed with delight over her story illustrations, especially when she read the stories to go with them. Sophia was careful to explain that the stories themselves were joint efforts with Vincent, except for the original dragon and mouse story, for which he was the sole author.

"What a gift you and your husband have," Agnes said. "It is actually a shame that only Lord Darleigh's nieces and nephews ever see these pictures and hear these stories. And they will be returning to their own homes within the week, you say? These little books of yours ought to be published."

Sophia laughed, pleased.

"I have a cousin," Agnes said. "Well, actually he is my late husband's cousin. He lives in London. He— Well. I will write to him, with your permission. May I?"

"Of course." Sophia closed her books. Agnes had not explained why the cousin might be interested in them, and she did not ask. She left the original Bertha and Dan story with Agnes when she returned home.

Agnes became her first real friend.

And the ladies of the sewing group became her first friendly acquaintances even though Sophia felt quite intimidated by the fact that they all, without exception, were far finer needlewomen than she. Actually, though, it seemed to her that that very fact endeared her to them, for they were all eager to help her and teach her and praise her efforts, and she did indeed improve under their expert guidance. She even started to enjoy plying her needle.

Vincent had been right in what he had said that afternoon when they had rowed to the island, she came to realize. Everyone needed friends of their own sex.

He had started to make definite friends among their neighbors. Mr. Harrison, a married gentleman no more than a few years older than Vincent—his wife was a member of the sewing circle—took him fishing one day with a few other gentlemen, and somehow they all devised a way for him to fish quite effectively. And Mr. Harrison had started to come to the house every few days to read the papers to Vincent, and the two of them would sit afterward, discussing politics and economics.

It was not, however, as if she and Vincent had drifted apart. They often sat alone together in their private sitting room in the late evenings, and they sometimes walked out together or practiced together in the music room. Once they went riding together, though they were not alone that time. The head groom hovered near Sophia, and Mr. Fisk rode beside Vincent. It was a lovely memory, though, because Vincent had been happy and carefree, and she had been exhilarated by her own daring, even though Vincent had told her if they crawled any more slowly they would be moving backward.

Sophia was returning on foot one afternoon from a sewing session when she saw Mr. Fisk striding alone from the stables toward the house. He had probably been watching the training session with Shep back in the paddocks. Mr. Croft was coming over every day now that the dog was nearly trained, and he and Vincent were growing more and more accustomed to each other and more and more able to move about as one harmonious unit. The only thing Sophia had found a trifle disappointing at first was Mr. Croft's firm directive that the dog was never to be considered a family pet, that he was never to be petted by anyone except Vincent or encouraged to follow anyone about or to sit with anyone except him.

It made perfect sense, of course. If the dog was easily distracted, then he could not be trusted to be Vincent's eyes at all times and under all circumstances.

Mr. Fisk nodded his head in Sophia's direction and would have hurried into the house before she came up to him.

"Mr. Fisk," she called. "Please wait."

She never knew if he liked her or not. She was a bit frightened of him, if the truth were told, though not in any physical sense. He would never harm her or talk disrespectfully to her. But old habits of mind did not die easily. Of course, he was deeply attached to Vincent, and he had definitely not thought her a worthy bride for his master and friend at first. She did not know if he still felt that way. It did not matter—except that, of course, it did.

He raised his eyebrows and stopped walking.

"It is going well?" she asked. "With Shep?"

"Croft thinks his job here is at an end, my lady," he said. "His lordship went all the way to the lake and back just now without anyone except the dog and without touching the handrail even once."

"The handrail is unnecessary, then?" she asked him.

"No, my lady," he said. "Anything that can help his lordship to a greater bit of freedom is worth having, and it is not wise for him to depend fully upon just one person or thing. People can die. So can dogs. Fences can fall down."

"I wanted to ask your advice," she said.

He looked at her a little warily.

"Now that the path has been finished," she said, "work will soon begin on clearing the wilderness walk and making it safe for my husband and fragrant too for his pleasure. The head gardener has suggested planting herbs as well as suitable trees and shrubbery. But I have another scheme in my head that may be utterly foolish and impractical. Anyone who hears it may well laugh at me. But *you* will know if it is foolish."

She bit her lower lip, but he said nothing. He just looked steadily back at her. He was intimidatingly large and broad.

"There is nothing much inside the wall along the east side of the park," she said. "Just grass, really, for the full two-mile stretch. And on the south side, the woods do not stretch all the way to the east wall. There is at least half a mile of bare land. In the north too the hills do not extend back all the way to the wall. There is a wide band of level land behind them. Altogether, you could walk along inside the wall, starting in the south, all the way around to the northwest corner without meeting any significant obstacle. That is almost five miles."

She knew. She had walked the whole distance one drizzly afternoon when Vincent was busy with his steward and none of his sisters fancied exercise in the outdoors.

"My lady?" He was looking mystified.

"Race tracks curve, do they not?" she asked him. "When horses race, they do not usually run a straight course from start to finish. They would run around curves without guidance, would they not, if none was given? Rather than keep running straight ahead, I mean, and crashing into the guard rail."

"If the curve was gentle enough." He was frowning. "Is that what you are thinking of, my lady?"

"Yes," she said. "Is it possible, do you think, Mr. Fisk? He could ride there without danger and for a considerable distance. He could even gallop. And if there is a rail on either side of the course, as there would have to be, he could run there too. He could run five miles if he wanted without stopping. Ten if he ran both ways."

He was looking full into her face, full into her eyes. She could not read his expression. He was a typical servant in that way.

"Is it a foolish idea?" She bit her lip again.

"Have you asked him?" he wanted to know.

She shook her head. "Not yet."

"The gardeners could not do it on their own," he said, frowning. "A whole lot more workers would have to be hired. It would cost a fortune."

"He *has* a fortune."

For a moment his lips twitched and he almost smiled. He surprised her then.

"You love him?" he asked, his voice abrupt, even harsh.

It was an impertinent question, but it did not occur to

her to reprimand him or even feel offended. She opened her mouth to reply and closed it again.

"He is my husband, Mr. Fisk," she said.

He nodded.

"It sounds possible to me," he said. "But what do I know? It also sounds like a huge project. It would be a dream come true for him, though, wouldn't it?"

"Yes," she said. "Thank you."

She turned sharply in the direction of the stables, leaving him standing there, staring after her. She felt flustered. He would think her an idiot. But—

It would be a dream come true for him, though, wouldn't it?

The training session was over, it seemed. Vincent and Mr. Croft were standing at the far side of the stable block, talking. Shep, the black and white sheepdog, was sitting quiet but alert beside Vincent, who held the short leash in his hand. Mr. Croft was just out of sight beyond the buildings.

". . . with its handrail was all your lady's idea," he was saying. "As well as the dog. And now the wilderness walk to be smoothed out and railed for you too?"

"I am very fortunate," Vincent said as Sophia slowed her footsteps, smiling.

"You have a whole houseful of ladies to look after your every need," Mr. Croft said. "What man would not envy you, my lord?" He laughed heartily.

"Yes." Vincent laughed with him. "Always women to look after me. And now my wife too. But gradually I am freeing myself. Or, to be fair, my wife is devising ways to free me."

And then Sophia wished she had not slowed down in order to hear good things about herself.

And now my wife too.

But gradually I am freeing myself.

He had not said he resented her. Quite the contrary.

He had given her credit for helping give him more freedom of movement.

And she had done it deliberately. At the start, she had
set out to repay him for all he had done for her by finding ways to make his blindness less irksome.

Had she succeeded all too well?

Oh, she did not want to think about that wretched
arrangement they had made. And he had told her not
to. But that did not mean it did not exist, did it? He very
obviously still longed for freedom.

"Good afternoon, my lady," Mr. Croft said as she
came into sight. He raised his hat to her and smiled and
inclined his head.

Vincent turned his face to her and smiled warmly.

"Sophie?" he said. "Did you enjoy your sewing
group?"

"I did," she told him. "Julia Stockwell brought her
new baby, and we spent as much time cooing over her as
we did sewing. Why do babies always have that effect
upon people, do you think? Is it nature's way of ensur-
ing that they are never neglected? How do you do, Mr.
Croft? Has Mrs. Croft recovered from her scalded
hand?"

"The marks are still there, my lady," he told her, "but
the worst of the pain seems to have gone. Thank you. I
shall tell her you asked. I think you had a winning idea
here, my lady. This dog took my lord all the way to the
lake and back just now without any mishap. And him
still very young."

"I believe, Mr. Croft," she said, "that when you described yourself as the best dog trainer in the county,
you did not exaggerate."

"Thank you, my lady," he said. "And today the dog
stops here."

"He does," Vincent said. "You will not be taking my

eyes home with you any longer, Croft. I need them with me."

Mr. Croft went into the stable block to retrieve his horse and gig, and Sophia and Vincent began the walk back to the house. There was no cane in sight. Only Shep beside his master. Sophia did not take his arm as she usually did.

My eyes.

"Sophie," he said, reaching for her hand, "how can I ever thank you?"

"For telling you about Lizzie and her dog?" she said. "But why would I keep it a secret?"

"And there is the path to the lake," he said. "And soon there will be the wilderness walk. There are to be herbs there, are there, and fragrant trees? Whose idea was that?"

"The trees were mine. I did not think of herbs, but they will work marvelously well. I think you will enjoy strolling there. And I have another idea," she added with a heavy heart. "I shall tell you about it later."

"The grand secret?" he said. "The one you mentioned at the lake?"

"Mr. Fisk thinks it is a good idea," she told him.

"Martin?" He turned his head her way. "You have spoken to him?"

"Just now."

"I am glad." He smiled. "He thinks you are good for me, you know. The first time or two he said it, he sounded almost grudging. Now he does not. He approves of you and admits that I made a good choice."

"Oh," she said, but the praise did not lift her spirits.

She was just another woman in his life. He loved his mother and grandmother and sisters, and she believed he was fond of her. But even so—just another woman to come between him and the independence he craved.

Shep stopped by the steps, and when Vincent stopped

too, the dog turned in front of him, led him to the bottom step and stopped again, and then led him up.

"We will go to the drawing room, will we?" Vincent asked when they were inside. "Is it teatime? We have not missed it, have we?"

"No," Sophia assured him. "I was careful to return in time. Everyone is at home today. We will miss everyone when they leave."

"I think they are all relieved and disappointed in equal measure," he told her. "Relieved that you are the wife they have always wanted for me, and disappointed that they are no longer needed to organize my life for me."

No. There was Sophia to do it for them.

Mr. Croft had spent the past two days in the house with Shep, training him to take Vincent to all the rooms he most frequented. He led them now through the hall and up the staircase and into the drawing room, where they were met with a chorus of boisterous greetings. Everyone was there, including all five children, all between the ages of two and five. Ellen's Caroline and Ursula's Percival were playing with Tab—Sophia had given permission earlier for them to fetch him from her sitting room since he never seemed to mind being hugged and mauled and lugged about like a prized toy.

He sat up and eyed Shep warily, arching his back and preparing to hiss. Shep looked disdainfully back and an understanding was struck, as it had been yesterday when the two animals had met for the first time—*you stay clear of my space, and I will stay clear of yours.*

Sophia seated herself on a love seat, and Vincent sat beside her.

His mother had been horrified at the idea of a dog leading him about without any other assistance, and she had been quite vocal in her opposition. She thought Sophia rather reckless of her son's safety. But she had seen the dog in action inside the house yesterday, and she had probably watched out of the window this afternoon with Vincent's grandmother.

Young Ivy, Ellen's two-year-old, came to climb onto Vincent's lap, and he gave her his pocket watch on a chain to play with. Sophia found it rather touching that he wore it when he could not see it to know the time, but he always did.

"Oh," Vincent's mother said just after the tea tray had been brought in, "there is a letter for you, Sophia. I had it put in your sitting room."

It always thrilled Sophia to have a letter. It was something that had never happened before her marriage and did not happen often now. But she had heard from Mrs. Parsons at Barton Coombs—her aunt and Sir Clarence and Henrietta had apparently gone back to London for what remained of the Season. And she had heard a number of times from Lady Trentham and once from Lady Kilbourne and even from the rather austere Lady Barclay, who was back in Cornwall, where she lived.

"Thank you." She smiled. She would read it later and then have all the pleasure of sitting at the small escritoire in the sitting room and replying.

"Tab has put on weight," she said as she drank her tea. "And his coat is perfectly sleek and shiny."

"You have put on weight too, Sophia," Anthony remarked.

"*Anthony!*" Amy tossed her glance at the ceiling. "That is just what every woman longs to be told."

"No, no," he said. "I did not mean that you are getting *fat,* Sophia. Just that you have lost that almost gaunt look you had when you came here. Your face has filled out to fit your features. The extra weight is becoming. I am going to button my lips now before Amy does it for me."

Vincent grinned her way, and his grandmother smiled

and nodded and even half winked at Sophia. His mother smiled and nodded too.

Was it so obvious to them, then, even though she had not detected any weight gain yet? How could she? She had been married less than two months. But it was undoubtedly true. She had listened to the women talk at the sewing circle, and she had all the right symptoms, if *symptoms* was the correct word for what was not an illness.

She looked down at her hands and hoped she was not blushing too noticeably. And she felt suddenly *miserable*. For though Vincent would surely be pleased at the possibility of having an heir, he did not really want to be saddled with either wife or child. He had never wanted it. Not yet, anyway. And there was one thing they had not considered. If they should decide when the time came that they would live apart, *who would have the child*?

She suspected they would remain together after all, but not with any degree of happiness. Not that happiness had been part of their bargain. Contentment, then. They would not live in perfect contentment.

Tab had come to curl up on the love seat beside Sophia, and Percival came to sit on her lap so that he could smooth one small hand over the cat's coat.

Sophia smiled at him and felt the soreness of unshed tears at the back of her throat.

18

❦

$\mathcal{V}$incent's sisters and their families were soon to return to their own homes, and his grandmother was going to move back to Bath in the autumn. She was missing her friends and her life there. For a similar reason, his mother was seriously considering returning to Barton Coombs and Covington House. Mrs. Plunkett could be persuaded to join her there, she was sure.

Vincent would be sad to see them all go. He was genuinely fond of his family, and even more so now when they no longer hovered over his every move and insisted upon doing everything for him that was within their power.

They had accepted Sophia and even grown fond of her, he believed. His mother spoke approvingly of what she had done for him during two short months, even though she had had her doubts about the dog.

He would be sad to see them all go, but he would be happy too. They would be able to relax into their own lives without having to worry every moment about his, and he would be alone with Sophia. He had told her even before they married that he thought they could be comfortable together, and they were. At least he was, and he thought she was enjoying her life with him too.

He hoped they could be comfortable together for a lifetime. He very much hoped it. Although he was becoming more and more independent—thanks in many ways to his wife's efforts—he could not quite imagine his life without Sophia. Indeed, the thought was too terrible to contemplate.

They were seated side by side on the love seat in their private sitting room on the evening of the day Croft had declared Shep's training complete. The cat was lying at his wife's feet, its tail curled over Vincent's foot. Shep was beside the love seat, close to him. He could trail his arm over the side and touch the dog's head. He could hear the dog heave a great sigh and settle to sleep. He could still not fully comprehend the wonder of it. It was almost like having his eyes back. Well, not quite, perhaps, but it was certainly going to restore a great deal of his freedom of movement.

He was not really thinking about either the dog or his independence, though, at the moment. He was listening to Sophia reading aloud from Henry Fielding's *Joseph Andrews,* a book they had both been enjoying for the last couple of weeks. She set it aside after she had finished a chapter.

"Living in a house with a large library," she said, "is a little like living in heaven."

"I might feel that *I* was in heaven," he said, "if I were not being tormented by an undisclosed secret."

"Oh, that." She hesitated. "You may think it very foolish or intrusive of me. I thought we might have half a race track built inside the east and north walls of the park and inside the walls on part of the south side too where there are no trees. It would be properly surfaced and railed on both sides and curved gradually at the corners so that a horse would round them without any particular guidance. It would be almost five miles long, and you would be able to ride along it and even gallop. And you would be able to use it as a running track too if you wished, your hand on the rail. Or even with Shep. *He* would undoubtedly enjoy the run. You could have a great deal of freedom there."

His first instinct was to laugh. It was a preposterously grandiose idea. Only Sophie . . .

He did not laugh. Instead, he visualized such a track in his mind's eye. Almost five miles long. Without obstacles. Shaped in such a way that a horse could walk it or run it with no real guidance. Shaped in such a way that *he* could run it. Uninhibited forward movement for miles. Fresh air rushing against his face.

Freedom.

"It would be too big a task for the gardeners," she said. "Workers would have to be hired. And a designer. It would probably take a long time to design and construct and would be costly."

He swallowed and licked his lips.

He could almost feel himself riding—alone. Taking his horse to a canter. To a gallop. For five miles. He could almost feel himself running, stretching his muscles, falling into a rhythm of movement, exhausting himself over five miles. Perhaps ten if he ran back again. Or just walking, striding briskly along with no fear of where his next step would take him.

He had been blind for six years. Why was it that only now . . .

It was because he had not met Sophia before now. That vivid imagination of hers was not just for fantasy.

"Mr. Fisk thinks it is a good idea," she said. Her voice was curiously flat, and he realized he had not spoken any of his thoughts aloud. "Perhaps you do not. Perhaps you think I am managing your life just a little too much."

He turned his head to smile at her.

"Will you ride there with me, Sophie?" he asked her. "We could take a picnic luncheon with us, for we would need to stop halfway to sustain ourselves."

"Oh," she said. "How horrid of you. I am not *that* slow on horseback."

"I will teach you to ride like the wind," he promised her.

"Do you think it is a ridiculous idea?" she asked. "Or one too many ideas? Should I mind my own business more?"

She was sounding strangely uncertain of herself. He thought she had got past that.

"I am in awe," he said. "Where do all these ideas come from?"

"I think from a lifetime of only being able to observe and never being able to *do*," she said. "I have twenty years of inaction to make up for."

"Heaven help me, then," he said. "You will be building me a flying machine next that will guide itself through the skies and find its way home again."

"Oh," she said. "Oh, Vincent, that *would* be one idea too many. But we could create some marvelous stories around the idea. We could—"

But he was laughing, and she stopped talking to join him.

"I think your idea is brilliant," he told her. "I think *you* are brilliant. Have you read your letter?"

"My—oh, my *letter*. I had forgotten it." She got to her feet. "It has been there on the mantelpiece staring me in the eye all the time we have been sitting here."

He heard her cross the room.

"I do not recognize the hand," she said. "I wonder—"

"There is a way of satisfying your curiosity, you know," he pointed out.

He heard a seal breaking and the rustle of paper.

"Perhaps," she said, "it is from one of your friends, Vincent, writing to you for me to read aloud."

It had happened a few times. There had been letters from George and Ralph.

There was a rather lengthy silence.

"What?" he asked.

"My uncle," she said. "It is from Sir Terrence Fry."

He felt instantly angry.

"He is back in England," she said, "and has heard of my marriage."

There was another lengthy silence.

"Come," he said at last, reaching out one hand.

She came to sit beside him again, though she did not take his hand.

"Is he congratulating you?" he asked. "Or commiserating?"

He could feel her hesitation.

"A bit of both, I suppose," she said. "He is happy that socially and financially I am secure for life."

And sorry that she had married a blind man. She did not say it aloud. She did not need to.

"He has no right." Her voice was trembling. "He has no *right*."

No, he most certainly did not. Vincent lifted a hand, found the back of her neck, and rubbed his fingers soothingly over it.

"He has spoken with Aunt Martha," she said. "Or, rather, she has spoken with him. She explained how I snared you."

"Did she, by Jove?" he said.

"But he is not sure he believes her," she said. "He wants to hear the story from my own lips."

"He expects you to go to London to wait on him?"

"No," she said. "He wishes to come here."

He opened his mouth to tell her exactly what he thought of that brazen idea. But he closed it again, the words unspoken. Sir Terrence Fry was her relative, one of the very few.

"Does he have a wife?" he asked.

"She died many years ago," she told him.

"Any children?"

"None that survived infancy," she said. "Only Sebastian."

"Sebastian?"

"His stepson," she explained. "His wife was a widow when he married her."

"And he has never communicated with you before now?" he asked her. "He never came to visit your father? He did not attend his funeral? Or your aunt's, his sister's?"

"He was out of the country," she told him. "He is a diplomat. And no, I have never met him or heard from him directly. Until now."

"Directly," he said, frowning. "And indirectly?"

"He wrote to Sebastian and asked him to call on me when I went to live with Aunt Mary," she said. "He wanted to know that I was well cared for there and happy."

"Did he?" He was still frowning. "And *did* his stepson call on you?" But he must have if she knew about the request.

"Yes," she said. "A number of times."

And for some reason he remembered asking if her Aunt Mary had any children, if she had any cousins in London. She had answered no, but there had been some hesitation, and he had noticed it then. Sometimes there was a world of meaning in hesitation.

"He is older than you?" he asked her.

"Oh, yes," she said. "Eight years older."

She had been fifteen when her father died. The stepcousin would have been twenty-three. Vincent's age now.

He massaged the back of her neck and could tell that her head was lowered farther than a reading of the letter made necessary. He guessed that her chin was against her chest and that perhaps her eyes were closed.

"Tell me about him," he said. "Tell me about those visits."

"He was very handsome," she said, "and amiable and full of vitality and confidence."

He waited.

"He was very kind," she said. "He befriended me and we talked and talked. He took me walking and driving in his curricle. He took me to galleries and old churches and once to Gunter's for an ice. I was terribly broken up over my father's death. He helped ease the pain."

He waited again. The air about them was charged with some terrible pain. He hoped it was not what he suspected it might be.

"I was very silly," she said. "I fell in love with him. It was hardly surprising, I suppose. Indeed, it would have been surprising if I had not. But I told him. In my foolishness I thought he had fallen in love with me too. I *told* him."

"You were fifteen, Sophie," he said, his hand pausing at her neck.

"He laughed at me."

Ah, Sophie. So young and fragile. At that age she would have been vulnerable even if the rest of her life had been as solid as a rock.

"He laughed and told me I was a silly, ungrateful little chit. Which I was. I would have been heartbroken anyway. I would also have been wounded and humiliated by his laughter and would have squirmed at the memory of my own naïveté. But I would have recovered. I think I would. I suppose it is not uncommon for young girls to fall hopelessly in love with handsome men and then to have their hopes and dreams dashed."

"Why did you not recover?" he asked when she did not continue.

"We were in the sitting room at Aunt Mary's," she said, "and there was a mirror. A long one. He took me to stand in front of it while he stood behind me explaining to me why it was absurd and even a little insulting of me to fall in love with him and expect him to return my regard. He made me look at my figure and my face and my hair, which was in a great bush about my head and down over my shoulders because I never could manage it. He told me I was a scrawny, ugly little thing. He told me he liked me well enough, but only as a little cousin he had promised his stepfather to keep an eye on. He laughed as he said it. It was an affectionate sort of laugh, I think, but it sounded grotesque to me. After he had left, I went to my room and found my scissors and hacked my hair off. He did not come ever again, and I would not have seen him if he had."

He wrapped both arms about her and drew her against him until her head was resting on his shoulder.

"Pardon my language, Sophie," he said, "but the *bastard*. I just wish I could have five minutes alone with him."

"It was a long time ago."

"He was *my age*," he said. "Your father had just died. Your aunt was neglecting you. You were fifteen. You were not even fully grown. And even apart from all that, you were a *human being*. And he was a *gentleman*. Oh, Sophie. My sweet Sophie. Even then you must have been beautiful. I know you are now."

She laughed against his neck and then cried.

And cried and cried.

That bastard. That . . . *bloody bastard*.

He fumbled for his handkerchief and put it into her hand.

"Sophie," he said when her sobs had quieted to the occasional hiccup. "You are beautiful. Take a blind man's word for it. You are the most beautiful woman I have ever known."

She laughed and hiccupped, and he laughed softly

into her hair and fought back the urge to weep with her. She blew her nose and set aside the handkerchief.

"Your shirt and cravat are all wet," she said.

"They will dry." He kept an arm about her shoulders. "Your uncle has not completely ignored you, then."

"No, I suppose not," she said.

"He is your family," he said. "Your father's brother."

"Yes."

"Let us invite him to come here, then," he suggested. "Meet each other at last, Sophie, and decide if you want to see him again after that. Do it in your own home and on your own terms. Let him see for himself if I have been entrapped by a wicked schemer and if you are trapped in a dismal marriage with half a man."

"He would not have taken any notice of me if I had not married," she said. "And a viscount at that."

"Perhaps," he conceded. "Or perhaps he always meant to check up on you himself once he was back in this country for some length of time. You were with one aunt, his sister, and then with another, and also with a female cousin that time, a young lady close to you in age. Perhaps he assumed you were where you ought to be and where you wished to be. Perhaps he thought he had done his duty by you simply by ascertaining that you were being well cared for by relatives."

"He never thought to ask me," she said.

"No, he did not."

He could hear her folding the letter.

"You have felt your lack of a family," he said, drawing her closer. "When you have been with mine, you have felt it. I am not wrong, am I?"

"No," she admitted after a short hesitation. "It is dreadful to be all alone in the world. Your family has been kind to me, and I have grown to love them. But— Sometimes there is an emptiness. Perhaps it would not weigh as heavily if I were truly without family, if they were all dead."

"Let your uncle come," he said. "Maybe it will not be a happy visit. But maybe it will. You will not know either way if you do not allow him to come."

He knew he would dread it with every fiber of his being. He did *not* feel kindly toward any member of his wife's family. But he had to remember that a few weeks ago she had to come here to meet all his family, knowing that the circumstances surrounding their wedding would predispose them to judge her harshly. But she had done it. And she had won them over even though he knew it had not been easy for her. She had been a quiet mouse for most of her life and had had to assert herself in order to be accepted here.

She sighed.

"I shall write to him tomorrow," she said. "I shall invite him to come in time for the harvest reception and ball. It is not very far in the future, is it?"

She had not given up on that idea, then? No, of course she had not. She had told too many people about it to back down now. Besides, Sophia was not the backing-down sort.

"Yes," he said. "Ask him to come for the ball. My family will all be back here for it. It will be fitting for yours to come too. It will be like a belated wedding reception. Perhaps we may even describe it as such. Perhaps you can even invite the Marches. They will probably say no, though I would not wager a fortune on it."

"Are you mad?" She drew a sharp breath.

"Probably," he conceded. "I have a distinct feeling they would *not* refuse. Their niece, Viscountess Darleigh, and all that."

"You *are* mad," she told him and laughed with what sounded like watery merriment.

He turned her head and kissed her.

"It must be bedtime," he said. "Am I right?"

"You are right," she said without turning her head to consult the clock.

His very favorite time of the day.

*S*ophia was sitting at the escritoire in the private sitting room the following morning. She was brushing the feather of the quill pen back and forth across her chin, thinking of how she would word the letter to her uncle. So far she had got as far as "Dear Uncle," having rejected "Dear Sir Terrence," "Dear Sir," and "Dear Uncle Terrence." She had achieved just the right balance between formality and informality.

Tab was lying across one of her feet, having abandoned his perch on the east-facing windowsill when she sat down.

She had not yet decided if she would also invite Aunt Martha and Sir Clarence and Henrietta to Middlebury Park. She was not sure what her motive would be for doing it. Holding out an olive branch? Taking an opportunity to gloat? Making a forlorn attempt to create a family of her own?

Forlorn, indeed. But quite impossible? She had grown truly fond of Vincent's family. But seeing their closeness, being a part of it, only made the emptiness of her own lack of family all the emptier.

And Vincent, bless his heart, understood that.

For a few moments she was distracted by memories of last night. He was always a vigorous, satisfying lover, especially since that afternoon on the island—she still thought of it every single day. It had been wonderful, and *he* had been wonderful, and ever since then . . .

Well.

But last night had been a little different from any

other time. Last night he had touched her and loved her with what she could only describe as tenderness.

Perhaps when he had spoken to Mr. Croft he had not meant quite what she thought he had meant. And perhaps he had. Perhaps . . .

Oh, she *wished* she could stop thinking.

"I received your letter yesterday," she wrote.

Progress indeed.

I was delighted to receive it?

"It was kind of you to write," she wrote instead.

Was it? Was it *kind*? It did not really matter, though, did it? There were certain courtesies that must be observed.

Why *exactly* had he written to her? Just because she was a viscountess now and her husband was a wealthy man? Because he cared just a little bit and feared that she was unhappy with a blind man? Because talking with Aunt Martha had made him suspect something of what her life with her aunt must really have been like?

Vincent was right. She really did need to see him and discover the answers to all her questions. But she did not *want* to see him. And yet she longed for him. He was Papa's *brother*. Sometimes Papa had used to tell stories from his childhood. Not often, it was true, but sometimes. And Uncle Terrence had always figured in those stories. They had been close friends as boys.

"I would be happy to see you," she wrote and then frowned down at the words. They would have to do. She did not want to start all over again.

And then she heard footsteps approaching the door from the outside. Firm, sure footsteps. Mr. Fisk's? A footman's? But whoever it was did not stop to knock on the door. Instead, the knob turned, the door opened, and Vincent came right in, with Shep panting at his side.

"Sophie?" he said.

"I am here," she told him. "At the escritoire. I am writing to my uncle."

"Good." He came closer and set a hand on her shoulder. There was a glow of color in his cheeks, and his lovely blue eyes were sparkling. "We walked to the lake—Shep and I, that is—and about it and along the alley to the summerhouse. We sat there for a while before coming back. I would have asked you to come too, but I wanted to prove something to myself."

"And you did," she said. "You do not look wet. You did not tumble into the lake, then?"

"Or fall and break my nose," he said. "You were still sleeping when I came up from exercising. Mama says you were late to breakfast. Are you feeling unwell?"

"Not at all." She set down her pen and got to her feet. "I am quite well. Indeed, I am more than well."

He raised his eyebrows.

She took his free hand in both of hers and kissed the back of it.

"We are going to have a child," she said. "I have not consulted a physician yet, but I am as sure as I can be."

He seemed to gaze very directly into her eyes, his own wide. His hand tightened in hers as she looked back warily.

"Sophie?" He smiled slowly and then laughed.

"Yes." She kissed his hand again.

He dropped Shep's leash, drew his hand free of hers, and reached for her. He wrapped her in his arms and tightened them so that she was pressed to him from shoulders to knees.

"Sophie," he whispered. "Really? A child?"

"Yes. Really."

She heard him swallow.

"But you are so small." He was still whispering.

"Even small people can have babies quite safely," she said.

She hoped she was right. There were never any guarantees in childbirth. But it was too late now for worries and fears.

He rested one cheek against the top of her head.

"A child," he said and laughed again. "Oh, Sophie, a *child*!"

They stood hugging each other for a long time. Her letter to her uncle was forgotten. Shep settled for a sleep at Vincent's feet. Tab was back on the windowsill, sunning himself.

19

*A*nd then, of course, only a few hours later, he had to have an attack of panic.

Sophia had gone off to the village with Ursula and Ellen. His sisters wanted something at the village shop, and Sophia was going to call on Agnes Keeping to show her some illustrations she had done for a new Bertha and Dan story they had concocted a week or so ago—about a chimney sweep's boy who got stuck inside the top of a tall chimney perched on top of a very tall building. One of her drawings apparently showed Bertha rescuing him from above, only her bottom and her legs visible, the rest of her hidden inside the chimney.

They were expecting Andy Harrison and his wife for tea later. In the meanwhile, he had a free couple of hours since his steward was away for the day on business. He decided to explore the wilderness walk even though work on it had only recently begun. No one had gone before him in the Lake District to smooth out the hills, after all. But then he had never tried walking those alone.

He did not walk alone today either. He felt that he had neglected Martin of late. Which was foolish of him, of course, since Martin was probably enjoying a bit more time to himself anyway. Vincent had heard a whisper that Martin was romancing the young daughter of the village blacksmith—it seemed appropriate.

He took Martin and his cane with him to explore the

walk and found it indeed rather rocky underfoot and overgrown to the sides once they had passed the work area.

"It does not take long for nature to reclaim its own, does it?" he said.

"Good for nature, I say," Martin said. "Humankind can do shameful things with it, given half a chance."

"You are thinking of coal mines and such?" Vincent asked him.

"More like those silly trees halfway down the drive," Martin said. "Clipped and shaped to look stupid, just like some poodles."

"The topiaries?" Vincent laughed. "Do they really look silly? I have been told they are pretty and picturesque."

Martin grunted.

"Large stone four paces ahead," he warned. "Pass it to the left. If you go right, you may roll all the way down the hill."

"Sophia has told me about the riding track," Vincent said. "You think it will work, Martin?"

"I don't suppose the Derby will ever be run on it," Martin told him. "But it will work. You should be able to go for a good ride there without all of us fearing you will break your neck."

"Sophia consulted you," Vincent said.

"She no doubt decided," Martin said, "that if it was an idea to be laughed at, it was better to have me laugh at her than you. She worships the ground you walk upon, you know."

"Oh, nonsense." Vincent laughed. "She is with child, Martin."

"That is what the cook and all the maids say," Martin said. "Something to do with the fullness of the face and the look in the eye and other such nonsense. They always seem to be right, though. I don't know how women do it. Know these things, I mean."

"I am going to be a father."

"If her ladyship is with child, then I hope you are, sir," Martin agreed.

And Vincent stopped walking and thought of how slender his wife was, how narrow her hips. And of how many pregnancies resulted in stillbirths or the death of the mother. Or both. And of how he would never see his child even if it lived, never be able to play with it as any normal father would, never . . .

Martin grasped his upper arm.

"There is a seat over here," he said. "It is pretty dilapidated, but it may bear your weight."

It was too late. There was no air to breathe, and he *could not see*. He clawed at Martin's hand, whether to prise it free or grip it he did not know.

The seat *could* bear his weight. He was sitting on it when he regained control.

In. Out. In. Out.

He was blind. That was all.

It was like a mantra.

It was the first bout of panic since that one in the carriage with Sophia. They were growing further apart. Perhaps eventually they would stop altogether. Perhaps the time would come when his unconscious as well as his conscious mind would finally accept the fact that he would never see again.

"Did I draw blood from your hand?" he asked.

"Nothing a bit of salve won't cure, sir," Martin told him. "It will give everyone in the kitchen something to tease me about. They'll pretend to think it was Sal who did it."

"The blacksmith's daughter?" Vincent said. "Is she pretty?"

"She is that," Martin said, "and a good buxom armful too. But a buxom armful is all I ever get, alas. She is after a wedding, that one, as sure as I'm standing here."

"And?"

"I'm not in any hurry," Martin told him. "Maybe I'll tire of her. Maybe she'll tire of me. And maybe I'll come to think that if the only way I can get under her skirts is to wed her . . . Well. I have not been brought that low yet, and if I say my prayers at night like a good boy the way Mam taught me, maybe I never will. She has the sauciest sway to her hips, though, Vince."

Vincent laughed. "When you say your prayers, Martin," he said, "you have to know what action you want. Otherwise God might be confused."

Interestingly, Martin sighed.

Vincent thought his legs would support him. He got to his feet, using his cane. The trembles were almost all gone.

Small women had babies all the time. Sophia had said it herself.

And one did not have to see in order to touch a baby. Or hold it.

Or play with it.

Or love it.

It.

Would it be a boy or a girl?

It did not matter. It absolutely did not matter. As long as it lived. As long as it was healthy.

And as long as Sophie lived.

Please, God, let her live. And there was no ambiguity in his prayer.

"I'll start saving for a wedding gift," he said.

Martin grunted again.

Vincent thought more cheerfully about his impending fatherhood as they came down off the wilderness walk. There was no point in thinking of all the things that could go wrong. And there was no point in lamenting the fact that he would never see any child of his.

At least there would be a child.

His and Sophia's.

And now of course she would stay and they would finally be done with that more-than-absurd suggestion of his when he was persuading her to marry him. For though they had thought of the possibility of a pregnancy delaying any plan they might have to live apart, neither of them seemed to have considered what they would do with the child when they *did* go their separate ways.

There was no way on this earth he would let anyone take a child of his away from him, even if he *would* never see it. And he would wager the whole of his fortune that nobody would wrest her child from Sophia either.

That meant they would have to remain together.

He was so glad that nonsense was done with. He thought Sophia would be glad too. Perhaps he would broach the subject with her later, and then they could finally forget all about it.

He could hear feminine voices coming from what he thought was the direction of the parterre gardens. He could hear Ursula and Ellen. Ah, and then Sophia. They were back from their trip to the village, then.

"Oh, look at *that,*" Ursula was saying as he came within earshot. "It is adorable. Is it a real place, Sophia?"

"Not really," Sophia said. "It is my dream cottage, the house of all places where I would like to live."

"I do love cottages with thatched roofs," Ellen said. "Oh, how *pretty* all these sketches are, Sophia. You have *such* talent. Just look at those flowers. Oh, and there is your cat. And a puppy sitting in the doorway."

"You do not prefer living at Middlebury Park?" Ursula asked, laughing.

"Ah, but Middlebury is reality," Sophia said. "The cottage is my dream. I will never live there, of course. It is make-believe. But oh, the peace of it. The quiet of it. The *happiness* of it."

Vincent felt a bit as though he were turned to stone. Martin seemed to have disappeared.

"I hope you are no less happy here in real life," Ellen said. "You *seem* happy, and we have never seen Vincent so contented."

"Ah, but we must all be able to distinguish between fiction and reality," Sophia said, "or we will be forever dissatisfied. Make-believe is just that. I live here in great contentment. I am the most fortunate of women."

"Well, I am much impressed with your sketches, Sophia," Ursula said. "The children are going to miss them when we go home, and the stories you and Vincent tell in such harmony. Ah, Vincent. You had better beware. Sophia is showing us a picture of the cottage where she will live when she can no longer stand living with you."

"Oh," Sophia said. "There you are. Have you been out walking?"

"I went up over the wilderness walk with Martin," he said, "and have lived to tell the tale. Did you all have a pleasant visit to the village?"

Sophia slipped a hand through his arm, and they led the way into the house.

His spirits were somewhere in the soles of his Hessian boots.

"I drew the cottage," she said, "because I have noticed the curiosity the children have about *everything*, and they have already started to ask, *the fairies at the bottom of* what *garden*? I thought to put the cottage on the cover of the first book in that series. Did you enjoy your walk? Did Martin go with you?"

She knew he had heard.

⸏ir Terrence Fry accepted his invitation.

So did Sir Clarence and Lady March. Henrietta was to come with them, though she was much in demand at summer house parties, where she was being besieged by the attentions of eligible gentlemen, all of them titled, none of them measuring up to her discriminating standards.

Sophia smiled at her aunt's letter at the same time as she felt a certain dismay. Did she *want* them to come? But she had invited them. She must welcome them warmly and be attentive to their needs.

Did she want her uncle to come?

She found that she dreaded his coming for one particular reason. She was afraid he would let her down. Perhaps he had not written to her out of any lingering fondness for her father's memory or regret that he had not made a point of seeing her before now. Perhaps he would not be able to give her any satisfactory explanation of his long neglect. Perhaps he was coming to show his displeasure with her for stealing Vincent away from Henrietta—if that was the story Aunt Martha had told him. Perhaps . . .

Well, she would have to wait and see.

And yet she longed for his coming. She was with child. Her son or her daughter would never lack for attention and love from all the relatives on his or her father's side. But what about *her* side? Would there be anyone there at all for her child?

Or for herself?

Vincent's sisters and their families had gone home but would return for the harvest ball. His grandmother was ready to return to Bath. She had even leased a house there. She would go after the ball. His mother was more and more inclined to return to Barton Coombs and her friends there, but she would stay until after Sophia's confinement, which was expected to be in the early spring.

The harvest ball had captured the eager attention of everyone for miles around, though it had actually stopped being called that. It was now being called a wedding reception and ball. A belated one. *Very* belated when it seemed common knowledge that the bride was a few months with child even though the very slight bump was not really visible yet beneath the loose skirts of her high-waisted dresses.

Her mother-in-law was helping with the plans, though really she had almost no more experience than Sophia did herself with such a grand event. Her main worries were for Vincent.

"Though you have had a remarkable effect upon him, Sophia," she admitted almost grudgingly when they were sitting together in the library, making lists of everything under the sun that needed doing—everything they could think of, anyway. There was always something else that kept occurring to one or other of them and sent them into flurries of near panic. "I do not know how you do it. And sometimes I wish you did not. Whatever made you think of a riding track in the park? And how is Vincent going to eat at a public reception or comport himself in a ballroom?"

"He will do both with the greatest ease, Mama," Sophia assured her. "He did it at Barton Coombs, and he will do it here. He will be among relatives and friends."

"I hope you are right," her mother-in-law said with a sigh.

The harvest ball, wedding reception, whatever one chose to call it, was set for early October. Summer slipped into autumn far too soon, as it always did, but autumn had its beauty too. The trees would turn color soon and shed their leaves, and before they budded out into green again, there would be a new baby at Middlebury Park. But it was too soon to dwell upon that yet.

Sir Terrence and the Marches were due to arrive on the same day, though they were not coming together. Vincent's sisters were coming a few days later, as was Viscount Ponsonby, who was visiting an elderly relative not far distant and had professed himself delighted to come to Middlebury for a few days.

"One grows hoarse from yelling into an ear trumpet," he had written. "My vocal cords need a rest, not to mention the rest of my person. I accept your kind invitation for no other reason."

Viscount Ponsonby saw the world through a satirical eye, Sophia thought as she read the whole letter aloud to Vincent. Did that come from his unhappiness, as it had come from hers? She did not know much about him except that he was one of Vincent's closest friends, one of the Survivors. There was not much sign of physical damage to his person except for his slight stammer. He had world-weary eyes, though. Yet he could not be older than thirty and was probably not even that.

The Marches arrived first, early in the afternoon. Sophia and Vincent went out to meet them, Vincent led by Shep.

"Aunt Martha," Sophia said, stepping forward as soon as the coachman handed out her aunt. And she hugged her for the first time ever.

"Sophia?" Her aunt's eyebrows rose in surprise, and her eyes swept over her niece from head to toe. "You have certainly done well for yourself. Middlebury Park is as grand as we were told. Almost as grand as Grandmaison Hall, where Henrietta recently spent two weeks at the special invitation of the Earl of Tackaberry."

"I hope your journey was not too trying," Sophia said.

"Lord Darleigh," Aunt Martha was saying as Sophia turned to greet her uncle, who was standing looking about him, his hands at his back.

"You have landed firmly on your feet, I see, girl," he said as she contemplated hugging him but rejected the idea. She smiled at him instead.

"I hope you have had a pleasant journey, Uncle," she said.

Henrietta was coming down the carriage steps. But she stopped suddenly and shrieked.

"Papa!" she cried. "A dog!"

"He is my guardian, Miss March," Vincent said. "He remains at my side at all times and is perfectly harmless."

"Mama?" Henrietta cowered on the bottom step.

"Henrietta had a nasty experience when she was a child," Aunt Martha explained. "She tried to pet a vicious dog from the village when we were on our way home from church, and it snapped at her and would have bitten her if her father had not beaten it off with a stick. Its owner also swore it was harmless, Lord Darleigh."

"I will take him along to our apartments," Vincent said, "while Sophia has you shown to your rooms. You will wish to refresh yourselves and perhaps rest for a while. I will be pleased to welcome you more fully in the drawing room at teatime. Rest assured, Miss March, that Shep will never hurt you or anyone else. He is merely my eyes. I am very happy you have all arrived safely. Sophia has been longing to have her family here with her."

And he turned and went back up the steps and into the house with Shep.

"His *eyes*?" Sir Clarence said, his eyebrows raised. "How very peculiar."

Henrietta stepped down onto the terrace and Sophia hugged her.

"Welcome to Middlebury Park, Henrietta," she said.

"I hope you are happy here, I am sure," Henrietta said. "You married a blind man to get it, and I hope it was worth it."

"Yes." Sophia smiled. "I married Vincent, and I am happy here. Do come inside. Uncle Terrence will be here soon."

She slid her hand through her aunt's arm and led the way inside.

She did not really wonder why they had come. Curiosity had brought them here, and the hope that they would find her regretting her marriage or that Vincent would be regretting it. Or that Middlebury Park would turn out to be not as grand as it was reputed to be. Or that in some way they could go back home comforted that their niece rather than Henrietta had married Lord Darleigh.

It must be a dreadful thing, she thought, to hug such unhappiness about oneself and defend it for a whole lifetime against all comers. It saddened her to know that she had an aunt and uncle and cousin who would never really be family to her. But for the few days of their visit here, she intended to smother them with attention and courtesy and even affection.

Her uncle arrived an hour or so later, and Sophia and Vincent went out again to meet him, Vincent with his cane this time. The carriage steps were being set down as they arrived on the terrace, and a tall, elegant gentleman came down them.

For a disorienting moment the breath caught in Sophia's throat and she thought that she must have been misinformed all those years ago. Her father had not died in that duel after all. It was only a moment, of course. This man's face was handsome but austere. He did not have the warm, smiling charm that had always clung about her father, even when he had had a mountain of debts and had just lost a fortune at the tables. On the other hand, he had a presence that was just as forceful in its own way.

But he looked so very much like her papa.

She slipped her arm free of Vincent's and stepped forward.

"Uncle Terrence?" she said.

He stood in front of her, looking her over from head to toe, rather as Aunt Martha had done. He removed his tall hat and inclined his head to her.

"Sophia?" he said. "Well, you are a dainty little thing and not at all what I had been led to expect."

Should she smile? Curtsy? Ask about his journey? Hug him? She felt paralyzed.

He held out an ungloved hand, and she placed her own in it. He raised it to his lips in a courtly gesture that had her biting her lower lip.

"On the only occasion when I saw your father after your birth," he told her, "he described you as his little mop-headed treasure who held him to life whenever despair threatened. Did he ever tell you that, Sophia?"

She shook her head. She was biting her lip hard. Her vision blurred and she realized her eyes had filled with tears.

"We often do not say what is in our hearts," he said, "to those who are closest and most dear to us." He patted her hand before releasing it.

She recovered herself.

"Uncle Terrence," she said, "may I present my husband? Vincent, Lord Darleigh?"

Vincent was holding out his right hand and smiling.

"Sir," he said. "I am delighted to make your acquaintance."

As her uncle stepped forward to shake his hand, Sophia's view of the carriage was no longer blocked. And for the first time she realized that he had not come alone. Another man stood framed in the doorway, halfway down the steps—a handsome, smiling young man.

"Sophia," Sebastian said with that characteristic emphasis on the final letter that she had once found heartwarming. "You have certainly grown up since I last saw you."

She felt as if all the blood must have drained away down to her toes.

"Sebastian?" She clasped her hands before her as he stepped down onto the terrace. He was broader in the chest than he had been six years ago. He was even more handsome than he had been then. He looked even more confident. His smile was even more charming.

"I could not resist coming with Father," he said. "I wanted to see what Viscountess Darleigh looks like. She looks quite as fine as fivepence."

"I hope you do not mind, Sophia," her uncle was saying. "Sebastian was quite eager to see you again. Darleigh, meet my stepson, Sebastian Maycock."

Sophia had never seen Vincent look icy cold. His nostrils were flared, his lips pressed into a thin line. His eyes looked very directly in Sebastian's direction. Sebastian was moving toward him, his right hand extended, an easy smile on his lips.

"Maycock," Vincent said, and the ice was in his voice too.

Sebastian's hand fell back to his side.

Sophia wondered if her uncle had noticed the change in Vincent's manner.

"Of course we do not mind, Uncle Terrence," she said. "We are happy to have both of you here, and there

are several empty guest rooms. Aunt Martha and Sir
Clarence arrived a while ago with Henrietta. They will
be coming to the drawing room soon for tea. Shall we
go directly there, or would you like some time in your
rooms?"

She slid an arm through his.

"They came, then, did they?" he asked, sounding
amused. "I am surprised you invited them, Sophia. But,
then, I am surprised you invited me. Surprised and
grateful. I am very ready for some tea. Are you, Sebastian?"

"Lead the way," Sebastian said.

Sophia could see that he was debating with himself
whether to lead Vincent in or not. But Vincent turned
without waiting for him, and found his way to the steps
and up them with his cane, Sophia and Sir Terrence just
in front of him. Sebastian brought up the rear.

$\mathcal{S}$ir Terrence Fry sounded like a sensible man. He
knew how to keep a conversation going, and it seemed,
on a first impression anyway, as if he was genuinely glad
to be here and to have met Sophia at last. Sebastian
Maycock sounded confident and charming. He soon
had Vincent's mother and grandmother eating out of
his hand, so to speak, and Lady March and Miss March
both simpered when they spoke to him, which led Vincent to conclude that he must indeed be handsome and
was probably wealthy too.

Teatime in the drawing room passed without incident. Vincent was delighted for Sophia's sake. If there
could be even a small measure of civility between her
and her family, he would be glad for her. But perhaps
there could be more than just that, as far as the uncle
was concerned, anyway. Vincent could detect no simi-
larity of tone or mind between him and his sister.

Of course, the man still had a great deal of explaining to do.

Vincent found the hour trying for one particular reason. He could have conversed with Sir Terrence with interest. He could have derived amusement from the often barbed remarks of the Marches. But he seethed with impotent fury over the fact that he had been forced to receive Sebastian Maycock beneath his roof and play genial host to him. But what choice did he have? The man had come uninvited, and he had come with Sophia's uncle. He had a claim to be here. He was Fry's stepson.

Vincent could cheerfully have slapped a glove in his face.

It had all happened several years ago, he tried to tell himself. Maycock might well have changed since then. He had been just a young man then. But he had been *twenty-three*, dash it all. He had not seemed one whit abashed when he had met Sophia again out on the terrace. He did not seem abashed now in the drawing room. Was it possible he had forgotten? Or that Sophia had exaggerated what he had said to her? But if he had said even half of what she remembered, his words would be unpardonable.

"I have to know," Sir Clarence said, his voice hearty and jocular, as though he spoke to a child or an imbecile, "in what way your dog is your eyes, Darleigh. The apple of your eye and all that, is he? Or is it a she? You had better not say that too feelingly in the hearing of your wife."

He laughed at his own joke, and Vincent smiled.

"Shep is a collie, a sheepdog," he explained, "and has been trained by an expert to lead me about just as surely as he would lead a flock of sheep if he had been differently trained. I suppose that means I am not very different from a sheep, for which fact I am more than thankful. I have regained a large measure of freedom since I have had him."

Sir Clarence laughed some more.

"One day he will spy a rabbit," he said, "and be off in pursuit, and you will collide with a tree or fall off a cliff, Darleigh. Wherever did you get such a mad idea?"

"From my wife, actually," Vincent said. "She heard of a child blind from birth who has a dog to lead her, and persuaded me to try one too. I have said that Shep is my eyes. But in truth it is Sophia who has that distinction. She brought me Shep, and she has had the railed path to the lake built and the wilderness walk in the hills behind the house cleared and railed. It should be finished before winter. And it is she who suggested the riding track that is being constructed inside the perimeter of the park so that I can ride safely and even go for a gallop. I heard you say, Sir Terrence, that your brother called Sophia his treasure. She is mine too."

"I am delighted to hear that she is showing a proper gratitude for your great condescension in responding to her rather bold advances when you were staying at Covington House, Lord Darleigh," Lady March said. "I am consoled. I was a little embarrassed and ashamed of her, I must confess, being both her aunt and her guardian at the time."

"On the contrary, ma'am," Vincent said, smiling in her direction. "It was I who was bold in my advances to Miss Fry, who declined my marriage offer more than once before I finally persuaded her to take pity on me."

"We are *extremely* happy," his grandmother said, "that she did. Sophia is like a bright little angel descended upon my grandson's home, Lady March. I commiserate with you for having lost her from your own home, but a girl must be expected to marry, you know, when she reaches a certain age. Vincent was fortunate to find her before anyone else did."

"Aunt Martha," Sophia said, getting up from her seat beside Vincent, "Henrietta, you must be longing for a breath of fresh air after your journey. Let me show you the parterre gardens and the topiary garden. The weather is being very kind to us for late September, is it not?"

"I will come too, if I may, Sophia," Sir Terrence said.

Vincent spoke quickly before his stepson could decide to join the party too.

"Maycock," he said, "my dog will be ready for some exercise after being cooped up in our private apartments most of the afternoon. Stroll down to the lake with me, if you will."

"Delighted," the man said—and he sounded it too.

❦

20

"Good old Sophia," Sebastian Maycock said, putting a peculiar emphasis upon the last letter of her name. "The dog was a brilliant idea of hers. I would scarcely know I was walking beside a blind man."

They were striding at a normal walking pace along the path to the lake. Maycock walked on the side with the rail. Vincent had Shep.

"I will not say I scarcely know I am blind," Vincent said, "but I *will* say my dog has given me back much of my freedom and confidence. And yes, it was Sophia who discovered that it could be done and persuaded me to give it a try."

"And you are having a riding track constructed?" Maycock said. "The park seems big enough to take it, I must say. You have a beautiful home here."

"Yes," Vincent agreed. "I am very fortunate."

They talked aimlessly and pleasantly as they walked. Under other circumstances, Vincent thought, he would probably like the man. He was friendly and good-humored. And perhaps he was judging him too harshly. Perhaps he had not intended to be cruel. Perhaps he had not known how those careless words spoken on one isolated occasion had hurt.

"Sophia always did have a lively mind," Maycock said when Vincent told him of her plan to have fragrant herbs and trees planted along the wilderness walk so that he could enjoy it even without sight. "I always found her rather amusing. I would take her to a gallery, and she would stand looking at an acclaimed master-piece, a frown on her brow, her head cocked a little to one side, and comment upon some detail that could be improved. This was soon after she went to live with that dragon, Aunt Mary, and just before I went to Vienna to join my stepfather."

Shep had stopped walking, and Vincent understood that they had reached the bank of the lake.

"Yes," he said, "she has told me about you."

"Has she?" Maycock chuckled. "She was a funny little thing."

"Funny?"

Maycock must have bent down to pick up some stones. Vincent could hear one skipping over the water.

"She was rather scrawny," Maycock said. "Thin with a pale, peaked face and big eyes. She would have looked like a boy if it had not been for all the hair. I think there was as much hair as there was Sophia, and she seemed quite incapable of taming it."

He laughed.

"Ugly too, I believe," Vincent said, turning to walk to his right along the bank.

"Eh?"

"She was ugly," Vincent said. "Or so you told her."

"Did I?" Maycock chuckled again. "And she remembers? She must do, though, if she told you. She *was* ugly, you know. I had promised my stepfather I would keep an eye on her, and I did. Aunt Mary was not doing it. She was a cold fish if ever there was one. Sophia amused me. I rather enjoyed taking her about London and talking with her. But I don't mind confessing that I was of-fended when she imagined I had fallen in love with her. I mean, it was ludicrous, Darleigh. My mistress at the time was one of the acclaimed beauties of the demi-monde. I was the envy of all the clubs. And there was Sophia . . . Well." He laughed again.

"She was fifteen," Vincent said.

"I beg your pardon," Maycock said. "I did not mean to be offensive, laughing like that. She does not look half so bad now, I assure you. You have bought her decent clothes, as Aunt Mary never did, and her hair is under control. She has put on a bit of weight too. I daresay it does not matter to you that you did not marry a ravishing beauty, though, does it?"

"I believe I did," Vincent told him.

Maycock laughed and then fell silent.

"Oh, I say," he said when Vincent said no more, the laughter still in his voice, "I *have* offended you. It was unintentional, old chap. She is a pleasant little thing. As soon as I knew my stepfather was coming here, I thought it would be good to come and to see her again. I liked her until she tried to make an idiot of me. I daresay you are fond of her. It is hard *not* to be fond of Sophia. She was fortunate to find someone to whom looks are not everything. I am happy for her."

Did he *mean* to be offensive? Amazingly, Vincent thought he probably did not. He was an amiable fellow, probably handsome and attractive to women. He was lacking only in the character department. Vincent stopped walking again and turned his way.

"Sophia had recently lost her father in a rather cruel manner," he said. "He had been her only rock in a precarious sort of life, and he was not much of a rock at that. She was being ignored by the aunt with whom she had been sent to live. She was fifteen with all the insecurities and vulnerability of youth in addition to everything else. And suddenly she had a friend, someone who talked to her and listened to her and took her about to interesting places. Was it surprising that she fell in love?"

"Oh, I say—"

Vincent held up a staying hand.

"*Of course* you did not love her in return," he said. "She was little more than a child. She put you in an embarrassing predicament when she declared her love. You had to explain reality to her. You could not let her continue in her delusion. And yet you did not want to hurt her. *Did* you?"

"She was a little scarecrow of a thing, Darleigh," Maycock said, chuckling again. "You ought to have seen her as she was then. You would have had a good laugh, especially at the idea that she imagined I was in love with her. I laughed about it afterward. I was deuced annoyed at the time. Good God, all those afternoons I had given up for her. I thought she would be *grateful*."

Vincent opened his mouth to say more. But what was the point? Even now Maycock could think only of the effect Sophia's declaration had had upon him. Did the fact that she still remembered not alert him to the fact that she had been deeply hurt?

How did one avenge that poor little fifteen-year-old Sophie? By pushing the man in the lake? It could probably be done. There would be the element of surprise, after all. But it seemed somehow childish. And it would not be satisfactory.

How else, though? He was *blind*.

And then he had the germ of an idea. He put it aside for the moment.

"There are boats in the boathouse," he said. "Perhaps you would like to take one out one day if the weather holds."

"I may do that," Maycock said. "There is nothing like a bit of exercise to get the blood pumping. I may take Henrietta with me. She looks decorative even if she does have a sharp tongue."

"What do you do for exercise?" Vincent asked.

"Ride? Spar? Do you go to Gentleman Jackson's when you are in London?"

"I am one of his star pupils," Maycock said. "I always drop my man. Sometimes he grants me a round or two with him, which he does not do with everyone, I would have you know. There is nothing like watching a decent mill, is there? Oh, sorry. You cannot watch, of course."

"You must come down to my exercise room one morning," Vincent said, and he indicated to Shep that they would return to the house. "My valet, once my batman, is also my trainer. He loves to spar. He is good at it too—he is built like a barn. It frustrates him that he almost never has anyone worthy of his skills close by. Perhaps—"

"It sounds as if he is my man," Maycock said. "You had better tell him to bring the smelling salts along, though, Darleigh. He will need them."

"I shall tell him." Vincent smiled. "Though it may be his opinion that *you* will need them."

Maycock laughed.

"I am glad I came," he said. "I am going to enjoy being here. And I must remember to assure Sophia that she is no longer ugly. Decent clothes and a decent hair style can do wonders, can they not?"

Martin would call him an idiot and a nincompoop and lunatic and other, even less complimentary, things, Vincent thought. Though, no, he would probably not when he knew the circumstances. The only thing Martin would not like was the fact that he would not be the one sparring.

It was the middle of the following afternoon before Sophia was alone with her uncle. She had shown the state apartments to her aunt and uncle and Henrietta, all of whom had agreed that they were really quite impressive, even if it *was* a shame that they were wasted upon an owner who was blind. She had had a brief conversation with Sebastian when he walked into the music room after luncheon while she was stealing a half hour to practice a particularly challenging exercise Miss Debbins had set her. Why her fingers had the annoying habit of turning into ten thumbs as soon as she sat on the pianoforte bench, she did not know. But if Vincent could conquer the harp—and he was well on his way to doing so—then she could conquer the pianoforte. She could at least learn to be competent.

"Sophia," Sebastian said, "you are becoming quite the accomplished lady."

"I doubt I will ever display these particular skills in public," she said.

"You used to sketch," he said. "Some of your drawings were wickedly clever."

"I illustrate stories now," she told him. "Children's stories. Vincent and I make them up together for the amusement of his nieces and nephews. And I sketch the pictures and make books of them."

"Do you?" He smiled, and his eyes crinkled attractively at the corners. "You must show them to me. I went to Vienna to visit my stepfather, you know, and stayed longer than I intended. The entertainments there were endlessly distracting. By the time I came home, the dragon was dead and you had gone to live with Aunt Martha. It must have felt a bit like being tossed from the frying pan into the fire. I ought to have gone to see you. We were fond of each other, I remember."

"I did not know you had gone away," she told him, turning on the bench to look more fully at him. "But I was glad you stopped coming, Sebastian."

"Because I called you ugly?" He pulled a face and then smiled again. "But you *were*, Sophia. Someone has done something with your hair since then and you have pretty dresses, and you are not quite as thin. Your looks have improved. I would not describe you as ugly now."

"But you see, Sebastian," she said, "I liked you, and I believed you."

"How could you not?" He laughed, a sound of sheer amusement. "Your glass must have told you that I spoke nothing but the truth. That was a long time ago, though. You come very close to being pretty now."

Ah. Praise indeed. She smiled back at him.

"You will be relieved to know," she said, "that I no longer love you, Sebastian. I must go and fetch my bonnet. I am to go walking with Uncle Terrence."

"Well," he said, opening the door for her, "I am happy to know you feel no lingering disappointment, Sophia. Darleigh must be more to your taste."

"Because he cannot see me?" she asked.

He laughed as though she had made a joke.

It was amazing what a difference five years could make to one's understanding. He was handsome; he was charming; he was amiable. He lacked all empathy for others.

Her uncle was waiting for her in the entry hall.

"I can see why Middlebury Park is considered one of the showpieces of England," he said as she approached. "Your mother-in-law showed me the state apartments a short while ago."

"And the park is just as magnificent," she told him, preceding him through the front doors and down the steps. "I shall take you to the lake, and if you are feeling energetic, we will walk about it to the cedar alley and the summerhouse. At a casual glance one might assume that the park ends with the trees beyond the lake, but it does not."

He offered his arm and she took it. He looked less like her father now that she had seen him a few times. He did not have her papa's charm of manner or endearing smile. On the other hand, he had elegance and perfect manners.

"We had better keep to the path while we can," she said.

The morning had been marred by a drizzle that had left the grass wet, but the clouds had moved off soon after noon and it was a pleasant afternoon with only a slight nip of autumn in the air.

"And the path is new?" he asked her. "It blends very well with the scenery. It was your idea, Sophia?"

"Vincent was confined to the parterre gardens unless there was someone to take his arm," she said. "It must not be a good feeling to be so dependent upon other people, must it? Or to be confined to one small plot of ground."

"Yet that is a child's lot in life," he said quietly, almost as if he was talking to himself. "Which is all well and good if the child is cherished and nurtured to an independent adulthood. One of the enduring pains of my life was losing three children in early infancy, Sophia. I used to envy my brother. No, *jealousy* is the more accurate word. We broke off with each other when we were still very young men. It was not his wild ways—they were his business. It happened when he stole—or so I described it to myself at the time—when he married the lady I had thought was mine. Did you know that of your mother? And they had you and you lived. I resented that. I resented him and I resented you. If you have hated me, Sophia, it is no less than I have deserved."

Her mind was numb with the shock of what he had said. Her father had never told her what happened between him and his brother. Her assumptions had not been the right ones. Had her mother ever regretted not marrying her uncle?

"I offered to take you when your mother left, you

know," he said. "Or perhaps you do not know. Already by that time my wife and I had lost two of our own children."

"You offered to *take* me?" She looked up at him in some amazement.

"My brother's way of life seemed hardly fitting for a young child," he said, "especially when your mother was no longer with you. But of course he said no. I do not blame him. I would have said the same thing in his place. But no bridges were mended between us. My offer and his refusal only seemed to make things worse."

They were silent while Sophia digested these matters. How little children knew about the adult dramas being played out around them.

"Whoever designed the lake," he said, "with the island just so and the temple, certainly had an eye to the picturesque. Are there boats?"

"Yes," she said, but she hoped he would not suggest going over there. She had not been since that afternoon when Vincent had taught her to float and when they had made love in a new way and she had fallen all the way in love with him.

They turned to walk past the boathouse and about the perimeter of the lake.

"We were a ramshackle family, Sophia," he said. "I do not know quite why it was, but none of us had a great deal of affection for any of the others, though your father and I were the best of friends while we were growing up. I suppose it was all as much my fault as my brother's and my sisters'. I have a tendency to be aloof. My wife once accused me of being cold, and I was wounded because I did not *feel* cold. But when I considered her accusation after the quarrel, I had to admit that my actions lent themselves to that interpretation. I would always rather hover at the fringe of any action than delve right in and become a part of it. Perhaps that is why I became a diplomat rather than a politician or a military officer."

Sophia said nothing. There did not seem anything to say.

"Ah," he said as they walked beyond the lake and past the trees on its far bank. "I see what you mean. And I see why the designer of the park put the alley here, out of sight of the house. A person can be private back here. It is a good place to stroll and think, or a good place to bring a book. And you see how my mind works? Those are the first things of which I thought. It is also a private place for lovers to stroll."

"Yes," she said.

"Do you stroll here with Darleigh?" he asked her.

"Yes," she said. "Sometimes."

A few times they had walked to the summerhouse and she had brought a book to read aloud while they sat there. Once it had rained a bit while they were there, and Vincent had remarked that the sound of rain on a glass roof must surely be one of the coziest sounds in the world. And he had drawn her onto his lap, and she had set her head on his shoulder, and they had sat in silence until the rain passed.

The memory could bring a lump to her throat, as so many memories did.

But he wanted to be free. She was just one more woman who wanted to look after him. And he had overheard the conversation she had had with his sisters about her drawing of the cottage that had once been her dream.

Yet she was with child. They would remain together. She would not leave him now, and she was as sure as she could be that he would not leave her.

They had a good life together. They were friends. They talked and laughed together. They were lovers. They were to have a child, whom they both wanted. They had family and good neighbors and a few close friends. They had . . . everything.

Why was *everything* such a heavy word?

"It is a good marriage, Sophia?" her uncle asked.

"Yes."

It *was*. She was not lying.

"I have sensed that it is," he told her. "It is quite clear that you are fond of each other. Did you choose him deliberately and go boldly after him?"

"Is that what Aunt Martha told you?" she asked.

"I would not blame you if it were true," he said. "It is how most of us get our spouses. But it was not so in your case, I would guess. I suppose Henrietta wanted him, or Martha and Clarence wanted him for her, and somehow you got caught in the middle and he married you. At least, that is my interpretation of the story they told."

"There was an assembly," she told him, "and Henrietta persuaded Vincent to take her outside for some air. She drew him along a little-used alley. I went after them with a shawl I pretended to think was hers."

He laughed softly.

"And there was a horrid fuss, I suppose," he said, "and Darleigh offered for you to save you from the wrath of Martha."

"I did say no," she told him. "But he persisted and persuaded me that our marriage would benefit him as much as it would me. It was not true, of course, but I married him anyway."

"No, it was not true," he said. "I believe he has benefitted more than you, Sophia."

"What nonsense." She laughed. "I might very well be in the gutters of London if it were not for Vincent."

He stopped walking in the middle of the alley and looked down at her.

"Tell me you are not serious," he said. "Martha did not threaten to turn you out, did she?"

"It was already done," she told him, "in the middle of the night following the assembly. I went to the church and the vicar found me there next morning. Vincent came to the vicarage when he heard."

Her uncle closed his eyes, and his free hand came to rest on hers on his arm.

"Ah, Sophia," he said, "I have been much to blame. Sebastian told me that Mary was neglecting you shamefully when you lived with her. I was busy in Vienna and dragged my feet about coming back to England to find out for myself. And then she died and Martha took you in. She had Henrietta, who was much the same age as you, and I chose to believe that you would have companionship and would be far happier than you had been. I ought to have known better. I really ought. I have asked discreet questions of a few acquaintances in London, but whereas they can all confirm Henrietta's presence at numerous *ton* events during the past few Seasons, not a single one of them has ever even heard of you. You were not given a come-out? You were not taken to any balls or other parties?"

"No," she said. "Aunt Martha was afraid people would remember Papa and how he came to his end."

"Ah," he said. "The fault is mine. But it is too easy to beg your pardon."

They had resumed walking and were drawing near the summerhouse.

"If people cannot beg pardon of one another," she said, "then nothing can be forgiven and wounds fester."

"Have you been deeply wounded, Sophia?" he asked her. "Have *I* wounded you?"

"Yes."

She heard him draw a slow breath and release it.

She was glad he did not choose to enter the summerhouse. He turned, and they strolled slowly back along the alley.

"And now," he said, "it is too late for me to do anything to really help you. You do not need my help. You have Darleigh."

"And his mother and grandmother and three sisters and their families," she said. "I have no one of my own, Uncle Terrence. Only Aunt Martha and Sir Clarence and Henrietta, with whom I hope for a cordial relationship though it will never be a warm one. And perhaps you."

"Your family has let you down abominably," he said. "Perhaps it would be better for you to turn your back on the lot of us, Sophia."

"As you and Papa did with each other?" she said. "As both of you seem to have done with your sisters? Families ought not to be like that. All I want is a family to love and a family to love me. My *own* family. Is it too much to ask?"

"I do not have much experience at warmth," he said.

"Can you try?" she asked him. "You said your greatest pain was the loss of your children. You have a niece. I can be no substitute for your own sons and daughters, but I crave your love. And I long to love you."

She swallowed and heard an embarrassing gurgle in her throat.

He stopped walking again and turned to her.

"Sophia," he said. "I do not believe I have ever known anyone as lovable as you. Perhaps my own children . . . But they are not here and never will be. I am not good at hugs."

"I am," she told him, and she put herself into his arms and wrapped her own about his waist and rested one side of her face against his shoulder.

His arms came tight about her, and they stood motionless for a long time before releasing each other.

"Forgive me?" he said.

"Yes."

"And let me be a part of your present and your future?"

"Yes."

"Do you love him, Sophia?" he asked. "Can you console me by telling me that it is a *really* good marriage?"

"Both," she said.

It *was* really good. They would remain together because of their child, perhaps in time because of their *children*. But it would not be just their children holding them together. Oh, she *would not* believe that. They would be a family. They would love one another as families ought. And she and Vincent would show their children the example of love and companionship and tolerance.

"Darleigh is a *very* fortunate man," he said.

She smiled and took his arm.

"We will miss tea if we do not return soon," she told him.

❧

21

Vincent edged out of bed very carefully. Sophia had only just fallen back to sleep. She had been awake since half past three, she had told him when he awoke just before six—she had looked at the clock to see what time it was. She had apologized if it was her restlessness that had disturbed him.

"Terrified?" he had asked her.

"*At least* that," she had said with something of a groan. "And excited. And . . . terrified."

The reception and ball were to take place in two days' time. As far as Vincent could tell, everything had been planned to death and organized down to the finest little detail. His sisters and their families were to arrive sometime later today, as was Flavian. Neighbors from ten miles about had been invited, some few to stay overnight on account of the distance. Of all the invitations that had been sent out, just one had been declined, and that only because the recipient had had the misfortune to fall off the roof of his barn when his wife had hullooed and waved the card from down below and distracted him. He had broken his leg in two places, poor man.

According to Andy Harrison and a few of the other men with whom Vincent had become friendly lately, there was going to be an eerie silence in the neighborhood after the Middlebury ball. There would be nothing, absolutely nothing, left to talk about. They had all enjoyed a merry guffaw at the prospect.

Vincent had hugged and kissed his wife and assured her that all would be well, that nothing would go wrong. Of course the orchestra would arrive from Gloucester. And of course all the food would be cooked on time and to perfection. *Of course* everyone would come. And of course it was appropriate and desirable that she lead off the opening set with her uncle. And she would *not* forget the steps or trip over her own feet or anyone else's. Miss Debbins had gone over the steps with her, and she had practiced in the music room with her uncle, an experienced and expert dancer, had she not? Of course he was not sorry she had put him through all this.

"What do you mean, anyway, Sophie," he had asked, "by saying *you* have put *me* through it all? Was it not *we* who decided it was time the tradition of grand entertainments in the state apartments was revived? Was it not *we* who decided upon the ball?"

"It is very kind of you to say so," she had said, her voice muffled against his chest. "But I fear it was me. I wanted to prove myself capable of being mistress of Middlebury. I wanted to show everyone that I could compete with all the viscountesses back through history."

"And you have done it admirably well," he assured her, kissing the lengthening curls on her head. "Or you are about to do it."

"That is the whole problem, though," she had said. "That *about to do it* part. Do go back to sleep, Vincent. I did not mean to wake you. I shall lie very still, though I doubt I will sleep a wink until after the next few days."

No more than three minutes later she was sleeping, and Vincent slipped out of bed and made his way to his dressing room. He heard Shep scramble to his feet and come to nudge his hand with a cold nose. He rubbed the dog's head and pulled gently on his ears.

"Good morning, old boy," he whispered, bending his head for the customary lick on the cheek. "Just a quick walk outside for you, and then I have an appointment to keep."

Actually he had lain awake quite a bit of last night too, but earlier than Sophia. Was he going to make a complete ass of himself? He had practiced with Martin for the last few mornings, and Martin had sworn the air blue, if only figuratively speaking.

"I don't know quite how you do it, sir," he had grumbled, "but you do, and I don't like it one little bit on my own account. I like it a whole lot on that smiling bastard's account, though. Spars with Gentleman Jackson himself, does he? I hope he was not merely boasting when he told you that. It would mean he has farther to fall."

It would also mean, if he had not been boasting, he would be a formidable opponent. And it was that fact that had kept Vincent awake, his stomach churning uncomfortably. Not that he feared getting hurt. He had grown up half wild. He had been knocked down in fistfights almost as often as he had done the knocking. He had always jumped back up and kept on swinging. No, this time it was the fear of being left feeling inadequate, of failing to accomplish what he had set his heart upon doing.

It was the fear that his blindness had unmanned him.

Pointless thoughts! But nighttime mind wanderings were the hardest to suppress.

Martin was already in the cellar when Vincent arrived there.

"You are sure about this, sir?" he asked. "I would gladly do it for you in the traditional way. I'll have him on his back watching stars through the cellar ceiling and all the ceilings above it in no time flat."

"Gentleman Jackson notwithstanding?" Vincent asked.

His valet said something unrepeatable.

"You do not have faith in me, Martin?"

"All the faith in the world," Martin told him. "But I don't know why you should have all the fun just because you are a bleeding viscount."

"And because the viscountess is my wife," Vincent said.

"Ah. There is that too," Martin conceded. "If it was Sal, no fists would do but my own."

Vincent grinned and would have said something about the continuing courtship between his valet and the blacksmith's daughter, who had still been holding out for a wedding the last time they spoke of her. But the cellar door opened above them, and a cheerful voice called down.

"Darleigh? Are you down there? And is your batman there?"

"Both of us," Vincent called back. "Come on down, Maycock. There should be plenty of light. Martin has lit the lamps."

"Ah, a wonderful cavern," Sebastian Maycock said, his voice closer. "This is where you do your exercising, Darleigh? And this is your trainer?"

"Martin Fisk," Vincent said. "Friend, batman, valet, trainer. He wears a number of hats."

"You look impressively large," Maycock said. "Those shoulder and arm muscles look as if they are kept in good condition."

"I do my best," Martin told him.

"So you think you can outspar me, do you?" Maycock laughed. "It takes skill as well as brawn. Did you know that?"

"I think I may have heard it mentioned a time or two," Martin said.

"Right," Maycock said. "You are stripped to the waist and ready, I see. I'll get my shirt and boots off, and we will go at it. Darleigh warned you to bring smelling salts and bandages, did he?"

"He did mention it," Martin said.

"A bout with no set rounds, then?" Vincent said. "A fair fight with fists only, no punches below the waist? To end when one gives in or is knocked down and unable to get up again within a reasonable amount of time?"

"That sounds fair to me," Maycock said. "I don't expect this to take long. I hope your cook serves breakfast early, Darleigh. There is nothing like a good sparring bout to whet the appetite. Try not to go down too soon, Fisk. Ready?"

"I am ready," Martin said. "There. I have gathered the lanterns together."

"Oh, spread them around again," Maycock told him. "There are too many shadows with all three of them in the same place like that. We will be careful to avoid tipping them. Darleigh, old chap, I would advise you to sit partway up the stairs. We would not want to hit you by accident, would we? It would not be sporting."

He laughed. The man did a lot of laughing.

"I think there is one detail you misunderstand," Vincent said. "It is not Martin who is to be your sparring partner, Maycock. It is I."

There was a short silence and then the laughter came again, uproarious this time.

"That is a good one, Darleigh," he said. "There would be a massacre here in one second flat. Right. Shall we get to it, Fisk? Spread out the lamps. It is dark down here."

"It is about to get darker," Vincent told him. "I apparently did not explain myself clearly. It is you and I who are to spar, Maycock. Clearly a fight between us would be ludicrous under normal conditions. You can see. I cannot. The light cannot be turned on in my eyes for the next little while, unfortunately, but it *can* be turned off in yours. And so we will be evenly matched and it will be a fair fight. I say *fight* rather than mere sparring bout for a reason. When you tell a grieving, vulnerable fifteen-year-old that she is ugly, Maycock, and when you force her to see for herself in a full-length mirror, you do more than hurt her. You destroy her. When you do it to the girl who has since become my wife, then you make an enemy of me and are deserving of punishment at my hands."

"Oh, I say." Maycock laughed again. "That was years ago, old chap, and it was nothing more than the truth. Would you have had me *lie* to her? Would you have had me tell her—Oh, I say!"

"The lamps are out, sir," Martin reported. "Three paces forward, slightly right."

"It is as black as sin down here," Maycock said, his voice outraged. "Light them again this instant, man."

"I would advise you to defend yourself," Vincent said, having moved forward three paces slightly to his right— the only outside help he would get. He used both fists and short jabs to locate his man, and then hooked a right to his chin.

"Oh, I say! This is not sporting."

"Are your hands tied?" Vincent asked. "Are your legs chained? Are your ears stopped?"

He jabbed at the naked chest before him, hooked with a left, cut upward with a right.

To his credit, Maycock recovered himself and raised his fists to protect himself. He danced about on his feet—and he danced away out of range. Vincent's free punches were at an end.

But of course, it was not really a fair fight. Vincent was experienced in the dark. He was experienced at using his ears and at using that sixth sense that told him when someone or something was close. Mostly it was sound—the slap of bare feet on the floor, breathing that became more labored. And, as often as not, a voice that protested or taunted, especially when Maycock landed a punch, which he did more than once, though nothing to really hurt. Nothing on the face. Vincent talked too. It was only fair.

"The trouble with you, Maycock," he said, "is that you are a man of surfaces. You see beauty and believe a person to be beautiful. You see plainness and believe a person to be dull and lacking in all the finer sensibilities. You would see an oyster and not even suspect that a priceless pearl was within."

Maycock was just ahead of him. He verified the fact with a series of fast left jabs, which the man countered in such a way as to leave his chin exposed to a swinging right. He went down like a log.

"Sheer luck," he said, scrambling to his feet. "I just wish I could have you in Jackson's Boxing Saloon for one minute on my terms, Darleigh. We would soon see who is the superior fighter."

"And Gentleman Jackson and all your friends and acquaintances would applaud your superior talents," Vincent said, knocking him down again.

It was hard to judge exactly where his chin was and where his face. Vincent had tried to avoid the face. There was a family to be confronted above stairs. There was a public reception and ball in two days' time. But he thought that this time he had connected with Maycock's nose.

Maycock got up again. At least he was no coward.

Vincent took a hard punch to the jaw, reeled for a moment, and danced back out of reach.

"You saw a lonely young girl, who was uncared for by her guardian," he said, "and you saw ugliness even though she worshiped you. I cannot even see the grown woman, but I do see all the beauty that is within her, and it dazzles my mind's eye."

"Perhaps it is cruel to be truthful," Maycock said irritably. "If you think it matters, Darleigh, I will apologize to her. I have already told her that she is no longer ugly."

The man just did not understand, did he? He was probably incapable of understanding. Vincent knocked him down again and he bobbed up within a second or two.

"I have seen her pain as well as her beauty," Vincent said. "The pain of believing herself to be ugly and unlovable."

"If you had eyes, Darleigh," Maycock said, "you would realize—"

Vincent knocked him down with a blow intended to keep him down.

It did.

There was silence except for the sound of his own heavy breathing.

"Maycock?"

There was merely a dull groan.

"A lamp, sir?" Martin asked.

"Yes, light one, please, Martin."

"He is not quite unconscious," Martin reported a few moments later.

Maycock groaned again.

"Here, let me help you up," Martin said. "Sit on the stairs here. I can sympathize. I have tried it with him, without any success. I used to knock him down as often as he knocked me down when we were lads, but that was when he could see. He is more deadly now."

Vincent had found a towel and was drying himself

off. He could tell that Martin was ministering to May-cock.

"Any damage?" he asked.

"Just a trickle of blood from the nose," Martin said. "It will look a bit like a beacon for the next day or two. A little red and raw about the chin. Not a single black eye. The chest and arms will be sporting bruises in a variety of colors for a while, but no one will see them beneath his shirt."

"I was brought down here under false pretenses," Maycock said.

"You were brought down here for punishment," Vincent told him. "I might have had Martin tie you down, you know. Instead you were given a fair fight."

"Fair!" Maycock said testily. "You made an ass out of me."

"I hope so," Vincent said and grinned. "The simplest explanation we can give upstairs, I believe, is a version of the truth. You and I had a friendly sparring bout after you very sportingly suggested we do it in total darkness."

"I do *not* enjoy being made a fool of," Maycock said.

"No one does," Vincent told him. "But only you and I and Martin need know it happened. And Sophia. I will tell her."

He heard feet climbing the stairs. The door at the top opened and then closed again.

"He was no sniveling coward," Martin said. "I am glad of that. Every time I heard him go down I willed him to get up again."

"*Was* it unfair?" Vincent asked.

"Not as punishment," Martin said. "He is not badly hurt. Just his pride. And he certainly does not get the point, does he?"

"I think he is incapable," Vincent agreed.

"You are going to have a nice bruise on your jaw,"

Martin said. "Here, let me press this wet towel to it. I said she looked like a boy, sir. When you told me you were going to marry her. Do you need to have a go at me too?"

"You have redeemed yourself since," Vincent told him. "And you did not say it to her and would never have done. Ouch! That is sore. Besides, she probably did look like a boy, my poor little scarecrow, with her shorn hair. It is growing."

"You don't want to exercise further this morning, I take it, sir?" Martin said. "I'll go on ahead to have your bathwater carried up, shall I?"

"Yes, please, Martin."

He flexed his knuckles, which felt nearly raw, and he flexed his jaw, which was going to hurt for a while.

He loved her, he thought. The idea popped out at him as if from nowhere.

Well, of course he loved her. She was his wife and they were comfortable together. They talked and laughed together. They were wonderful in bed together, and she was a few months with child by him. Of course he loved her.

But, no. That was not what that sudden thought had meant.

He *loved* her.

And she still dreamed of her cottage in the country.

Sophia had slept late, and now it seemed to her she would never catch up. Though what there was to catch up with, she was not quite sure. With just two days to go to the reception and ball, everything that needed to be done had been done, and now it was simply a case of waiting for everything to happen and hoping that nothing would go wrong and that nothing had been overlooked.

Nothing *had* been overlooked. They had even ridden yesterday, she and Vincent, to call upon Mr. and Mrs. Latchley—he was the unfortunate tenant farmer who had fallen off his barn roof. Yes, they had *ridden,* she on one side of Vincent, mounted on a sidesaddle on the quiet mare to which she had graduated, Mr. Fisk on his other side, and Mr. Fisk had even remarked at the end of the return journey that they could scarcely have walked the distance in less time.

She liked Mr. Fisk after all. For all his blunt, gruff manner, she often thought she detected something resembling a smile back inside his eyes when he looked at her.

They had persuaded Mr. Latchley to allow them to send the traveling carriage to bring him and his wife to Middlebury on the day of the ball. They would find him a sofa in a safe corner of the ballroom, they had promised, where he could recline and rest his splinted leg while he watched the festivities and chatted with his neighbors. Mrs. Latchley in the meanwhile could dance and stroll about with her friends. They would stay overnight, of course, and be taken home the next day.

Sophia was not hungry. She would miss breakfast, she decided, though she knew she ought not. She had a baby to feed as well as herself. Perhaps a little later. In the meanwhile she would steal a few minutes for herself outside. It looked like a chilly morning, but it was not actually raining. She took a cloak with her.

She strolled in the parterre garden for a while, reluctant to go farther. Her family and Vincent's were late risers by her standards, but they would be up soon, if they were not already. She must not be gone too long, then. And there were more people arriving today.

She had family of her own! She tested the new thought, and found it as warmly satisfying as ever. She had an *uncle.* She had an aunt and uncle and cousin besides, and they would remain a part of her life because she would refuse to let them go. Some might call her foolish. They were not particularly likable people, none of the three of them, and they had certainly not been good to her, beyond the fact that for three years they had provided a roof over her head and food for her stomach. But she would not hold a grudge. She simply would *not*. Just as she did not hold a grudge against Sebastian. He was an amiable, weak, rather self-absorbed man, and he certainly had not been worthy of a young girl's devotion, but he was somehow a part of the small dregs of her family, and she was content that he be there.

She was about to return to the house when she became aware of someone hurrying up the driveway on foot. A woman. She turned onto the straight stretch between the topiary trees, and Sophia, seeing that she was Agnes Keeping, went to meet her. It was early for a morning call, but it was a welcome one.

"Agnes," she called when they were within earshot of each other.

Her friend was smiling brightly and waving a folded paper.

"I could not wait until a more respectable hour," she said, all out of breath. "The post came early, and so I have come early. I have heard from Dennis after I had given up hope of ever hearing from him again. Men are the more hopeless of correspondents, are they not?"

Sophia smiled, and they both stopped walking. Who was Dennis?

"Dennis Fitzharris," Agnes explained. "My cousin-in-law. The publisher."

Ah, the cousin. But Agnes had not said he was actually a publisher. Sophia raised her eyebrows.

"He wants to publish your first Bertha and Dan story," Agnes told her. "And he wants to look at more.

Here. Read for yourself." And she thrust the folded letter into Sophia's hands.

He did indeed. He wanted to publish the book. He liked it, both the text and the pictures. He thought it would delight children, and he thought there would be a fair market for it as there were so few books published just for children, especially books that were so thoroughly and amusingly illustrated. He suggested publishing it under the name of "Mr. Hunt, Gentleman," since Viscount Darleigh would doubtless not wish to have his title associated with something so apparently trivial, and Lady Darleigh would not wish to be considered vulgar. He offered a sum that sounded to be generous enough as an advance against future sales.

Sophia looked up into Agnes's smiling eyes and smiled back. *Grinned* back, actually. And then they were both laughing and hugging each other and dancing in a circle on the driveway.

"Is it *vulgar* to be an authoress?" Sophia asked.

"Dreadfully, my dear," Agnes replied. "It is even worse to be a book illustrator. Is there a word more derogatory than *vulgar*? If there is, you are it, or would be if you allowed your name to appear on the cover of your book."

"The cover of my book." Sophia stared at her arrested. "*My* book. Mine and *Vincent's*. Oh, Agnes!"

"I know," Agnes said. "Wonderful, is it not? But I must hurry back. I told my sister I would be gone no longer than half an hour. I have promised to help her sew new trim onto her best evening gown for the night after tomorrow, and she is convinced the job will occupy both of us for the whole day, horrid thought."

She turned and hurried back the way she had come, and Sophia made her way back to the house.

"Have you seen my husband?" she asked the footman in the hallway.

The footman believed his lordship was with Mrs. Pearl and Lady March in the morning room, but as Sophia hurried along the corridor of the west wing, he was just leaving the room and closing the door behind him.

"Vincent," she cried.

He looked in her direction, cocked his head to one side, and frowned.

"What is it?" he asked. "You sound distressed."

"Merely breathless," she told him. "The postman just brought a letter to Miss Debbins's house, and he wants to publish us, Vincent, though not under my name because it would be vulgar."

His expression did not change except that his frown perhaps deepened.

"He?" he asked her. "The postman? *What* would be vulgar?"

"Using a woman's name on a cover," she explained. "Apparently it is not done. And you might consider it trivial to have your title there. So he suggests just plain Mr. Hunt, Gentleman."

"Kind of him," he said, grinning suddenly. "Sophie, who on earth is *he*? And *what* on earth are you talking about? What do the postman and Miss Debbins have to do with whatever it is?"

"Nothing whatsoever," she told him.

He laughed outright and, after a moment, she joined him.

"The letter was to Agnes Keeping," she told him. "She sent a copy of *Bertha & Dan and the Adventure of the Cricket Ball on the Church Spire* to her late husband's cousin in London, do you remember? And it turns out that he is a publisher and that he loves the book and wants to buy it and publish it under the name Mr. Hunt, Gentleman to save you from embarrassment and me from vulgarity. He wants to *publish* it, Vincent, for children all over the country to read and look at. And he wants to see more."

The smile was arrested on his face.

"He wishes to publish your books, Sophie?"

"*Our* books."

"Then it had better be under the names Mr. and Mrs. Hunt or not at all."

"Do you think?"

"I think."

And then his smile deepened again and he opened his arms—he had neither Shep nor his cane with him—and she threw herself into them. They closed tightly about her, and he swung her off her feet and about in a wide circle. He set her down a considerable distance from the morning room door and facing in the opposite direction.

He was laughing. So was she.

"Are you happy about it?" he asked.

"Are you?"

"Yes."

"Me too."

And then her smile faded. The light was not brilliant in the hallway, but there was quite enough of it to show her that the left side of his jaw was swollen and discolored.

"What happened?" She cupped her hand very lightly against that side of his face. He winced and pulled back.

"I collided with a door?" He made the answer sound like a question. He also raised one hand to touch the area gingerly with his fingertips.

She took the hand in hers and turned it over, palm down.

"Your knuckles too?"

"It was a heavy door," he said.

She took his other hand from his side and held it in both of hers.

"A *very* heavy door," he said.

"What happened?"

"A sparring bout in the cellar," he told her. "Maycock came down this morning, and we thought it would be diverting to spar with each other. Maycock suggested very sportingly that we make the odds more equal by doing it in darkness, and Martin doused the lamps. Maycock came out of it rather worse than I did, unfortunately for him, but it was to be expected. I have had more experience with darkness than he."

He grinned at her.

She searched his blue eyes, which gazed so nearly directly back into hers.

"It was not a friendly bout, was it?" she asked him. "It was about me?"

He did not answer for a while.

"You were fifteen, Sophie," he said. "You were hurting and fragile, and he trod all over your heart with nailed boots. Worse, he trod all over your self-esteem. He convinced you that you were ugly when you were in reality one of the most beautiful little creatures ever created."

"Oh, Vincent." She felt a tear drip off her chin to be absorbed by her cloak. Another was trickling down her other cheek. "It was all a long time ago. He means no harm, you know. He just does not have strong sensibilities. There was no need to punish him."

"Yes, there was," he said. "I may be without sight, Sophie, but I am still a man. And when my woman needs defending, I will defend her."

My woman. She had a momentary image of a caveman, hanging on to his woman by the hair with one hand while in the other he wielded a club to beat back caveman number two. Perhaps she would sketch it one day.

But she understood his need to be as other men

were—Vincent Hunt, who had always been a leader among boys, at the forefront of every game and wild exploit. He had probably been at the forefront of every youthful fistfight too. She could not squash him by telling him that Sebastian was really not worth his wrath.

"Thank you," she said softly. "Thank you, Vincent. Do you have any ointment on those knuckles? Or on your jaw?"

"Martin knew better than to suggest any such thing," he told her.

Another male thing, she supposed.

"Well," she said, "I shall kiss them better."

Which she proceeded to do.

He had fought for her. In the darkness. And won. And then concocted a story to explain all the bruises and raw knuckles so that no one would know the truth except the three men who had been in the cellar. And now her.

She ought not to be pleased. Nothing was ever gained by violence. His generosity in marrying her and his kindness since then had healed her. And she had grown up in five years. The violence had been unnecessary.

She was pleased nonetheless.

Vincent had fought for her.

Because she was his.

And because she was one of the most beautiful little creatures ever created.

22

Sophia was dressed for the ball. She did not believe she had ever felt so excited or so sick or so altogether delirious in her life before. She *knew* she had not, in fact.

"You *see*, my lady?" Rosina said just as if Sophia had been arguing with her. "I *told* you."

"You did indeed," Sophia agreed, gazing back at her image in the pier glass in her dressing room. Rosina was standing behind her shoulder, and she was somehow reminded of another occasion when she had stood in front of a full-length glass with someone behind her.

Sebastian had taken her aside yesterday after luncheon. His nose had been looking a little less bulbous than the day before, and the bruises on his chin and both sides of his jaw had looked more blue than black. He had spent the day before laughing good-humoredly at all the teasing to which he had been subjected and declaring that the next time he challenged a blind man to a friendly sparring bout, he would make sure it was out of doors at noon on Midsummer Day.

"Sophia," he had said when they were alone together, "Darleigh is under the impression that I hurt you quite grievously when you were still at Aunt Mary's. I could not altogether avoid hurting you. I had not realized you were developing tender feelings toward me, and I could not encourage you to continue with those sentiments. To me you were still just a child, you know, and I did not see you that way."

"No, of course you did not," she had agreed. He was quite right. But that was not the point.

"You understood, surely," he had said, "that when I said you were ugly, I was just teasing you."

The easiest thing would be to say yes. It did not really matter after all this time, anyway. But she would make what Vincent had done yesterday seem foolish. Besides, it *did* matter. The effect of his words had lived with her for years after they were spoken.

"No, Sebastian," she had said. "I did not understand that, for you were *not* teasing."

"Oh, I say." He had looked uncomfortable. "Well, perhaps you are right. You had embarrassed me, and I was annoyed because I did not know quite what to say to you. And you really were a funny-looking girl, you know. You are very much improved now. Please accept my deepest apologies. I probably did you a favor, anyway. You probably took yourself in hand as a result of what I said, did you?"

What was the point of withholding her forgiveness? He had been smiling endearingly at her, his nose slightly glowing. And Vincent had punished him.

"Your apologies are accepted, Sebastian," she had said. "And you do not look so pretty yourself today, you know. Perhaps you will look better tomorrow."

She had laughed and held out her right hand toward him, and he had taken it, laughing heartily with her.

"I am *so* glad I got to be your maid," Rosina said now. "There is *so* much I can do with you."

Before she could wax even more rapturous, there was a tap on the dressing room door, and Vincent stepped inside.

"My lord." Rosina curtsied.

"Rosina," he said, and she withdrew.

He always dressed neatly and elegantly. But tonight, in his black, form-fitting tailed evening coat with silver embroidered waistcoat, pale gray knee breeches with white stockings and linen, and black shoes, he looked nothing short of magnificent. The knee breeches were slightly old-fashioned, but Sophia was very glad he wore them. He certainly had the legs to show them off, and the waist to show off his waistcoat, and the shoulders and chest to make his coat look as though it must have been sewn around him. His fair hair, slightly overlong as usual, had been brushed into a neat style, but soon it would be its usual unruly, attractive self.

"You look extremely handsome, my lord," she said.

He laughed. "Do you think?"

"I think."

"Tell me." He gazed across at her. "Describe yourself."

"I look ravishing," she told him, and there was only a very little self-mockery in her tone. "My gown is a bright turquoise, the skirts all soft and floaty and trimmed with a wide flounce at the hem. It is low at the bodice and the back and has little puffy sleeves. My dancing slippers and my gloves are silver, my fan Chinese bamboo and finely wrought and delicately painted. And my hair, Vincent! Rosina has magic in her fingers, I swear."

"Am I going to have to double her salary?" he asked her.

"Oh, at least that," she said. "She has made it look *long* when really it has only just started to grow below my chin. I have no idea how she has done it. It is all sleek at the sides and swept up at the back, and all the curls are gathered high on the crown of my head so that there appears to be a great mass of hair there. And she has let a few curls wave artfully over my ears, and I suspect there will be some along my neck before much time has passed. There must be a whole arsenal of pins in my head, Vincent, though I cannot see a single one in the mirror. And Lady Trentham's hairdresser was quite right—and Rosina too. The style does show my neck to advantage. And I *do* have good cheekbones. I look older. More grown-up, that is. More . . . Hmm."

"Beautiful?" he suggested. "Impossible, Sophie."

"Yes, I suppose so," she agreed.

"You cannot possibly be more beautiful than you already were," he said.

She laughed and he grinned at her.

"Happy?" he asked.

Her smile faded.

"Ask me again at the end of the evening," she told him, and the baby chose that moment to perform what felt like a sideways somersault. "If no grand disaster strikes, the answer ought to be yes."

"Come." He reached out a hand toward her and drew her against him.

"Don't squash my hair," she told him.

He lowered his head and kissed her. She kissed him back and clung to him, her arms about his waist.

"Don't squash my waistcoat," he murmured against her lips and deepened the kiss.

She drew back, picked up her fan, and took his arm.

There were guests to receive.

*S*ophia had described the scene. Vincent had had the state apartments described to him before, but he had not come here often. They had not particularly interested him except that he knew they gave great pleasure to visitors and there was a certain satisfaction in knowing himself to be the owner of such magnificence.

This evening's description, of course, had more life to it than it ever had before, partly because Sophia was the teller, and partly because the apartments were being used as they had been intended to be.

The grand salon had been set up as a card room and sitting room for those who wished to withdraw from the bustle of the ballroom for a while. There were four tables and a number of sofas. A fire had been lit in the large marble fireplace. The walls were paneled with narrow bands of oak alternating with wider panels with painted scenes. The high coved ceiling was also decorated with paintings. There was gilding everywhere and a single large chandelier hanging from the center of the ceiling, every candle lit for the occasion.

The small salon, exactly half the size of its grander neighbor, was similarly decorated. It was set up with refreshments—dainty savories and sweets, wines and liquors, lemonade, tea.

The state dining room was to be used later for supper and toasts and speeches—and a four-tier wedding cake, which had been his grandmother's idea. A wedding cake with Sophia several months pregnant and beginning to show, if his hands were to be believed!

He hoped it showed. He was bursting with pride—and with suppressed terror.

The ballroom was twice the size of the grand salon and not unlike it except that where there were painted panels in the salon, there were mirrors in the ballroom. And there were three chandeliers overhead and an orchestra dais at one end and a floor that gleamed with polish and French windows that opened onto the terrace.

It must all be magnificent indeed to behold. But it was more so than usual tonight, of course, because it was filled with guests. Oh, it was not the sort of grand squeeze so beloved of hostesses in London during the Season, he supposed, but all his family and Sophia's were here, and all their neighbors. And Flavian.

Everyone was glittering with jewels and waving with plumes and glowing with color, Sophia reported. She had heard that it was fashionable in London ballrooms for even the youngest of girls and the spottiest of youths to affect an air of ennui. Henrietta had practiced the look when she first made her come-out. No one had that look tonight.

"Not even your aunt and cousin?" Vincent asked when she reported on the fact as the last trickle of arriving guests had been greeted at the doors and had passed inside the ballroom.

"No." She laughed. "They are too busy looking superior. But they are enjoying themselves too, Vincent. They are very important people here. Our neighbors are looking upon them with deference and admiration. Aunt Martha's hair plumes must be four feet tall, and they are nodding in very stately fashion."

"I detect a bit of the caricaturist in that remark," he said.

"Well, perhaps *three* feet tall," she conceded. "She is talking with everyone. So is Sir Clarence. If he puffed his chest out any more, his waistcoat buttons would all pop off in unison. Oh, dear! Please stop me."

"Not for worlds," he told her. "And Henrietta?"

"Setting her cap at Viscount Ponsonby," she said, "though it looks as if he has solicited the hand of Agnes Keeping for the opening set."

"Talking of the opening set," he said.

"Yes." Even over the buzz of animated conversation about them, he heard her draw a deep breath. "Where is Uncle Terrence? Ah, here he comes."

"Shall I give the orchestra the signal to strike up a chord for the opening set, Darleigh?" he asked. "It looks to me, Sophia, as if this is going to be a grand success of an evening."

"If you will," Vincent said. He took Sophia's hand in his and raised it to his lips.

"Enjoy yourself," he said.

He stood in the doorway listening to the music and the rhythmic pounding of dancing slippers all hitting the wooden floor at the same time. His own foot tapped and he smiled.

He was not left alone. Neighbors came to compliment him upon reviving the old tradition in such grand fashion, and they stayed to chat. His grandmother came to take his arm for a while. Andy Harrison's wife brought him a glass of wine.

He had come a long way in a few months. Thanks to Sophia. Though not entirely. He must not be unfair to himself. He had exerted himself. He had pulled himself free of the smothering protection of the female members of his family—without hurting them, he believed. He had worked hard with Shep so that he had a far larger measure of freedom of movement than he had had in the past six years. He had spent long hours with his steward, both in the man's study and out on the land, learning the ins and outs of his estates and taking an active role in the decision making. He had got to know his neighbors and his laborers. He had made a few real friends. He had gone fishing. He had helped Sophia recover from the terrible trauma of the past five years, and even perhaps from the insecurities of the fifteen before that. He had brought her contentment, he believed, even if not active happiness, and some pleasure, both in and out of the marriage bed. He could now play the harp without wishing every moment that he could simply hurl it through the nearest window. He might even be reasonably competent upon it within the next year or so. He was soon to be a published author.

That last thought made him grin. His toe was still

tapping. Sophia was apparently dancing a set with Flavian.

He was very much enjoying having one of his fellow
Survivors at Middlebury. They had sat for a couple of
hours or longer in the parterre garden yesterday, hud-
dled inside their greatcoats against the unseasonable
chill of the day. Sophia had joined them there after a
while, and Flavian had commented that it was a pity
Vincent would not be able to join the rest of the Survivors at their annual gathering at Penderris Hall next
spring.

"But it is so that he can answer a higher c-calling," he
had said, amusement in his voice. "Congratulations are
in order, Lady Darleigh. Or am I n-not supposed to
know?"

Flavian had not had to be told, of course, that Sophia
was with child.

"What do you mean," Sophia had asked, "that he
cannot go? Of course he will go. He must."

"It will be soon after your confinement, Sophie," Vincent had said. "Wild horses would not drag me away
from you so soon, you know."

She had been silent for a while. So had Flavian.

"Well, then," she had said, "everyone must come here
instead. Would that ruin everything? *Must* it be at
Penderris? I know it is where you all spent those years
and where you naturally choose to gather. But *must* it
be there? Is not having you all together more important
than the place? Vincent, *may* we invite everyone here?
Would *you* come, Lord Ponsonby? Or would you rather
go to Cornwall, even if it means being without Vincent
for one year?"

"We can and we will, Sophie," Vincent had said.
"But—"

"No *buts* about it, Vince," Flavian had said. "You
will be awarded the year's prize for b-brilliance, Lady

Darleigh. With all our seven heads put together, we would never have seen the solution. W-would we, Vince?"

"Perhaps everyone else will disagree with you," Sophia had said.

"P-perhaps," he had agreed. "There is one way of finding out."

"Have you heard from Ben?" Vincent had asked him. "Has anyone?"

"He has fallen off the face of the earth," Flavian had said. "Just as you did back in the spring, Vince. His sister has been seen in town—the one with whom he is supposedly staying in the north of England, that is, b-but Ben was not clinging to her skirts when she was spotted. Perhaps he is tramping through heather in the Lake District as you were and will emerge with a bride. I rather hope not. It may prove c-contagious."

Now the dancing was in full swing, and Vincent relaxed in the conviction that Sophia would be happy at the success of all her efforts.

That was all that really mattered tonight—that she be happy.

It was all that mattered *any*time, he thought a little sadly.

Sophia was happier than she ever remembered being in her life. Not a single thing had gone wrong all evening, and it was close enough to the end to make her relax and decide that nothing *would* go wrong.

Though something still might, of course. There was still a big moment to come.

She had danced every set. She had also seen to it, as had Vincent's mother and sisters, that everyone else danced too who wished to dance. There were no wallflowers allowed at the Middlebury ball!

Even Henrietta had danced every set, all but one of them with gentlemen she must have considered inferior to herself. Viscount Ponsonby was the exception. He had danced the third set with her.

He had danced twice with Agnes.

The supper had been perfect. The state dining room had looked quite dazzlingly magnificent, and the food had been perfection itself. There had been toasts and speeches—one by Vincent. And there had been the cake, which they had cut into before it was sliced by the servants and set on trays for them to take about to make sure that everyone had a slice. Vincent had come with her, though he had neither held the tray nor dished out the slices of cake. He had charmed everyone with his conversation instead. It was amazing that he had more or less hidden inside the walls of the park for three years, Sophia thought. In the past few months he had grown enormously popular, just as he had used to be at Barton Coombs.

There were two sets remaining after supper, the first of which was a waltz. It was the only one all evening, since even now it was not a really well known dance out in the country. But Sophia knew it—she had practiced the steps with her uncle in the music room. And Vincent had watched it danced out in the Peninsula and knew the steps. He had been present when she had waltzed with her uncle, and she had seen his foot tapping in time to the music Miss Debbins played.

It was announced when she was at his side. He was smiling genially about him, though she guessed that it must have been a trying evening for him. Though perhaps not. He seemed to enjoy talking with everyone. Perhaps the fact that he was standing in his own state ballroom added to his enjoyment.

But how sad it was that he could not see all the splendor or participate in the more energetic of the activities.

"It is a waltz, Vincent," she said.

"Ah." He smiled. "You must dance it, then, Sophie. With your uncle? You practiced with him."

"With you," she said. "I mean, I must dance it with you."

She took his hand in both her own and backed a short way onto the dance floor.

"With me?" He laughed. "I think not, Sophie. That *would* be a spectacle for everyone to behold."

"It would," she agreed and backed up one more step.

No one else had yet stepped onto the floor, and they had caught the attention of those people who were close to them, and awareness quickly spread. The volume of conversation decreased considerably.

"No." He laughed. "Sophie—"

"I want to waltz," she said. "With my husband."

Someone—Mr. Harrison?—began to clap his hands slowly. Viscount Ponsonby joined him. And soon it seemed that half the guests in the ballroom were clapping in time with one another.

Oh, dear. Sophia had not intended this moment to be half as public. But it was too late now to do it differently.

"Waltz with me," she said as softly as she could.

Not softly enough.

"Waltz with her," Mr. Harrison said—it was unmistakably he this time.

And then it became a chant from their segment of the ballroom.

"Waltz with her. Waltz with her."

"Sophie—" Vincent laughed.

So did she.

And he walked out onto the empty floor with her.

"If I make a thorough spectacle of myself," he said just loudly enough to be generally heard, "would everyone be kind enough to pretend they have not noticed?"

He laughed again.

And the orchestra played the opening chord and did not wait for anyone else to take the floor.

It was very clumsy and awkward at first, and Sophia was terrified that she really was going to cause him great humiliation—not to mention herself. But she had practiced the steps very carefully. She had also, with her uncle's full collaboration, practiced leading without appearing to do so.

His feet found the steps, and his fingers spread against the back of her waist and his other hand nestled her own within it more comfortably. His head came up and he smiled very nearly into her eyes. He danced her into a spin and she laughed and had to make an effort to keep them both on their feet and within the confines of the dancing floor.

It was probably not the most elegant demonstration of the waltz ever performed. But it was wonderful nevertheless. And they had the whole floor to themselves. Whether that was because everyone else was terrified of being collided with or whether it was because everyone was enjoying watching, she did not know. She was aware at one point that most people were clapping to the rhythm of the music.

"Vincent," she said after a few minutes, "will you ever forgive me?"

"Maybe after a century or so," he said.

"Seriously?"

"Well, maybe after a decade."

And then he spun her again, but she was ready for it this time and steered them safely.

"I have always, *always* wanted to do this," she said.

"Waltz?"

"Waltz with *you*."

"Oh, Sophie," he said, and his hand tightened slightly at her waist. "I am so sorry I cannot—"

"But you can," she told him. "You can see with every part of your being except your eyes. Tell me you are enjoying it."

"I am," he said, and he drew her so close that she almost brushed against him. "Oh, I am."

Candlelight was wheeling overhead. Colored gowns were a kaleidoscope of pastels about the perimeter of the ballroom. Mirrors multiplied the candlelight and the twinkling of jewels to infinity.

"Such sounds and smells," he said. "I will never forget this moment. Sophie. I am actually *waltzing*."

She bit hard on her upper lip. It certainly *would* be humiliating to have all their guests see her weep. And then somehow her eyes focused upon his mother, who was standing with Ursula close to the doors. Tears were openly trickling down her cheeks.

And then there was a break in the music, and before the next waltz tune began, other dancers joined them on the floor.

*W*hen Sebastian Maycock came to ask Sophia for the final set of the evening, Vincent gave her as much freedom of choice as she had given him before the waltz.

"My wife has already promised the set, I am afraid, Maycock," he said. "To me."

He could almost feel her look of surprise.

"Yes, I have," she said with scarcely a moment's pause. "But thank you for asking me, Sebastian. It looks as if the elder Miss Mills is without a partner. The lady in green."

"You are *not* contemplating dancing the Roger de Coverley, are you?" she asked when Maycock had apparently taken himself off to solicit the hand of Miss Mills.

"I am contemplating a quiet stroll on the terrace with

my wife," he said. "It is probably too cold out there for you, though."

"I shall send someone for our cloaks," she said and promptly deserted him.

She was back a few moments later, and only a couple of minutes after that she murmured thanks to someone and handed him his evening cloak. He could hear the sets forming on the floor. The noise level had increased. It was to be the final set.

It seemed they were the only ones out on the terrace. His ears told him so, and Sophia confirmed the fact when he asked. It was not surprising. Though it was not a really cold night, the breeze was nippy.

"Happy?" he asked as she tucked an arm beneath his and guided him in what he guessed was the direction of the parterre gardens.

He heard her exhale.

"Happy," she said. "Everything has gone well, has it not? More than well. Oh, Vincent, we *must* do this more often. Perhaps when your friends come next spring. They will come, will they not?"

He did not answer her.

"Sophie," he said, "you will stay, will you not? I mean, for the baby's sake? I could not bear to part with it as well as with you, and I do not believe you could bear to leave it with me. Could you?"

"Oh, of course not," she said. "Yes, of course I will stay. I am only sorry—"

"I am *very* sorry about your cottage," he said. "I know you would love it and your life there more than anything, but—"

"Oh, Vincent," she said, "I would *not*."

"But when you were showing your sketchbook to Ursula and Ellen out here in the garden—"

"I sketched it for our *stories*," she told him. "I did not intend for it to look like my dream cottage, but that is how it turned out. And then I could not resist putting Tab in the picture. Yes, it is a dream of a cottage, Vincent. When my life was so desperately empty and lonely, and when I thought myself ugly and unlovable, I thought nothing could be more desirable. But compared with the reality of my life now, it is . . . Well, it is *pitiful*."

"You mean," he said, "you no longer wish for it? Even if you were not increasing?"

"No," she said quite emphatically. "How could I? But, Vincent, I *wish* I were not a woman."

"What?" He laughed. He was feeling a bit light-headed actually.

"Just another woman interfering with your freedom," she said.

"Whatever are you talking about?"

"You said it to Mr. Croft," she said. "The day he left Shep with you. You said I was just another woman looking after you and interfering with your independence."

"I am sure I said no such thing," he told her indignantly, trying to remember what exactly he might have said. "How could I unless I had been lying through my teeth?"

"But you said it," she said. "I heard you."

"Sophie," he said, "my mother and my sisters loved me to distraction and did everything for me and quite inadvertently *stifled* me. You came along with your wonderful ideas and did just the opposite. You gave me my freedom back and a large measure of independence. You silly goose, whatever you overheard on that day, you must have misunderstood. I would *never* have said you took away my freedom. *Never*, Sophie. You brought light back into my life."

"You do not *mind* that I will have to remain here, then?" she asked him.

They had stopped walking, he realized.

He heaved a great sigh and *wished* he could remember the exact words he had spoken to Croft.

"I love you, you know," he said.

She was still holding his arm. She tipped her head sideways to rest her cheek against his shoulder.

"Yes, I know," she said. "You are always very good to me. And I love you too."

"Ah, the inadequacy of words." He sighed again. "And the deceptive nature of words that have so many different meanings that they become virtually meaningless. Do you remember that song I sang at Covington House? *I'd crowns resign to call thee mine.* Remember that line?"

"Yes." She slipped her hand from his arm.

"I would do it in a heartbeat," he told her. "If I had a crown, Sophie, or multiple crowns, as in the song, I would give them all up. For you. That is what I mean when I say I love you."

He heard her swallow awkwardly.

"But you do not have a crown."

"I would give up Middlebury Park, then," he told her, "and my title. If I had to make a choice between them and you, there would not even be a contest. It is easy to say, I know, when there appears to be no danger that I will ever have to make that choice. But I would do it if I had to. There is no doubt in my mind. I love you."

"Vincent." One of his hands was in both of hers.

"It was not a part of our agreement, was it?" he said. "I am perfectly happy to make do with contentment, Sophie, if you do not want to be burdened with more. Really I am. And we *are* contented, are we not? It is just—Well, I am selfish, I suppose. I wanted the pleasure of saying it. Of telling you. It really does not matter if—"

"Does not *matter*?" She half shrieked the words and threw herself against him with such force that she almost knocked him off his feet. Her arms came about his neck. "You have just told me you love me to all eternity and it *does not matter*? Of course it matters. It matters more than anything in the whole wide world and throw the sun and moon and stars in for good measure. I love you so very, very, *very* much."

"Do you, Sophie?" His arms came about her and he hugged her to himself. "Do you, my love?"

"Add a few more *verys*," she said.

"You had better save a few for me." He laughed against her hair, which felt as if it was breaking free of the bonds Rosina had imposed upon it.

She lifted her face to him and he kissed her.

Sounds of merry conversation and laughter and a vigorous country dance came from the ballroom somewhere behind them. In the distance an owl hooted and a dog barked. A light, chill wind caught at the edges of their cloaks.

All of which Vincent ignored for the moment, for he held all the world clasped to himself. Ah, yes, and the sun and moon and stars too.

And all eternity.